DEEP CUTS

EDITED BY

Angel Leigh McCoy

E.S. Magill

Chris Marrs

Cover art by Anja Millen

Evil Jester Press

New York

ISBN-13: 978-0615750897
ISBN-10: 0615750893

Published by Evil Jester Press
Printed in the United States and the United Kingdom
First Edition
First Printing: February 2013

10 9 8 7 6 5 4 3 2 1

This book is dedicated to the women who write horror—
past, present, and future.

READ ORDER

129	15	39	51
133	67	155 (12)	77
229	185	25	95
211 (8)	219 (10)	115 (14)	139
			169
			195
			235

TABLE OF CONTENTS

MAYHEM

MENACE

MISERY

Editors' Foreword

If you were lucky enough to grow up with records, you probably remember handling the vinyl by its edges, trying not to smudge oily fingerprints on it and messing up the purity of the music. If it was a much-loved record, you had your favorite songs, ones that seemed to belong only to you—and not the ones regularly played on the radio, the "hits." No, your songs required moving the needle to the grooves closer to the center or to the record's flipside. These songs earned the moniker *deep cuts*—songs buried deep in an album's playlist.

We're using that *deep cuts* concept for this anthology and applying it to an idea we conceived while at a World Horror Convention sitting together at a table with a scrap of paper and a pen dug up from the bottom of one of our purses. The idea was to recognize great horror stories by women writers.

But, we had a dilemma: we didn't want to do a book of all reprints, and we didn't want to exclude men writers. We did want new stories and new voices. That's when we came up with the idea of having our contributing writers, women and men, recommend great horror stories by women writers through a mini-essay. We've come to call these recommendations *deep cuts*.

So, this book accomplishes much more than your typical anthology. There are new stories and recommendations for stories you should hunt down and read. We even included stories by three of today's great women horror writers—Nancy Holder, Yvonne Navarro, and Mehitobel Wilson.

So why the focus on women who write horror?

When it comes to women horror writers, most readers (or writers) don't associate women with extreme horror. Well, that's their initial reaction: women don't write that stuff. But if you make them pause and think it through, they'll suddenly start coming up with the names of women horror writers who do write that stuff. It's probably social convention that clouds their memories for those first few moments.

1

Much of Nancy Holder's current work is Young Adult, but there was a time when she was part of a group of writers who were taking horror to literary extremes: "I became a Splatterpunk because someone turned to me at a con and said, 'Of course, women can't write splat.' I think sometimes we're still considered somewhat unusual. But I love seeing more women in all aspects of horror publishing—editors, agents, executives, artists, writers."

Women have been integral to the horror genre since its gothic inception. There are so many great stories out there that have already been published, but that are languishing in a literary purgatory. We wanted to remind everyone of these stories by digging them up out of their moldering graves and singing their praises once again.

◉

During the course of putting together *Deep Cuts*, we were asked why the request for a recommended woman horror writer and her story? Why not have an anthology of stories written only by women? While there isn't anything wrong with anthologies containing only stories written by women, we wanted to do something different. We wanted to have an anthology honoring women writers that wasn't gender exclusive.

Coming up with a way to do that wasn't an easy task; we kicked around many ideas before we decided on the recommendations method. And, as an added bonus, they tied-in with our *deep cuts* theme, as a good number of the recommendations are for women writers of whom, otherwise, you may not have heard. The same goes for their brilliant stories. By asking that submitters include a recommendation with their submissions, we felt we could achieve our goal of honoring women, no matter the gender of the person submitting. We believe we were successful in this and hope you do, too. Hopefully, you'll discover, or rediscover, some of the horror genre's lesser known but talented women writers, as we did.

◉

The response to *Deep Cuts* has been phenomenal. Not only was our Kickstarter fully funded, so we could pay beyond pro rates, but we also received more than 250 submissions. We used Sub-mittable.com, an online submission tracking service, to keep it all straight, or we'd have been lost! Fortunately for us, Submittable has a voting system. Each of us read every story and then voted on it. Yes, No, or Maybe. By the time we'd finished, we had a fairly clear idea of which stories had made it into the final stage of decision-making. We eliminated two-thirds of the stories in the first voting round. Then, we settled in to do the really hard work.

The editors all converged at a writers retreat (in a haunted house, no less) to discuss the remaining third of the stories and choose which would make it into the anthology. We had so many amazing stories to choose from. We talked for hours, analyzing and arguing; and ultimately, we got our list down to sixteen stories that didn't put us over our word-count limit.

Our original intent was to choose only stories that were "extreme" horror, but we learned that a story doesn't have to have a lot of blood and guts to be "extreme." Our submissions taught us that, and we're thankful for the lesson. We ended up choosing stories based on their emotional or conceptual intensity instead.

Most importantly, we chose stories for their merit, and in our final list of authors, we have nine women (including our three spotlight writers) and ten men. We had anticipated an equal split, but we refused to artificially force that balance. We discussed it and opted to be true to our standards and take the very best stories, independent of the author's gender. We were delighted that more than a third of those chosen from the slush pile turned out to be women writers, and maybe that's a fair representation of the gender split in the Horror community. One can only conjecture.

After being chosen, each of the writers underwent an intense line-editing process with us as well, and the stories were all further polished to an obsidian shine. This is something that not many anthology editors take the time to do but that we felt was an important part of our process. The resulting quality of each story was naturally enhanced with revisions done by its writer, and we're deeply proud to present them here.

◙

We the editors would like to say how pleased we are with the final line-up. Now, we offer them to you, our readers, with the hope that you enjoy them as much as we enjoyed choosing and editing them. We thank you for buying this copy of *Deep Cuts,* and thank those of you who received a copy because you supported our

Kickstarter. Thank you all very much.

So, join us as we knock the needle over a few grooves to find and recommend those *deep cuts* by women horror writers.

Warning: Cuts May Be Deeper Than They Appear

—Angel Leigh McCoy, E.S. Magill, and Chris Marrs

Introduction

Lisa Morton

"...if our authoress can forget the gentleness of her sex, it is no reason why we should; and we shall therefore dismiss the novel without further comment." – From *The British Critic*'s review of Mary Shelley's *Frankenstein; or, the Modern Prometheus*, April 1818

"Modern female horror writers...are not as good as modern male horror writers. That is an unassailable fact." –From an internet discussion forum, 2009

In the nearly 200 years that have passed since the publication of *Frankenstein*—arguably the most important horror novel of all time—Mary Shelley would undoubtedly have been gratified to see what advances women have made in general. We've been granted the rights to vote and own property, birth control has given us more voice in choosing whether to conceive or not, and we are no longer confined to deciding between housewife/mother and spinsterhood. You'll find us everywhere from your local police department to the boardrooms of major corporations.

And yet those of us who practice the craft of dark fiction sometimes still feel like it's 1818.

Peruse any internet site where horror fiction is discussed, and you'll invariably find the "Can women write horror?" thread. At its most tolerable, it will appear as a "List your favorite female authors!" topic; just as often, though, it's presented as some variant of the 1818 criticism of *Frankenstein*—that women either are or should be too gentle to write that nasty horror stuff.

Of course, there are still plenty of men out there who don't think women should be writing *anything*. Take, for instance, the esteemed literary novelist V. S. Naipaul, who believes that women live too much in "sentimentality, the narrow view of the world" to

5

write truly worthwhile fiction (guardian.co.uk, June 02, 2011). Other genres have their own problems, which have been the stuff of much discussion among their respective communities recently: Female science fiction authors are so often stalked at gatherings that many conventions now routinely post anti-harassment statements; fantasy critics have decried their authors' tendency to describe female characters in terms of their breast size; women who write in the comics field recently initiated legal action against an online stalker; and those who specialize in computer hacking not long ago attended a major trade show in which the event's security made a game of passing out cards that suggested one way of earning points to get a woman to show her tits.

Ugly, isn't it? Oh, but wait…it's about to get much worse.

Because, as awful as all those scenarios are, and as much as they reveal that some men aren't interested in women as anything other than sex objects, at least—in fantasy and science fiction circles—readers aren't accustomed to picking up books that feature graphic depictions of women being viciously raped, mutilated and murdered.

Unfortunately, there really is no question that horror is the most misogynistic of literary genres. Buy and read any stack of horror books, and chances are you'll come away wondering why any woman would *ever* want to write in this genre. Horror, after all, is where you'll find "extreme fiction," a sub-genre that is almost solely about rape, dismemberment, and killing, nearly all directed at women. Rape may follow mutilation, with those offensive arms and legs removed so that the female form is rendered down to nothing but the sexual organs (and the parts required to keep those operating). I once saw a post on a discussion board defending this obsession with rape on the basis of how horrifying it was in real life; when I responded that I could instantly think of about 973 other real-life things that were horrifying that I rarely or never saw mentioned in horror novels (including the rape of *men*), I killed that thread pretty quickly.

Even in books that don't cater to these violent male fantasies, female characters are often treated in an offhand or openly derogatory way. One midlist author with a fervent fan following has used the word "bitch" so often in referring to his female characters that I was once tempted to write him and suggest that he also use "cunt," "pussy," "whore" (or "ho"), "twat," "snatch," "slit," or "slut" just to break up the repetition.

At some point, the question must become, "Why?"

Why has the horror genre become home to such savage and blatant sexism? Part of the answer is obvious and has already been mentioned: Horror allows men the stage on which to act out their ultimate fantasies; the other end of that scale is pornography, and I have often espoused my notion that extreme fiction really should be considered pornography and not horror, because the ultimate intention is to provoke a physical reaction, not to horrify.

But beyond that, one has to wonder if men aren't—subconsciously, deeply—threatened by the presence of women in a genre that we not only started, but are better equipped to excel in.

Yes, that's right: I just suggested that women should make better horror writers than men. And here's why:

Those of us born into female bodies learn from a young age to deal with fear and blood. Some of us may be molested (and yes, I know boys are molested, too, but the number of girls who suffer sexual abuse is around three times as many as boys). Some of us may grow up watching fathers abuse our mothers; most of us grow up aware of how dominant our father is. All of us who survive pre-adolescence will reach a day when we experience the shock of seeing blood gush from between our legs, only to be told this is a normal process that will occur once a month for the next forty or so years. All of us at some point or other will experience fear at the greater physical strength men wield over us (and don't tell me that proves how right those internet pundits are about rape as a useful horror trope). If we choose to give birth, we'll understand all too well that life begins in pain and blood. We will learn that we can only succeed by asserting ourselves, something we've been programmed not to do…or we'll simply never be seen.

We, the women writers, have an intuitive grasp of the mechanics of fear and blood, in other words.

And we can look back to the women who gave birth to this genre and advanced it: Ann Radcliffe, who so perfected the art of the Gothic novel that she was known by the likes of Keats as simply "Mother Radcliffe"; Mary Shelley, who practically invented both the horror and science fiction genres; Shirley Jackson, who wrote what may just be the most famous horror story of the twentieth century, "The Lottery"; and Anne Rice, who redefined vampires—and the horror novel—forever, with *Interview with the Vampire*.

So, beyond those shining examples…why aren't there more women writing horror? If we have the nature, the nurture, and the examples that should make us the perfect horror writers, why are horror reference guides in 2012 (like the American Library Association's *Readers' Advisory Guide to Horror*) noting that "horror is still a very male-dominated world" and confining the discussion of "Ladies of the Night" to five of us?

You might find a few clues lurking in the small essays on female horror writers that accompany each of the stories in *Deep Cuts*. Here's a list of the authors who are cited as having influenced and inspired the contributors: Tanith Lee, May Sinclair, Diana Wynne Jones, Frances Garfield, Shirley Jackson, Roberta Lannes, Caitlin R. Kiernan, Melanie Tem, Joyce Carol Oates, Lucy Taylor, Elizabeth Massie, and Monica O'Rourke. At least three of these authors are primarily known for writing in other genres (or, in the case of Joyce Carol Oates, for writing in *no* genre). Several of these writers have never had a major publishing deal (at least not for their stand-alone work). I confess that I've never heard of May Sinclair (although I intend to seek her out now). Once again, the ladies don't seem to have an easy path to horror fame.

More interestingly, though, at least three of these writers—Lannes, Taylor, and Massie—are mentioned for their extreme fiction, which my own experience with their work affirms can rival the most gut-churning the men have to offer. So much for the "gentler sex."

And one of these women—Shirley Jackson—was mentioned no less than three times. The authors who admired Jackson herein all discuss how her work found horror in the ordinary (an idea that was still fresh when these authors all first read the story) and suggest once again the extraordinary importance of "The Lottery" in the history of the horror genre.

Yet, Jackson is routinely omitted from lists of the great horror writers…lists that often include far less important male writers.

I'm not sure how to remedy a situation this completely ridiculous, other than to urge my sisters in dark fiction to keep working, regardless of the seemingly impossible task set before us. *Deep Cuts* proves that our work *is* affecting some of our readers, that they are remembering our tales long after they've read them and admitting to the influence we've wielded. Surely, it's only a matter of time before the lists can no longer deny the importance of women to the genre, when we're accorded our proper place in this dark history.

In the meantime—fuck the haters, and sing loud and proud, bitches. Oh, I'm so sorry—that wasn't very gentle, was it?

MAYHEM

E.S. Magill on Nancy Holder's
"Crash Cart"

In the world of literature, the short story is guerilla warfare. A novel is a full-on campaign with multiple battles, and the troops its cast of characters. The short story, on the other hand, is a quick, direct hit that retreats to the shadows once the job is done. The best are those read in one sitting, the strongest effect produced that way, said Poe.

I'm a connoisseur of the short form—especially when it comes to horror. That's where the genre rocks. Don't get me wrong. Great horror novels abound, and I have an affinity for old-school '70s horror novels.

So, my bookshelves are loaded with anthologies of horror stories—in part because I was fortunate to work in a bookstore during those heady days of horror in the late 1980s and early '90s. As I unpacked boxes of books in the stockroom, a lot of those anthologies never even made it to the bookstore shelves. They went home with me, and a lot of my paycheck was left behind in that store. Kirby McCauley, Martin Greenberg, Jeff Gelb, and John Skipp & Craig Spector edited the likes of Roberta Lannes, Douglas E. Winter, Richard Laymon, and Lisa Tuttle. Forget movie and rock stars, I grow giddy over writers.

The tour de force of those anthologies was Ellen Datlow and Terri Windling's *The Year's Best Fantasy and Horror*. The covers were beautiful, conjuring up fantastic worlds from the start. Inside, treasure—summations of that year's fantasy and horror in all its shapes and forms and always the obituaries to remember those fallen comrades of the dark pen.

And the stories!

Twenty-one years of this anthology series grace my bookshelves. Lots of stories read but many still waiting. One Saturday morning, sitting at my desk in my home library with a steaming mug of coffee, I randomly plucked from the shelf nearest me the "Seventh Annual Collection." Mind you, by this time, the anthology was no longer being published, its editors on to other projects—something I mourn to this day. There was nothing like it, and while today there are various incarnations on the theme, I still long for the original. So that morning, I opened that volume to the table of contents and scanned titles and authors.

"Crash Cart" Nancy Holder.

A story I'd never read, *sitting on my shelves for over a decade*. I know Nancy Holder. We both live in San Diego. I've taken her writing class; she's come to my house for a party; we move in the same circles. But I hadn't always known her personally. Long ago, Nancy Holder was a byline in the anthologies I loved. A storyteller I respected—especially because she was a woman horror writer. She had no qualms about dabbling in the Splatterpunk phenomenon— a maligned sub-genre of horror whose criticism I vehemently protest.

I cracked the book to page 302 and started reading.

What I want to write here are the expletives I blurted as I read the story. That's the type of critique to do it justice. Instead, to be polite and professional, I'll yield to literary jargon: well-drawn protagonist; a disturbing thematic concept; well-paced storyline; a plot with deftly executed twists.

Well, that just told you jack about a story that blew me away. So, screw it, I'm going back to my original comments:

Holy fuck! One twisted mother of a story. A sick premise that shocked me to the core. A conclusion that left me stunned. Goddamn.

I hope there weren't any spoilers in my description.

Here was a guerilla of a story, lurking on my shelves only to jump me when I wasn't expecting it, leaving me reeling for the rest of the day and to this day. I read "Crash Cart" to my husband. I told others about it. "Do you know this story?" I asked. Not even my fellow horror writers knew the tale, and it was in a respected anthology.

Which got me thinking about all the short stories out there— lost to time. I contemplated the fate of short stories published and passed from memory, and I came to the realization that horror stories written by women were probably even more lost than those by men writers.

And I knew then that something had to be done because stories likes Nancy Holder's "Crash Cart" deserve to be remembered and reread.

Crash Cart

Nancy Holder

Alan sat for a long moment with his eyes closed, allowing his fatigue and disappointment to wash through him like a gray haze. Felt himself drifting and sinking; if he didn't move, he would fall asleep. He opened his eyes and picked up his soup spoon, and was shocked at the amount of fresh blood on the sleeve of his scrubs. Perhaps he should have changed into fresh ones.

Then he looked down at his bowl of cream of spinach soup and winced: it looked just like the stuff that had backed up through the feeding tube in Elle Magnuson's stomach two hours ago as she lay dying. That crap seeping out, then the minor geyser when her son tried to fix it.

Christ, why the hell had her family done that to her in the first place? All the Enfamil had done was feed the tumor, for weeks and days and hours, and the last, awful few seconds. Code Blue, and they had yelled and screamed for him to do something, even though everyone had spoken so rationally about no extraordinary measures when she had been admitted. Her daughter shrieking at him, shouting, crying. Her son, threatening to sue. Par for the course, Anita Guzman had assured him. She'd been a nurse for twenty years, and *hombre*, she had seen it all.

Dispiritedly, he slouched in his chair. He had really liked that old lady. Her death touched him profoundly; his sorrow must show, for no one came to sit with him in the cafeteria. He looked around at the chatting groups of two's and three's. How long before he became the type of doctor for whom nobody's death moved him? Par for the long haul, years and years of feeding tubes and blood. Why had he ever thought he wanted to be a doctor?

Maybe she had been special, and they wouldn't all be this way. Maybe that's why the feeding tube and the shrieking and the threats. It was so hard to let go, of certain people especially.

He pushed the soup away, marveling that he had been stupid enough to order it in the first place. He really had no appetite for

15

anything. Which was bad; he had hours to go until his shift was over. He didn't understand why they worked first-year residents to death like this. He never had a chance to catch up; he always felt he was doing a half-assed job because he was so tired. What if he made a mistake that cost someone their life?

What if he could have done something to save Elle Magnuson? She'd been terminal; he knew that. But still.

Alan unwrapped a packet of crackers and nibbled on one. They would settle his stomach. Maybe. If anything could. Last Tuesday, when he had asked Mrs. Magnuson how she was feeling, she had opened her bone-dry mouth and said, "I sure would love a lobster dinner." And they looked at each other—no more lobster dinners for Elle Magnuson, ever, unless they served them in the afterlife. Jesus, how had she stood it? Spiraling downward so damn fast— her other daughter hadn't made it from Sacramento in time. It had been a blessing, that last, brutal slide, but it didn't seem that way now.

He dropped the cracker onto his food tray and wiped his face with his hands.

"Oh, God, Jonesy! *God!*" It was Anita. She was bug-eyed. She flopped into the chair across from his and picked up his soup spoon. "You're not gonna believe this!"

Before he could say anything, she threw down the spoon and grabbed his forearm. "Bell's wife was brought into the E.R."

"What?"

"Yeah. And he comes flying in after the ambulance, just *screaming*. 'I want my wife! Right now!' " She imitated him perfectly except for her accent. " 'I want her out of here!' "

Shocked, Alan opened his mouth to speak, but Anita went on. "Then they strip her down, and she's covered with welts, Alan. Cigarette burns. Bell's absolutely ballistic. And the paramedics drag MacDonald—that new ER guy?—over to a corner and tell him there are whips and chains on their bed and manacles on the wall, and in the corner, there's a fucking *crash cart*." She gripped his arm and leaned forward, her features animated, her eyes flashing. "Do you know what I'm saying?"

He sat there, speechless. Eagerly, she bobbed her head. "A crash cart," she said with emphasis. A crash cart with the paddles that restarted your heart. A crash cart that brought you back from the dead. In the Chief of Surgery's house.

For his wife.

He reeled. "Holy shit."

Her nails dug into him. "He would torture her so badly, she'd go into cardiac arrest. Then he'd bring her back."

"With the crash cart?" His voice rose, cracked. He couldn't believe it. Bell was his mentor; Alan looked up to him like a father. Occasionally they talked about getting together to play chess. This had to be an April Fool's joke. In January.

"Believe it, *mi amor.*" Anita bounced in her chair. "He's in custody." Alan stared at her. "I'm telling you the truth!"

"Bullshit," he said savagely.

"Is not! Go see for yourself. His wife's been admitted."

Numb. Scalp to sole. He ran his hand through his hair. A joke, a really stupid joke. Sure. Anita was Guatemalan, and she had this very strange sense of humor. Like the time she had stuck that stuffed animal in the microwave. Now, that was just sick.

"C'mon," she said, grabbing his wrist as she leaped to her feet. "Let's go check her out."

"*Anita.*"

"C'mon. Everyone's going up there."

He'd often wondered what Dr. Bell's wife was like; there were no photos of her in Bell's office. He had imagined her beautiful, talented, supremely happy despite the fact that she and Dr. Bell had no children.

He jerked his hand away. "No," he said hoarsely. "I don't want to see her. And I think it's gross that you—"

"Oh, lighten up. She's unconscious, you know."

"I'm surprised at you." Although in truth, he had peeked in on other patients whom doctors and nurses had talked about—the crazies, the unusual diseases, even the pretty women.

"Oh, for heaven's sake!" Anita laughed at him and let go of his arm. "Well, *I'm* going. I have twenty minutes of dinner left. It's room 512, if you're interested. Private. Of course."

"I'm not interested."

"Suit yourself." She grabbed his cracker packet and took the uneaten one, popped it in her mouth. "Eat your soup. You're too skinny."

She flounced away. At the doorway of the cafeteria, she saw more people she knew and greeted them with a cry. "Guess what!" and they followed her out of the cafeteria.

Alan sat, unable to focus, to think. He couldn't believe it. He just couldn't believe it. Not Bell. Not this. It was a vicious rumor; he knew how fast gossip traveled in the hospital, and how much of it was a load of crap.

His stomach growled. During the long minutes he sat there, the soup developed a film over the surface. A membrane. He stared at it, thought about puncturing it. Making an incision. Making it the way it had been.

With a sigh, he covered it with his napkin. Rest in peace, cream of spinach soup.

He jumped out of his chair when St. Pierre, a fellow resident, clapped him on the shoulder and said, "Jesus, Al, you hear about the old man?"

"Yeah." He wiped his face. "Yeah, I did."

Then he went to the men's room, thinking he would vomit. Instead, he cried.

◉

At one in the morning, he went to the fifth floor. The nurses were busy at the station; he wore a doctor's coat and had a doctor's "I belong here" gait, and no one challenged or even noticed him.

The door to 512 was ajar. There was no chart.

A dim light was on, probably from the headboard.

He stood for a moment. Gawking like the other sickos, like someone slowing at an accident. *Shit.* He turned to go.

Couldn't.

Pushed open the door.

He walked quietly in.

She lay behind an ivory curtain; he saw the outline of her in her bed. The lights were from the headboard, and they reflected oddly against the blank white wall, a movie about to begin, a snuff show. He walked past the curtain and looked sharply, quickly to the right, to see her all at once.

Oh, God. Black hair heaped in tangles on the pillow. IV's dangling on either side. An oxygen cannula in her nose. He drew closer. Her small face was mottled with bruises and cuts, but it could have been pretty, with large eyes and long lashes, and a narrow, turned-up nose. He couldn't tell what her mouth was like; it was too swollen.

She stirred. He didn't move. He was a doctor. He had a right to be there. He flushed, embarrassed with himself. All right, call it professional curiosity.

Gawking.

There were stitches along the scalp line. Jesus. He reached toward her but didn't touch her. Stared at her bruises, the long lashes, the poor lips. He saw in his mind Dr. Bell manacling her to the wall, doing…doing things…

…making her heart stop, *my God, my God, what a fucking monster…*

But what about her?

He wouldn't let that thought go farther, wouldn't blame the victim. He'd been commended last month for his handling of the evidence collection for a rape case. Dr. Bell had written a glowing letter: "Dr. Jones has shown a remarkable sensitivity toward his patients."

Dr. Bell. God. *Dr. Bell.*

How could she? How could she let him? Until her heart stopped. Until she was clinically *dead.*

Mrs. Magnuson had clung to life with a ferocity that had proven to be her detriment—cream of spinach—making her linger and suffer, almost literally killing the fabric of her family as they began to unravel under the strain.

He stared at her. And suddenly, he felt a rush of…

…anger…

…so fierce he balled his fists. The blood rushed to his face; he clenched his teeth, *God,* he was so pissed off. He was—

"Jesus." Shocked, he took a step backward.

She stirred again. He thought she might be trying to speak, coming up from whatever she was doped up on.

In the corridor, footfalls squeaked on the waxed linoleum. He felt an automatic flash of anxiety, a little boy sneaking around in places he shouldn't be. Mrs. Magnuson had called him "son" and "honey," and he had liked her very much for it.

The footfalls squeaked on, and he shook his head at his reaction. There were few places in the hospital he was actually barred from entering. His mind flashed on Dr. Bell shuffling through the morgue like some demented ghoul; sickened, he shut his eyes and decided to leave.

Instead, he found himself standing closer to her. His hand dangled near all those black curls; and for an instant, he thought hard about picking up some of those curls and pulling—

—hard.

"Jesus." He spoke the word aloud again and wiped his face with his hand. What the hell was wrong with him?

He had a hard-on. He couldn't believe it; he stepped backward and hurried from the room.

◉

Down the corridor, where the physicians' showers were, he washed his face with cold water and dried it with a paper towel. His hands shook. He staggered backward and fell onto a beechwood bench that lined the wall. Across from him, gray lockers with names loomed over him: Jones, Barnette, Zuckerman. Dr. Bell had no locker here; of course, he had his own office, his own facilities.

Hurting her.

Jesus. He buried his face in his hands, still shaking. Mrs. Magnuson would be absolutely incapable of believing what he had been thinking while he was in 512.

And what had that been?

He stood and walked out of the room. It was time to go home; he was overtired, over-stimulated. Too much coffee, too much work. Losing the old lady. Mrs. Magnuson. She had a name. They all had names. But what was *her* name?

Mrs. Bell. Ms. Bell. What was the difference?

He hurried back down the corridor and back into 512.

She lay behind the curtain; the play of shadow and white somehow frightened him, but her silhouette drew him on. He almost ran to her; he was panting. He had another erection, or perhaps he had never lost the first one. He was propelled toward her, telling himself he didn't want to be there, didn't want to, didn't. She was unconscious: Sleeping Beauty.

He touched her forearm. There were bruises, cigarette burns. Scars. Didn't her friends wonder? Did she have no friends? Bell was so friendly and outgoing, kind. He would have had lots of parties. He talked about barbecuing. His special sauce for ribs.

His chess proficiency, teasing Alan in a gentle way, telling him how he'd beat him if they ever played.

Beat him.

Alan found a place that had not been harmed and pressed gently. He moved his hand and pressed again.

On top of the bruise.

Pressed a little harder.

His erection throbbed against his scrubs. His balls felt rock-hard; God, he wanted…

…he wanted…

He pressed again, this time on a cigarette burn. Touched his cock. It was so hard. He was short of breath, and he wanted her so badly. He wanted…

He pinched the burn with the tips of his fingers, his short nails. He felt so dizzy, he thought he might fall into her bed; he hoped he would. Swimming through something hot and active and moving, with volition and something so powerful, he stretched out his hand and cupped her breast. Squeezed her nipple. Squeezed harder.

She stirred. Her two blackened eyes fluttered open. He did not remove his hand. More blood was rushing to his cock, if that were possible. He was swaying with desire. The room spun. Those black eyes, staring at him, filled with tears as she smiled weakly.

"It's…okay," she whispered.

He jerked his hand away and drew it beneath his chin as if it had been severely injured.

"It's okay," she said again.

"I…I…" He averted his head as bile rose in his throat; he was sick to death; God, what had he been doing?

Her voice came again: "It's okay." Pleading. The hair rose on the back of his neck.

Oh, Christ, she wanted him to hurt her.

He wanted to do it.

At this time, the vomit flooded his mouth; he ran from the room.

○

He didn't take a shower or change his scrubs. In the cold light of his car, he avoided the rearview mirror. He dropped the house keys twice. His mouth tasted of sickness; he thought of Mrs. Magnuson's cream of spinach soup.

His roommate, Katrina, who was also a doctor but was not his girlfriend, had left on the TV without the sound; a strange habit of hers—she did that when she studied. There was a note that someone had called about the bicycle he wanted to sell. The bicycle. His patient had died and he had molested—

—tortured—

—crash cart—

He opened the fridge and grabbed a beer. Put it back and got Katrina's bottle of vodka out of the freezer. Swigged it. He felt so sick. He felt so disgusting.

There were sounds in her room. Deliberately, he reduced his noise level; if she asked him what was wrong, he wouldn't be able to tell her.

Because he didn't know.

◎

An hour later, puking his brains out. Katrina hovering in the background, muttering about God knew what. Praying to the ghost of Mrs. Magnuson, dreaming of Ms. Bell.

Of her versatile heart.

Of the power and the need of that heart

that so often stopped…

that so often started.

Oh, God.

"What happened tonight?" Katrina was asking, had been asking, over and over and over. "What happened?"

"Lost a patient," he managed between bone-rattling heaves. His knees knocked the tequila bottle, and it arced as if they were playing Spin-the-Bottle; they had agreed to be platonic, and it had never been a problem. He liked her enormously, respected her.

"Oh, God, Alan. Oh." She stroked his hair. She had a glass of water at the ready; she was solicitous that way. If she'd known what he had done, she would probably move out. At the very least. Maybe she would have him arrested and thrown out of medicine.

"Mrs. Magnuson." He had told Katrina about her.

"Oh, I'm sorry." Soothing, sweet. He could feel himself shriveling inside. He was sick.

He was sick.

"Alan, drink this water." Rubbed his back, rubbed his shoulders.

It's okay.

He sobbed.

◎

A few hours passed; he dozed, then slept. Finally at about seven, he woke and realized he hadn't been very drunk; except for a draining sensation of fatigue, he was all right. Katrina had left him some toast and a couple of aspirin and a note that said, "I'm really sorry. Hope you feel better."

He showered and changed his clothes, forced down the toast but not the aspirin, had coffee, and drove to the hospital. He had to talk to her, to apologize, to make what couldn't be right, right.

No one paid him much notice when he went to the hospital— a few bobbed heads, a mild expression of surprise that he was back so soon. He pushed the button for the staff elevator; as he waited, a young nurse whose name he couldn't remember joined him. She said, "Did you hear about Dr. Bell?" His terse nod cut off the conversation.

The elevator came. They both went in. He pushed five and stood apart from her, his hands folded. He watched the numbers; at four she left with a little smile. She was very pretty. As pretty as Ms. Bell might be.

The doors opened. Her room was to the left.

He turned right and walked into one of the supply rooms.

Got a hypo.

He put it in his trouser pocket and headed back toward the left. Perspiration beaded his forehead, and his hands were wet. He felt cold and tired.

Filled with nervous anticipation.

Sick, Sick. He was almost to her room. He felt the hypo through the paper wrapper. He was going to stick it someplace. Into her shoulder, maybe, or her wrist.

Or her eye.

His erection was enormous; it had never been this big, or hard, or wanting.

God. He sagged against her door. Tears spilled down his face. He held onto the transom and took deep breaths.

He was going to go in there, and she would want it.

"No," he murmured, but he was about to explode. "No."

"Hey." He started, whirled around. Anita Guzman stood in the hall. "You okay?"

"Man." He wondered if she could see his erection; as she stood looking at him, it started to go down.

"They're going to fry him," Anita hissed, lowering her voice. "Fucking fry that *chingada* asshole."

"What?" he asked faintly.

She blinked. "You don't know." She made a helpless shrug. "I had to pull an extra shift. Alan, Bell's wife died last night."

His heart jumped. "No."

She nodded vigorously. "It was her heart. They took her to ICU but—"

"No." He ducked his head inside the room. The ivory curtain was there, the form stretched behind it. He walk-ran toward her, his chest so tight that his breath stopped.

The dark curls, the small face. He whirled around. Anita stood in the doorway. He said. "But she's still here."

"No. I had the room wrong," she whispered, wrinkling her nose in confession. "Mrs. Bell was up on the sixth."

His stomach cramped, and the room began to tilt crazily; with a trembling hand, he gripped the edge of the bed. "Then...who is this?"

Anita came around the curtain and barely looked at her. "I don't know. But it isn't Bell's wife. This place is full of battered women, you know? Well, I gotta get back." She gave him a wave, which he didn't return.

Not Bell's wife. Not Bell's work.

But partly his.

Dr. Bell, so kind and generous. Dr. Jones, so sensitive.

This place is full...

The woman opened her eyes. Her gaze met his, held it, would not let him look away. His penis bobbed inside his underwear.

"It's okay," she murmured. Her broken mouth smiled weakly. "Please. It really is."

Sandra M. Odell on Tanith Lee's "The Princess and Her Future-Asia: The Eighteenth Century"

Tanith Lee snuck into my dreams to whisper dark and wondrous things in my early teens, and "The Princess and Her Future-Asia: The Eighteenth Century," from her collection *Red as Blood: Or, Tales from the Sisters Grimmer*, has stayed with me ever since. Here is a retelling of "The Frog Prince," told with one eye on the shadows and the other on the rich details woven into the telling. The princess does indeed lose her golden ball in the well, and it is returned by a prince, but that is where the similarities end. Tanith Lee draws the reader in with her deft use of setting, offers a cup of honeyed wine, and only after the drugged wine has taken affect does the reader realize she can't move, and there are other shadows in the corners of the page. And the fairytale will never again be the same.

◧◧◧

The Poison Eater

Sandra M. Odell

Doby eats half a pack of cigarettes without so much as flinching. Camels, breaks them in half and eats them filters and all. Same with a Marlboro Menthol Spence pulls out of a pack he unwraps himself. Three bites, chews, and washes it down with a swig of Mountain Dew.

A swallow of dish soap, then an air freshener stick, then cigarettes. The rest of us stare.

Doby burps and wipes his mouth with the back of his hand.

"Pay up."

We do, even Spence, though he doesn't look happy, which is messed up because this was his idea in the first place.

Doby stuffs the wad of ones into the front right pocket of his jeans.

Spence frowns. "So, that's it?"

Marty's Mart closed at one so we have the back lot to ourselves, us and a couple of cats sniffing around the dumpsters. The night smells like garbage, Scotch broom, and diesel exhaust from the semis passing by on the 422 overpass on their way to Akron. That's all the world does any more is pass Youngstown by. And my folks wonder why I want out so bad.

"That the best you can do?" Spence says.

Doby's got to be pissed, I would be, but I can't really tell in the shadows. All we got is the moon and the streetlights on the corner for light. "Like what?"

Spence can be a real jerk sometimes, and the mosquitoes are getting to me, so I say, "Stop being an ass. He did it, didn't he?"

"Big deal, he ate soap and a couple of cigarettes. I got a kid cousin who can do that, then he shits himself for a week and it's all good."

D-Jay, Carlos, and the rest nod like they agree. Doby's face looks bunched up, like maybe he's gritting his teeth. Spence reaches into his backpack. "You want a real pay up? I got something for you."

He pulls out a fat white plastic bottle with a blue cap and sets it in front of Doby. I catch the edge of the label in the light. Bleach?

"You think you're the man and shit, let's see you down some of this," he says.

That's too much for me. "C'mon, man. That shit's poison."

The others look about how I feel, even D-Jay, but not Doby. Doby cuts a look from Spence to the bleach and back.

Spence taps the lid and smiles like a shark. "He's the one who said he can eat anything, made a big deal of it, so let's see him do it."

He's playing Doby is all. Before I can tell Spence what he can do with his bottle, Doby reaches into his jacket and pulls out a thin yellow and blue can. "All right. You want it so bad, let's make it interesting." He tosses the can into D-Jay's lap. "But you gotta make it worth my time."

D-Jay picks the can in his lap like it's a snake. "Cigarette lighter fluid?"

This time Doby taps the cap on the bleach bottle. Even in the shadows, his smile is cold and crazy. "Squirt it in, as much as you want. Ten bucks a swallow."

Suddenly the night's real quiet. No trucks, no mosquito buzz, no nothing. Spence isn't smiling so much now.

I stand up. "All right. That's it. You guys are crazy if you think—"

"Siddown," Spence says to me without looking away from Doby.

"He's not going to do it, and you're a 'tard for thinking he will. I got better things—"

"You pussying out, Connor? Sit your ass down."

Everybody's looking at me, even Doby. I want to kick Spence in the teeth, want to pour the bleach down his throat, and watch his stomach eat its way out his ass. Spence is a 'tard, but Jenna says she loves him. Besides, Mom wants me to hang with him so the baby has a father when it's born, like anything I do will keep Spence around.

Pete and Jamal and Eddie look like they want out, too, but Spence leads the pack. If I back out in front of him, I do it in front of all of them, and then word gets around school.

Maybe I'm the 'tard. I sit down.

Doby nods and smiles like a razor, white teeth in a dark face.

"Show me the money," he says.

We dig in pockets and wallets and come up with a wad of bills Spence passes to me. Bastard. I count it out. "Sixty-five bucks."

"Seven swallows," Spence says.

Doby shrugs, nods. "Whatever."

Spence looks even whiter, if that's possible. He's got to know Doby won't do it, but it's his turn to put up or pussy out. Doby's playing him now.

D-Jay's always been Spence's bitch, but he just stares wide-eyed from Doby to the lighter fluid in his lap until Spence punches him in the arm. "Do it."

D-Jay flinches. "I, uh, I…"

"Squirt it in," Doby says again.

Eddie squirms and says, "Listen, I got to get goin'—"

Spence twists off the bleach cap like he's wringing Doby's

neck. The smell cuts through the dumpster stink. "Do it," he snarls at D-Jay, and D-Jay does. His hands shake so bad he squirts lighter fluid down the side of the bottle before he gets the red nozzle inside. The smell of the two together has me rethinking if I should leave.

Doby grabs the bottle, swirls it around. "Seven swallows."

Spence kind of nods.

Doby brings the bottle to his mouth. He's not going to do it; he can't do it. I'm reaching for the bottle, Hayden and Jamal telling him to stop. Doby tips the bleach back, and we're groaning and swearing and gagging as he chugs it down. The smell fills my head, coats the back of my throat; my stomach twists and burns. Somehow my cell phone is in my hand, and I'm calling 911, but I can't look away. Four, five, six...

"Nine-one-one. What is the nature of your emergency?"

Seven.

Doby lowers the bottle and smacks his lips, looking straight at me. "Pay up."

"Nine-one-one. What is the nature of your emergency? Caller, are you there?"

I wait for Doby to scream or hurl or burst his stomach or something. He lifts his eyebrows and holds out a hand.

"Hello? Caller, are you there?"

Eddie drops his phone. I close mine, and pass the cash to Doby.

Spence stares, mouth wide open, and then gets all pissed because he got owned. "You crazy or something?"

"I'm sixty-five bucks richer than you, that's what I am," Doby says.

Spence grabs the backpack and stands. "Well, you call or do whatever you want. I'm not stickin' around for the ambulance when you explode. I didn't do nothing."

He looks around like he'll kick the shit out of anyone who says otherwise, then takes off without looking back. D-Jay, too, then the rest one at a time until it's Eddie, me, and Doby.

As Doby arranges his money into one roll, my cell goes off, so does Eddie's. I check the number: 911. Eddie looks at me like I'm supposed to know what to do, but I got no ideas, so I hit silent and stuff the phone in my pocket.

Eddie won't look at Doby. "You should really go see a doctor or something, man."

Doby stands, kicks the bottle of bleach over, and it suddenly smells like a Laundromat on a Saturday. "I'm fine."

"No, seriously, Dob. I can drive you."

"No thanks."

Eddie doesn't look like he wants to take Doby anywhere, and talking wastes time. I wipe my hands on my jeans. "We got to get going before they send the police or something."

That's all Eddie needs. He takes off, and it's me and Doby.

Doby zips his hoodie. He lights a cigarette, a Camel. "What are you waiting for?"

I have no idea. Spence put him up to it; I didn't do nothing but hold the money. It wasn't my fault, yet I can't just leave him. "Maybe you should stick a finger down your throat or something. I got a pencil if you want."

Doby takes a drag, the ember making wicked shadows across his wide nose and cheeks.

"You really need to get to a doctor." It sounds lame, but I can't exactly knock him down and drag him to the emergency room when that might mess him up more. What's the number for Poison Control? How long do I have before he starts screaming? Maybe there was more water than bleach, and the lighter fluid was really vegetable oil.

Doby French inhales another drag. "I said I'm fine."

Lit end first, he eats the cigarette in two bites and walks away.

◎

I catch hell when I get home because 911 called my house when I wouldn't answer my phone, and Mom was late for work because she waited for me. She takes my phone and tells me Dad is going to "set you straight" when he gets home from his back shift. Later, Dad rolls his eyes and tells me not to worry Mom so much.

I don't expect to see Doby at school the next day, but he shows up for homeroom like nothing's wrong. He looks straight at me on his way to the back row in math like he's daring me to say something.

Carlos lets on how Spence rags on Doby in American history, but won't go near him. "Not like Spence gave a shit first off, but I feel where he's coming from," Carlos says around a mouthful of fries at lunch.

"That's bogus, man." I finish my cheeseburger, roll the tomato up in the lettuce for a salad burrito.

"I'm serious. What he did, that was messed up. I mean it."

"You scared of Doby?"

"What? Oh, hell no." Carlos downs his milk.

"You totally are, aren't you?"

"Gimme a break."

"I'm serious. You're just like Spence."

Carlos stuffs his napkin in the milk bottle, doesn't look at me. "What you think?" he says almost too soft to hear over the cafeteria noise.

Yeah, me too.

We talk about something else.

Five minutes before the end of lunch, I walk by Doby on my way to drop off my tray. He's alone at the table, earbuds leading to a hoodie pocket, tearing apart a slice of pepperoni pizza and eating it a greasy piece at a time.

He doesn't look pale or sick or anything. "Hey, Dob."

Doby stops eating just long enough to make me think he hears me, but doesn't look up.

As far as I know, Doby's an okay guy. He's odd man out, even dweebs think he's not cool enough to make up for being smart, but I don't have a hard spot for him or nothing. Really never gave him much thought until he mouthed off to Spence. "You got, um, a partner yet for the environmental presentation?"

He pulls out an earbud and stares up at me with that same look from math. He's the kind of thin my dad calls no-chin pencil neck. My dad's a dork sometimes. "No. Why?"

"Just asking. I mean, I looked at the packet and started taking notes, but I don't have a partner yet. You interested?"

Doby finishes his pizza, wipes his hands on his jeans. "Sure, I guess."

Why'd I ask? The warning bell sounds. Benches and tables scrape across the floor as everybody hurries towards the garbage cans. Carlos cuts us a look from across the room, but doesn't stop. Jenna is too busy with her friends to pay attention to me, not like she ever does at school anyway. Spence glares at us, his arm around my sister like she's his property.

"Yeah, um, okay." I hitch up my backpack, take a step towards the garbage cans. "See you in class and we can set something up?"

Doby shrugs. "Whatever."

I don't stick around.

Two days later, I'm out the door with the escape bell and on my way to the bus when I see shit going down by the planters out front. Carlos, Justin, and a couple others have Doby cornered, knuckling him in the arm, getting up in his face. Some nearby keep an eye out for school security. The rest pretend not to watch.

Doby is pissed, gut you and leave you to bleed pissed, his face all flushed and shoulders hunched tight. He wants to hurt them bad. I feel it in my stomach, the way he wants to grind their faces into the cement. Carlos and the rest keep pushing him to make the first move, but Doby doesn't do shit back, never does, which only makes it worse.

I'm moving before I realize it. Next thing I know Doby is at my back, and I'm leaning into Carlos, talking low, "Wassup, man? C'mon, you don't wanna do this, huh?"

Everyone's watching us. "What the fuck, man?" Carlos says in my ear, his breath hot and sour against my cheek. "This got nothing to do with you."

"I know, I know, right? So leave off and we're cool." I don't want to do this for a whole bunch of reasons. I've known Carlos since the third grade, he's a bud, but treating Doby like the meat of the week is all because of Spence's dare and that's not cool. I don't play that. "So, why you doing this?"

"I heard he's talkin' shit about me."

"Doby doesn't talk shit, man, you know it. He didn't do nothing to you, right?" I step closer so he can feel me, letting him know I'm not going anywhere. I keep my hands flat against my legs so I don't make fists. I keep it on the low. "What's really going on?"

I see the memory of the weirdness in his eyes, his frown. "He went and said…"

"You hear him say anything, huh?"

That's when Carlos looks over my shoulder. I don't have to turn around to bet money he's not looking at Doby but at Spence. I tell him, "You ain't Spence's bitch, man. I got it, you know. Leave off, huh?"

I slide my left foot back.

Carlos finally looks away, jerks his head to the side. "Yeah, man, be right there," he says to the distance.

I didn't hear anyone call him. I back up half a step. He does, too.

We bump fists, and it's over. Carlos and the others head to the buses and cars. I think I see Spence watching from beside his car at the end of the bus line, but I can't be certain. Doesn't matter. I knew he was watching.

I'm twitchy; my shoulders ache from coming down. I turn around. "Listen, I—"

Doby puts a chunk of blue and white in his mouth. He chews it like a thick wad of gum. One of those dishwasher gel packs? Had to be gum. Had to be. He drops his skateboard and rolls off without a word, eyes wide and hating. I breathe through my mouth so I don't smell detergent.

◎

Doby sucks as a partner. He doesn't do much except tell me when I'm wrong, like he knows all about mercury levels in fish. At the library, he sits with his feet on the table and listens to music, doesn't crack a book or log on to the net, and corrects everything I do. Thing is, he's right every time, which pisses me off even more.

Jenna flips me shit. "I don't think you can get any more retarded than asking Doby Chuckman to be your partner."

Like she has room to talk. I bet she's going to end up working part time at Taco Bell and taking night classes at the community college for her GED while the rest of her friends walk come June. I tell her where to get off. Mom gets on my case; it's bad for the baby.

It's all about the baby anymore. What about me? I may not be the smartest in my class, but the recruiters liked my test scores back in February and took down my name. Mom freaked, and Dad told me he could get me a job at the recycling plant. Screw that. No way I'm sticking around.

◎

Doby doesn't show up for science for two days. Eddie says he hasn't seen him all week. I'm sweating. The presentation draft is due tomorrow, and I was stupid enough to give him my thumb drive when he said he'd check the references. For five bucks Anna gets me Doby's address from the office during third period, and I catch the express transit after school.

As soon as I step off the bus, it starts to rain. Great. I'm soaked and set to finish everything myself by the time I get to his house, fuck Doby and his freak stomach, the rusted cars and sacks of garbage in his yard, then the front door opens and I swallow everything I was going to say.

A small guy with a face like a hemorrhoid, puckered and mean, squints up at me through the screen door. "What?"

I can see the resemblance. His dad? "Yeah, uh, is Doby home?"

"Doh-ber-min! You got someone at the door!"

Doby's named after a kind of dog? That's messed up.

The man turns away. "Come on in. He's in his room, end of the hall. Mind the cat."

The cat is sad, all bald patches and bug-eyes. It hides under the coffee table piled with newspapers and garbage and hisses at me on my way down the hall.

The far door has posters of Tony Hawk and 50 Cent. I knock. Doby opens it, a paler shadow in a house of shadows. "Wassup?"

I'm still angry, but this place looks like it has enough anger. "Hey, man."

Doby looks me up and down. He steps to the side and motions for me to come in. "Hey."

The room smells like sweat, cat pee, and pot. A bed, a dresser, a couple of broken down chairs. Piles of clothes and junk make it hard to walk. Can hardly see anything with the light off and the blinds closed. "Where you been? Haven't seen you in school."

He pushes magazines and clothes off of one of the chairs, then drops onto the bed. "Not feeling good."

I sit, put my backpack at my feet. "That sucks."

He shrugs.

Does he have a stomachache? I want to ask, maybe as a joke, I'm not really sure.

"Doh-ber-min! I know I told you to take out the garbage, dammit!"

Doby gets that look again, the hurt you, hate you, make you bleed look he had at school. An ugly look. It busts through the wall beside me, grabs Doby's dad, and snaps his pretzel neck.

Doby is up off the bed, gets his hoodie, stuffs a bottle in the pocket. "C'mon."

He scoops up the bag of trash on our way out. I say goodbye

to his dad because I don't want to be rude. His dad smokes and watches wrestling, doesn't answer. He does yell something after Doby slams the door behind us, I don't catch what. Doby doesn't turn around.

We walk. Doby looks straight ahead, working his jaw the same as my dad when he's pissed. I can't get any more soaked. I didn't come to hang out, but I don't want to up and split. Doberman. A dog gets kicked all the time, you want to do the right thing and help. "You okay, man?"

Doby pulls out the bottle and has it open and two swigs gone before I smell pine and see enough of the label to realize it's not iced tea. "Yeah."

The question tumbles out of my mouth: "Dude, what's wrong with you?"

I expect him to tell me to mind my own business. Instead he snorts and takes another drink.

"Are you trying to kill yourself?" Do I stop him? Knock him over and call 911 this time like I should have done at Marty's Mart?

Another drink, half the bottle gone. "What's it to you?"

That catches me by surprise. I'm not his friend, not really, I don't think. "I dunno. I just think it'd be a waste is all. You're smart; you could be someone." I look around at the rundown shoebox houses with pastel siding, the 7-11 next to a boarded-up liquor store, a dead end street in a dead end town. My dad could have made it out, but he quit college and came back to Youngstown when his dad died. Mom wanted to be a nurse; instead, she got married and works at fucking WalMart. "I mean, Youngstown ain't worth dying for."

We cross against the light, cars laying on the horns as they swerve around us. "It's all I got," Doby says. "All I'll ever have."

I shake my head. Water drips into my eyes. "Not me. I walk with my paper next year, and I'm gone, no looking back."

"Really?"

"Yeah."

We don't say anything for a couple of blocks. "You ever get angry, Connor?" he says.

I nod. "Yeah."

He looks at me full on, not from the side, not with a snarl. "I mean pissed, hate someone mean."

That's harder to answer. Those feelings are like a genie. I got this fear that if I admit to it, I'll never be able to stuff it back in the bottle. "Once or twice, I guess."

Half a block more. Where are we? No idea.

"I do," he says. "I hate all of them, the fucks, the dorks, the douche bags." He finishes the bottle and throws it into the bushes. "This is food, right, for when I want to kill them. All of them. I might still someday."

"Dude."

"Give it all back."

That last part is as dark as his look. What does he want me to say? I think of the kicked dog, how it can turn on you without warning, and don't say anything at all.

Doby pulls out the cigarette lighter fluid, squirts a stream into his mouth. I try not to watch, but it's like a wreck on the overpass and I can't look away. He pulls my thumb drive out of a back pocket. "Here."

I take it. "Thanks."

He brings out a plastic packet of green pellets, the label a cartoon dead mouse holding a lily. "Whatever."

◎

I turn in the presentation rough and get to work on the finished project. Doby corrects me and eats bleach tablets.

Jenna starts having contractions. Mom says they're Braxton-Hicks or something. Spence gives me the eye if I'm around when he picks Jenna up for birthing classes at the hospital. He only talks to me once, when Jenna's upstairs getting ready and Mom's in the kitchen. I'm on the couch with a Dr. Pepper and chips. Spence stands in the doorway watching me play *Halo 2*.

"Hey, Connor."

I don't look up. "Hey."

"You still a pussy for the freak?"

I give a Brute Spence's face and press down hard on the fire button, blowing his ass away. "Bite me."

"Pussy," he says.

I hear Jenna coming down the stairs and suddenly he's all smiles. Mom tells them goodbye from the kitchen, and they're gone. Then she nags me to get off the game and clean the cat box.

Doby and I don't hang out so much as go for walks a couple of nights after the library closes. He drinks lighter fluid and listens to his music. Him and me, we're not from the same neighborhood but not that far from the same life. We don't talk much. It's better that way.

This is how Spence finds us. Maybe he didn't set out looking for us, I don't know, but we're cutting through the back lot at Marty's Mart and I hear him over the traffic: "Hey, freak!"

It's late, but not as dark as it was the last time we were here. I see his sneer as he walks over to us, the glitchy eyes. The bastard's tweaking. I wasn't home when he picked Jenna up. Was he tweaking with her in the car?

"Wassup, freak and pussy. Freakin' pussy." He jangles his car keys in time with his steps like some sort of Clint Eastwood wannabe.

"Whatever." I nudge Doby with my elbow. "C'mon."

Doby doesn't move. He puts the can of lighter fluid back in his hoodie pocket.

"What you got there, freak?" Spence says. "What is it this time, huh? Gasoline?"

"Fuck you," Doby says, his voice low and hard.

Spence rattles his keys. "Ooh, big man."

"Fuck. You." Lower, harder, ugly.

Spence is close enough I smell the beer on him. Pictures of Jenna wrapped around a tree, in a body bag, the baby in a little casket, are lightning behind my eyes. The anger and what I want to do to him comes hot and fast, and scares me enough to speak up. "Get lost, Spence." To Doby, "Let's go, man."

That Goddamn sneer. "You suck him off yet, Connor? His dick taste like bleach?"

Doby explodes. He knocks Spence to the dark rainbow asphalt, drives a knee into his chest and grabs handfuls of red hair. I can't move. I can only watch as Doby slams Spence's head against the pavement. Spence bucks, punches Doby in the side of the face, the ribs, again, and again, but Doby doesn't care. He's all hate, and scariest of all, Spence is swearing but Doby doesn't make a sound.

A nightmare. Doby pulls his left sleeve up with his teeth and begins to gnaw on his wrist, his own freaking wrist, like a, oh God, like a dog. He puts a knee in Spence's face, digs around his pants pocket, brings out a Swiss Army knife. He flips out a blade and saws at his wrist until it glistens, flows. He drops the knife and jams his wrist into Spence's mouth. "Drink, mutherfucker."

I couldn't be half as frightened if he'd screamed it.

Spence gags, jerks his head to the side.

Doby wrenches it back and clamps a hand over Spence's nose. "I said drink, you cocksucker. Swallow it." I can't see Spence's mouth, only Doby's hand and wrist with a black line oozing around it. "Swallow."

Doby puts all his weight on Spence's face. There's a terrible sucking, puking sound that goes on forever, then Doby takes his wrist away.

Spence coughs, and I swear he tries to scream but all that comes out is foam. Black and blacker, it shoots out like he's puking up his soul. His eyes roll back, and in the bare light I see the veins of his face crawl like worms trying to escape acid rain. Doby's hate and anger and ugly eat Spence alive. He spasms and shakes. His insides pool around his head, ooze foamy and stinking in my direction. He stops moving.

I wanted Spence dead, but not like this. Right?

"What?" The word hangs up in my throat. "What did you...?"

Doby slides off, licks his wrist, looks at me sidelong. Looks at me like a dog kicked one-time-too-many-ready-to-turn.

He holds out the lighter fluid. I can move again, take a step back.

Doby smirks and looks sad at the same time. He goes through Spence's pockets, takes his wallet and keys, grabs the knife. Then he's sucking on the blue and yellow can on his way to Spence's car. I hear the squeal of tires and see the flash of metallic blue less than a minute later.

Got to get home. Spence's dark and foamy spreading towards my feet. Home. Veins like worms. Mom and Dad. Home.

Jenna is sorting through baby clothes and chatting on the computer when I stumble through the door. She looks up from something with strawberries and ruffles. "Wassup?" she says.

I sag against the wall, try not to puke. Shaking like I'm going to fall to pieces on the outside the way my life has on the inside.

She frowns. "You okay?"

"Everything okay down there?" Mom calls from upstairs.

"Yeah, just Connor," Jenna says. To me, "Gawd, what happened with you? You look like crap."

I stagger towards the couch. Does she see what happened? What I let Doby do?

Mom, "Any word from Spence?"

Jenna fiddles with the touchpad. "Not yet. He said he'd text when he got home. Probably stopped to get cigarettes."

I gag, make a sound, not a word, and Jenna looks my way again. "What?"

"I-I…"

"You look like crap. Sit down before your fall down."

Veins like worms, and the baby, oh God, the baby.

It's over, my life is over. The genie is out of the bottle. Turn and run, no idea where. Try to outrun the taste of lighter fluid as Youngstown closes in.

Samael Gyre on May Sinclair's "The Victim"

As a *deep cut*, "The Victim" by May Sinclair fits the bill nicely. It is from 1922 and touches upon both modern gruesome and subtle psychological horror while playing against expectations of genre and presenting a chilling set of implications to consider. It is a neglected gem, originally published by T. S. Eliot alongside "The Waste Land" in his *Criterion*. That her fine dark fiction has been overshadowed by her poetry is a shame; it's time to revive interest in her groundbreaking prose. Her work is well worth seeking out. She straddled the Victorian, Gothic, and Modern periods of literature and chose ghost stories to demonstrate her vision. She mixed oblique psychological terror, the erotic, and outright horror with an elegant directness. In "The Ditch" I tried to do the same.

◎◎◎

The Ditch

Samael Gyre

The ditch scares the hell out of me.

Which ditch?

The one you end up in. The one that catches you when you trust the shape and forget its contents. The one where your life's story comes to a sordid end.

The ditch is closer than most know.

Life is like driving in a car. As long as you're on the highway, moving along in comfort with music, and snacks, and conversation, coffee or soda to sip on, sun shining, protected from cold or rain, you ignore the passing ditch, but it's there.

And you can be in it in a blink.

One second you're fine. The next, you're in the ditch broken, bleeding, and blind to life's joys. Pain goes from a black cloud barely noticed on the horizon to a cloudburst drenching you in an inescapable, suffocating world. You condense into life's last drops in the ditch. You become run-off. You become toxic spill. You're in the ditch before you know it's coming, and maybe you realize the ditch was always there as you draw your last breath—your eyes dull, as you beg someone to go for help.

And if life's so fragile, I thought, putting up my thumb along old reliable Route 66 somewhere outside a town in Ohio, how come we cling to it? Why not think of life as lightly as we think of a snot rag?

Truth is, some of us do.

A Cadillac de Ville, four-door limo style, once chocolate brown but now more the shade of dried mud, veered toward me and hit the berm, splashing gravel as it skidded to a stop. I picked up my backpack and trotted over. Opening the front passenger door, I bent down to look in. My breath clouded now. Snowflakes fell, just a few so far. It would be a blizzard the diner's radio had said.

She was older than I am. Small, with a weathered face and sun-streaked brown hair. Her smile melted years off her. Her eyes looked lively. "Where you headed?" she asked in a smoke and whisky voice.

"More away than toward," I said. "Can you take me maybe to the next town, ma'am?"

"Ooh, ma'am, is it? A polite one. Sure, hon, hop in. I can take you as far as the border, if you want."

Borders. Lines to be respected. Crossed.

"Sounds good. Thanks." As I slid in and set my backpack on the floor between my legs, I caught a whiff of something. It was bitter but sweet. My nose itched.

"Patchouli," she said. "Wards off demons."

"It's nice," I said, wondering if I meant it, then wondering about which part of what she'd said alerted me to possible lies.

"It's retro. Sixties, they tell me." She spoke easily, her voice edged with roughness but still warm. "Not that I remember them. If you remember them, you weren't part of them, huh?" She laughed back in her throat but with good humor. "Not that I'm old enough anyways."

Nervous, I thought. Drawing attention to her age meant she

wanted me not to notice. She's breaking the ice. I should say some things, put her at ease. "Well, ma'am, I'm not old enough either but I'll tell you, I read about those years, and I think it was a shame, what Nixon did. Seems to be how power works, though."

She nodded and avoided a pot hole I had not seen coming. She knew the area, I realized. Drove it often. "You live around here? I mean, you don't hafta go out of your way for me. Border's a ways off."

"I go back and forth a lot." Her body, under the hoodie, sweat shirt, jeans, and work boots, looked lean from work. Some women take good care of their bodies. For others, it's the other way around.

I thought about the coasts. "Don't we all?"

She laughed. "Looking for some work?"

"I do odd jobs when I need money. Doesn't come up often. Got used to being on my own."

"What do you do for food?"

"Dumpster dive." I said it proudly, like I'd discovered it, even though I'd last eaten in a diner favored by long-haul truckers. "You'd be surprised how good you can eat from what gets thrown away."

"I guess I would."

"I wonder if that's what manna from heaven really was: Wasted, discarded food from midden heaps."

She glanced at me, her frown one of assessment, but said nothing.

I wondered if I had revealed too much of my thoughtful side. Many did not like intelligence, I'd found.

To cover, I switched from the abstract to the concrete. Opening a pocket on my backpack, I pulled out a twenty dollar bill. I set it on the dash. "For gas."

"Oh, that's not necessary. Please. I offered you a ride. It's fine. It's on the house."

"No, it's all right. Money's tight these days, gas costs money, and I don't have much use for it."

She drove for a few moments as if I weren't there. I felt her go away and come back. Then she nodded. "Okay. Thank you."

"Not a problem." And it wasn't. Money, of all things, is always there for the taking, wherever you look. It's the real stuff that's getting hard to find, like love, loyalty, and joy. And don't even mention faith, hope, and charity. Those sisters are long gone on permanent vacation, probably to some secret location. Maybe they fled to an undiscovered village in a jungle. A jungle yet to be slash-burned for cattle pens so the rich can choke down more hamburgers and hasten their own coronaries. Or maybe they're in a gulag, there are so many these days, or pirates have them in the brig of a black ship. Wherever they are, they're likely being tortured to death, ground up to feed the roses or sharks.

People are strange and hate themselves.

We drove for a while in silence.

As we crossed a rickety bridge she asked if I liked country music. I hate it with a passion because it reminds me of my father pounding my mother to a pulp to the whine of steel guitars and nasal accents but said, "Sure," and she turned on the radio. It was set to a station that played mostly old stuff like Cash, Owens, and Pride. Their songs I liked. They spoke about real people, real situations. They were not all plastic cowboy hats, plastic hair, and plastic emotions.

I still prefer Metallica and Marilyn Manson, though. Blunt, strong, and unflinching are the ways to sing. Make a joyous noise unto the nothingness. Isn't that what some book of holes said? Cry in the wilderness.

Yes, the wilderness is indifferent to suffering, but no one wants to hear you whine. Suffering in wilderness is the next best thing to suffering in silence. Ask society.

"How are you going to kill me?" she asked then, slowing and putting on her right turn signal. She drove off the highway, bumping the car down off the verge onto a dirt road that scraped across barren fields toward a stand of trees in middle distance blur.

"How—what?" I was startled but also hurt. Did I seem such a beast?

"It's okay to tell me. I won't fight. Unless you need me to. I know how men can be."

I stared at her, seeing how pretty she might once have been, seventeen and confident. She had retained the confidence but the years had burdened her with a heavy radiance, a glow like weight. She had gravitas that half-blinded. She was hard to get a good look at.

Reaching the trees, I felt their shadows crowd the car into a held breath. It was not a bright day, and those woods blocked any chance of one. Dense underbrush moved without wind. Bark peeled like leper skin. Leaves clotted the rutted path she drove on. The heavy old car bottomed out a few times as if crushed from above. I thought about the Bataan Death March, how fallen people had been flattened into the ground.

She gunned it over the high spots, each time with a smirk. Maybe it was a cringe.

"It's just up here," she said, gesturing with her face, keeping her hands on the wheel.

I expected a rustic hunter's cabin, or maybe a squatter's shack made of mismatched scrap wood, parts of old signs, and duct tape sticky and peeling like a hobo's awful luck. Instead I saw a squat white building with a steeple and thought, holy shit, a church.

It slouched, its stained glass dull from years without care, but still, there it stood proclaiming the revelatory word of real estate for an absentee landlord.

She pulled up, looked over at me, and smiled as she cut the engine. She left the keys in the ignition. "You can have the car, after." She got out.

My scalp tingled. When I opened my door my legs did not at first respond. My heart beat fast. Shutting the car door, I trotted to catch up to her—second time that day, I realized—as she mounted the seven steps leading to the high, narrow doors.

She glanced back, gave me another smile that was almost coy. If it had not also been challenging it might have stiffened me. She pushed open the doors. I reached her and we both walked in, she with a purpose, me from inertia.

We swim in slipstreams, drawn by any passing ship.

"What makes you think I'm the kind of guy who'd do a thing like that?" I asked. "Like what you're asking."

My voice echoed, and I winced at its aural slap. It felt like a rebuke. I was a little boy shouting out in church. Heads turned, eyes glared at me.

Keep them in my head, I thought. Those memories are no good if they get loose.

This church was empty. Some of the pews lay canted or fallen. All were grimy. On the wall behind the altar cobwebs made the crucifix into a Celtic cross or maybe a guilt-catcher. The carved dead man hung cocooned. Spider Christ, I thought.

"He's not going anywhere," she said, laughing.

I watched her the way you'd watch a rabid dog. She stood her chosen ground in work clothes, her hair loose, her hands empty. "How will you kill me?"

I looked away from her gaze. "Why would I kill you?"

"Someone has to."

"Maybe, but not me. I don't have to do anything. So why me?" She just smiled.

"Wrong place, wrong time, is that it? Story of my life, huh?" My chuckle conveyed no mirth.

She stared and smiled, calm and steady. "Purity shows through skin. Did you know that? Here." She started taking off her clothes.

"Wait."

She did not wait and soon stood naked. "See the glow? That's purity. I'm old but I'm a virgin."

"Fine by me." Truth was she looked pretty good for being older. Belly sagged a little but her breasts were small and shaped well, and her thighs and ass seemed tight. She was muscular, lean.

Yeah, I could be with that, a voice in my head said.

She smiled bigger. Had she heard my thoughts?

My heart pounded enough to make me twitch as she approached me. "Go ahead." She took my right hand and closed the fingers, folded down the thumb. "Hit me as hard as you can. Hit me in the throat. Break my jaw. I'm a woman, but you're a man."

"Lady, damn it." I stepped back and tripped on the edge of a pew. As I flung my arms up to grab for balance, one of them struck her an uppercut under her chin. She spun back and fell down.

"Oh, god yes," she said.

My arm ached where I'd hit her. I got up and stood over her.

"Kick me. Stomp my throat. Kick my guts out. You can kick me in the ass, in the teeth. Think how good it feels to do that. Think how you've always wanted to."

Shivering, I raised my hands, palms out. "Look, I'm not into this, whatever it is." There was a brighter glow coming off her now to rival the moonlight. It made me a little dizzy, a little breathless. "If we could just—"

"You can fuck me if you want. As long as you kill me after. Or during, or even before, I don't care." She opened her arms and legs and smiled. It was a sweet smile, no guile. She looked like she genuinely wanted me.

44

I was so scared a few drops of urine dribbled from me, marking my jeans, and yet I wanted her somehow. Sexuality was older than any of our rules and guidelines. Older than our feelings. It takes over.

"You see?" She caressed herself. "All yours."

My body reacted even if I did not, especially when she half-closed her eyes and reached down to run a finger along her labia, bottom to top, slowly.

"See how clean I am? Laser."

She would be smoother than the silk of inside thigh skin, my voice said. One of my voices. Maybe it was hers, in my head already. I felt pressure from her gaze.

"Lady, please. Get dressed. Let's get out of here." I sounded like a scared little boy now, and it angered me. I took a step away from her.

A growl sounded from the altar.

Dog? Raccoon? Could a bear have mistaken this old church as a good place to hibernate?

Was it winter? I shivered again. My breath made clouds that evaporated. My cloth coat from a Goodwill store had snowflakes on it from outside. They had not melted.

Another growl swiped everything out of my mind but alertness and a tinge of fear. I wanted to run. Instead, I watched her go to the altar, walk around it, and shove the podium over. It crashed and rolled to one side exactly like a guy in a bar fight going down unconscious.

"What the hell?"

"Gotta show them who's boss," she said.

"Show who? What are you talking about?"

"Relic demons. Guess my patchouli is wearing off. Want to run out to the car and get the bottle from the glove compartment?"

Okay, she's crazy, my voice said. Naked or not, and as small as she was, she scared me. "I'm outta here. You're a head case, lady."

Another growl, louder and longer, stopped me.

"It doesn't like when you move," she said. "Can't you see it?"

What do you say to a crazy naked lady and her invisible demon? "I can hear it," I said.

"That's a good start."

She watched me for a moment. I watched her. I wondered if she felt the cold. She did not shiver. Her nipples were pert though.

45

Then I noticed her breath did not cloud, either. How could that be? Was she cold inside and out already?

"Kill me and he'll go away."

Back to that again. "I don't want to kill you."

"Fuck me, then."

"No, lady. Look, no offense."

"My name's Clara Mitchell."

Hell of a time to introduce herself, I thought.

Time stretched or tilted. Stained glass windows with dust cataracts dimmed as dark finished itself off outside. Wind blasted the church, rocked the steeple. Blizzard's hitting, I thought. We might be buried in here.

She leaped at me, fingers clawed, eyes flashing. Her mouth was open. She tried to bite me as I slapped her aside.

I pushed her harder the next time she came for me. She moved so fast I barely had time to react. I felt cornered even though I stood in relatively open space.

Her fury subsided as quickly as it had pounced. Her gaze roamed the far reaches of the church where shadows pulsed like sacs of spider eggs. When her eyes focused on something I could not see, she smiled.

Creeped me out.

Shaking, I sat on a pew. It creaked but held. I panted, adrenaline ebbing now. My chest hurt. My hands and feet tingled.

"Tie me up and burn the church down around me," she said then. "Fire cleanses."

"I thought you said you're pure."

"You can see it glow." She touched her body again, ran her hands over it. Her nipples hardened. A blush formed at the base of her throat and spread. "I love how flesh feels."

Still her breath did not cloud.

Mine did.

I felt like I was on Stephen King's idea of a *Candid Camera* revival. Or that *Scare Tactics* show, only with better production value and on cable, for the nudity. It was faintly ridiculous and altogether frightening.

I started to tell her something, but I giggled instead. The sound shocked me but also struck me funny. My voice had gone high-pitched, wild. I laughed until I could not stand straight. I was trying to deal with too much at once. It was cutting me down to splinters of myself.

Hysteria, I knew.

Not funny, gagging on hysteria. Mean things were getting loose inside me, trying to dig their way out.

Wiping tears from my eyes, I caught my breath and stood up again. What the hell? I had been bent over slapping my thighs and vomiting laughter as if it were poison. I'd been braying like a donkey on acid. I'd fallen over, sprawled on the floor, an ache in my right shoulder, curled into a fetal ball moaning out laughs I did not have breath for. I'd been gasping, clenched and tortured by hysterical giggles that left my ribs bruised, my lungs quivering, and my head aching.

Her crazy was seeping into me, I thought. Maybe I breathed it in, or maybe she sent out crazy waves.

I had to get out of there.

I took a shaky step and felt abandoned. I looked for the woman, the naked Clara Mitchell, and saw nothing in the church but debris, cobwebs, and my own breath. The small clouds I made were luminescent in the faint light still filtering through the storm and dusty stained glass. Her puddle of clothes was gone.

The sky rumbled, and I thought about thunder snow. An omen, one of my voices told me.

At the tall, narrow doors I glanced out and saw the dirt path covered by a foot of snow. No car, no tracks. Had I passed out? Had she driven off while I lay gasping? Wouldn't I have heard the car? How much time had stepped over me?

Trees groaned under the weight of snow. I heard branches cracking. Falls of snow were snatched by winds playing tag through the trees. These white flails looked like ghosts dying all over again. I felt sorry they were being shredded.

Shivering, I closed the doors and turned back to the debris. Going to the altar area, I broke wood from the podium and moved the empty font. It was ceramic, about the size of a bird bath. I filled it with crumpled hymnal pages to light a fire. I sat on a carved wooden chair and huddled at my bowl of light and heat, feeding it now and then with pieces of wood I broke off the pews and altar.

My stomach echoed the sky, then gave a long moan, like one of those snow ghosts lamenting its brief, meaningless flight.

I opened a tin of beans from my backpack and set it at the edge of the fire. When the beans warmed I ate them slowly, savoring each bean.

As I chewed I thought about the woman. Where had she gone? The storm was bad. Roads would be impassable. It was no night to be driving. Would she end up in the ditch? Or maybe she already had. Time was not behaving well for me.

I was dozing when she came back in. Still naked, no snow or ice on her, not blue from the cold, and glowing the brighter in the dark church.

"Oh, you have a fire going," she said. "Good."

"You hungry?"

"Not anymore." Her smile was wistful, a trickle of blood at the corner of her mouth. "It could have been you."

I nodded. "Want to sit by me and warm up?"

"Is that how you're going to kill me?"

"Yeah." I nodded again. "Sure." What else could I say? "That's how I'm gonna kill you."

"Okay," she said. I watched her walk like a cat toward me, soundless, naked. She stopped so close to me I could have kissed her belly without tilting my head. Her fingers combed through my hair, sending a cascade of tingles down my spine, into my groin.

When she pushed at my forehead, I lay back, obedient as a little boy with his mommy.

She was ice cold and weighed about as much as a handful of air. She lay on me, and her kiss was colder than deep space, hotter than lightning. It numbed me from the center of my skull outward until my skin felt only her will. Her eagerness to die. No, to be killed. That lust for inflicted death.

That's what scared me.

I struggled then. My hands came up to grip her throat. Squeezing was easier than letting her go. I twisted at her as if trying to pull her head off. I snarled and bit at her breasts. Her nipples made my tongue burn the way a pepper does. When I bit down it was like eating snow. My teeth left no mark on her. I swallowed empty cold.

My cock hardened in transubstantiation, and she freed it. She slithered onto me and I rose to meet her. I tried to split her. I hammered upward like a lumberjack racing to chop down a tree, then rolled on top of her. I pinned her, rage and lust brimming.

Inside she was that weird mix of cold and hot. It spurred me to more exertion even as my fists began hammering at her face and shoulders. Each punch felt solid but left no mark.

When I came my semen evaporated into wisps of grey smoke that wormed into the air above us. I wanted to cry.

Nothing I did hurt her in any way that I could see. I thought about that for a long time, and finally I had to tell her I did not know how to kill her.

"No one ever does," she said. "And yet you'll do it. You'll see." She snuggled into a fetal position, a faint smile making her lips look kissable.

I was afraid to nod off but exhaustion tore at me. I let myself doze only after stoking the fire as high as I dared. I used my blanket but shivered anyway.

She slept beside me, changing positions now and then. She was so still and quiet between bursts of movement that each twitch startled me. Unless she moved, I began to forget she was there. She still glowed faintly.

When I woke it was bright and silent. She was not there that I could sense. I pissed on my fire's embers and went outside to find a white world of snow. It looked pretty. It looked pure. It glowed in a healthy way.

I walked out to the main road and waited for the plows to come along. One did by late afternoon, and the crew gave me a ride to the next town. I remember passing a wreck and thinking, I'll bet there's a Cadillac under that snow mound. I asked what was known about the wreck. "Was it a vintage Caddy?"

The snow plow driver assured me it was a Ford 150, and no one had been killed in it. "Juss kids out rammin' around, skidded off, couldn't get their daddy's truck out uh the ditch."

Sounded about right, I thought.

"Any women killed around here lately?"

"What, with this here storm? Nah, ain't been since that one over toward Dayton. Seen her with my own two eyes, yessir, what a damn mess. Big fat woman, I'll tell ya, wheel about went clean through 'er. Hadda pry her off with one uh them there jaws uh life things."

Well, that wasn't it.

I asked him about that little abandoned church in the woods, expecting to hear it had burned down years before. Probably I was still thinking in terms of stories I'd heard.

"Oh that? Yeah, old chapel, some reverend built it when times

49

was good, then his congregation drifted off the way they do and he left, what? Oh, year or two back. Pity, nice little place. Always thought about I might could salvage some uh that stuff from there. Some uh that there wood's rare now. Why you ast?"

"No reason. Just saw it and wondered about it."

So that wasn't it, either.

We got to town, and I thanked him. He took a twenty from me without a blink or word, and I walked to a coffee shop. I never did find out where Clara Mitchell came from, or what her story was. Had business of my own to attend to. Had places to get away from and things I'd done to shrug off.

I know you want this to end with the snow plow driving off the road into the ditch with Clara Mitchell's ghost, or whatever it was, showing up to lead me to perdition, but, I'm sorry, that's not what happened. All that happened I already told you.

It was just one more thing for me to get as far from as I can. Before I end up in the ditch, too.

Or maybe I'm already there. Maybe I'm just like Clara Mitchell but don't know it. Sure seems like I've been on the road a long time. You don't suppose the better part of a man can end up in the ditch long before the rest of him, do you? Like maybe I'm mostly dead inside already and just waiting for my person shape to give up the running and fall off the road.

Or get knocked off. Either way, that would finish it.

Unless it wouldn't.

That's why the ditch scares the hell out of me.

It's where I left my wife and kids, too. I don't want them to hate me for running away. I tell myself I went for help. What I really did was run from their blood. Their smashed bodies.

Maybe Clara Mitchell is the woman we hit head-on when I drifted into the wrong lane while trying to find a radio station. Maybe I put her in the ditch, too. Maybe I'm responsible for helping them all die.

All I know for sure is I've got to keep moving.

Sara Taylor on Diana Wynne Jones's "The Master"

When I was fifteen I picked up Diana Wynne Jones's collection of stories *Unexpected Magic* while between novels. The dreamlike quality and uncertainty of "The Master" made my skin crawl almost as much as the unknown woman with her throat ripped out that the narrator describes at the beginning of the story. I love the duplicity of Jones's characters, the dichotomy between what is thought and what is said, and what is said and what is done.

◧◧◧

Practical Necromancy

Sara Taylor

When we got to the viewing, Mallory threw herself into Mom's coffin. Alice tried to pull her out without causing a scene, but she held on by handfuls of Mom's hair, shrieking and crying. She kicked Alice off and clung to the tie that Dad never wore when he was alive, until the sexton and two of our cousins pried her off and carried her into the back.

No one said anything. They were all too stunned, and the undertaker rushed forward to neaten our parents in their caskets. Mallory sobbed the whole way home. When I went to get her for dinner, I found she'd gathered up everything of Mom's and Dad's and brought it to her room—the photo albums from when they were dating, the wedding pictures from the wall in the hallway, the hairbrush from their bureau, Dad's razor, and Mom's bath towel with the brown splotches from where she'd cut herself shaving her legs the day they had the accident. Mallory lit candles everywhere, more than there'd been at the church, but even though she was still crying, she'd stopped screaming. I just told her to blow them out before she came down.

After dinner, she wanted to visit their graves, but Alice said no. It was too far, too dark, and she was too young. She didn't start screaming again, so we weren't surprised when she tried to climb out the bathroom window when she went for her pre-bed shower. I figured we should have let her go, but you can't argue with Alice. When I heard the front door creak open around eleven p.m., I just rolled over and went back to sleep.

Mallory's eyes were red in the morning, and there was dirt under her fingernails and caked into the creases on her hands and knees. I asked what she'd been up to, but she didn't say anything.

She'd stopped talking completely.

I thanked god for it, at first. She did her chores when I told her to, she ate what we gave her, and she didn't pitch a fit when I borrowed my favorite skirts back. It was what I'd always wanted, a generally clean house without any fighting. Alice was busy with getting control of all the paperwork my parents had left behind, and when she wasn't doing that she was busy with her boyfriend Doug, who had more or less moved in the night we got the bad news.

But then I started feeling cheated. This wasn't my Mallory— my water-balloons full of cherry Jell-O, bed sheet tents in the hallway, baby frogs in the bathtub, ice cream for breakfast Mallory. I mentioned it to Alice one afternoon, while she was hunkered down in a drift of blue-inked insurance forms on the dining room table.

"There's something wrong with Mal," I said.

"If she's mouthing off too much, smack her and give her extra chores," she answered without looking up.

"That's just it. She isn't mouthing off."

"Hide the chocolate chips, then. She only behaves when she's sneaking junk and doesn't want to get caught." She signed her name, flipped the form over, and picked up the next one.

"That's the weird thing. She's not sneaking junk. This afternoon I gave her chicken and broccoli for lunch, and she just ate it. No complaining, no bargaining, no faces even."

"Maybe she's finally growing up," Alice said.

"This isn't growing up. This is turning into a robot!" I shouted. "This is like *Stepford Wives*! This is like *Invasion of the Body Snatchers*!

Something is wrong with our little sister!"

"Annie," she finally looked at me, "what does it mean that when Mal finally starts acting her age instead of her shoe size, you freak out? Maybe she feels like Mom and Dad's death was her fault and by eating chicken she can atone for it. If she's eating chicken without fighting you, just thank god and keep feeding her chicken."

She went back to her forms, so I left her alone.

That night I couldn't sleep. Every time I drifted off I snapped back awake to lie there, not quite conscious, listening to sounds just on the edge of my hearing. Around two a.m. I woke up all the way, annoyed as hell. Doug was sleeping over. I assumed what I was hearing was their fault, and I rolled out of bed to go and give them a piece of my mind.

The hallway was dark, so I almost walked into Mallory before I saw her. She was standing outside her door, perfectly silent and eyes wide open. I jumped back and shrieked a little when I realized she was there.

"Mal, for the love of Christ, why are you up?" I hissed. She tilted her chin up so she could stare right at me, and the ambient light was just enough to make her eyes shine in the dark. She didn't say a word.

Doug was suddenly behind her. He must have come out when he heard me scream.

"She's probably sleepwalking, Annie," he said, and put his hands on her shoulders. "I'll take her back to her room. What are you doing awake?"

"I heard things, and I figured it was you guys. How do you know it's sleepwalking? She's never done it before."

"You three have been through a lot recently. It's probably just the wind; the creaking woke Alice up earlier." He turned Mallory by her shoulders and gently pushed her back towards her bedroom. I went back to my own bed, but I was almost asleep before I realized that I hadn't heard him go back to Alice's room.

◉

The next morning things were almost too normal. Alice was at the dining room table surrounded by drifts of paper when I came down, and when I asked, she said Mal had finished her chores early and gone down to Fisher's Lake. I ate some eggs, found my bathing suit, and wrestled a bike out of the garden shed so I could follow her.

It was a nice day, the kind of clear-blue-sky day you only get a dozen or so of a year. The lake was down a long dirt road from our house, about two miles, and the gravel made a pleasant crunchy sound under the tires.

As I coasted down the last long hill, I scanned the lake, but couldn't see Mallory at all. There was no one else either; it wasn't hot enough yet. Then I caught sight of her, laid out on a towel just above the waterline. She had borrowed one of Alice's bathing suits, an excuse of a bikini, and was soaking in the sun. I dropped my bike next to hers and wandered down.

"What are you doing up here?" I asked. She squinted at me, but said nothing. "You always said that tanning was for bimbos and idiots who want skin cancer." Still nothing, not even a smile. "Come on. Let's get in the water."

I reached down to help her up, but she ignored my hand and flipped over onto her stomach.

"Suit yourself. Alice is going to be pissed if you borrowed her bikini without asking." I dropped my towel next to her, took off my clothes, and set off for the center of the lake.

Once the bottom dropped out from under me I stopped, swung my legs up, and floated on my back with the sun turning the inside of my closed eyelids red. Water filled my ears and strange sounds filled my head, echoes and thrums that I could pretend were whales and fish swimming hundreds of feet below me.

A churning broke through the underwater sounds, and I bobbed up to see Mal paddling to me through the clear tea-colored water. Her hair spread out behind her like a curly cape, drifting on the surface.

"Changed your mind then?" I asked. She put a hand on either shoulder and pushed me under.

Okay, I'd been as annoying as possible lately, trying to get a response out of her, so I guess I deserved the dunking. The bottom was two yards down, and when my feet touched, I tried to bob back up. She kept her hands on my shoulders, and my feet churned up soft silt, sliding and sinking into the bottom, but not getting enough resistance to push off. I whacked at her arm, trying to signal my surrender, but she ignored the tap-out. Lungs burning, I flipped back-first towards the lake bottom, dragging her with me. She let go the moment I pulled her head under water, clearly not ready for it. I kicked away, gathered my feet under me, and shot to the surface.

"What the hell was that?" I screamed when I'd gotten my breath back. She was treading water awkwardly, gasping and scraping hair out of her face. "Were you trying to drown me?"

She didn't answer.

I swam back to shore, dried off, and pulled my clothes on. As I picked my bike up, I looked back. Mallory was standing at the edge of the lake. Alice wouldn't like me leaving her, but she was old enough to take care of herself.

"You're back quick," Alice observed, as I slammed into the house.

"Mallory tried to drown me," I barked, and stalked to the kitchen.

"What did you do to her?"

"Me? Nothing! And she's wearing your bathing suit." I pulled a tub of yogurt out of the fridge. "She's been acting weird, Alice. You can't ignore it any more. There's something wrong with her."

"I don't blame her. There've been times I've wanted to drown you myself. We're not going to recover on your schedule, Annie. Not everything is clear-cut and controllable. Leave her alone."

When Mal got back, Alice gave her an earful about taking the bikini without asking, but Mal just stood there and stared at the floor until Alice gave up. I'd taken a book into the living room. Mal plunked down on the chair across from me and stared at its cover. I ignored her until it got to be annoying.

"You can apologize any time," I said.

She didn't answer, just sat.

"This whole silence thing is getting annoying, Mal. If you're practicing to be a nun, great, start talking and I'll help you fill out the paperwork. If you're trying to drive me crazy, congratulations, you've succeeded. If you're psychologically distressed and this is a desperate, uncontrollable cry for help, blink twice and we'll get you a shrink." She didn't even grin at that, so I went back to my book. I could feel her staring at it still. It made the hair on the back of my neck stand up. I wondered if we were about to have a repeat of the lake, Othello style with one of the couch pillows. When I reached the end of the chapter, I closed the book and found my shoes.

"I'm walking into town. Want anything?" I asked Alice.

"Nope. But ask Mallory if she wants to go. It might cheer her up."

"Wanna go?" I called back to the living room. She was looking at me still, but of course, she said nothing. "Nah, she doesn't feel like it," I told Alice.

We live in the woods a couple of miles outside of town, just far enough for privacy but close enough to be able to walk it when we're really out of milk. As I set off down the driveway, I felt a weight on my shoulders. When I looked back, Mallory was at her bedroom window, watching me. I broke into a jog. Just to get there faster, I told myself.

○

That night I fell asleep almost as soon as I turned off the light, but around three a.m. I jolted awake, completely conscious all at once, like jumping into cold water.

Mallory was standing over me.

She hadn't made a sound, but I'd woken up anyway. Her hair was hanging down on either side of her face like vines, and her eyes were glinting. A dark shadow, looming over my bed. Watching me sleep.

I choked on my own air.

"The hell you doing?" I hissed at her.

She didn't move.

"Go back to bed and stop creeping me out."

Her hand rose, brushed up my shoulder towards my neck. I noticed then what I hadn't noticed in the lake: her skin was ice cold, soft and dead-feeling. I shuddered.

"Get the hell out of my room!" I jumped out of bed and shoved her backwards towards the door. She went over with a soft thud: Doug cushioned her fall. He had been standing in the hallway, outside my room.

"Here," I said, and pulled her up. Doug looked at me blankly. I felt a chill run through my gut. I stepped around him and helped Mallory to her feet, guiding her back to her room. When I turned around he was still there, staring at me. His gaze followed me as I went around him to get to my own room.

"Go to bed, dude. She'll be all right." I closed and locked the door and leaned there, listening, until I heard his footsteps go slowly down the hall to Alice's room. As I drifted off to sleep I thought I heard, again, a door creaking open, but I couldn't tell whose it was.

◉

The next morning I told Alice about it, while she was slumped over coffee. Doug left for work at half past six every morning, so if I wanted to catch her alone, I just waited until I heard his car pull out of the driveway.

"Did Doug tell you about last night?" I asked her.

"What happened last night?" She had a vague, puffy look without makeup, and the steam rising off her mug made her squint.

"On Tuesday night I ran into Mallory in the hall, and last night I woke up and she was standing right over me. And every time she's there, he's there."

Alice shook her head slowly. "He never mentioned it to me."

"I told you something was wrong with Mallory."

"Sleepwalking is perfectly normal, Annie. Quit with this obsession over Mallory." She slugged her coffee and trudged upstairs to get dressed.

That night I waited for Mal to take her pre-bed shower, then I hid in her massive closet, snugged in behind her collection of second-hand prom dresses. The room was still full of Mom and Dad's stuff, but she didn't light all the candles at once any more. She was back before long, and I heard the light click off and the rustle of sheets as she got into bed. I counted to one thousand three times before sliding out from behind the dresses and over to the crack between the doors.

Mallory's bed was opposite the closet, between two windows, and for a few moments all I could see was deep shadow and the vague square shape of the mattress. Then the cloud cover shifted, filling the room with a dim glow.

She was sitting up in bed, the light summer blanket spread neatly over her feet and legs, hands at her sides. At first I thought she'd fallen asleep sitting up, but the moonlight glinted off her eyes. She was staring in my direction, and it felt like she could see me straight through the closet door. I had thought I'd just watch her for a bit to see if she really was sleepwalking, but suddenly I realized that I was trapped in that closet until she went to sleep.

I waited, kneeling on the floor with my eye glued to the crack for what felt like hours, but she never once looked away. If she blinked, I didn't see it. A few times I dozed off, only to jerk awake when I started to overbalance, hoping she hadn't heard me, but she didn't move.

Her clock faced away from the closet door. I didn't have a watch, but I guessed it was two a.m. when Doug came into her room. The creak of the floor pulled me out of one of my upright catnaps, so it seemed to me like he'd suddenly materialized. Mallory didn't look at him, just kept her gaze fixed on her closet door. He kneeled by the edge of the bed, so their heads were on level, and turned her face so their mouths met.

I was too shocked to move and nearly burst out of the closet to ask what the pervert thought he was doing with my little sister. When he didn't do anything else, I kept still. It wasn't exactly kissing. He was breathing hard, like he was giving her mouth-to-mouth, and Mallory just drank it in. When he pulled away, she gave a gasp like she'd just chugged an entire bottle of water at once. His head dropped forward like he was overwhelmed by the force of her underage mouth. I felt sick, wondering what he would do next, and if there was anything in the closet long and hard for me to whack him with. While I was still groping around for a weapon, he got to his feet. As he turned to go, the moon slid behind clouds again. I couldn't see anymore. The floor creaked a little, and then I heard the sound of his bare feet sticking to the wooden floor in the hallway as he walked down it and the click of Alice's door closing.

The moon came out again, but the only thing I saw was Mallory's eye, no more than a foot away, staring directly into mine.

I jumped, stifled a scream, and sprang out of the closet and across the room. Her eyes followed me, barely more than glints in the dim light.

"I was just...I wanted to borrow...I fell asleep..." I gave up and bolted for the door. She followed me with measured steps but stopped at the threshold of her door. "Good night," I whispered as I skittered into my room.

I shut and locked the door, sliding my dresser in front of it: there was no way in hell I was waking up again with her standing over me. I locked my window for good measure, said every prayer I remembered from when I was little, and got into the bed.

As I closed my eyes and tried to settle down, I heard soft footsteps come out of Mallory's room and stop in front of my door. The knob rattled, then turned, but the door thudded into the dresser. She tried it again, and again the dresser held it closed. I smiled to myself and settled in to sleep. She couldn't get to me.

I heard her footsteps again, going slowly down the hall and into the empty room next to mine—our parents' room—and coming to stop right where the head of my bed pressed against the wall. There was silence for a moment, and then the quiet scratching of her nails against the wall. She stopped after a few seconds, then took it up again—*scritch, scritch scritch*—right above my head. I closed my eyes and rolled over, but even asleep I could hear it. It only stopped when the light through my blinds turned golden, and the springs of Alice's bed creaked as she and Doug got up.

◎

I waited until the front door slammed shut before going down and finding Alice.

"Look," I said, "I know you think Mallory's just fine, but I watched from her closet last night. She's not sleeping. She's just sitting up in bed staring into space."

"Just listen to yourself: 'I watched from her closet last night?' If I get a shrink for anyone, Annie, it'll be you."

"Okay, it's a little weird. But then Doug came in and started giving her mouth-to-mouth or something. He's sucked out her soul, or he's feeding on her youth, or he just really likes tongue."

Alice had been staring, bleary-eyed and tired, into her coffee, but that woke her up.

"That's just gross. Don't even make stuff like that up." She stood to go upstairs.

"But it's true!" I said.

"It's sick and weird is what it is. And it's crazy. Doug's just as likely to be making out with Mallory in the middle of the night as he is to be feeding off her life force, which is not at all. Knowing the way she usually behaves, I'd think you'd be down here telling me she was sucking out his life force, rather than the other way around."

"Okay, maybe saying he's feeding on her life force is a little ridiculous, but I was there and I saw mouth action. Lots of it."

"Annie, stop this. There is nothing wrong with our sister. Doug is not making out with her in her sleep or sucking her soul out through her mouth, and you're going to drop this now. Do you hear me?" She left the kitchen, and I followed her to the stairs.

"But Alice—"

"This is the last conversation we're going to have about this," she said. A few minutes later I heard the shower come on.

I went back to the kitchen, plunked down in one of the chairs, and watched the early light moving through the trees in the backyard. Something had to be done. The question was what? Briefly I considered cutting Doug's throat while he slept, but immediately discarded the idea. Alice would wake up, it would be way too messy, and I didn't think I could bring myself to cut anyone's throat. Something that didn't involve blood, that wouldn't necessarily be associated with me. I'd waited long enough for her to just get better; she wasn't going to as long as he was doing things to her.

One of Dad's old computers was set up in a corner of the kitchen for anyone to use, and I trudged over and sat down in front of it. One eye on the door and one ear cocked towards upstairs, I opened the Web and started searching "brake lines."

◎

Dad's red-handled cutters clunked against my leg every step of the walk into town. They barely fit inside my pocket, the point occasionally digging into my leg. I didn't run into anyone, and I didn't really think about anything specifically, especially what I was about to do. I did wonder, as I passed the gas station that marked the edge of town, what on earth people did before Google.

Doug's blue Ford Ranger was parked at the far end of the gravel lot outside the welding shop where he worked, which was on the edge of a small industrial park full of glasscutters and auto mechanics and metalworkers. I saw no one as I wandered down the central road. None of the buildings had windows, but I looked around anyway before I crouched under the front of the truck. The cutters were sharp, but my hands were small. It took a bit to get all the way through one, and most of the way through the second. I slipped them back in my pocket afterward, scuttled out from under the truck, and headed towards home without looking back.

Alice got a call from the hospital while she and I were doing the dishes. Doug had pulled out of the parking lot, made it all the way out of the industrial park before his brakes failed and slammed into the stoplight post. He was alive, awake, but not talking or responding much to anyone. She grabbed her purse and ran out, telling me to make sure that Mallory went to bed at a decent time.

I waited until I heard Alice's car pull out before I went upstairs to find Mal. She was sitting on her bed, a book open in front of her, staring at the wall.

"I took care of Doug," I said. "You're going to be all right now."

She looked at me, looked through me it seemed, but didn't say anything.

"You can start talking again. You'll be all right." I sat down on the bed and put my arm around her, but she just kept staring. Her skin was cold against my arm, made my flesh crawl. When she didn't respond, I let my arm drop away.

"Maybe you'll feel like talking tomorrow," I said weakly. Had I gotten it wrong? "Alice said to go to bed on time, okay?"

Before I left, I glanced down at the book. "Whatcha reading?" I asked, and flipped it cover-side up without losing her place. *The Forbidden Art* was printed large across the front, white on black. It didn't have a library barcode. She must have ordered it through one of our local bookshops. Mom and Dad wanted us to figure out religion for ourselves, but I had a feeling that even they wouldn't like her reading this.

"Mind if I borrow it?" I asked, and tucked it under my arm as I stood up. Of course, she didn't say anything.

I left her sitting on the bed, her eyes boring into my back as I walked out. Nothing had changed with Mallory. Maybe it was because Doug was still alive. Maybe I didn't just have to get her away from him but had to get rid of him entirely. That would be hard to do with him in the hospital with nurses everywhere, but I'd think of something.

There was a doubt niggling at the back of my mind. What if I'd made a mistake? What if Doug wasn't the reason Mallory was acting weird? But I'd seen him. And hadn't he turned up every time she'd gotten out of bed in the night? The two had to be connected, cause and effect.

The other thing I didn't want to think about was that I might not be getting my sister back. That she might be gone, that she wouldn't start acting normal even once Doug wasn't around. And then there was this book. None of us had noticed her with it, probably because she hadn't wanted us to notice it.

I locked my bedroom door and checked my closet after getting ready for bed. I didn't expect her to be hiding there, but then I didn't expect her not to be. I really didn't know what to expect anymore.

The Forbidden Art was heavy, printed on thick paper, probably to make people feel like they were getting their money's worth. I didn't want to read it myself, but I felt like Mom would want me to get it away from her. I stared at the book for a second, stood it on its spine on my desk and let it fall open. The pages ruffled, then rested right in the middle of a chapter titled "Reincarnation and Reanimation." I flipped to the title page. *Practical Necromancy and Blood Magick* was printed in smaller type beneath the title.

Mom had said once that people believed crazy things if they thought it would give them what they wanted. I knew Mallory was too smart to think that some book she'd gotten off eBay would let her bring our parents back to life, but really it wasn't much different than wishing on dandelions, only on a larger scale. Maybe Mal *had* tried, half expecting it to work, but realizing she was never getting them back had pushed her over the deep end. Or maybe it had gone wrong in some other way. "Blood Magick" sounded nasty, sounded like it could go bad even though it wasn't real.

I closed the book and again dragged my dresser in front of my bedroom door. I thought magic was silly and magick even more so, but Mallory was acting weird. I'd rather feel silly in the morning than wake up with her standing over me again. I got in bed and turned out the light.

Alice came home a few hours later, quietly as possible, but I still heard her car in the driveway, her steps on the stairs, her door closing and the rustle of her undressing. Even with her home, the safety of having her in the house, it was a long time before I fell asleep.

At two a.m. I jerked awake. I couldn't figure out what had woken me up, but then my bedroom door bumped quietly against the back of my dresser. She was trying to get in again. I listened to the *bump bump*, then to her footsteps walking slowly away. A few moments later the scratching came, right over my head.

"Nice try," I called to her. "I'm not letting you in if you're going to be a creep-ass jerk, Mallory." My voice quavered, and I cleared my throat before saying more firmly, "Now get back in bed!"

The scratching paused. Her footsteps went down the hall and down the stairs. The back door creaked open and smacked closed.

That worried me. I debated going down to figure out what the hell she was doing versus staying safe where I was, when I heard a scraping from the aluminum siding below my window. I shot up like I had current passing through me. I got up and went to the window. I pressed my forehead to the glass so I could look down.

She did it like climbing boulders, wedging her fingers in and pulling herself up by her skinny arms. Her face looked up at me, her eyes glittering in the moonlight. I screamed for Alice, then jerked the window open and leaned out.

"Get down right now, or else!" I shrieked at her, but she kept coming. I smacked the window shut and darted to my closet for something to fend her off, to knock her down. I flung my clothes onto the floor and wrenched the dowel out of place. When I turned back, she was a black shape against my window, clinging with one hand to the top of the frame and smacking the other palm against the glass. The bedroom door thunked and rattled against my dresser, Alice's shouting muffled by the door. Mallory raised her foot and gave the glass a kick, and it shattered.

As she stepped into the room, I raised the pole and jabbed straight at her middle. She caught it in both hands and jerked it away. She came towards me, bare feet crunching on the broken glass. I wrenched at the dresser blocking the door. As it began to slide, Mallory put her hands around my throat. Her breath sounded like a file on iron, like rocks in a food processor, but that was the only sound she made as her hands pressed tighter. I grabbed her wrists and tried to push her off me.

The door burst open, the dresser shrieking across the floorboards, and Alice stumbled in. My lungs burned and my head swam. Alice was screaming, I was screaming, but Mallory still had not made a sound.

Alice was on Mallory, arms around her neck in a chokehold. We staggered across the room and toward the window, locked together in a kind of macabre dance. I swung my body, kicked at Mal's ankles, then I went limp.

There was a moment of satisfaction as the surprise showed on Mallory's face. Her hands loosened. The back of my head hit the floor with all my weight behind it. Alice was still hanging on around her throat, shouting at Mallory to calm down, to stop. The glass crunched under them. They were right by the window. There was a moment when I believed that Alice would get her down, would stop this craziness.

Mallory bent forward, whipped her head down. With a thin shriek Alice pitched over Mallory's head and out the open window. The wet thud as Alice hit the ground was almost instantaneous.

For a moment Mallory stood there, looking first at me and then out the window—back and forth, deciding who to go for first. Then she climbed up onto the window ledge, the jagged bits of glass still embedded in the frame crunching as she stepped on them. She climbed head-first down the outside of the house, like a bat.

I pulled myself up on hands and knees and managed to hang my head out the window. Every single piece of glass in my skin felt white hot and sickening. My vision blurred.

Mallory was crouching over Alice, who lay on her back, limbs twisted, body crumpled, but sobbing with adrenalin, trying to get her breath back. She tried to turn her head away as Mallory put her mouth to hers, but Mallory was stronger now. It looked like mouth-to-mouth, except for the way Alice's feet and hands twitched, like she wanted to run away or fight it off. Mallory pulled away suddenly, triumphantly.

I heard the rasping of her breath over the rushing in my ears. My vision narrowed from the edges in, then everything went black.

I woke up the next morning with a crushing headache, but in my own bed, in my own pajamas. There was a lump throbbing on the back of my head, but no glass in my feet, though the parts of my skin I couldn't easily see felt pulled tight, as if by a thousand tiny scabs. The floor was clean, the dresser pushed back against the wall where it belonged, my clothes hung neatly in my open closet. The window was glassless, though covered over with a thick sheet of plastic.

Mallory was at the kitchen table when I stumbled down, her head bent over a book. Alice was hunched across from her, cup of coffee between her hands, peering into it as if trying to see the future.

"Hey guys, do either of you know what happened to my window last night?" Simple reasons existed. I could have just had a wild dream.

They both looked up at me, their eyes blank, their faces empty.

"How's Doug?" I asked, figuring that, if anything, would get Alice talking. She just stared at me. "You went and saw him last night, didn't you?" I prompted. She raised her coffee to her mouth and drank, put it back down and stared at me, silently.

As I got up and went back upstairs to get dressed, I could feel the pressure of their eyes on my back, like the pressure of Mallory's hands on my throat the night before.

Michael Haynes on Frances Garfield's "Come to the Party"

I love ghost stories, and Frances Garfield's "Come to the Party" has a wonderfully increasing air wrongness that suffuses the environment the characters inhabit. It reads, in a way, like "Hotel California" put into prose but with a deeper sense of surrealism. Originally in Stuart David Schiff's *Whispers*, I read it in *100 Hair-Raising Little Horror Stories*. The story having a connection to the writing life only deepens my affection for it. The characters are originally searching for the home of one of their publishers, who is having the author in to sign flyleaves for her book. A book, which one of her traveling companions reminds her, was rejected by a dozen other publishers. Garfield had reason to be familiar with the writing scene; she and husband Manly Wade Wellman were published in *Weird Tales* and other venues. Her published works are few, though; I only wish there were more.

○|○|○

Awaiting the Captain's Ghost

Michael Haynes

Lillian prayed that the men trudging down the path from the main road to her home were beggars or deserters or simply lost. Three men coming together to her home on an errand was too frightful to consider.

She bustled away from the front of the house. If they knocked, she would come to the door but she would not stand and wait. Upstairs she went, to Alice's room. She had boxed up most everything from here already. The rag doll Alice had loved sat on top of the dresser, orphaned. Lillian hadn't been able to bear consigning it to the cellar. She pulled the sheets from the crib. Little flecks stained them, and Lillian suddenly wished she were anywhere but here.

From below, a heavy pounding on the front door. She dropped the sheets and closed her eyes, a distant wailing growing in her mind, until the knocking was repeated.

The three men stood there when she swung the door open. They wore ragged clothes, and one of them went shoeless. Clots of dried blood stood out from the grime coating his feet.

"Yes, gentlemen?"

None of the men spoke immediately. The April afternoon sun was well past its peak, already half-hidden behind the magnolias. The air was painfully still and quiet.

At last one of them, the one with a beard, said, "Mrs. Conner?"

"Yes."

He swallowed. "Mrs. Jacob Conner?"

Lillian's vision swam. She reached for the door frame and focused on the eyes of the man who spoke. "Yes," she said. "Yes, I am Mrs. Jacob Conner."

He nodded. "I'm Sergeant Taylor, ma'am. John Taylor." He broke their shared gaze, brought a hand to his head, and rubbed his hair. When he lowered his hand, he did not look straight into her eyes. "These are Lee Brooks and Martin Clay. We've come with word of Captain Conner."

Behind the men, cicadas began their chorus. The chattering sound grew louder, and a trickle of perspiration slid down Lillian's back.

"What word?" she asked, her tight throat allowing barely a whisper.

"Mrs. Conner." And then he looked at her eyes again. She almost begged him to look away. "I am sorry to have to inform you that Captain Jacob Conner was slain at Selma on the second of April."

The words hung in the air. When Lillian did not reply Taylor went on, haltingly. "The three of us served with Captain Conner, ma'am. I knew him a bit. He was a good man, and I am sorry for your loss."

Lillian licked her lips with a tongue so dry that it felt as if no moisture was imparted by the act. "You men must be exhausted." The words felt distant, as if another person were speaking them.

"May I offer you the hospitality of our home?"

The two men—boys, really—behind Taylor glanced at each other, but he did not look back at them. "Yes, ma'am, thank you kindly."

She took her hand from the doorframe and though her legs felt weak, Lillian did not fall. "Come inside," she told them, turning away.

She left the men in the sitting room and went to fetch a bottle of brandy, the one they had saved for the day Jacob returned home. The cellar door was locked, and she retrieved the key from its peg. Her legs trembled when she stood at the top of the narrow stairs beyond the opened door. She kept her hands against the walls for support and counted the steps, the counting a focus to keep from fainting. *Seven, eight, nine…*

The air down here was heavy and unmoving. She found the bottle, tucked off to one side among a few bottles of whiskey. Back up the stairs, counting again all the way. *Eighteen, nineteen, twenty*…The walls gave her body something to hold onto; the numbers did the same for her mind.

Taylor cleared his throat as Lillian poured the strong drink. "Your husband and I spoke several times about your home." She glanced up from her work. "I grew up here in Butler County and knew the road which runs along your land."

She carried glasses to him and one of his comrades. Taylor took a short swallow and nodded appreciatively. "Thank you."

Lillian listened to the still-heavy breathing of the men, the clank of glass on glass as she poured two more measures, the distant hum of cicadas. No breeze flowed through the room, and the house—even with four live souls in it—felt dead. The house that was to have been hers and Jacob's…and their daughter's.

"Captain Conner had me swear once…" Taylor's voice broke through her reflection. He paused and downed the rest of his drink. "He had me swear to be the one to bear you news if he were killed."

She looked at him. His face was flushed and sweat dripped down his temples, towards his cheeks. How many times Jacob had looked just that way, drenched in the Alabama heat. If it had been Jacob's sweat she would have brushed it aside, caressed his skin. Kissed the spot and tasted the salt.

Lillian saw that Taylor noticed her gaze and tore herself away.

"More brandy?" she asked, reaching out with the glass she had poured for herself. He hesitated just a half second before taking it from her hand, his fingers brushing against hers along the curved glass. She turned quickly, heat rising up her own face.

She took the bottle and added more to the other two men's glasses and poured an inch for herself into the sergeant's original glass.

Lillian sat and looked across at them. She raised her glass. "To Jacob," she said.

They echoed her motion, her words. She took a long drink and closed her eyes as the warm liquid slid down her throat. When she opened her eyes few seconds later everything was the same, everything was still broken.

She poured more brandy into her glass. "Selma, you said?"

"Yes, ma'am. It was while we were retreating. The city was overrun by Wilson's forces. We made the Alabama River at the southwest side of town. Jacob...Captain Conner...had us halfway across. A sharpshooter cut him down. Him and two others we were running with."

The crash of breaking glass intruded. One of the men behind Taylor had dropped his brandy, the one called Clay. Amber trickled across the floor.

Clay's hands were trembling, and he would not meet Lillian's gaze. He bent his head and rested it in his hands. "He was helping me when he died, Mrs. Conner." The words trickled past Clay's fingers. "I'd lost my sense, was swimming all the wrong way. Captain Conner, he grabbed me. He was dragging me with him. There were shots. And then he didn't have me no more."

Lillian bit her lip to hold in the curses coursing through her. The taste of blood seeped onto her tongue, and she downed the rest of her glass to chase it away. The brandy touched the wound on her lip, adding one more layer to her pain. Tears gathered in her eyes.

"Excuse me, gentlemen." She rose and turned away. Behind her, the men got to their feet as she made for the doorway.

Lillian stood by the front window, breath ragged, memories and illusions and hopes for the future swirling through her. In the sky, clouds scudded in from the northwest, threatening to overrun the sun's position.

"Why, Jacob? We could have had another chance. I needed

you."

Dust blew across the path the men had walked to her door, the path she had waited two years for her husband to return to her by. But he would never return, dead in a river miles from their home.

Lillian shut her eyes and leaned against the window's frame. The glass rattled softly with the oncoming breeze. Tastes of blood and brandy lingered on her tongue. Somewhere, not too far, not too close, a rumble of thunder rolled.

Behind the thunder, another sound, a tune and words to go with it. *There is a fashion in this land...* The voice of her Aunt Caroline, singing, when Lillian had been young and Caroline had lived with her parents.

A bitter laugh bubbled up her throat. "The knight's ghost," she whispered. Lillian hadn't thought of the song for years, but she recalled every word: The young woman who went with her son down to the seashore to meet her husband back from the war. The men she brought home with her. The cellar.

And—oh!—the young woman's husband had come back to her. He had returned, though just for one night. And she might forgive Jacob if just for one night. She would tell him about Alice, she would hear his voice and see his face and, if she could not touch him...if she could not touch him, then at least they would have that time together in spirit.

Lillian opened her eyes and found the sky darkened by clouds, near the color of night. Her tongue found the injured spot on her lip and played with it.

Her mind made up, she returned to the sitting room. Taylor was pouring the last of the brandy—Jacob's brandy—into a glass held by Clay. And for a moment she doubted her senses, wondered if the shattered glass and the news that, but for these men's actions, her husband might still be alive were all a dream of heat and misery. But, no. There on the floor, a faint stain and a glint or two from fragments of glass someone had failed to retrieve.

"A storm is blowing in," she told them. "And I fear it will be night once it has passed. Can I offer you men the honor of your Captain's home for the evening? Or are you expected elsewhere tonight?"

Taylor shrugged his shoulders. "Things are...rather disorganized, ma'am." He glanced back at the men. They gave no sign. "We welcome your invitation."

She smiled tentatively, as a young widow should. "If you all could help me in the cellar, we can have another bottle. I fear it won't be as fine a drink as the last, but…"

Taylor strode towards her. "I can help you, Mrs. Conner."

Lillian nodded slightly. "There are crates blocking the rack where the bottles are stored." She smiled again, a touch more broadly. "There has not been anyone to partake of it here these past years, and I let other things pile up. We could make shorter work of the retrieval were you all to help me."

"Yes, ma'am." He gestured, and the other two stood.

Down the steps in single file, the broad shoulders of Taylor nearly touching the walls on each side as he led the way.

"D'you have a lantern?" he asked at the base of the steps.

"I don't," Lillian said. "But with the door open, there's light enough, once you let your eyes adjust. The rack is towards the rear."

She showed the men a pile of old crates sitting in front a set of shelves at the rear of the cellar. She moved two crates herself before letting her knees buckle and dropping a third to the ground.

Brooks picked it up. "Might want to rest, ma'am," he told her with a voice rough as tree bark.

She went to the wall and put her back to it, feeling the chill of the cold earth. The three men continued to work. Soon the whole of the shelving, bare since the day Jacob had built it, would be visible. Slowly, Lillian worked her way back toward the stairs.

One of the men, Brooks by the sound of him, cursed. "Ain't nothin' here," he muttered.

She hurried up the steps, fast as she could, hearing all three of their voices from behind. At the top, she threw the door shut and locked it. Moments later, the door shook as fists banged on it.

"Mrs. Conner, what in the devil is going on?" called Taylor. The words, harsh though they might have been meant to be, were soft through the dense timber.

She walked away, letting them curse, letting Taylor pound at the door. No two of them would be able to get side by side in those stairs. And if she thought rightly, none of them would be strong enough to break it down by themselves.

The tune her aunt had sung returned to her again. "Take here the keys," the ghost would say, "and ye'll relieve my merry young men." And that she would, if Jacob were to command her to do so.

72

For the moment, the key went on a stand in a corner of the room.

Outside, rain pattered against the walls of the house. Though it was but early evening, Lillian climbed the stairs. She passed by Alice's room without a glance and went straight to the room she shared with Jacob. Up there, the noise from the cellar was only sporadically audible.

Lillian left the door to their room open so as not to impede Jacob's ghost. She took off the clothes she wore, layer by layer, and replaced them with only her one sheer nightgown, a gift from Jacob on their second anniversary. She lay down and tried not to think of anything. The alcohol made this easy, and before long, she was asleep.

○

No spirit arrived in the night.

She woke once in the middle of the darkness to complete stillness. Only a few clouds remained to drift in the sky, and the moon's light filtered in through magnolia leaves.

"Jacob?" she called. But no one replied.

She did not stir again until the sky was bright. Below, she heard sounds from the men in the cellar. There would be a loud bang, a pause of half a minute or so, and then another crash.

Lillian dressed for the day and went to that door. One of them must have heard her approach.

"Mrs. Conner." It was Taylor who spoke, but his voice too was rough, as if he had been screaming in the night. "Mrs. Conner, I know you hear me. You need to be letting us out of here, ma'am. Someone will come if we stay missing."

"I pray he does," she replied.

"What's that?" Taylor asked. "I couldn't hear you."

She walked away, then, and went about the rest of her day, only occasionally wishing for a respite from the sounds of the men and their attempts to free themselves. The noise of shattering glass let her know they had found the whiskey.

That evening, she left the house's front door ajar an inch or two. She knew nothing of the habits of shades and wanted to make the path as easy as possible for her husband, for she was certain he would return to tell her to free his men. He would come, and she could let him know how their daughter had died late in March, the fever taking her after almost a week.

She could not bear the thought of decades alone in this house. So she would ask if he could tell her future, like the knight's ghost had. Would she marry another man and have children with him as the lady of the song had? If not...well, if not, then she might make her stay in this house shorter than God would have expected. There were ways of that.

She wore the same nightgown as before, but tonight she foreswore the bed sheets, lying on top of them and letting the hot, heavy air be her covering.

But again, no spirit arrived in the night and dawn came to Lillian with sadness and curses.

There was no banging and crashing from the men in the cellar on this day, though they shared curses of their own. When they screamed, Lillian screamed back at them until her throat burned and her ears rang.

"We have our own families!" one of them cried through the door. She couldn't tell their voices apart any longer. Theirs and hers were a chorus of agony, drowning out the cicadas.

"You'll see them again! As soon as I've seen my Jacob. I swear you'll see them again." She sank to a chair and hugged her arms tightly around herself, cold despite the rising heat of the afternoon.

Though she was cold in the day, fire burned within her at night, and when she went to bed, she left the nightgown where it lay. She tried to sleep but could not still her thoughts. Owls and other night creatures called outside, and the light of the full moon worked its way across her view of the sky. Even once the moon had passed beyond her window's reach, she waited awake. She was there, still watching, when morning light blossomed in the sky.

Three nights and no spirit had arrived.

Lillian fell asleep then, as day passed, and she woke past midday with sweat on her bare skin.

She bathed and dressed and wandered downstairs. There was silence beyond the door to the cellar.

Had it all been for naught? She went to that door and stood by it.

"Is that you, Mrs. Conner?" The voice was weak, that of a soldier left behind. Left to die. "Please, whoever is there. For the love of God, please open the door."

Lillian ran her hand across the door's beams and considered retrieving its key, doing as this man asked, even if her husband had

74

not come to her.

She hummed a bit of the melody of her aunt's song: *They shot the shot, and drew the stroke and wade in red blood to the knee; no sailors more for their lord could do than my young men they did for me...*

Was this why Jacob had not come? Unlike the knight's men, certainly her husband's men could have done more. Not foundered in the river, forcing Jacob to give his life for theirs. Not left his body behind when maybe he could have been saved.

Weak beating against the door. "Please," said the voice.

"No," she said, so quiet that her voice could not have carried into the cellar. "Not today."

Though she had barely been awake, fatigue hung heavily over her through the next few hours. The occasional scratches and thumps at the cellar door drilled into her aching head.

She went back to bed, not bothering to change out of the clothes she was wearing. She spread her arms across the bed and her legs, too, reaching out for all of its four corners, covering it.

She drifted back into sleep while day was still light and awoke to howls outside and a dark sky.

There, between her bed and the window, stood Taylor and Clay and Brooks. They looked at her with malevolent eyes. The pale moonlight shone through them.

Lillian had just a moment to recognize them for what they were, and then, they were upon her. They made not a sound and neither did she.

Hours later, when the dawn came, the room was empty, and the house, once full of life, was home to not a soul.

R. S. Belcher on Shirley Jackson's "The Lottery"

I remember being in English class—Mrs. Burton's fourth period, I believe, when I was first introduced to Shirley Jackson. The story was called "The Lottery." It's short—twelve pages, but in those twelve pages, Jackson, changed the way I perceived horror, taking it out of the dark shores of Poe's kingdom and showing me that the dizzy vertigo of fear works even better when it is wrapped in the trappings of our calm, ordinary, "normal" world. Her work made horror personal, made familiar things seem ominous, and taught me that you can't hide from terror in the bright sun. Many of my horror stories, like "Hollow Moments," are anchored in the familiar harbor of the "real world," and I thank Shirley Jackson for teaching me that horror, at its most visceral, is personal and as familiar, and as inescapable as your own backyard.

Hollow Moments

R. S. Belcher

The dark, sticky things LaGrue whispered to me while we were alone in the box would never wash off, but I was thankful for the rain anyway.

I flashed my gold shield to two transit cops, shook the rain off my coat, and walked down the stairs to the platform of the Metro. Lieutenant Montgomery and Chief of Police Glasse were standing by a small triangular column illuminated with posters advertising the Kennedy Center. The D.C. Crime Scene Investigation Unit was swarming over a subway car that was part of the Orange Line.

"Morning," I said.

Montgomery nodded and handed me a paper cup of coffee.

Chief Glasse frowned. He was a burly black man with salt-and-pepper muttonchops and a gut that looked more muscle than flab.

"You look like you're half in the bag, Detective Pang."

"Thank you, Sir, and might I add that you look exceptionally radiant this morning yourself."

Both men chuckled.

"That was good work on LaGrue," Glasse said. "We need quick closures like that when the damn media gets wind of the weird ones."

Stanley LaGrue's family, bloody and raw, was there, behind my eyes, pounding on the walls of memory for attention. Closure.

"Thanks," I said and sipped my coffee.

"I understand you worked the psycho in the interrogation room for twenty hours straight before he rolled," the Chief said.

"Uh-huh," I replied, looking for my notebook in the pockets of my raincoat.

"You had any sleep since then, Detective?"

"Yes sir," I replied as I flipped open my notebook to a clean page and clicked my pen. "About two hours and forty-five minutes, not including the ride over here. What do we have?"

"Weirdest damn thing I've seen in a long time," Montgomery said. "About 8:15, this guy puts his fiancée on the Orange Line. He remembered it was this car, Number 23." Montgomery was a big white guy in his early fifties. He used to play football in college, and it showed. He wore a little American flag pin on the lapel of his suit coat.

"So, he's walking away when he remembers he has her debit card. He jumps on another car of the same train just as the doors shut, so he can give her the card at the next stop—here.

"He goes straight to Car 23, but she's not in the car. There were no stops in between. He freaks out at what he sees in the car and grabs a transit cop at the next stop."

"I'm confused," I said. "Is this all for one missing person?"

"It isn't one missing person," the Chief said. "It's everyone on that subway car. About 120 people we estimate. Gone between two stops in less than five minutes."

Cops can't stand stuff they can't easily and neatly catalogue. The Chief hated it because it wasn't something that fit in a box on a form.

"Gone," he said again.

◉

I stepped around the working crime scene technician in a Metro Police windbreaker.

It was bright inside the subway car after the cave-like shadow of the metro station. The walls and the seats were beige plastic and orange vinyl. Metal poles ran from floor to ceiling for standing commuters to steady themselves. A map of the multi-colored subway lines of the Metro system was attached to the wall near the doors at opposite sides of the car.

With latex-gloved hands, I kneeled and picked up an overturned Diet Coke can. Most of its contents had become a dark stain on the carpet. The can was still sweating and cool. Near the can was an umbrella with rainwater still beading on its white-and-blue panels. A cereal bar with a single bite out of it lay near cell phones and briefcases, gym bags and paperbacks. Purses with fortunes in cash and plastic sat abandoned. Laptop screens burned brightly. Newspapers scattered, open to today's sports or finance or funnies.

I felt weight, heavy on my chest. It was like standing in the wake of a neutron bomb, no traces of humans—blood or struggle. The car's interior suddenly seemed too bright, the ceiling too low. Sometimes crime scenes hold the charge of the event. You can call it ghosts or vibes, but whatever it was this place had it bad.

I realized I was holding my breath.

"Detective, you might want to finish up," a voice called to me from beyond the open doors. "They're about to move the car out to the yard so we can go over it without holding up the line anymore. It's a mess all over, hell of a morning rush."

I made my notes, eager to be out of the car.

◉

A uniformed cop led my last interview out of the noisy and crowded squad room. Everyone was in—all shifts, all departments. It was a madhouse. We were working it at our end and the FBI, Department of Homeland Security, CIA, NSA, and CDC were all working theirs. It was on every network.

Chief Glasse paused at my desk for a few seconds between meetings with the Feds and the mayor's people.

"Ben," he said. "You work this as hard as you worked LaGrue.

You stay on it until you hear different from me."

I nodded and got back to it.

I typed up the interview with another family member of the lost of Car 23 and drained my sixth cup of black coffee. Virgil Whitehurst sat down in the chair beside my desk. "Solved it yet?" he said.

"Well, so far I've got about fifty interviews with people who are all scared as hell over what happened to their loved ones. No solid connections between the missing people, other than most of them took the Orange line daily to and from work. Oh, and almost everyone hated their jobs and dreaded the commute. I anticipate major arrests within the hour."

Whitehurst smiled. He was a slender man with heavy "Clark Kent" glasses. We had both joined the department seventeen years ago.

"Same with the folks Perry and I've been interviewing."

Whitehurst nodded. "Press is getting lots of 'no comments' from the Chief and the Feds about this being some kind of terrorist thing," Whitehurst said around a yawn. "Lots of talking heads saying this is an alien conspiracy or a cult like those psychos who gassed the subway in Japan. What do you think it is?"

"I didn't do it," I said. "Other than that, I really don't know."

I had taken pressure and caffeine as far as they could go. I needed to crash. I grunted good night to Virgil, grabbed my coat, and headed for the parking lot.

I vaguely remembered the trip home.

I walked into my apartment, stepping over the three-day pile of mail and automatically clicked on the TV just to have some noise. I could care less about the dirty laundry overflowing the hallway closet. My dad would have had a coronary if he saw my place.

I fell asleep on the couch, the TV babbling. I dreamt of hands pulling at me, grabbing me, the smell of dead cigarettes. The phone, ringing far away. I fought hard to reach it.

Bright sunlight was stabbing through my blinds and into my eyes. The TV was droning on as it had done all night long. I answered the phone.

"Pang, Homicide," I said without even realizing I wasn't at work

"Ben? Virgil. It happened again."

Crystal City is an island of blue steel and mirrored glass towers that hold the offices of some of the most powerful corporations in America. I was one of thousands of cars locked into the arterial clog of morning rush hour on the G.W. Parkway. I mechanically started and stopped with the flow of the traffic. Time seemed stretched and frozen all at once. Empty time, wasted time.

Virgil was waiting for me when I walked in the lobby.

"We have seven people vanished out of an elevator between floors," he said. "Same deal as the subway—personal items left behind, no signs of violence or struggle. At least this time we got a witness."

"Who?"

James Debois, seven-years-old, was sitting at a table in the corporate break room. A uniform cop talked softly to him while he played with his bright blue Power Ranger action figure—not a doll, an action figure.

Whitehurst drifted over to me and nodded toward the boy.

"The kid is scared of something," he said softly. "We got him calmed down, but he's not talking. His mother is Sharon Debois. She's a customer service rep for a travel agency on the 16th floor. James was sick, so she had to take him with her to work."

I walked over to James and sat down across from him.

"James, this is Detective Pang," the officer said as she stood and shook my hand. "He's a very nice guy, and he's here to help us find your mom. He needs to talk to you and ask you some questions, okay?"

James's chocolate-brown eyes looked down at his Power Ranger for guidance or escape. He squirmed in his chair.

"'kay," he muttered.

The officer smiled and excused herself to go get James a soda. I asked for anything with caffeine.

"Pang," James said looking up at me. "That's a funny name."

"Yeah," I replied, "it's Chinese. My dad stuck me with it. You can call me Ben if you like."

"You from China?" James asked.

"Nope, New York. My grandfather was from China, though."

This seemed to satisfy James. He showed me his Power Ranger.

"You like it? Momma got it for me today 'cause I was sick, and I had to come with her to work. Momma wanted to stay home with me, but she had to go."

"You and your mom were in the elevator with the other people, right?" I asked.

"Um-hum." His gaze retreated to his toy.

"My friend Tray, he says policemen take people to jail for not doing nothing. Am I in trouble?"

"Nah," I said. "We try to help people and catch bad guys. You haven't done anything wrong, James. You're cool."

"You like being a policeman?" James asked.

"Yes," I said automatically. "Listen, James, this is important. I know you're scared, but I need to know what you saw. I need you to be brave for me like a Power Ranger would be. Can you do that?"

The kid nodded. I opened my notebook and scribbled a few notes to myself.

James's little face twisted as he tried to think of the words. His hands fidgeted with the toy and fear welled up in his eyes, darkening them.

"The Wall People got her. Got all of them."

"Who are the Wall People, James?"

"Don't know," he said clutching his toy tightly like a charm. "They're just hands coming out of the walls. Lots of hands. They don't got no faces. They pulled Momma into the wall. They pulled all them people into the wall."

My mouth was dry and I felt a little dizzy. My internal compass was spinning wildly.

"Did they come through the little panel in the top of the elevator car, James?"

"No," he said softly. "They just came out of the walls. I only saw them for a second. They had already grabbed Momma and the other people. They were hard to see."

I leaned over the table to look into James's eyes.

"Did they try to grab you, James?"

"Nuh-uh," he said shaking his head.

"This is important. Are you telling me the truth, James?"

The boy nodded. His eyes were damp.

"Are the Wall People going come get me now?"

"No," I said numbly. "I promise I won't let anybody get you

James, and I'm going to try to find your mom, too."

I left the boy with a police artist. I asked James to help the artist draw the Wall People for me.

◉

Back at my desk I stared blankly at the computer monitor, the lines of the standard report screen burning into my retinas. I drummed my fingers on the desk and tried to remember something from yesterday.

Something about somebody coming to get them. *Coming to get them.*

I rubbed my eyes and looked at the clock over the doorway to the squad room. I had been staring at the screen for twenty minutes.

I tapped the keyboard and brought up the report Whitehurst's partner, Perry, had done yesterday. It was an interview with the wife of one of the missing from Car 23.

My eyes watered with fatigue as I re-read the report I had absently skimmed yesterday evening.

"Mrs. Jetter said her husband had been suffering from work-related stress for the past few months and had been making irrational statements about people following him and being out to get him," the report said. *"Mrs. Jetter assured the detective these suspicions were unfounded. However, she believes her husband may have run away or done harm to himself."*

I picked up the phone and dialed Louise Jetter's number.

"Thanks for seeing me on such short notice," I said, as Mrs. Jetter ushered me into her home.

Louise Jetter had the haggard look of someone who was one pill away from a nervous breakdown. She had been pretty once, now she was just handsome.

"Have you heard anything from William?" she asked after offering me a cigarette with a shaky hand.

"I'm afraid not. Actually, I was following up on the statement you gave yesterday. You said your husband had been exhibiting some…strange behavior lately?"

Mrs. Jetter nodded curtly and exhaled smoke thorough her nostrils.

"Yes. William was given a lateral transfer to a new division last year in lieu of being downsized. There was a lot of stress at the new job, and he really didn't care for the work. He hated it, actually."

"And that was when this behavior started?" I asked, scribbling notes.

"At first he would just sit and stare at night," Mrs. Jetter said, frowning as she remembered. "We stopped having conversations. He would stare at the television, but I could tell he wasn't paying attention to it or anything else. Then came the nightmares, and then he went on about the people following him."

"What did he say about these people?"

Mrs. Jetter looked at me oddly, crushed out her cigarette and immediately lit a new one.

"You aren't taking William's delusions seriously, are you, Detective?"

"At this point, we're looking into any possibilities. What did your husband say exactly?"

"Well, he said he would look up, and they would suddenly be there. He said no one else saw them. He said they were like ghosts or something—shadowy, made out of smoke. He said he could never see their faces but knew they were watching him.

"Once we were on a long car trip to see our daughter at college, and William suddenly screamed and nearly lost control of the car. He said he looked in the rearview mirror, and one of them was in the back seat. That was when I asked him to get some help, but he just became more withdrawn, more depressed. It was like he'd given up."

She began to cry, but it was obvious she was used to it. She kept it together; she had been mourning her husband for a long time. She wiped her eyes with the back of her hand and took a long drag on the cigarette.

"Mrs. Jetter, did your husband ever say that these people were trying to grab him or touch him?"

She blinked several times and looked at me with a little bit of fear in her tired, wet eyes.

"Yes. How did you know that? William used to wake up screaming, crying like a baby. He said he felt like they were suffocating him, trying to drag him down into some awful dark place."

I handed her the sketch James Debois helped our artist to draw.

A forest of odd-angled arms and oversized clawing hands the color of ash growing out of the plastic-paneled walls of the elevator, wrapping themselves around the mouths, arms, and legs of the victims.

The shadowy arms and hands didn't look like limbs attached to a human body; they were reminiscent of both tentacles and wisps of milky smoke.

The artist had left the victims' faces blank, but my mind could fill in the details. Eyes wide with terror, desperate attempts to scream—clawing against the hands that could not really be there. Fighting like panicked drowning victims to resist the pull; then they were under, beneath dark, unforgiving waters. Gone.

Mrs. Jetter stared at the drawing. The tears slid down her gray face and this time she did not have the will to push them aside.

"This is like one of William's dreams," she whispered.

As I was driving back to the office, the dispatcher patched through a call.

"We got a hit on a credit card belonging to one of our people from Car 23. It was used in a restaurant in Chevy Chase about twenty minutes ago," Montgomery said. "I've got uniforms on the way."

◎

A half- dozen police cars were already in the parking lot of the Mongol Horde Barbecue and Mega-Buffet, when I arrived.

I jumped out of my car as four burly, uniformed cops wrestled a slender man through the double glass doors. He was kicking, squirming, and screaming unintelligibly as the cops struggled to hold on to him. They slammed him against the trunk of a police car and tried to wrestle cuffs on him.

He got an arm free and took a wild swing at one of the cops. This resulted in him being bounced against the trunk a few times and pinned under 600 pounds of unhappy cops. They got the cuffs on him, and I walked over.

"Sonovabitch," one of the cops said wincing as I approached. "Freak took a bite out of me."

The man's eyes were wide. He didn't blink. It was like looking at a terrified animal—no comprehension, no recognition. His features were hidden behind a mask of Egg Fu Young and gravy, smeared like war paint across his screaming face. Foam and bits of food flew from his lips as he shrieked. One of the cops handed me the perp's wallet. The man continued to howl like a wounded dog.

"Malcolm Karchai," I said, reading the name off his driver's license and comparing the smiling young professional in the photo to the lunatic a few feet from me.

"Mr. Karchai, can you understand me?" I asked, leaning close to his face, half mashed against the car's trunk.

"More, more! All, all!" The rest was animalistic growls as he was wrestled into the back of the car. "No! No prison! No cell! No! No! Death! Let me die here! They'll come for me!"

The door slammed shut, and Karchai went back to making sounds and thrashing about.

I found the first officer on the scene.

"That one of the guys that went missing on that subway car yesterday morning?" he asked as he wiped his brow with his sleeve.

"Yeah, what happened in there?"

"He comes in for the buffet. The cashier said he acted he didn't understand how to pay, and she had to talk him through how to use the credit card in his wallet. She thought he was high or something. Anyway, he starts cutting the line, grabbing handfuls of food off the buffet, acting like a wild man, like he's starving or something. The owner called 911. What happened to him?"

I stared at Karchai's calm, sane likeness on the license and shook my head.

◎

Malcolm Karchai died on the way to be interrogated. He spasmed in the back of the police car. The cops hit the rollers and rushed to the hospital, but before they got there, he "just stopped living," as one patrolman described it to me.

I waited alone outside the Medical Examiner's office for the District. A few times I thought I was falling asleep. Suddenly I felt cold hands that smelled like ash clamp over my mouth and nose. I jumped bolt-upright in my uncomfortable plastic chair, wiped my eyes and looked at the clock.

How many hours of my life had I spent like this? Waiting. Sitting. Watching a clock. Emergency rooms, courtrooms, interrogation rooms, traffic jams. Wasted time.

How long had I hated this? For a long, long time.

Any illusions about saving the world were long dead for me. I was a record keeper, a census taker, and sometimes night watchman; the clerk keeping score of the number and variety of inhumanities people could chalk up. Seventeen years of my life spent mopping up other people's messy, broken lives. Their empty lives sucking dry the marrow of mine.

Do you like being a policeman?

How do you change the inertia your life has accumulated?

Whenever I had to wait a long time I wanted to start smoking again. I was just starting to go around the corner to bum a cigarette from a morgue attendant when Dr. Gaffney, the M.E., ambled through the swinging doors of the morgue, a brown folder wrapped with rubber bands cradled under his arm.

"Well, Ben, this one was truly worth the wait," he said, shaking his head. "I don't know what exactly happened to that poor joker but his insides are a mess."

"What have you got?"

"Well for starters, he is positively identified as your missing subway passenger, Malcolm Karchai. Dental and fingerprints confirm that.

"His stomach contents show the breakfast he had yesterday before he left to take the subway. He has beard stubble consistent with someone who hasn't shaved for a day."

"Cause of death?" I asked as I scribbled. What Gaffney said stopped me from writing.

"From examination of the lungs and airway, I would say affixation caused by suffocation."

"Doc," I said, putting away my notepad and pen, "those cops didn't lay a hand on him in the car."

"I'm sure they didn't, Ben," Gaffney said. "The hemorrhaging and condition of the lungs I saw were consistent with death sometime in the last twelve to eighteen hours, no sooner than that."

"You're saying he's been dead for half a day or more? Doc, he was the liveliest dead man I've ever seen a few hours ago."

"I saved the best for last," Gaffney said, his grin widening. "Tox screen shows no drugs in his system. He was clean as a whistle. Examination of his brain tissue showed massive decay, however. His gray matter looked like something you'd see in a corpse dead for months, Ben."

◉

My brain felt half rotted away too as I drove home from the

morgue. After all the years, all the things I've witnessed, you'd think I'd have developed enough calluses on my eyes that nothing could surprise me anymore. Gotcha.

I felt a sharp sadness for James Debois and Mrs. Jetter. Whatever they imagined had happened to their loved ones, I was beginning to suspect it would turn out to be worse.

I glanced at my watch; it was still early enough to swing by Louise Jetter's home. William Jetter had seen the Wall People coming, and maybe, somewhere in his personal effects would be something I could use, like a good cop, to make sense of all this.

It was a thin lead, but it was better than going home to an empty apartment and trying to sleep.

As I pulled into her cul-de-sac, I saw Louise Jetter standing under the streetlight at the bottom of her driveway, gesturing franticly to a uniformed officer in a dark unmarked police car, who had obviously just arrived.

"Detective Pang," Mrs. Jetter cried, "there's someone in my kitchen. He looks like William, but it isn't my husband. He...he scared me the way he was talking...his eyes..."

"It's alright, Mrs. Jetter. Stay here with the officer."

Fifteen years on the job and I never had to use my gun for real. I snapped it out of its holster, jacked a round into the pipe, and trotted up the drive toward the front door. My heart, made of lead, was thudding heavily against my breast.

Inside, the house was dark. A faint blue illumination came from a night-light plugged into a hallway outlet. I held my flashlight away from my body and tried not to think how badly my hands were sweating as I moved down the hall. Everything seemed disjointed, jerky, like a film stuttering off the reel.

I heard a tinkling sound, like glass, and some scuffling coming from the kitchen. I held my breath and stepped into the kitchen, my flashlight and gun sweeping the room.

William Jetter sat hunched over a bowl of cereal at the kitchen table. He looked up at me and milk drooled down his chin, like he forgot how to close his mouth. He had thin, white hair that swirled in wild wisps around his gaunt face. His eyes reflected yellow pinpoints in the beam of my flashlight, like a cat's.

"Want...a...bowl? It's good," he said.

I switched on the kitchen lights. He didn't blink.

"Mr. Jetter?" I asked, keeping the gun leveled at him.

"Yes. I am…William Jetter," he said.

"No," I said, shaking my head slowly. "I don't think so."

"Very good," he said. "You are an enforcer?"

"I'm a cop," I said softly.

"Cop," he said, rolling the word around in his mouth like a newly discovered wine.

"I want you to stand up and clasp your hands behind your head," I ordered.

Jetter, or whatever this was, stood and did as I asked. I moved slowly towards him.

"Where is Mr. Jetter?" I asked as I cuffed him.

"Dead," he said.

I heard the front door crash open and the thump of boots on the hall carpet.

"Freeze, police!" the SWAT commander shouted from behind his AR-15.

His expression was stone. No fear, no surprise—nothing. "Cop" was the only thing he said to me before he was dragged away into a sea of black fatigues and Kevlar armor.

◉

Of fifteen detectives, two-dozen uniforms, twenty feds, the Mayor, the Chief of Police, and more politicians than you could kill with a term limit bill, I was the one they sent into the box with Jetter.

"Why him?" A guy from Homeland Security asked with obvious contempt in his voice. "This is an issue of national security. The president is getting updates on this. I think someone who has—"

"Pang goes in," Chief Glasse interrupted. "Because I say he does. He's good with the crazies."

The fed obviously wasn't used to being cut off.

"Fine Chief, it's your ass."

The rest of the parade stayed behind the two-way glass. I walked in alone with my notebook and a mug of coffee.

Jetter was sitting at a stainless steel table, running his fingers along the scratches and the graffiti on the surface. He looked up at me and made an attempt at a smile, reminding me of a stroke victim.

"Cop," he said.

"I'm Detective Pang. You understand you can have a lawyer

present with you if you would like Mister..." I paused and sat down in the chair across the table from him. "What is your name?"

"We are not allowed to have names, only work designations."

"What do you mean, 'not allowed'?"

"If you are caught using a name, you are punished. You receive less nourishment. Less sleep," he said as he ran his hands along the table. "This surface is exquisite. The way the light reflects off it, the texture, what is it?"

"It's just a table. Not a very nice one either," I said.

"This would be a treasure beyond compare where I come from."

"Where do you come from?"

He seemed to have difficulty with the question. When he responded it was like the words were sharp and painful in his mouth.

"Sometimes we see you, your world," he said. "You are like wind to us, bringing warmth and color and then you are gone. They say you are imaginary, a product of our minds not functioning properly, but I think that our worlds are side-by-side and that sometimes they slip into each other. Either that or I am mad. If your world is madness, then I welcome it."

He stopped playing with the tabletop and looked at me with hunted animal eyes.

"Our existence is work and sleep, shadow and dust. The food has no taste—something you eat before you return to your tasks. The sky has no sun or rain or clouds or that beautiful thing you call a moon. We work to maintain a sleeping cube and to receive our portion of food. The only pleasure in my world, the only hope, is in death.

"They punish those who do not conform. They are locked away where there is not even the toil of labor to distract them. They sit and they rot in the darkness, first inside, then out."

"Are you saying you come from Hell?" I asked.

"We are not allowed the luxury of believing in Hell."

He tilted his head at a strange angle as he looked at me.

"Do you enjoy being a...cop?"

"No," I said, "I hate my job."

"Then why do you do it?"

"It's...my job. I started out doing it because of my father. He wanted me to be in the family business – big-shot, just like him.

What I wanted didn't matter, so to piss him off I became something I knew he would hate."

"You have spent your life doing something you hate to punish your father?"

"Yeah, I guess I have. When he died we hadn't talked for twelve years."

I tried to find the words to explain, but they weren't there.

"It's my job. It's a living."

"It does not sound like…living," the shadow man said, "In our world, they give you the illusion of choice. Here, you have real choices; you can do or not do whatever you want. There is no one watching over your shoulder, but so many of you Window People act as if there were. You do what is…expected of you.

"I don't understand how someone could not be happy here."

"Window People?" I said.

"The ones like this body. They open themselves to us. This Jetter slipped between your world and ours, and I caught him. I was very fortunate. Only one of us can fit in your skin. There have been so many Window People lately, so many of you falling. So many of you spend more time in our world than yours."

"The people on the subway, in the elevator. They were windows for you."

"Yes, they were hollow inside. We use them as our means of escape.

"You can't do this," I said. "Those people had lives. You and the others have stolen them."

"Lives?" he replied. "This is what I do not understand. They hated so much. They were so empty. They had become more of our world than yours. They called to us. We ended their pain."

"You don't have that right. At what point is a life irredeemable?"

The shadow man nodded in agreement, "We will suffer punishment for what we have done here."

"What punishment?"

"They will find us and take us back. Whatever they do to us, it will be worth it. To have played with children, to smell flowers, and taste the sweetness of lips. The suffering will be worth a day here."

"I think we're done for now," I said. I didn't know what else to say. I stood and walked towards the door.

"Cop?"

I turned.

"Live," he said. He smiled again. This time he got it right.

◉

We found them the next morning, during rush hour on a muddy section of underpass that was part of the 495 Beltway, near the Maryland border.

Bodies everywhere.

They were covered with white sheets while the technicians processed the crime scene. News and traffic helicopters circled in the sky over the scene like vultures preparing for a feast. The scene, from above, was being shown live on networks across the planet, analyzed and talked about over and over again to dead-eyed, vapid faces basking in a phosphor dot light and shadow.

"It's them," Whitehurst said. "Looks like all our missing from Car 23 and the Crystal City elevator. Working on cause of death right now, but it could be a while."

"Suicide," I said. The words didn't fit in my mouth very well and they sounded alien in their lack of inflection. "This was suicide."

Virgil stared at me strangely, but I really didn't care. I took out my notebook and pen and started doing my job.

It was afternoon by the time I got to the city jail to see the shadow man who'd replaced Jetter. A deputy looked up from a mound of paperwork long enough to tell me the guy was dead, found this morning in his cell, about the same time as the others at the underpass.

"Sorry," the jailer said with a dry sound that might have been a chuckle, "you just missed him."

Outside the jail there was traffic on the street as far as the eye could see.

Exhaust swirled in the hot air and settled in the back of my throat. The rumble of car engines was interspersed with the bleat of horns.

I got in my car and put the key in the ignition. I didn't turn it.

Everything was gray. Gray buildings, gray sky, gray exhaust, gray faces drifting past my car window.

For a moment, my eye jumped to the rearview mirror—a flash of movement in the back seat, like smoke. But nothing was there.

The sky rumbled and the downpour began.

I climbed out of the car. I tossed my notebook in the gutter and walked down the sidewalk towards home. People ran for doorways or their cars. I raised my face to the storm and opened my eyes.

The traffic edged by. Dead people in rolling coffins, hurrying toward the meaningless ends of desperate lives. Sealed up against the rain and the dirt and the heat by glass and air conditioning, preserved like mummies.

I passed a shop window and saw the shadow step between the curtain of raindrops and umbrellas on the sidewalk, reflected in the glass. Always there, always longing, with eager grips that choke like stale cigarette smoke.

I remembered playing in the rain. I was nine. My father was yelling at me to come inside, to stop being a fool. I had laughed at him and embraced the storm.

The memory drenched me all the way down to the dry crevasses in my soul.

Stephen Woodworth on
Roberta Lannes's
"Good-bye, Dark Love"

When I first read Dennis Etchison's *Cutting Edge* anthology back in 1988, one of the tales that impacted me the most was not by a superstar contributor such as Peter Straub or Clive Barker, but rather by an author of whom I'd never heard before. That story was "Good-bye, Dark Love," the writer Roberta Lannes. While the graphic depiction of necrophilia in "Good-bye, Dark Love" is more stomach-churning than the grossest Hollywood gore-fest, the emotional violence really gives the story its punch-to-the-gut potency. As in all of Lannes's superlative short fiction, the damage that her characters do to each other's minds and souls proves far more horrific than wounds inflicted on mere flesh. With the ice-pick incisiveness of its vivid prose and psychological insight, "Good-bye, Dark Love" introduced me to the work of an artist whose talents transcend both genre and gender.

Mr. Casey is in the House

Stephen Woodworth

Martin swirled the cockroach around in the popcorn cup, watching it skitter in circles, and slowly tilted the cup upside down. The insect scrambled for purchase as it slid down the slick-coated wall of the container, then dropped into the sizzling oil of the popper with the crackle of frying bacon.

Another thrilling Saturday night at the glorious Royale Cinema, the city's last remaining second-run movie theater.

Charlene snapped her gum. "That is *so* gross."

"Just doing my part for pest control." Martin peered down at his test subject, which, amazingly, still scuttled around the circumference of the popper's metal tub, seeking a way out.

Charlene leaned against the candy case and went back to daubing puce polish on her fingernails. "I read that torturing small animals is one of the tell-tale signs of a serial killer. You wet your bed, too, Martin?"

He bugged his eyes and leered at her. "Only when I dream about keeping your head in my fridge."

"Freak!" The girl recoiled to the opposite end of the concessions stand. "I hope Ms. Sprague cans your ass." Although barely older than her teenaged employees, the manager insisted on being called *Ms.*

"B.F.D. if she did." Martin nodded toward the vacant lobby and chucked the popcorn cup in the trash. "This place is doomed anyway."

The Royale's October "Slasher Classic" Fright Fest was a bust. Serves 'em right for playing wussy crap like the original versions of *Psycho* and *Halloween*, which had, like, what? Three drops of blood between them? As resident expert on splatter films, Martin had tried to tell Sprague to go for the *Saw* and *Hostel* movies if she wanted some *real* horror, but did the manager listen to him? Of course not. No wonder the owners were planning to bulldoze this firetrap and put up condos.

"Yo, Martin!" Randy called from the box office. "We got a couple green tickets here!"

Martin abruptly snapped to attention. He slapped the lid on the popper shut to hide the frying cockroach, then buttoned up his grease-spotted red vest. "Green tickets" was their code word for cute chicks.

Two girls in their late teens entered through the theater's swinging glass doors, one in a mini-skirt and platform shoes, the other in low-rise jeans and a camisole. Martin leaned forward as they approached the concessions counter and smiled.

Charlene intercepted them. "I can help you over here."

The two girls veered toward her to place their order. Charlene filled their fountain drinks with her right hand while waving the left back and forth to dry her nails.

Martin glared, clenching his jaw. She did that just to tick him off…and she did it a *lot*.

A flat, toneless voice pierced his brooding. "Popcorn. Large."

Martin looked over and found a gaunt man with stringy black hair standing at the counter. The guy was pale even for a Goth, and his bony frame all but disappeared in the shapeless drapery of a black trench coat. He looked only twenty-something, but his hard, flat expression seemed etched by far greater experience.

Martin pulled a fresh popcorn cup from the dispenser behind him and scooped it into the mound of white kernels they'd made before the first feature. He glanced up at the guy's reflection in the mirror mounted on the back wall of the concessions stand. "Want butter on that?"

The man stared at him with unblinking eyes, whites filigreed with bloodshot capillaries, pupils dilated to hollow blackness. His lips formed soundless words.

Junkie, Martin decided. He pumped greasy "Golden Flavored" oil onto the popcorn and passed the cup across the counter.

The dude handed him a twenty and suddenly snickered for no reason at all. "Thanks, Martin."

That creeped him out. How did the freak know his name? Then he remembered the stupid name badge pinned to his vest. *Duh.*

"Good movie, *Martin*," the dude went on. "George Romero. Ever see it?"

At that, Martin had to grin. "You bet I have. Wish we were showing it now." He fished the guy's change out of the register and jerked his head toward Charlene. "Idiots here wouldn't know real horror if it puked on 'em."

The dude smiled his appreciation. "You can say that again."

He grabbed the popcorn and wandered off without taking the change.

"This is your brain on drugs," Martin chuckled and shoved the cash in his pocket.

A few other teenagers showed up before the start of the second feature, mostly couples hoping to make out in the darkness of the near-empty theater. As always, the moment the opening credits started to roll, Ted, the projectionist, came down to the lobby and thrust his plastic tumbler at Martin. "Half Coke, no ice."

Martin half-filled the cup with undiluted soda, leaving plenty of room for Ted's rum. The gangly projectionist grabbed it and headed back toward a door marked "Employees Only."

Martin ground his teeth as he unbuttoned his vest. Damned if he was going to get stuck working in this dump like that lush. Having to live with his uptight parents and brain-dead sister was already driving Martin nuts.

Bored to the point of unconsciousness, Martin filled a cup with Coke for himself. "I'm going in to watch the movie."

Charlene rolled her eyes. "Like you haven't seen it a zillion times already!"

Ignoring her, he stepped out of the concessions stand and pushed through the double doors leading into the auditorium. The aroma of beer and pot smoke saturated the theater's darkened interior. That was another advantage of the Royale: lax security.

Navigating through the shifting illumination reflected from the screen, Martin made his way down the center aisle toward the front rows. As he slouched in a seat upholstered with crushed velvet, he shared the viewpoint of little Michael Myers, staring through the eyeholes of a clown mask as the boy stalked and stabbed his older sister. Fortunately, the film was dark enough that the picture camouflaged the large tear in the Royale's screen, a flap of fabric lolling from the hole like a lascivious tongue.

Wussy as the original *Halloween* was, Martin enjoyed filling in the movie with his own gory details. He pictured Mikey driving the blade right into his naked sister's navel and nipples—with some decent makeup effects, that would be awesome.

Rob Zombie had done an okay job putting some guts into the remake, but even that kind of splatter had started to bore Martin. So cartoony and fake, he could tell the girls getting killed weren't being hurt at all. Martin wanted to know what it *really* felt like to do someone like that. How do you hold someone still while you're cutting 'em up, anyway? What if a dead girl gets all rigor mortis on your erection while you're still inside her? And what does a human liver taste like, with or without fava beans?

To satisfy his curiosity, Martin had been checking out some really gnarly autopsy photos online, and had gone from watching cheesy low-budget flicks about Berkowitz and Manson to poring over true-crime books about them. He fantasized about one day collecting serial-killer memorabilia like the lead singer from Korn, stuff like Gacy's clown drawings or Bundy's VW Bug. Man, that would be *sick!*

Not that Martin could bid for those kinds of trophies anytime soon, especially if he couldn't even hold onto a slave-wage job at the Royale. He didn't want Sprague, She-Wolf of the S.S., to catch him loafing, so he joined the crowd that left during the closing credits, before the house lights came up. As the patrons filed out the auditorium's double doors, the manager emerged from her office in her usual pantsuit and pumps to supervise the Royale's closing ritual. Martin pretended to tidy the concessions stand so she wouldn't ask him to help sweep the theater.

"Go ahead and cash out, Charlene," Sprague said. Barely out of high school herself, she'd made manager before she was twenty by having a bug up her butt the size of Missouri. "Randy, why don't you start on clean-up?"

"You got it!" He propped open one of the theater's double doors and wheeled a garbage can into the auditorium.

Martin saw Randy return to the lobby just a few minutes later, before Sprague had even finished counting Charlene's register drawer. The ticket seller clutched at his stomach, his face ashen as he shuffled over to the manager.

Sprague glanced up from thumbing through a stack of fives and frowned. "What is it?"

Randy scanned the lobby, where a few audience members still lingered. The two green tickets gossiped with Charlene, while another girl waited for her boyfriend to get out of the bathroom.

Randy leaned closer, and spoke in a low, unsteady voice. *"Mr. Casey is in the house."*

Martin saw Sprague blanch, and felt the hair on his own scalp prickle. "Mr. Casey is in the house" was the code signal cinema employees used to inform management of an emergency, such as a fire in the building, so the patrons wouldn't panic and trample each other stampeding toward the exits.

Sprague hastened Randy into her office, out of earshot of any customers. Unobserved, Martin sauntered over to the open door of the auditorium and stepped inside.

Brass lighting fixtures with fluted chimneys of frosted glass, relics of the Royale's heyday in the '30s, illuminated the theatre with a dim, jaundiced glow. Once bright crimson, the carpeting along the center aisle had blackened to maroon, and soft drink stains and pancakes of dried chewing gum dotted its length. A fresh yellow splat marked the spot in the aisle where Randy had barfed.

Only one audience member remained in the cavernous auditorium. The dude slumped in an aisle seat, second row from the front, his head lolling over the edge of the backrest. It was not unusual at the Royale to find bums or druggies who'd passed out during the show. The spreading wetness under the guy's chair might simply have been a sloshed soda or beer.

Martin halted halfway down the aisle. Beside the overturned popcorn cup at the man's feet, white kernels had scattered over the spilled liquid and turned scarlet. A knife lay on the floor by the figure's limp right hand, the blade drizzling redness. Martin didn't need to see the freak's face to know who the dude was, for he had already recognized the stringy black hair and pale skin.

◎

"Did you see him that night? I mean, see his *eyes*, up close." Charlene hugged herself as if the stuffy lobby had become a mortuary freezer.

Randy shook his head. "Not until…you know. They were still open."

"Well, you could tell he was a freak." She shuddered. "The cops say he killed those girls they've been finding along I-5. He found out they were onto him, so he cut up his mom, then came here to off himself."

Randy looked at his feet and shrugged. "Guess he did us a favor."

"Yeah, but why did he have to come *here*? I'm so creeped out I didn't even want to come to work."

Sweeping up the flattened popcorn kernels that littered the lobby, Martin paused to grin at her. "Hey, he's the closest thing to a celebrity we've had here. I think it's cool."

She made a face. "You would."

After the psycho committed suicide, the Royale had closed for a couple of days to allow the police to conduct their investigation. Tonight the staff had reopened the theater, and naturally the killer was all they could talk about.

"And how do you know so much about the dude, Charlene?" Martin jeered. "Been Googling everything you can about him, haven't you? Admit it—you're just as into the whole thing as I am."

"Whatever." Unable to think of a snappier comeback, she took a sudden interest in wiping down the candy case.

Martin's grin widened. He'd never actually managed to shut her up before.

Although he'd said it to tweak her, Martin honestly *did* think it was cool that, after months of reading about guys like Henry Lee Lucas and Jeffrey Dahmer, he'd met an actual serial killer, face-to-face. The guy sounded like a top-notch sicko, too. The local paper gave his name as Virgil Aldon Barnett, and the cops figured that he'd murdered at least sixteen women before butchering his mom. Although the reports withheld details "out of sensitivity to our readers," the stuff they hinted at was juicy enough: The articles mentioned that at least one victim had been decapitated and that semen samples had been recovered "from inside the body cavity" of another. Detectives and reporters speculated that self-loathing over the viciousness of his final crimes may have driven him to take his own life.

Now Martin wished he'd talked to the dude more while he'd had the chance. At the very least, he should have gotten a better look at Barnett's body. Maybe even grabbed the guy's knife before the cops got it. Heck, Martin would have settled for the murderer's empty popcorn cup. That's one souvenir you'd never find on eBay! Damn! When would he have an opportunity like *that* again? If only he hadn't been so squeamish about getting close to the corpse.

Ironically, the killer's suicide gave the Royale such notoriety in the local press that the "Slasher Classic" Fright Fest became a huge overnight success. Local teens lined up around the block to be part of the first audience in a theater where a genuine slasher bled to death. The packed house resulted in a bumper crop of trash, and Ms. Sprague asked for a "volunteer" to stay late, clean up, and secure the premises. Charlene immediately said she wouldn't go anywhere near where the dead guy had been, while Randy peered down at the carpet, his mouth twisting, evidently hoping the manager wouldn't notice him.

Martin gave a crooked smile. "I'll do it."

Everyone looked at him as if horns had sprouted from his forehead. Ordinarily Martin would never have offered to work late.

But tonight was different—it might be his only chance to see the remaining bloodstains before they cleaned everything up.

"Look, you want me to do it or not?" he snapped when no one

said anything.

Ms. Sprague spread her hands to indicate the empty lobby. "Hey, it's all yours. But I better find it clean in the morning. And don't forget to block the doors before you go."

Randy and Charlene punched out on the time clock and left with Sprague, who locked the Royale's entrance behind her and took the keys. The push bars on the doors would allow Martin to exit, but once he did he'd be shut out of the building. Only a few lights remained on in the lobby for his benefit; his final duty for the evening would be to flick the switch in the circuit breaker box that would turn them off.

Relieved to be rid of the others, he popped in his earbuds and blasted Cannibal Corpse and Psycroptic into his skull while he shuffled around and bagged garbage. He worked just long enough to be sure that Sprague wouldn't come back for something, then went through the double doors to see Virgil Aldon Barnett's blood for himself. Martin swore that the theater still reeked of it—a rusty odor he could taste on his tongue as he drew closer to the aisle seat in the second row. Once the cops had finished their investigation, Sprague asked Randy to swab the floor with a couple gallons of bleach, but the stain beneath the chair had permeated the cement so badly that the usher could not mop it away. Sprague said she might have to call in a special crime-scene cleaning service to sanitize the place.

The ruined seat was still bolted to the floor, and Maintenance hadn't sent anyone to remove it yet. Randy had covered the chair with a black plastic trash bag and stretched thick strips of silver duct tape across the armrests to keep people from sitting there until it could be replaced. These precautions hadn't deterred some thrill-seeker from occupying the corpse's seat. The duct tape dangled from its sides in curlicue tangles, and the shifting weight of the chair's recent occupant had rent a large hole in the plastic cover.

Martin told himself that he wasn't going to wimp out this time. He probed the open lips of the tear with quivering fingers, until he touched the velvet upholstery. The cushion was still sticky, gummed with what felt like the trail of a giant slug. Martin recoiled, cursing, and wiped his hand on his vest with prissy anxiety.

A bead of sweat dripped into his eye, and he brushed it away. It certainly wasn't heat making him perspire. Sprague had lowered the thermostat to keep the larger audiences comfortable during the Indian summer weather. With only Martin's body to warm the cavernous space, the theater had turned numbingly cold, yet he stood motionless in front of the forbidden aisle seat. An overwhelming urge seized him to rip off that stupid plastic bag and sit in Virgil Aldon Barnett's place.

The fact that he wanted to cozy up to that gore—wanted it badly—tripped Martin out. He busied himself with his closing chores to keep from thinking about it. Ms. Sprague would have been astonished at how quickly he cleared up the half-empty soft drink cups and crumpled candy wrappers. He just wanted out of there.

From the utility closet in the lobby, he grabbed two L-shaped wooden blocks from a stack in the corner and returned to make a final check of the auditorium. Local homeless people often viewed the Royale as a dirt-cheap motel, so Martin gingerly checked behind the threadbare, red velvet drapes hanging on either side of the screen, searching for hidden vagrants. He didn't know what he'd actually do if he found one, but he kept hold of the wooden blocks as possible weapons, just in case. Last of all, he checked the dark niche beneath the screen.

Satisfied that only he and the cockroaches remained, Martin crossed over to the fire exit. Testing to make sure the door was firmly latched, he wedged both blocks in between the door and its push bar handle to keep anyone from using a coat hanger to open the door from the outside. Now all he had to do was get the other pair of blocks from the closet, jam them in the door handle on the front entrance, and leave this dump.

He got about halfway up the center aisle when the house lights went down.

Total darkness engulfed Martin. Not even the exit sign stayed lit.

He groaned. Randy's little joke, no doubt. Ha-ha, very funny. Martin put his hands out at arm's length and inched his way forward.

A circle of light flickered on in the square window of the projection booth, a cone of dancing cinema light frosting forward to the movie screen. As the soundtrack slurred up to speed, a girl's shriek cleft the air. *"Get offa me! Oh, God—"*

The scream made Martin jump with its suddenness, but it

didn't frighten him. It was a horror movie, after all. He raised a hand to block the shimmering light from the projector trying to spot Ted, the alcoholic projectionist, up there in the booth. Maybe the lush had arranged his own private screening.

Martin turned to see what was showing. It definitely wasn't either *Psycho* or *Halloween*. The picture was shot with a jerky handheld camera from a killer's point of view. No masks here, no coy cutting to Hershey's syrup swirling down the shower drain. Just a skinny, buck-naked teenage prostitute, pinned down in the back of a night-darkened SUV. Other than the few intelligible words Martin heard, her dialogue consisted of either pitiful yelps or guttural choking as the spidery male hand at her throat throttled her. Tears speckled the heavy eyeliner and blue eye shadow, overdone cosmetics that made the adolescent look like a kid who'd played with Mommy's makeup kit.

The camera showed little interest in her face, choosing instead to focus on the carbon-steel hunting knife that unzipped her bare belly. Martin gawked in dumb fascination as the lens plunged into the entrails bursting through the slit midriff, winced as if *he* were the one nuzzling his face in the slick innards as the dying girl squirmed at her body's violation. The theater's iron stench thickened around him.

Martin had never seen a movie like this—more like a snuff film than a teen screamfest. He wondered what it was. Had Sprague finally taken his advice and booked some torture porn for the Royale?

The screen remained a blurred smear of burgundy as the viewpoint protagonist wallowed in gore. It…bothered Martin more than the other flicks he'd seen. The violence didn't have the jaunty, music-video editing or the exaggerated funhouse shock value of splatter. Instead, the ordeal dragged on, the girl dying by degrees, until her shrieks became grating white noise. And the longer it went on, the more Martin *felt* it, as if someone were nuzzling his own guts.

The shot grew so grindingly monotonous that Martin couldn't keep his eyes from wandering. And that's when he saw the silhouette outlined in the aisle seat, second row.

Good movie, Martin.

Martin flinched, for the voice hadn't come from the sound system's speakers but from inside his head. It played in his brain like a memory, echoing the brief conversation he'd had with Virgil Aldon Barnett. But its intonation was entirely new—sinuous and insinuating.

He stared at the back of the shadowy figure's head. There *couldn't* be anyone else in the theater. He'd checked. There was nowhere Randy or Tom could have hidden from him.

I knew you'd appreciate my work, said the voice that he might have mistaken for his own thoughts. *You and me—we like real horror.*

It didn't occur to Martin until then that he should say something. "Y-you...you're not supposed to be here."

The voice ignored the interruption. *The others, they don't understand. My mom sure didn't.*

The scene onscreen abruptly cut to another location, with no attempt to bridge the transition with exposition or narrative logic. This time, the set was a tiny bedroom with pressboard paneling, the kind found in mobile homes. The camera looked down upon a nude female form on the bed, but this body belonged to a much older woman. The breasts and hips fleshy and rumpled, and the stomach bearing the stretch marks and C-section scars of multiple pregnancies. But something else was different: the body's skin remained livid when a hand swung into the camera's view and slapped the flabby tits, and the arms stayed as stiff and still as manikin limbs while the unseen cinematographer ground his pelvis against the prostrate woman.

The camera panned up the woman's torso, and Martin gagged. The neck ended in serrated tears of sawn skin, sinew, and spine, leaving only a gaping vacancy on the bloodstained pillow. But the lens focused on a bookshelf about a foot above the bed. There, among thrift-shop knickknacks and ceramic figurines, rested the head of a trailer-park Medusa, her disheveled salt-and-pepper hair still partially rolled in pink plastic curlers, the color drained from her face along with the blood that oozed from the stump beneath her doubled chin. Her filmy, half-lidded eyes had rolled up toward the ceiling, unable to watch the spectacle even in death.

Doubled over by nausea, Martin braced himself against the seat nearest him and heaved, but couldn't seem to draw enough breath to vomit. He thought he'd seen everything—after all, he'd rented DVDs about guys like Edmund Kemper and Ed Gein, complete with buckets of corn syrup gore. But he hadn't realized just how much of the reality the directors left out. Here, he could almost feel the rubbery hardness of the lifeless breasts, the cold stiffening of the labia in the beginning stages of rigor mortis.

"Y-you've got to go," Martin stammered, trying to convince himself that this guy was only a bum looking for a place to flop for the night. "Or I'll call the cops."

He wished he had the wooden blocks back—any weapon, in fact—but doubted they would make any difference. His gaze again fixed on the figure in the second row aisle seat. The head no longer lolled against the back of the chair but now tilted upward, peering avidly at the screen. Martin got the crazy impression that the celluloid images up there did not originate in the projection booth, but instead radiated out from the silhouette like an aura of atrocity.

Know why I killed myself, Martin? the echo in his skull asked. *Not from remorse, no matter what people would like to think. No, I couldn't stand the thought of spending the rest of my life in jail, never again to know the joy of torment, the ecstasy of annihilation...*

Martin spun around, the coruscating light from the projector dazzling him as he turned his back on the screen. He intended to run up the aisle and out of the theater, but the extremes of bright and dark disoriented him. The upward slope of the auditorium floor seemed to seesaw beneath him, tilting like the base of an upended cup, and when the blinding afterimages cleared from his eyes, Martin found himself skittering like a terrified insect *toward* the screen. He skidded to a halt mere feet from the second row aisle seat.

But the movie doesn't have to end. Now I can watch, and you *can be the star.*

The set onscreen morphed into a different location—a different bedroom—this one decorated in girly pinks and pastels and Hello Kitty crap. Martin didn't need to see the bare body of the tween girl on the bed to know who it was.

"Rochelle," he croaked.

He had never seen nor ever wanted to see his kid sister naked. Now she was splayed out before him like any movie screen queen, arms lashed to the headboard with nylon rope. Except she was no Bijou Phillips or Linnea Quigley—this was a twelve-year-old whose preadolescent chest had barely begun to bud breasts. She thrashed on the mattress, bawling, her baby-fat face bunched in agony. Beneath her bony ribcage, her punctured bellybutton welled red over the bulge of her tummy.

So, how about it, Martin? the whisperer goaded. *Are you a poser or a player?*

A sickening excitation stirred in Martin's crotch; it seemed he could feel his erection penetrate the wound, its shaft lubricated with blood. Although he would never have admitted it to anyone, Martin was still a virgin, and he'd always fantasized that his first time would be with a hot girl his own age—a green ticket—who'd welcome his touch with a sultry smile and deep tongue kisses. Not this—this fear, revulsion, and hatred. And certainly not with his *sister.* Sure, she irritated him but *this*—

"Go to hell!" Martin clapped his hands over his eyes, shouting defiantly at the shadow in front of him. "I won't watch any more! I'm not *like* you!"

The moment he said it, though, it occurred to Martin that he might be—probably was—imagining this whole thing. If so, his own mind had produced everything he saw on the screen…which meant he *was* like Virgil Aldon Barnett.

He'd shut his eyes, but the festival of depravities continued to unspool before his vision, as if his hands and eyelids had become transparent. Martin started to cry, and he let his legs fold up, expecting to sink to the floor. Instead, he found himself supported—comfortably cushioned for the next feature.

"I'm *not* like you!" His fingers clawed into the hollows beneath his brows, but he couldn't look away from the movie screen. "*I don't want to see!*"

The film rolled on…

Kids were already camped outside the Royale when Randy arrived at eleven in the morning to prep the theater for the first matinee. Evidently, neither school truancy laws nor the Fright Fest's "R" rating could stop the teens from trying to sneak into what the locals had dubbed the "Serial Killer Cinema."

Since the discovery of the killer's body, Charlene had flat refused to enter the auditorium, which left Randy as the only other person on the day shift to unlock the theater exits and make sure that Martin the Slacker had actually cleaned the place the previous night. As the sole staff member who'd actually seen the ear-to-ear gash gaping beneath the dead man's jaw, Randy didn't relish the thought of going in there again, but at least it was easier than having to deal with the hot dogs and popcorn at the concessions stand.

As he pushed open one of the double doors, the taint of blood in the air made Randy feel like he was going to hurl again. He'd have to gas the place with Lysol. The queasy sense of *déjà vu* swelled when he saw a dark-haired figure seated in *that* chair—the one with the tattered black trash bag still draped over it. The fleeting notion that somehow Virgil Aldon Barnett's body had returned nearly sent Randy running from the theater.

But he quickly saw that the guy in the chair was not the dead serial killer. This figure rocked back and forth and made little mewling sounds as if weeping. And he wore the ill-fitting red vest of a Royale usher.

"Martin?" Randy moved down the center aisle toward him. "You spend the whole night here, buddy?"

His steps slowed when Martin didn't answer. He suddenly dreaded the thought of seeing Martin's face, particularly as the words Martin muttered grew more distinct.

"No more, please. I don't want to see any more…"

Martin's profile phased into view like a moon emerging from eclipse. He pressed his balled fists to his temples, trickles of blood and clear, viscous fluid running from between the knuckles. Crimson drips trailed down his cheeks in lieu of tears.

The vacant gouges of the sockets gaped as if they still had eyes.

"Please, stop. I don't want to see."

Randy reflexively glanced in the direction that Martin stared. He saw nothing but the Royale's blank white screen with its sagging rip. Randy backed away, his chest heaving, and ran up the aisle.

He nearly slammed into Ms. Sprague as he barreled out into the lobby.

"What is it?" The manager's expression darkened from quizzical to apprehensive. "Is something wrong?"

Randy was about to blurt what he'd seen, but he noticed that Charlene had already unlocked the front entrance and started to take tickets from the patrons who surged into the lobby. Two teen girls—the green tickets from earlier that week—had returned for an encore performance, giggling with excitement as they approached the double doors of the auditorium.

For the second time that week, Randy steadied his breath and bent to whisper in Ms. Sprague's ear. *"Mr. Casey is in the house."*

MENACE

Chris Marrs on Yvonne Navarro's "Santa Alma"

I lived in a small town on a little island until my mid-teens. It was during the pre-Internet era, so I relied on the public library for my horror fix. Although well-stocked, they only carried bestselling authors. So, my introduction to horror was through King, McCammon, Koontz, and Barker, and I thought Anne Rice was pretty much it for women horror writers. I knew about Shirley Jackson and Daphne du Maurier, having studied a short story by each in English class. Also, Ms. Mary Shelley, of course. Imagine my delight when, after having moved to a bigger town on a larger island, I walked into the public library for the first time and discovered not only that a plethora of additional horror writers existed, but there were more women writers than I had initially thought. And talented women writers at that. Yvonne Navarro is one of those writers.

Her story, "Santa Alma," sneaks up on you, carries you along with its lyrical and moving prose. At first glance, it appears unassuming but, in the capable hands of Yvonne, you realize too late that this isn't a gentle whimsical ride. With deft turns, she takes you down past the upfront horrors and drops you into the terrifying heart of choices, or lack thereof, and their far-reaching consequences.

If you haven't read any of Yvonne's work, I highly recommend her novels *Mirror Me* and *AfterAge*. There are scenes in both which made even this jaded horror reader squirm. So, to Yvonne, I say thank you for sharing your talent with us and for being a part of this anthology.

Santa Alma

Yvonne Navarro

Jonas Scharffen saw the woman by the back wall of the *Monasterio de la Encarnación*.

She was there—

—and then she wasn't. Headlights cut across the sidewalk as some lost late-night tourist started to turn onto the *Calle de Encarnación*, then realized it was a one-way street. As he watched the car retrace its path then continue down the *Calle de la Bola*, Jonas thought about the vision he'd seen and decided she had to have been a dancer. Maybe she was one of the women who'd been at the *Café de Chinitas* on the *Calle de Torija* before he'd gotten there tonight, because he certainly would have remembered someone wearing a dress that looked like it was made of layers of ruffled, white clouds. He turned back, rubbed his eyes and strained to make sense of the darkness—perhaps she had turned the corner. But no, there *was* no corner, not for another fifty yards. No one dressed as she had been could run that fast, and certainly not him, wobbling along the streets of Old Madrid on aged legs and fueled by too much *sangría* and too few *tapas*. Perhaps that was his trouble—not the alcohol, the lack of food, or even his age, but that there were too many things in his life that he couldn't outrun.

Suddenly, Jonas wanted to go back to the *Café de Chinitas* and ask the owner, the staff, everyone—did they know her? Had they seen this woman, with her silver-dusted hair drawn tight behind an exquisite Spanish lace comb? But it was such a long way back…even beyond the *sangría* in his stomach, Jonas was weighed by too much grief and guilt, an overwhelming combination and surely one that invited hallucinations.

Trudging homeward in the hot darkness, he was unable to turn his bleary thoughts away from the woman in white. He had seen her for only a moment, yet now it seemed like much longer. She had danced, had she not? Flamenco, and even Jonas, outsider that he was, could recognize the steps of *Sevillanas*—God knows he had seen it enough times in his nightly hauntings of the *Café de Chinitas* and the other dance clubs in Old Madrid, the darker and smokier the better. In these places, he could feed his lifelong addiction to alcohol and try ever uselessly to drive away the keening of old ghosts in his head and heart.

The thought of a drink made Jonas stop and shiver. Whether it was because of the disappearing woman or his own pain, the pleasant, numbing high he'd had was gone, evaporated by the July heat and too much thinking. It was easily twice as far to the dingy room he rented in a private residence on the *Calle de Lazo* as it would be to return to the *Café de Chinitas*, and turning back wasn't so much a conscious choice as a necessity. He *needed* the drink, the disassociation from reality, the eventual forgiving oblivion; tomorrow's hangover meant nothing but handfuls of aspirin and treating patients at the free clinic—the only place that would hire him—while he waited for the cover of darkness so he could start all over again.

Like the woman in white, the memory of the return walk eluded him. Then the café was there, like an old, dark friend welcoming him with a comforting embrace, one whose breath was thick with cigarette smoke and whose intimate kiss was tangy with wine. His blood sang with the familiar disastrous desire—God, how he *needed*, how he had *always* needed.

Jonas slipped in through the unlocked back door and headed to his usual table at the far right of the stage, where he could sit and drink himself into a stupor as he listened to the local guitarist pick out a song. Earlier there had been two couples on the stage, paid dancers whose bodies had arched and trembled as they followed the intricate music and danced a *Rumba*. Now the touristy lights were dimmed and the front entrance was locked, and Jonas's glass of the house's cheapest *sangría* barely touched his mouth as a middle-aged woman took the stage. Her wild dark hair, heavy eyebrows and full lips bespoke of Romani heritage, and everything inside Jonas soured—the red wine, the simple plate of *jamón serrano* and bread he'd eaten three or four hours ago, his *soul*.

She was good—more than that, *excellent*—and her sturdy heels followed the rhythm perfectly as the guitarist played "Belingonero Flamenco."

Her eyes flashed as she whirled, the movement lifting her patterned skirts high and showing shapely legs. Halfway through the song, a young man with pale skin and dark hair joined her in mid-*pasada*, and for some reason Jonas felt that her gaze changed—every time she turned and met Jonas's eyes, her darker ones seemed to stab at him. When she lifted her arm in the usual flamenco curve and the loose sleeve of her blouse fell back, was he really seeing a crescent-shaped scar above her right elbow, the signature of his handiwork on so many young woman in 1970's Czechoslovakia? No, of course not; she would have been barely a teenager then, perhaps only fifteen—

The perfect age for sterilization.

Jonas slammed the wine glass on the table and stood. The only thing he could think of was escape—no amount of alcohol would dull his guilt when unspoken accusation swayed only a few feet away.

"Jonas, is something wrong?"

Caught, he turned to face one of the few men he would occasionally drink with, Carles Herrero. Like Jonas's, Carles's face was aged and weathered beneath a thinning cap of gray hair, and his fingers were stained with nicotine; unlike Jonas, his expression was free of remorse, his eyes clear. Jonas had lived in Madrid for two years, and he had talked with Carles off and on; Carles was the closest thing he had to a friend in this country, perhaps in the world. No doubt, Carles considered himself just that, but the truth was he knew absolutely nothing about the real Jonas Scharffen.

Jonas had been very careful about that.

"Is something wrong?" Carles repeated and inclined his head toward Jonas's glass and the puddle of wine that had splashed around it. A mere ten feet away the couple went into another round of *pasadas*, heeled feet flashing upward at the start of each pass.

Jonas tried to speak, but for a moment nothing would come out; finally he sank back onto his chair and motioned reluctantly at Carles to join him.

"It's her," he finally managed. "The dancer. She…reminds me of someone."

Carles's eyebrows lifted. He wasn't prone to prying and this was a large part of the reason Jonas could tolerate his company. Still, even Jonas had to acknowledge the invitation he'd just extended. "Someone you used to know?"

Jonas shook his head and waited while the server, a sexless teenager with short, pallid hair and sallow skin, poured Carles a

117

glass of the house *sangría,* then drifted away.

"No." His voice was raspy, and he cleared his throat and took a sip of wine, quickly concocting a half-truth. "A woman I saw dancing on the street tonight. Outside the *Monasterio de la Encarnación.*" He didn't say anything else as he watched the couple finish their dance then go together to a table on the other side of the room. After it closed to the public, the café's dimmed lighting always showed a haze of cigarette smoke floating just beyond the stage, and before she faded into it, the woman turned and inexplicably gazed in his direction a final time. The summers in Madrid had never bothered Jonas, but her penetrating look was enough to make him sweat beneath his simple cotton shirt.

He turned back to Carles, then started. His friend's face was drained of color, and he was staring at Jonas in dismay.

"What is it?" Jonas demanded. Dear God, had he said something, given Carles some unintentional clue about the things he had done?

"You have seen her," Carles said. He was whispering, but with the music ended, Jonas could hear him clearly. There was no mistaking his next words. *"Santa Alma."*

Jonas frowned, confused and relieved at the same time. "'Saint Soul'? What are you talking about?"

He waited, but Carles didn't answer. Instead, the other man glanced around the café, a faraway expression on his face; at last he turned back to Jonas, and his eyes were full of pity.

"Jonas, you are my friend," he said. "But we are not close, so I know nothing about whatever it is that you have done—" He held up a hand to stop Jonas when he would have spoken. "And I don't want to. I would prefer to remember our conversations—*you*—as they have always been."

"What are you talking about?" Jonas asked again. The skin at the back of his scalp was crawling. "Who is this woman?"

"Not who, *what.*" Carles looked at his hands. "Do you know what night it is?"

"Wednesday," he said. "July 27th."

Carles nodded. *"Sí.* It is the anniversary of the death of St. Panteleon."

Jonas frowned, unable to make the connection. "But what does a Grecian saint have to do with the woman I saw? She was a flamenco dancer."

"St. Panteleon was a physician—"

"I know that." Stress had made Jonas snappish, and he lifted the wine glass, hiding behind a long swallow.

"In the *Monasterio de la Encarnación*, there is supposed to be a vial of his dried blood," Carles continued calmly. "Legend has it that on this night every year the contents liquefy, and while the church won't officially acknowledge this, the local priests will talk about it if you ask. What they *won't* talk about is *Santa Alma*, the woman in white who appears the same night."

Jonas sat back on his chair, involuntarily searching the shadowed corners of the café for the dark-haired Gypsy dancer. She was gone, but the dread she had stirred inside him remained, and Carles's next words only deepened his uneasiness. "The locals believe that she comes to claim the souls of men who have done evil. Those who report seeing her…" He shook his head instead of finishing.

"What?" Jonas demanded.

"They disappear," Carles answered.

"That's ridiculous," he said. Still, a pulse had begun a sickening beat in his temple. "If they disappear, then how would anyone know about her?"

His friend's mouth turned down. "Because they always see her once beforehand, and they always stop somewhere before she takes them. Just like…you. It's as if she intends that others should know of her presence."

"No one's taking me—or my soul—anywhere," Jonas said, but his tone held no conviction.

Carles leaned forward. "Jonas, I will stay with you," he offered. "Until it passes and it is *mañana*. We will not leave the café, and so you will be all right, *sí?*"

Jonas squeezed his eyes shut and drew his hands across his rough face, feeling a two-day growth of beard. How ironic that his fingertips remained sensitive, still the hands of a fine surgeon after all these decades. Age had mapped its lines upon his face and skin, but even the drink had not unsteadied that touch, that *skill*. How much good could he have brought about with his natural feel for a scalpel, the instinctive ability to carve with a minimum of movement and destruction? Yet, instead of saving life or continuing it, he had chosen alcohol and, in his own dark way, stolen the very thing he was supposed to preserve.

"No," Jonas said, opening his eyes. "Though it is kind of you to offer." He started to say something else, then blinked as everything in the café somehow...*sharpened*, as if God had dialed up the contrast in this minuscule part of His Kingdom so that Jonas could appreciate it. It was late, well beyond the two a.m. closing time to which the tourists were held; only the locals knew that if you went around to the back of the eighteenth century building in which the *Café de Chinitas* was located, you could get in after hours when it was darker and more...earthy. The performers went from the well-rehearsed professionals of earlier to those who danced because their spirits demanded it, like the Gypsy woman of a few minutes ago and her younger partner. The stage lights were shut off, and the others were dimmed, draining away the commercialism the café maintained during regular business hours—the red plates and painted chairs now looked sensual and warm, the bright tablecloths mellowed out, the flamboyantly decorated wall behind the stage turned dark and exotic beneath the stucco arches on either side of it. Jonas found it suddenly beautiful, and it wasn't difficult to understand why. The *Café de Chinitas* had been the focal point in his dismal existence for the last two years, the only place where he had, except for Sundays when it was closed, the barest of social contact with other human beings. In a way it had been his life, and he supposed that what he was experiencing now wasn't much different from the way a drowning man was said to see his life flash before his eyes before he finally died.

"No," he said again to Carles. He felt drunk with the loveliness of the café, awed that it felt like an hour had passed when he knew it had only been seconds. Jonas stood and offered his hand to Carles across the table, seeing the sorrow in the old man's eyes. "You are a good friend," he said quietly. "But it is time for us to say good-bye."

"Good-bye," Carles repeated. "Not just...good night?"

Jonas shrugged, unwilling to admit what they both knew. They shook hands, and although he had touched thousands of people—patients—the delicate, papery feel of Carles's ancient skin was, in that moment, unique and wonderful, something alive and like nothing else in the world. If only Jonas had had this same admiration for humanity in his youth. He let go of Carles with reluctance, nodded a final farewell, and strode out of the café, wishing he could go with his head held high. Unfortunately, he was fresh out of false courage.

Such a beautiful Spanish night. The full moon floated overhead like a huge heavenly spotlight, effectively washing out man's weaker electrical ones as it shone on the old buildings and beautiful flowerbeds lining the streets. Perhaps he could take a final walk and stop by his rented room—then he could return to the *Monasterio de la Encarnación* and await the appearance of *Santa Alma*. Jonas had no doubt that's where he would find her, and he knew also that he would seek her out. The thought of fleeing was simply…not there, as if the concept of escape had been utterly erased from his brain. There were, however, papers in his room that would condemn him if he did not return, and others found them…but then, why would he care? He had no family upon which to bring shame, and Jonas had long ago eradicated anything that would incriminate anyone else—the others would have to bear their own burdens of penance. Would it not be fitting, and perhaps enlightening, for the world to learn of the unspeakable crimes he had committed?

Let them know…let them *learn*.

Jonas's feet had a will of their own, and this time, they carried him not to the back of the *Monasterio de la Encarnación*, but around to the high, wrought-iron gates guarding the convent's front. How strange to think that nuns slept in one section of this seventeenth century building, while elsewhere, in its reliquary chamber, were stored the bones of saints…and the infamous vial of St. Panteleon's blood. Had the blood, as Carles had claimed, returned to its liquified form tonight?

"Yes," said a female voice from behind him. "It has."

Jonas turned slowly and faced the woman he'd seen earlier in the evening. Close up, she was lovely beyond description, and there was no mistaking the resemblance. His heart, already shattered in so many places, crumbled a little more. This was what had so crushed him earlier in the café, what Jonas had refused to admit to Carles, and to himself, until now: the middled-aged woman in the café had looked and danced like Nadia—the only woman he had ever loved and who had died because of what he had done. How fitting that his destroyer could have been her twin.

"You've come to kill me," Jonas rasped.

She shook her head and turned, slipping in a graceful circle around him, her every movement clearly in time to a score of music he could not hear. Layer after layer of pure white ruffles shimmered in the moonlight, and it was impossible to tell where the glowing fabric ended and her skin began. Pearlized castanets flashed on her fingers but made not the slightest sound. Her hair was silver, her lips as pale as her skin—even her eyes were colorless but still, somehow, filled with compassion. She was like a deadly albino angel and he had never seen anything so beautiful.

Eerily graceful, she circled him twice, then stopped. "I have not come to punish you, Jonas Scharffen. I have come to *save* you."

Jonas was terrified, but still he frowned. "But the legends—"

"Are just that," she interrupted. "Tales built of things about which man has no true knowledge." Her smile still held that strange hint of kindness. "Like so much of what mankind insists, the beliefs are only partially correct."

"Then what…?"

"Forgiveness requires remorse," she said. "Regret and sensitivity for those you have wronged. You have all this." Her unblinking gaze was fixed upon his. "But it also requires admission of guilt, and acceptance."

"I know what I've done," he said in a low voice. "And I know what I am."

"But you have admitted it to no one." Now her voice had an edge of ice. "And you have not accepted your own actions. You have not accepted that *you* are to blame for the things you have done."

Jonas shook his head vehemently and felt himself stumble with the movement. He grasped one of the iron fence bars to steady himself, then released it in horror—it felt too much like the bars of a prison. "No. I was only following orders from the government—"

"Did someone cover your hand with theirs and guide your blade?" she demanded. The moonlight in her eyes reminded him of gleaming metal. "I think not. No one wielded the knife but you, Jonas." Her voice was barely loud enough to be heard, yet something in the tone stopped him from arguing. He was lying—to her, to himself. Jonas knew it, but he had the passage of years to give him the strength to maintain that deception. Or so he thought.

"What are you?" he asked. "An angel or a demon?"

"Neither." She tilted her head to one side. "If you must label me, I suppose you would call me a guide. I am sent to lead you to salvation, in whatever way I must. But for redemption, perhaps you need to remember."

Before he could reply her hands flashed forward and crossed, then her arms lifted in the classic start of flamenco. At the apex of the movement, the pearl-colored castanets clacked smartly, the first sound Jonas had heard them make. She spun and her dress left a blur of white fire across his vision that made him recoil and rub his face. Music suddenly filled his ears, the fiery sounds of a gifted flamenco guitarist, and when he scowled and opened his eyes—

It is twenty-five years ago and Nadia's laughter fills his soul and makes him cry inside.

Another café, this one in Czechoslovakia and nameless, a tiny back-street place deep in Central Prague that the Roma keep carefully hidden from the secret police. No one here would sneer and insult another by calling them "Gypsy" or "thief"—in this place, the people could laugh and dance and drink without fear.

The aromas of strong coffee and pilsner beer beat at Jonas's senses along with the smells of pork sausage and cabbage, plus the sweeter scent of Roski from platters scattered throughout the room. Nadia whirls in front of him, outrageously patterned skirt spreading like a huge, colorful bird as she tries to convince him to join her, she will teach him flamenco, the traditional dance of her forbidden heritage. But he is uncoordinated at best, at worst paralyzed from the terror building inside his chest like a wild thing because he knows what is coming—

As the door shatters and a dozen uniformed men with weapons storm into the café, he grabs Nadia's hand and pulls her aside. "She's with me," he tells the captain of the militia. "I am Dr. Jonas Scharffen." The young military man hesitates then passes Nadia by, his brutal grip snagging the wrist of a much younger Romani girl, easily half the age of Jonas's beloved.

"Jonas, what have you done?" Nadia cries. "I trusted you—we all did!"

"Keep your voice down," he hisses. "I did it for you, so that we could be together and not have to hide."

"But Jonas, these are my people!"

"They won't be harmed," he tells her, believing this. "The government will have them sterilized and released. They won't be hurt—"

Nadia's mouth twists while, around them, the women scream and the men hurl curses as the militia forces them to line up, then begins herding them out of the café like goats. Her arm is warm beneath Jonas's fingers and even amid the chaos it brings memories of the previous night, when her soft body had moved against his and her mouth murmured endearments.

1

"How could you?" She looks around wildly. "You are just like the Gadjo—you think of the Roma as breeding machines to be eliminated." She pulls away from Jonas, the touch that had been so warm now rough and hateful. "I will stay with my people and share their fate. You have destroyed what we had, Jonas. I could never love you now."

"But they knew about this place already!" Jonas reaches for her. "You think I had more to do with it than that?"

"Then you should have warned us." Nadia's gaze is full of loathing. "You are an evil man, Jonas Scharffen. God forgive me for ever sharing myself with you."

"Do you remember now?"

A different voice, a different time. Jonas squinted at the warm darkness, and the woman Carles had told him was Santa Alma stood patiently a few feet away. He said the first thing that came to mind. "It wasn't my fault. The secret police already knew they were there. If I hadn't cooperated when they came to my office that morning, they would have accused me of consorting with the Gypsies."

"And weren't you?" she asked softly.

"What does that matter?" Jonas balled his fists at his sides, an old man's pathetic gesture of defiance. "I wanted to *save* Nadia, not condemn her."

The look that Santa Alma gave him was full of false surprise. "And did you, Jonas Scharffen? Did you save the woman you loved?" Before he could reply, her castanets flashed over her head again, another blur of pure white, and—

The room is white and silver, painted walls and sanitized metal, filled with tubes and wires and equipment, cold and flooded with unforgiving fluorescent light. He has been at this for what feels like years, but in reality it has only been slightly more than a week, eight days of cutting and tying, of changing—limiting—the lives of the Gypsy women the militia bring to him from the holding quarters in the main hospital. One is finished, and her arm is marked, and they roll her away; another cart is pushed inside, and someone else takes her place within his queue. Jonas works like a machine and nothing is wasted, not his movements or the sterilized scalpels or the minimal sutures he so deftly works into their bodies. To him, they are faceless beings, not human and certainly not women—they are nothing, no more than animals to be controlled. Jonas glances at the anesthesiologist and sees him look down at the latest patient; his gaze automatically follows the other man's, and he gasps for air behind his surgical mask as the sound of his breathing becomes huge, more than enough to drown out the hiss of the nearby respirator—

On the table before him, the unconscious woman is Nadia.

"Did you save her, Jonas?"

"I did what I had to do," he said hoarsely. He couldn't meet her eyes, couldn't bear to see what he knew would be disappointment rather than accusation.

"That's not what I asked," she said gently.

"No."

"Then what *did* you do?"

For a long time, he said nothing. Then, "I…killed her."

"But you didn't mean to."

Jonas opened my mouth to agree, the denial rising automatically. After all, wasn't that what he had been telling himself for years?

"Yes, I did," he said suddenly. "I knew exactly what I was doing. Nadia hated me for what I'd done, wouldn't have anything to do with me. So I took revenge." How strange to hear this most brutal of truths after a quarter century of poisonous self-denial, but suddenly Jonas couldn't stop. "I had her opened up, and she would have been fine…but I cut both of her ovarian arteries. She bled to death on the table, and I watched her die."

Santa Alma said nothing, and Jonas couldn't bear to meet her colorless gaze. He stared at the ground instead and realized that his feet were swallowed in darkness, as though he were standing over an abyss. Perhaps he was, and wouldn't oblivion—even damnation—be better than what he had endured for the last third of his life?

The woman's voice, like plaintive music that could not be ignored, made Jonas lift his head. "And the others, Jonas Scharffen…what of them?"

"I always told myself that they were better off," he admitted shakily. "That although what I did might be wrong, the Czech government would have taken more drastic steps, perhaps even exterminated them if I hadn't done my part. It was bad, but not as bad as it could have been."

"And you believed this."

"I…" The sidewalk tilted momentarily, no doubt thanks to the alcohol. A lot of things were thanks to that, and maybe this was something he also needed to admit. "I drank," he said. "To make myself believe that. I've been drinking all my life."

Her next question was hardly more than a whisper, and yet…it was thunder. "And do you, indeed, believe that?"

Jonas stared at her, unable to answer. Rather than ask again, she offered him her hand. "Dance with me."

He shook his head and grimaced, would have backed away had the wrought-iron fence not been behind him. "No, I can't—I don't want to."

Then her hand, the skin as frigid as snow, grasped his, and she pulled him forward and into a dancer's embrace. Jonas's feet found a rhythm to music inside his head, and it all came back, so many nights in that café with Nadia, so much laughter and joy. Santa Alma's face was only inches from his own, and she looked so much like Nadia that it hurt him to breathe. Then her features blurred and rearranged themselves, and she resembled another of the women who'd often come to that nameless café, Nadia's sister and someone else who had been "saved" by his scalpel. Jonas blinked, and her face changed again, and again, and again, faster and faster until he could see nothing in the blur but the dark eyes of a thousand women filled with barren pain.

"All right!" he cried. He yanked free and staggered a few feet away, trembling. "I was *wrong*—I didn't do it to help them, I did it to help myself! Because of my drinking the government was the only place I could find work. Nadia was the only person who ever believed I could stop, *and I killed her.*" His legs would no longer hold him, and Jonas sank to his knees in front of the woman in white, welcoming the bite of the rough concrete through his slacks. "Whatever it is that you're going do, for God's sake—just get on with it!"

She stood over Jonas, silent as a ghost, letting him wait until he thought he would explode with fear. In a few moments, the church bells all over Madrid would begin to toll the start of another day.

Santa Alma spoke. "Atonement will cost you a year, Jonas Scharffen, and the time will feel like an eternity. The blood in St. Panteleon's vial must be revitalized yearly by a soul seeking forgiveness, but that soul's desire must be strong enough to conquer all other earthly cravings. Do you have the strength to carry this through?"

I can choose forgiveness, Jonas thought. A spirit free of the crippling guilt that not even the drink could extinguish. "And if I say no?"

There was no change in her expression. "Then you will be as you are," she said simply.

And what was that? Alive, yes…but old and drunk, suffocated by his own conscience. He would not live much longer, but he would be condemned forever. He bowed his head.

"I wish to be forgiven," he said in a low voice.

"You will die."

"I'm going to die anyway," Jonas said. "Better now and saved, than a decade from now and damned."

Santa Alma nodded, then closed the distance between them. When she reached for him, Jonas saw that her palms were coated with scarlet, a startling display of stigmata. Still, the old physician never hesitated as he grasped her hands, never flinched when fire shot through his body as his dry, shaking flesh touched hers.

And as the bells tolled the onset of another year over Madrid, the cloud of light that Jonas had first seen earlier that evening enveloped him in blissful pain and restitution, then spun into sparkling red—

—and finally winked out.

C.W. Smith on Shirley Jackson's "The Summer People"

Shirley Jackson's "The Summer People" is easily one of my favorite horror stories. I liked "The Lottery," but "The Summer People" was more my style. Telling a good horror story in which nothing is explained requires a peculiar talent. More often than not, stories built of such bare stuff as "The Summer People" suffer from missing ingredients. Jackson was a master of detail (the chilling opening paragraph of The Haunting of Hill House is proof enough of that)—and Jackson was also a master of how detail operates within a story. We learn about the vacationing couple in "The Summer People," but what do we ever learn about the threat? The danger is palpable, but what is it? We're terrified and we can't say what of. Shirley Jackson taught me that vivid description isn't the only way to shred a reader's nerves.

Sanctity

C.W. Smith

Sounds of the child carry throughout the single-wide trailer and permeate the long night. The child's mother stares up from her pillow to the ceiling with her eyes half closed. She knows better than to tend to the child when it cries like this. She knows his different cries. This is the one she's most afraid of.

Four hundred miles away, the child's father stares into a glass. He knows the child is restless again. He feels its need like an itch at the tip of his nose—followed by the rain of nails in his guts. The child isn't the cause of that distress, only the sensation at the end of his nose; but the molten drip of his digestive fluids follows the itch, and it follows every time. The attacks have been more frequent lately, but money's been hard to come by. Buck "Nero" Mulligan wraps his torso in his arms and waits for the storm to pass.

The crying child pounds his tiny mattress. His leaden fists have not grown twice their normal size *or have they*? The force is enough to lift the crib. It comes down hard between arcs. It's percussion for the crying. It echoes throughout the trailer park and explodes the night.

The crickets stop singing and depart for safer posts. The oldest woman in the park, whom the kids adoringly call Old Racist Bitch, whose underpinning is a veritable cat farm, suffers another stroke in her sleep. The last thing she sees in her mind's eye is a nude Mexican doctor on top of her administering CPR. He yells for help until he tells her he is God and he's come for her at last. She screams louder and never again.

Horace Dayton is bench pressing milk jugs filled with cement in his kitchen when the crying and concomitant pounding proves too much. He doesn't give two shits about kids, he's planted no fewer than four himself in various gardens statewide. The sound of them crying though sends his teeth to a grind. The newcomers in what used to be the Askins' trailer are too much. The woman is too sickly to be any fun and the baby has interrupted his reps three nights in the span of a week. H.D. wipes his hair back and grabs his Harley tank top from the aquarium. He leaves his door unlocked because his dog is awake and his dog is a thoroughbred asshole.

The mother, once known as Ann Chopin but for the rest of her human term simply mother, hears approaching footfalls outside. She removes her prostrate form from the bed's twin mattress with a jolt and the shriek of dead springs.

The mother opens the door before Horace can knock.

"You must leave!" she commands.

Her order is inaudible. Horace reads her lips and interprets what she says as a threat and an encroachment on his civil liberties.

"Woman," he says. *Woman* was the word his daddy used to invoke the female's full attention, and Horace swears by it too. "If you don't shut that baby of yours up, I'm liable to come up in there and take care of it myself."

In response to their highly evolved sense of danger, the dozen or so cats who've set up shop under Old Racist Bitch's trailer rush home through the door they've made in the bent siding. Sensing an opportunity, some proceed upward through the kitchen cabinets.

"Stranger, my baby is real sick. He'll fall asleep once he's done, but 'til then he has to cry it out. Ain't nothing that can be done."

Horace isn't deterred. Horace has matter of face never been deterred in his life. He dropped out of school. Beat his old man half to death with his own belt. Bit chunks out of two bosses and a cop.

"Woman, this is your last warning. You shut that rat up or I will." Horace flexes to prove his point. The long scars on his arms, souvenirs from broken-bottle fights, swell twice as wide.

She takes a step back to make way for Horace's inflated pecks but stands her ground just the same.

"Sir, I suggest you go home and you relax. Turn your TV up real loud. Listen to some rock music. Please, just leave us be! It ain't safe."

Horace shoves the woman to the side. She crumples like a pile of sticks. When she's on the ground she appears to have melted so there's nothing left of her but her nightgown. Despite appearances, she's in there. Beneath fabric heavier than she is, and as much as she'd love to be melted away to nothing, she's in there.

Horace follows the racket to the back room. The chair propped up against the knob surprises him. A crazy sight, though he's seen far stranger. One night as a child in Des Moines, under a half moon, he watched an elderly man morph into a possum. The possum-man ravished Horace's mother before disappearing in the cornfield behind their house, never to be seen again. Horace tosses the chair aside and storms into the room.

"Aight, listen up! Sandman's here, so put a cork in it!"

Four hundred miles away, Nero Mulligan falls out of his barstool. The bartender picks up the phone, but a look around the bar compels him to return the receiver to the cradle. He pours himself another beer while Nero seizes.

Less than forty feet away, Ann Chopin reaches for the doorknob to help herself up and wonders how far away she can get before the child comes after her.

"What in the blazes is this?" Horace bellows.

The baby stands in the cradle fuming. Two empty plastic bags rest at his shit-stained feet. A modicum of white residue is left in the corner where Junior couldn't get to it; otherwise, the bags have

131

been sucked clean.

Junior grips the bars of the cradle and pulls them apart. Splinters shred his wee little hands but he doesn't notice. With his features twisted by withdrawal, with his eyes red, with splashes of long-dried white beneath his nose and around his mouth, Junior has the face of a rabid bat. Horace has momentary and coinciding flashbacks to the possum-man and juvenile hall. He and Junior rush each other.

The trailer begins to wobble. Ann starts for the truck, but stops when she hears the scream. Junior begins to reel her in by their invisible umbilical chain. He pulls so hard she nearly throws up her reproductive organs. She intuits via the fiber-astral filaments linking mother to child that Junior has rifled through the felled man's pockets and has turned up a pair of twenties. She follows the psychic leash toward the trailer. She remembers what her family pastor said long ago about a mother's blood oath to her child. Every life is sacred. Every mother must surrender her life to her child, even if, *especially* if her recreational drug use turns her child into a cocaine-dependent psychic vampire.

The baby is hungry. He begins to cry again about the time she reaches the bottom of the plastic steps leading up to the front door. The child's cries carry throughout the singlewide trailer and escape into the endless night.

Colleen Anderson on Shirley Jackson's "The Lottery"

As a child, I was assigned Shirley Jackson's "The Lottery" for a class. I was already writing fantasy, though rather badly. Her horror story snuck through that barrier, before people understood what the genre was all about, besides the schlocky werewolf and vampire movies. When you read a great deal, sometimes only the most brilliant stories shine through the years. And Jackson's was one of those. The horror was more real because the place seemed like an everyday town, the people like you and me. And yet, they were complicit in their agreement to a brutal ritual. Everyone took part for fear they would be the victim. The Lottery stands to this day as a disturbing morality tale about how easily it is for us to slip into bestial behaviors. I find many of my own tales deal with morality from the resonance of "The Lottery" in my mind.

Red is the Color of My True Love's Blood

Colleen Anderson

My hand touches the cool metal of the door knob. I've been humming a tune. The problem is when I do this I sometimes zone out, forget what I was doing. And I've been to Jordy's door so many times before that it's almost automatic.

But what's different today is that my flight was canceled due to the weather and I thought I'd surprise him with dinner. I push the door open with my shoulder and carry in the bag of groceries.

Music drifts like a wraith down the hall, and amber light capers over the living room walls illuminated by a fire crackling in the fireplace. The scent of sharp pine resin mixed with an odd metallic smell fills my nose.

I turn right into the open layout kitchen, maneuver the bag onto the counter, then return to the living room. I check the logs in the fireplace and warm my hands for a minute, staring into the fiery dance. The axe is lying in the middle of the floor. I take a few moments to absorb the heat, the scent, and the space of Jordy's home. Soon this will be mine too. I pick up the axe and prop it against the fireplace, near a fresh pile of wood brought in to dry. There is a sticky residue on the handle. Back in the kitchen, I wash my hands.

I smile; just like him to put a fire on and then forget its ambiance as he goes back to his thesis. He's so close to the end now, which will be a cause for celebration on several levels. Not only will he be done with years of school and have his PhD but I'll get to move in. We both agreed it would be less distracting for him in these final stages if I moved in after his defense. But that's now only a month away and we've been distracted enough by each other as it is. I'd love to just crawl into his bed and wait for him there but it could be hours until he notices.

I'm still humming, unpacking the crusty baguette, the head of lettuce, the basil and crimson tomatoes for an al dente pasta sauce, and am reminded of Jordy's thesis. It's a fascinating subject and really, how we first met. He's looking at the psychological and mythical symbolism of the color red. Every color has its significance but he's always been drawn to red. Perhaps I have too.

Maybe that's why he noticed me with my spiked, red only-a-bottle-can-give hair. That and my photo show, Nature's Rainbow. Each image of nature focused on a different color; the wild green of trees with young leaves, the blue of a gentian against a lake reflecting the sky, the red of an apple amongst turning leaves. He had wandered in, his dark wavy hair falling over one eye, spending so long before each picture, especially the ones with red. My show had had two photos for each color, the second one played out a juxtaposition of manmade objects with nature; the blue of a car against the backdrop of sky, a red lacquered wood-handled knife spattered with blood from a slaughter—to show how humans encroach upon nature.

Jordy's thesis goes into more depth than my show, more history. He could have written a book on each color but said red was the most vibrant. It's the lifeblood, and looking around his place I see accents of scarlet embellish each room. The rust red wall in the living, the trim on the counters is cinnabar. The carpet is beige with random speckles of dark ruby, which I've never noticed before. When something is drawn to our eyes we suddenly see it everywhere.

A thin, cherry border encircles each dinner plate, and his cutting board is red marble. I've laid out the ingredients and put the pan out but I better check to see how he's doing before I start. I should let him know I'm here.

I stop for a moment. Something seems odd, out of place. But then I'm what's different at this time, my schedule disrupted. I smile. It's worth it to get to spend a few moments with Jordy. He doesn't complete me necessarily but he makes me happy, is counterpoint to my thoughts. Where I see patterns and shapes, he sees lines and symbolism. We mesh well like that. He is like a great scarlet balloon rising into a summer sky and bringing joy. His laugh always lightens me.

Jordy is one of those people who likes to work with extra stimulus, music playing or a radio talkshow in the background. I like the opposite, a cone of silence in which to concentrate or sort out the natural sounds. But I guess I'm the only one who believes that as more than one person has commented on my humming. It's a subconscious thing; I don't even notice most of the time.

I like the glow from the fireplace, the warmth, and the softly sinuous shadows. It makes me think of centuries ago when people lived in the mysteries of color. Jordy said Christian religion used red to represent saints, and of course blood, the active humors and the earthly connection. Even Catholic cardinals, like the bird, wear red. Brides in China, and women in India do as well. Studies have shown people get fired up, (fired up!) by red but interestingly orange is used on inmates because it supposedly calms them. Or is it just that they're easier to spot if they escape? Maybe I'll do a series next on colors tied with emotions. Green is jealousy. Yellow is cowardice.

Color is so integral to many things, and the patterns and shapes of color form my focus in photography. People or places don't matter as much as the colors they embody. Blue for calm, black for death, white for spirit. So many ideas attached to what nature provides. Blood is red. Red is anger, love, war, passion. Blood is used to curse, to heal.

Jordy said numerous cultures use blood for rituals, such as voodoun. Some just try to predict the future, or contact a dead granny to find out where the jewels are buried. Yet, other rituals call on gods and spirits for knowledge and retribution. Curses are always about getting even, a punishment to fit the crime. If justice can't be brought upon the perpetrator, then the curser can get those from the other side to mete out an eye for an eye. People make up so many things.

One night we both had too much wine, laughing about all the superstitions attached to colors. When Jordy knocked over the glass, slicing his finger on the shards, I held my hands to my face in mock horror. "Blood sacrifice," I giggled.

Instead of wiping away the blood crawling from the small cut, he chased me around the living room with his finger held up like the wand of doom. "I'll teach you," he yelled, laughing. "I'll curse you."

He caught me as I pretended to cringe in dread. My face clasped gently between his palms, he leaned in and kissed me, blood smearing my cheek. Into my kiss, Jordy whispered, "I'll curse you to always love me."

And I do. I love him like I've never loved anyone else, but only because we're compatible, understand and trust each other. I loved him from the beginning. And we both are fascinated by color. I uncork the pinot noir, pour a small amount and take a sip, toasting our lives to be. The wine needs to breathe and I set it aside to walk down the hall.

I peek into the den on the left, expecting to see Jordy chewing his knuckle as he works through his concluding chapter, but he's not there. Only the bluish glow of the monitor's screensaver shows he was in the den. The air is dead here, papery. He spends more time on his laptop than sitting at a desk.

Maybe Jordy took one of those cerebral naps as he calls them, the ones he claims sorts out his thoughts but which I think are just procrastination. Still, he's done some amazing work and the end is very near. I love him as much for his brain as his awesome humor and great body.

The music contours the bedroom and spills out the open door

on the right; unusual if he's sleeping. I slow. Should I wake him?

As I reach the door, I pause with my hand on the wall, not wanting to disturb him. The light is low. Why would he be burning a pillar candle beside the bed if he's napping? Then I see Jordy's tight little ass moving up and down, up and down. I am glued in place. Slowly, I filter what I can't comprehend. He says, "You are my firebrand. God, how I burn for you," and a small feminine laugh follows.

I'm doubling over, clutching my stomach as though he punched me. A gut shot, the air is sucked from me and I back out the door. Our endearments. The words he says to me. The special phrases. My vision begins to fog with a red haze.

I'm back in the bedroom. I don't recall moving. I see only red. I smell salt and musky sex and something else, something coppery, metallic. They don't perceive me as I draw near. Humming, I raise the axe over my head as Jordy's head turns. The axe falls, of its own gravity and volition, sheering off his lower jaw, spattering scarlet everywhere. It sounds like he's gargling and I realize I've severed Jordy's lying tongue. He's a mess, no longer pretty. Still attached to red, carmine, carnelian, ruby. It's always there. I can't leave him like this and the axe blade falls again, biting with lover's passion into his neck. My last kiss. He twitches and falls. Blood geysers, oozes, blends with his burgundy sheets.

A keening comes from beneath him, high pitched, like a teakettle. Humming, I let the blade shut her up too. I keep expecting to hear metal hitting wood but it is only a thunking, wet meaty sound. There is blood, so much blood, a red speckled pattern upon the carpet, and something gray. Jordy's wasted his brains. Too bad. He was brilliant.

The haze in my vision begins to recede.

What have I done? There is cloying gore everywhere. I gag and back out of the room. The punishment should fit the crime or there will be hell to pay. People say these things, the clichés, the color codes, the blood curses. I didn't mean to do this but red overcame me. I've gone too far, immersed myself. Red is everywhere in Jordy's apartment.

I stare at the fire, let the axe thud on the carpet. Red-handed, I stumble to the kitchen, wash the sticky residue off my hands. But everything is going black. I don't see red, just black, an end, a finale. The punishment should fit the crime. I stumble toward the door, humming.

◉

My hand touches the cool metal of the door knob. I've been humming a tune. The problem is when I do this I sometimes zone out, forget what I was doing. And I've been to Jordy's door so many times before that it's almost automatic.

But what's different today is that my flight was cancelled due to the weather and I thought I'd surprise him with dinner. I push the door open with my shoulder and carry in the bag of groceries. Music drifts like a wraith down the hall, and amber light capers over the living room walls illuminated by a fire crackling in the fireplace. The scent of sharp pine resin mixed with an odd metallic smell fills my nose.

I turn right into the open layout kitchen, maneuver the bag onto the counter, then return to the living room. I check the logs in the fireplace and warm my hands for a minute, staring into the fiery dance. The axe is lying in the middle of the floor. I take a few moments to absorb the heat, the scent, and the space of Jordy's home. Soon this will be mine too. I pick up the axe and prop it against the fireplace, near a fresh pile of wood brought in to dry. There is a sticky residue on the handle. Back in the kitchen, I wash my hands.

James Chambers on Elizabeth Massie's "Crow, Cat, Cow, Child"

I read "Crow, Cat, Cow, Child" by Elizabeth Massie in her collection *Shadow Dreams* after meeting Elizabeth at a convention. The piece stood out among a gathering of excellent stories because it reminded how powerful and affecting short horror fiction can be. "Crow" relies on the depth of its characters and their convictions to draw readers in, engage them in social debate, rouse their empathy, and ultimately conflict and horrify them. It concisely but fully informs us of the protagonist's illusions before forcing us to share her agony when they're shattered. And when they are, the act is accomplished by one who has suffered his own tragic disillusionment. At the core of the story is the beating heart of all horror fiction: How do we preserve our humanity in a cruel world, living among people who can be even crueler still? And all this in only 25 pages.

◘◘◘

Lost Daughters

James Chambers

Three young women in black party dresses stood by the side of the "suicide bridge." They were looking into the darkness over the guardrail. Drew dropped his Audi to a crawl as he passed them then stopped, put it in park, and watched the women in his rearview mirror. His tail lights gilded them electric red. It was well after midnight, and there were no other vehicles or pedestrians around, but they paid him no attention.

He opened the door, stepped halfway out of the car, and called against a chill wind, "You ladies okay?"

Together, the three turned and looked at him.

Black streaks of makeup ruined by tears lined their cheeks. Their dark hair was mussed and wild. Their stylish dresses were torn ragged along the hem and spotted with dry leaves and flecks of mud. They were barefoot, and their feet were scratched and streaked with blood and dirt, but the youngest, who wore a beaded shawl across her exposed shoulders, held a single pink sneaker. It was torn across the front, and it dangled from her right index finger by a frayed lace. The women possessed the inherent beauty of youth—but spoiled and bruised. They weren't much older than Drew's two daughters in high school.

"Did you have an accident? Are you hurt?"

The women didn't answer.

"Want me to call someone? The police? An ambulance?"

The women only stared. Drew thought maybe he'd frightened them by stopping.

"I'm not going to harass you or anything. I'm on my way home from work, and I...thought you might need help."

Nothing.

"You want me to leave you alone? Fine. Whatever. It's none of my business why you're out here, but people sometimes throw themselves off this bridge. You're not going to do that are you? Tell me you won't, and I'll go. Tell me you're not here to kill yourselves."

Nine people in the last two years, and more before then, had dropped themselves onto the desolate railroad tracks more than a hundred feet below the bridge, a guaranteed lethal descent.

Times were tough, Drew knew well enough. The recession claimed its victims. Drew had worked down the hall from one of them for six years: Carmine Price. Drew and Carmine were analysts, and then Carmine wasn't—he was laid off from his six-figure, eighty-hours-a-week job, and then he came to this bridge, over which Drew drove almost every day. His funeral was still vivid in Drew's memory. Sometimes when he was out shopping he ran into Carmine's wife and three kids, and they always looked trapped in a state of shock, as if they would never come to grips with their loss. *These women have people who'll be haunted the same way if they lose them over the side of this ugly bridge*, Drew thought.

Drew sighed. "Have it your way. But if you won't talk, at least listen. Whatever you're thinking of doing, there's nothing that could've brought you here tonight that's worth throwing your life away over it. You can get help. Call a hotline. People care what happens to you. You're young, and life will get better. So, please, come off the bridge."

The women seemed still as statues. The wind ruffled their dresses, teasing dead leaves from the fabric and scuttling them along the pavement. It embarrassed Drew how the women stared at him, their dark eyes gleaming like hot coals in the glow of his taillights.

"Dammit, say *something*. All right?" Drew said. "If you won't let me help, then whatever happens to you, it isn't on me. Okay? It's your choice."

Drew waited for a reply, but none came. He shrugged and got back in his car, intending to call 911 and let the police deal with it. Before he closed the door, though, the woman Drew took to be the oldest stepped forward, and asked, "Are you going through Quantuck?"

Drew popped out of the car again. "Why?"

"You could give us a ride."

"No," Drew said. "You can use my cell phone. Call a cab or a friend to pick you up. I'll wait with you until they get here."

"We have no friends. We have no money for a cab."

"Well, I'll help you, but I'm not giving you a handout."

The woman scowled. "We don't want money. We only want a ride."

"I'll call your parents so they can come get you." Drew took his Blackberry from his pocket. "What's the number?"

"We can't call them," the woman said.

"Why not?"

The women exchanged glances with each other, but no one answered.

Drew noticed then that they had no purses and gave them a closer look. Their fingernails were long, chipped, and polished the color of dried blood, and their fingertips were stained with something dark. Each woman wore a single piece of jewelry. A silver-weave choker with a red gem dangling from a silver chain adorned the oldest woman's neck. The one with the shawl wore sharpened hook earrings of tarnished brass, and the other wore bracelets made of rusted iron. The choker and the bracelet half obscured what Drew took for scars: a ring of raw skin under the choker, and pink furrows beneath the bracelets.

"How did you wind up on this bridge?" he asked.

The second woman stepped up. "Our shitty boyfriends took us on a date then dumped us here because we wouldn't put out."

"Please give us a ride," the youngest woman said.

"I'll help you get home," Drew said, "but no ride."

Drew didn't like refusing. He imagined his daughters stranded this way, and he felt bad for the women, but he saw too many unwelcome possibilities if he let them into his car. A sharp ache stabbed the back of his eyes, a headache building. He often got them after a long day, which meant almost every day; this one's first pangs had come on before he left the office, too drained to finish the quarterly reports sitting on his passenger seat. He massaged his temples and tried to rub the pain away.

It was so late, and he wanted only to go home.

He gazed at the heavy darkness beyond the edge of the bridge. Wind whistled through it, and Drew thought of sleep.

"Listen." The oldest woman inched closer. "We're screwed if we're not home before sunrise. Our step-father doesn't know we're out. Our little sister isn't even supposed to be with us. If we have to call him to come get us, he'll *kill* us, for sure. And we'll never get home on time if we walk. All we need is a ride."

Drew shook his throbbing head. "I won't do it."

"If you give us a ride," the oldest woman said, "I'll make it worth your while. A guy like you going home from work this late, you must be stressed out, right? I mean, you must be the kind of guy who works *all* the time, no life outside the office, hardly ever see your family—your *wife*. When was the last time you were alone with her? All that work, all that time—maybe you tell yourself you do it so you can give them the life they want, but really, isn't it easier when you're not there? Then their problems don't become your problems, and you've already got so much stress at work, you don't need more at home too. The worst part is what you're really afraid of is losing your job even though you hate it. Maybe someone you know—someone like you—jumped off this bridge. Maybe *you've* even thought about jumping just to escape all the shit you have to deal with. It would be so easy to fall into the darkness. What kind of life is that? Someone should be there to make you feel good. So...you do something nice for us, I'll do something...*nice* for you."

Drew was stunned, speechless.

A wicked glint in the woman's eyes made him shiver.

So did the black space behind her, the emptiness beyond the bridge.

What the hell did I walk into here?

"Don't embarrass yourself." Drew struggled to contain his outrage. "I'm not interested, and I'm old enough to be your father. You should show some respect for someone who stopped only to help you."

The three women rolled their eyes and snickered.

"We know what you want," the youngest said.

"Forget it," Drew said.

He started to get back in his car, but the oldest woman grabbed his shoulder. Her touch was cold and stiff. "Give us a ride."

Drew opened his mouth to say, "No," but he couldn't. He was frozen in place.

The woman didn't look strong enough to hold him, yet he was unable to break her grip. He could barely move. She plucked his Blackberry from his hand and dropped it on the road. The other women joined their sister.

"Give us a ride," all three said.

Their voices echoed in Drew's head: *Give us a ride.*

He didn't want the women in his car, didn't want them anywhere near him, but when the woman let him go, instead of getting in the car and driving away, Drew straightened his jacket, opened the driver's side back door, and then let the sisters slide onto the backseat. The youngest paused before she got in and hurled the torn pink sneaker over the side of the bridge. It spun into darkness. Drew waited for the noise of it crashing below, but if the sound came, it was too faint to hear. He shut the back door and then settled in the driver's seat and latched his seatbelt. With the driver's door closed, the quiet in the car enhanced the nearness of the women. They had brought with them a scent like smoke and fresh mud, sea salt and wet dead leaves.

Drew licked his lower lip. His mouth was dry.

"Where in Quantuck?" he heard himself say.

"Start driving. We'll tell you," the oldest sister said.

Drew tapped the gas. The car finished its interrupted journey across the bridge, and Drew drove east along a connecting road.

"Don't you know that bridge's reputation?" he said.

"We know," the youngest woman said.

"Of course, we know," the second woman said.

"How could we not know?" the oldest said.

All three giggled, a shrill sound.

"Why were you really there?" Drew asked.

"Like we told you," the oldest woman said. "Our boyfriends dumped us."

"Like that, in the middle of the night?" Drew said. "Where'd they go?"

"Who cares?" she said. "Pigs."

Drew drove, and the two older sisters whispered over the head of the youngest, sitting wedged between them. Drew couldn't make out what they were saying; they sounded like hissing snakes.

"At least, tell me your names," he said.

The youngest raised her eyes to meet Drew's stare in the mirror. "I'm Venge."

The second sister said, "I'm Grudge."

"I have no name," the oldest told him.

Grudge and Nameless resumed whispering.

Venge leaned forward and touched Drew's arm.

"Do you have any food?" she said. "I'm so *hungry*."

Drew pointed to a gold foil bag beside his briefcase and reports stacked on the passenger seat. Printed on it in red ink were a heart-shaped store logo and the words: Gwendolyn's Gourmet Chocolates. "There's some candy I bought for my daughters."

Venge snatched the bag and dragged it into the back seat. It rustled as she removed one of the boxes. She undid the ribbon tied across the top, opened it, and then peeled away the crinkly paper under the lid. Drew watched in the mirror as she popped a chocolate into her mouth and chewed. Right away, she made a sour face and then spit the half-chewed candy onto the floor and gave a disgusted groan.

"No good!" She chucked the open box against the dashboard, spilling chocolates around the front of the car. She pressed her face close to Drew's and sniffed him. "You know our names. What's yours?"

"Drew Cahill." The words came before he could stop them.

"I'm so hungry, Drew." Venge ran her finger along Drew's neck, scraping him with her nail. Then she licked her fingertip.

"Before we go home, we're going to eat you up."

She smiled and pulled her shawl tighter on her shoulders. Glimpsing her in the rearview mirror, Drew thought he saw rows of sharp teeth in her mouth, but she closed her lips as she sat back in the shadows. He told himself he couldn't have seen what he thought and wished he'd gone home early that night. He should've never stopped on the bridge; he should've ignored the women, told himself they were only out for a walk or waiting for a ride, that they weren't his responsibility. He should've rationalized his indifference and driven past them without so much as slowing down. A year ago, that's what he would've done, but tonight he couldn't—not once he saw them leaning on the rail, their faces pale against the darkness over the side.

He *had* to stop.

He had to *know* they weren't going to jump.

The moment he saw the women, he'd thought of the last time he saw Carmine. Leaving his office, his personal belongings collected in a cardboard box, a framed picture of his family face down on top—and his face so pale Drew had thought he might faint. He had wanted to walk him out to his car, maybe even drive him home to make sure he got there safe and sound. But too many people were watching, and no one else stepped forward to help the *losers*. That's what they called the ones who lost their jobs; Drew didn't want to get too close, afraid he might be seen as one of them. *Afraid it might be true.*

Afraid all his work and time were wasted, and he would be discarded too.

Yet if he'd helped, maybe Carmine would've made it home.

Home.

It seemed so far away to Drew now, and the night so late.

He had to be back at work in only a few hours.

…home…

A question that had been nagging him sprang to mind: Whose torn sneaker had Venge tossed from the bridge? He doubted it belonged to any of the sisters. He should've looked over the side, into the darkness where the women had been looking when he first saw them. Maybe it was better he hadn't.

"What do you mean you're going to eat me?" Drew asked.

The older girls stopped whispering and leaned forward between the seats.

"She means what she says," Nameless told him. "We've been

145

out all night. We're hungry. We want to eat. But not until after you take us home."

"That's sick," Drew said. "That's nothing to joke about."

"I never joke about eating," Venge said.

Her two sisters laughed.

"You're all crazy. Get out of my car. Now!" Drew tried to swerve to the side of the road and stop the car, but the women's words—*give us a ride*—resurfaced in his aching head and forced him to keep driving. He couldn't lift his foot from the gas, or turn the car, or move his hands on the wheel.

Nameless leaned between the seats. "Take us home."

"I don't know where your home is," Drew said.

"I told you. Go to Quantuck."

"Where in Quantuck?"

"We'll tell you how to go," Grudge said. "Turn left at the next traffic light."

"No," Nameless said. "Go straight."

"I want to go the back way."

"It will take too long. We'll go the right way."

"Right, wrong." Grudge gave a dismissive wave. "They both get us there, don't they?"

"No, no, no, he should take the road that passes by the cemetery," Venge said. "That's the fastest way—*and* it goes by the cemetery."

"Hush," Nameless said. "The cemetery is way out of our way."

"The cemetery *is* nice at night," Grudge said. "And it's such a dark night. I say we go that way."

"No. Go straight," Nameless told Drew,

"I know Quantuck," Drew said. "Tell me the address. I can find my way there."

All three of the sisters replied, almost in unison, "Shut up! Drive where we tell you."

Venge whispered to Drew, "We have to find our own way home. If Father knows we snuck out, he'll stop us from wandering again."

Drew clenched the wheel and followed the road. Traffic was sparse even for this time of night. All the shops were closed, and the late-night diners and fast food restaurants looked dead and full of vague shadows. There wasn't even a cop on patrol as there almost always was on this road at night. Not that it mattered. Drew couldn't have asked for help even if there was any to be had. The second he thought about stopping, the pain in his head spiked, and the women's words filled his mind again, locking his body behind the wheel.

They passed three more lights. Nameless told Drew to take the next left. Grudge argued, and her sister clamped a hand over her mouth to silence her.

Drew turned left, and they came to a fork in the road.

"Go right," Nameless said.

Grudge shoved her sister's hand from her mouth. "No, go left."

"This way is boring," Venge said. "Let's go by the cemetery."

"Morning comes fast," Nameless said. "You want to get home before sunrise or do you want to be punished?"

"I don't want to be punished."

"Then forget the cemetery."

"But I'm *soooo* hungry," Venge said.

"We'll eat later. We have to get home before father knows we snuck out," Grudge said. "Go left."

"No, go right," Nameless said.

Drew stopped at the crux of the intersection.

"Left," Grudge said.

"Right," Nameless said.

"Go back a block and take the left so we can go by the cemetery," Venge said.

"Shut up," Nameless said. "Don't listen to them. Go right."

Grudge snapped at her sisters, and Venge complained again that she was *so hungry*. The pain behind Drew's eyes spread to his whole head. Pangs of nausea squirmed in his stomach. The car was idling. If only he could move he could've taken the keys and run so they couldn't use the Audi to chase him. He would have a good head start, and he was fast. He ran five days a week. His legs were longer than theirs, and they would never catch up running barefoot—except he couldn't unwrap his fingers from around the wheel. He couldn't unfasten his seat belt or reach for the door handle. His body simply refused.

"What..." he said. "*What* are you?"

The women stopped arguing. Their deep, cold eyes and sudden smiles filled the rearview mirror, and now there was no mistaking the rows of jagged teeth hidden behind their soft lips. Drew didn't want to believe it. Maybe their teeth were filed, like a body modification thing, or they were fake, like custom vampire fangs Drew had worn one Halloween in college. He could almost buy that if not for how large their teeth were—and that he was no longer in control of his body. Had they hypnotized him? How? But that didn't feel right. His mind veered toward darker answers and groped for the right word—*demons, ghosts, monsters.* But Drew didn't believe in any of those things.

Venge said, "We are spiders, spinning our web."

Grudge said, "We are lovely shadows breaking your heart."

Nameless leaned between the seats. Her breath brushed over Drew's neck. "We are lost daughters."

They all laughed then.

"You know about daughters, don't you?" Nameless asked Drew. "I smell your daughters on you. Leah and Gabby. They're good daughters. They ask you for only one thing above all the things you give them. Do you give them that one thing? Hmm? Do you, Drew?"

Drew couldn't answer. His thoughts disintegrated into the pain swirling in his head.

"No, you don't," the woman said. "Do you know what that one thing is? I'll give you a hint: It's not fancy chocolates. Got a guess?"

In his mind, Drew heard echoes of Gabby and Leah scolding him for working so late, for spending so much time at the office, for always coming home and leaving again while they slept. He heard Heather lecturing him: "No one gets to the end of their life and wishes they spent more time at work." He'd told them he'd try—he'd promised them...*promised*...and as often as he had, he'd broken his promises.

"Oops, guess not." Grudge giggled. "Now you'll never know. You'll never see Leah and Gabby again, never know what's going on in their lives, and you won't be there for them when they really need you most. All daughters have a dark side, Drew. They have secrets, you know, and secrets always turn toxic sooner or later."

"*Hungry,*" Venge said.

Drew found his voice then, only a whisper. "How'd you know my daughters' names?"

Nameless inhaled, flashing her jagged teeth. "Their scent is all over you. I could follow it to your house and pay them a visit.

Would you like that, Drew?"

Drew shook his head.

"Then turn right."

Drew stepped on the gas and took the right fork. The sisters resumed bickering. Every turn was an argument, every intersection a dispute. Drew trawled the night while the sisters fought. They were cruising around a residential neighborhood of winding streets, steep hills, and dead ends. There were no streetlights, and the houses were dark. Beyond reach of the car's headlights was a deep, patchy grayness only a shade removed from black by the ambient light reflected off the overcast sky. It was passing 3 a.m. Heather would be worried Drew hadn't called or answered his phone. He turned down another desolate road.

"You're taking us the wrong way," Grudge said.

"What do you know?" Nameless said.

"What I know," Venge said, "is we *should've* gone past the cemetery. My stomach is *growling*, and we'd be home by now."

"Oh, will you *please* let it go," Nameless said. "You could stand to miss a meal or two."

"Like you're so smart. Can't even find our way home," Venge said. "Our step-father will have the door locked up tight by the time you get us there. Then what'll we do?"

"Shut up. Everything will be fine," Nameless said.

Time seemed to slip away faster now, and the fuel gauge fell below a quarter of a tank. Drew had meant to fill up on the way home. He didn't know where he would find a gas station open this late, and he wondered what the sisters might do if he ran out of fuel.

"Here!" Nameless said. "Turn left here."

Drew sensed that in spite of the sisters' arguing and all their misdirection, every turn was taking them closer to their home, a place Drew didn't want reach if he could help it. Mustering all his willpower and concentrating on Leah, Gabby, and Heather—remembering their faces, their voices—he was able for a moment to silence the sisters' commands in his head. It was enough that he could turn right instead of left, and he felt triumphant. His skull throbbed like it might split apart, but he'd defied the women and broken their control. Then Nameless smacked him in the back of his head so hard he jolted forward and cracked his nose against the steering wheel.

"Drive where I say!" she shrieked.

Drew rubbed his nose with the back of his hand. It was running and sore, and it amplified the pain beating inside of his skull. He found a tissue in the console and wiped it. His errant turn had taken them into an industrial area. Sprawling old buildings and fences topped with barbed wire raised deep, complicated shadows alongside the road.

"Go straight then take the next right, and we'll be back on track," Grudge said.

"That's one way," Nameless said.

"What's another?"

Nameless didn't reply.

"I thought so," Grudge said.

When the turn came, though, Drew focused on his wife and daughters, and once more broke the sisters' control; he forced himself to punch the gas and drive straight through the intersection.

The intensity of his headache exploded.

The sisters were on him in seconds, spilling into the front seat, crowding him, pinching him, drawing blood with their fingernails, screaming in his ears—and blocking his view of the road. The car swerved and jerked. It jolted over a sharp bump. Drew hit the brakes, bringing them to a shuddering halt halfway up the curb, only inches from a telephone pole. The interior of the car swam with shadows, and then Nameless was in the passenger seat, while Grudge and Venge had returned to the back. Nameless held her finger against Drew's neck. Her nail dug into his skin like a saw tooth.

"You're wasting our time! Drive where we say, or we'll eat you here and now," she said.

"You're going to eat me anyway," Drew said.

The woman let out a low hiss then sniffed around Drew's neck. "Drive, or one night we'll go visit…*Heather*. She's sitting up with the TV on wondering why you aren't home yet, why you haven't called. She smells so…*sweet*. And after we see her, we'll go visit Leah and Gabby…unless…you…drive…*now*."

Drew felt near exhausted. The sisters' voices returned, roaring inside his head, and he couldn't gather the energy to resist them again, so he drove. They directed him along crooked routes that detoured and overlapped until they came to the edge of the industrial zone and passed rows of run-down houses.

"There," Nameless said. "Go left up that hill."

Grudge and Venge said nothing.

Drew accelerated up the hill. The trees and brush alongside the road were thick and unruly, and they grew denser and more scraggly as the car ascended.

"Park by the house at the top of the hill."

The higher they drove, the more cracked and pitted the street became. The car jounced as it strained up the incline and rolled to a dead end. Ensconced among pines and elms tall enough to blot out the sky stood a three-story Victorian in an overgrown yard filled with wild shrubs and rangy weeds. Not a single light glowed inside or out. The house's black windows were grimy and cracked. Its shingles and shutters hung askew, and paint was peeling from its trim. A weedy, gravel driveway faded into the shadows beside it. Drew parked at the mouth of the drive and shut off the engine. The sisters exited the car. Venge opened the driver's side door and yanked Drew out. She dragged him onto the front lawn. Drew struggled but he couldn't get free. Venge didn't look even half strong enough to pull him around how she did, but Drew felt as if she hadn't only grabbed his body but had reached inside it and latched onto some intangible, essential part of him.

The front door of the house swung open.

Impenetrable darkness filled the entry. An odor of burning drifted out on a wave of heat and haze. A musty, earthy scent followed, and then the doorway exhaled stray winds.

Grudge smiled. "See? Father doesn't even know we were gone."

"I'm so hungry." Venge looked at Drew and parted her lips, uncovering her teeth.

"There's no time." Nameless pointed east. Glimmers of dawn already brightened the sky, deepening the silhouettes of trees and houses. "Drew made us late. We have to go while the door's open."

"No. I'm hungry, and I *want* him," Venge said.

"Then you shouldn't have argued so much about which way to go," Grudge said. "Now the sun's almost rising."

"You argued too. *Both* of you! And you let him take us the wrong way. If you'd listened to *me*, we could've gone to the cemetery and gotten here in plenty of time." Venge pressed Drew against the ground and knelt on top of him. Her mouth widened; her teeth protruded as if they might pop loose from her jaw. "I'm going to eat."

"No!" Drew shouted. "Stop!"

Grudge pulled Venge away and spilled her onto the lawn. "Me first!"

"Why are you doing this to me?" Drew said.

Nameless shoved Grudge aside with Venge and bared her teeth.

"Because small crimes get punished too," she said.

"What did I do?" Drew said.

"What you did, what you didn't do, what you're going to do, it's all the same thing. You weren't there when we needed you. You let us go. You let us die, *Father*." Nameless slapped Drew. "You let us fall into the darkness. You'll do it again and again and again."

"Please," Drew said. "I don't know what you're talking about."

"You think helping us tonight makes up for anything? You think it makes it better?"

Nameless's fingers dug into Drew's chest. Her nails tore his shirt and stabbed his skin.

"You'll stand there and stare into the blackness one day. I know you will, because you could see us, and we could see you. Who can say what will happen when that day comes?"

Her head jolted sideways. At first, Drew thought she was leaning in to bite him, but her head bobbed as if her neck was broken, and then it snapped back into place. The raw streak of scarred skin on her necked peeked out from beneath her choker. Grudge knelt down beside him; blood streamed from the scars on her wrists and dripped off her hands. A trickle of blood and foamy, white saliva trailed from the corners of Venge's lips. Nameless lifted Drew until her teeth were inches from his neck. Her mouth split so wide and looked so deep, Drew thought she might decapitate him with a single bite. He thought of the bridge and the darkness over the side and that if he jumped, he would only be breaking a machine, a construct of organic gears, tubes, and wires that would scatter on the ground and wait to be collected and repaired. But that wasn't right, that wasn't true, and there was something horrible waiting down there in the darkness. He thought of Leah and Gabby, their faces drawn and haunted like the faces of Carmine Price's children. Or, worse yet, Leah and Gabby standing on that bridge by themselves like the three sisters he'd stopped to help. A reservoir of darkness he'd barely known was inside him broke. It leaked out and stained his thoughts. Nameless seemed to savor the exact moment.

A fierce burst of heat and wind blew down from the open door of the house with a sound like a long, low growl. Shocked, Nameless glanced at the open door. The odor of burning intensified and mingled with the stench of something old and rotten, something long dead.

"No," Nameless said. "Not yet!"

"We're sorry, Father!" Grudge said. "We didn't mean to stay out all night. It was so hard to find our way home."

"They made me go with them!" Venge said. "I didn't want to, but they made me!"

Nameless let go of Drew and dashed toward the door. "Please! Don't punish us. We made a mistake, that's all. We promise it'll never happen again. Give us another chance!"

Grudge and Venge followed their sister, rushing to the house.

Drew wriggled onto his belly. He rose onto hands and knees in time to see the first ray of morning sunlight break through the trees and touch the gaping black entrance of the house. It lit up the saddle and crept inside, and then the door slammed shut while the sisters were still several steps from the front porch. A burst of shadow erased the dawn twilight, leaving Drew blind for a moment. From inside the house, a low, deep sound reverberated. Laughter. Then the stink of the place faded. Drew's sight returned. His mind cleared, and his headache subsided. Where the sisters had been running stood three gnarled and stunted trees bowed toward the house. Their branches were scattered with torn, black leaves. On the smallest tree fluttered the weathered remnants of a knit shawl. The others bore gnarled scars in their bark. They looked like they'd been growing forever out of the cracked front path. In the light of the rising sun, the trees cast strange, moving shadows that seemed to stretch toward the house's front door.

Drew had come so close, saved only by the sun and the wrong turns he'd made that delayed them enough for it to rise before the sisters fed.

A breeze rustled the three trees, and they made sounds like whispers and groans. Drew leapt to his feet and ran to his car.

He drove fast into town, filling up at the first open gas station he found. The morning paper fresh on the news rack showed a headline about another suicide at the bridge—a young woman who'd jumped last night around the time Drew left his office. He stared at the article, afraid to touch the paper, then paid the attendant and sped away. He reached home in time to cook a special breakfast for his wife and daughters, who were surprised and happy to see him, and after his daughters left for school, he called in sick and skipped work to be with them that afternoon.

He wanted to make the most of the time he had left.

Ed Kurtz on Elizabeth Massie's "Abed"

Of all the short fiction pieces I have ever read by the multitude of women writers in our genre, none stands out so starkly to me as Elizabeth Massie's "Abed." Reading Massie is like a master class in horror literature, from her superb novel *Sineater* to some of the finest short stories in any genre, but "Abed" in particular strikes at the soul. At once shockingly gruesome and compassionate, she takes the form of "extreme horror" and imbues it with heart and humanity. Not many writers are capable of such a challenging juxtaposition—the form is typically reserved for pure shock value—but Massie succeeds in jangling the reader's brain with pure horror while simultaneously pulling heartstrings, forcing a close, almost claustrophobic siblinghood with poor, doomed Meggie. A classic.

Mules

Ed Kurtz

When the A/C unit finally blew the curtain hard enough to wrap it around the steel casing, the puke-yellow glare from the streetlight stabbed directly into Mary-Jo Ford's eyes and forced her awake. Chagrined, she tried rolling over, away from the window, but the frigid motel air raised cool goose pimples on her back and she could hear some woman hollering in the parking lot, and then there was the matter of the smell.

Mary-Jo groaned, slid up to lean against the headboard, which was screwed into the wall. She threw a crusty glance at the clock on the nightstand—also screwed in—and saw it was only half past two in the morning. She felt disoriented, and it took her a minute to remember where she was.

Presidio, Texas was where she was. Just across from Ojinaga, where she'd been. And from the smell of things, Hank had gone and shit the bed.

"Christ Jesus," Mary-Jo muttered. She leaned over to switch on the lamp. The light from it was somehow worse than the streetlight outside. Everything here was yellow, aged beyond further use.

Hank sprawled out on the queen bed, half under the sheets and half dangling out, like a photograph of somebody drowning. Mary-Jo knuckled the corners of her eyes, blinked away the white spots, and immediately saw the mess soaking through the top sheet.

They'd had some crazy nights together, Hank and her—crank, crystal, grass laced with Christ knew what—but this was the first time she'd ever known him to shit himself in his sleep. She pinched her nostrils closed and made a hog-calling noise.

Whoo-ee.

Last night was a celebration, all right; there'd been Chivas Regal and a rock so fat she had to break it up to fit the smaller crumbs in the pipe. They talked about snagging one of the girls working the rooms downstairs, roll around a bit and maybe take some pictures with the Polaroid, but she was spent before they could get together enough to put the plan to action. And by then, she didn't much care anymore. Hank was flying high and Mary-Jo crashed hard and fast. She didn't know when Hank followed suit, but now she was up and he was still down and she was going to have to do something about the goddamn stink.

She threw a punch at his shoulder, hard. His torso gave with the impact, sank back. His thin, sandy-blonde hair spilled down over his stubbly face.

"Hell, Hank," she grunted. "You got to wake up. This ain't hygienic like."

She thumped a knuckle against the crown of his skull. He didn't so much as moan.

Mary-Jo said, "Ah, no. Ah, hell."

The woman outside shrieked louder still, railing against the cops to whoever would listen and quite a few who would rather not. Mary-Jo brushed Hank's hair away from his face and peeled back his eyelids with her thumb.

He was, as she suspected, dead.

◎

They'd met Octavio at the dentist's office on Blv. Libre Comercio in Ojinaga, as prescribed, the afternoon before. The dentist was Octavio's uncle. Under the flickering bulb in the one-john bathroom, he unzipped a blue and white duffel and showed them what they'd come for: a pile of condoms packed fat with Mama Coca.

Mary-Jo thought they looked like little white sausages. Octavio brought them a two-liter bottle of orange soda to help get the pills down, called Hank and Mary-Jo his *poco mulas*. The soda was gone before they managed to swallow just two each. The rest took up another two bottles and most of the remaining daylight.

Mary-Jo hated the orange soda, and the fact it was warm only made it worse.

In the evening, after sunset, she and Hank waddled back to the Impala parked crookedly on the boulevard and said nothing as he turned back toward the border. When the border patrol grilled him, he could barely speak. The officer searched the Impala, found nothing of interest. They rolled on through, back into the good old U.S. of A., a couple Cads of blow, wrapped tautly in greased latex, resting painfully in each of their bellies.

◎

"God almighty," Mary-Jo sobbed, hunkered down on the edge of the bed farthest from Hank's body. She let herself have a good cry. There was never anything quite approaching love between them, and she had no inclination to embellish their history now, but they'd had some good times. A mess of bad ones, too. But most to the good.

When at last her tear ducts dried up and the shuddering relented, she went round the bed to the bathroom and washed her face, trying to remember not to pick at the scab at the corner of her mouth. Hank hated that. The picking, not the scab itself.

She then started a hot bath, and while the faucet sputtered into the tub, she took a damp towel back into the main room for what she hoped was going to be the worst part of it—looking for the product among the mess on the sheets.

It was, after all, bought and paid for. She still had to deliver.

Gagging, Mary-Jo went to work. She found it necessary to take a break every five minutes or so, to duck back into the bathroom and breath in the hot steam. And when, at long last, she was done, she was distressed to discover the product Hank swallowed back in

157

Ojinaga was still inside him.

"I'm so sorry, baby," she said softly, frantically waving her hand an inch from her face, "but that's gonna have to come on out."

First, she lowered him into the scalding bathwater, underpants and all. The water burned her hands and quickly fogged with filth. She let him soak for a bit while she tended to balling up the soiled sheets and double-checking the door was locked up tight.

Then she withdrew Hank's butterfly knife from the pocket of his jeans on the floor. A scalpel, she realized, would have been better suited for the task at hand. But who carried a scalpel around with them?

She fought against his weight for a few minutes, struggled to keep his face above the water. He kept sliding down, stopping only when the murky water slapped against his swollen eyelids. It didn't matter, and she knew it didn't matter, so she just pulled out the plug and watched as it all swirled nosily, chokily, down the drain.

His body gleamed, shone wet in the fluorescent light. She studied the tattoos dotting his flesh, the one for his mama he'd gotten in County from a Lowrider with a homemade gun. It was on his left bicep, and on the same place on his right was one spelling out *Libby*, who he said she shouldn't worry about. *Libby's gone, baby*, he said.

His mama was gone, too. Everybody Hank loved was gone, to hear him tell it, and everyone who loved him. Mary-Jo didn't know for sure if she ever did, or if she did now; she'd never said as much. She was afraid it might be a lie. She was afraid that, someday, he would get her name inked on his skin, only to coo softly to some other bitch that *Mary-Jo's gone, baby, Mary-Jo's gone*. If she had the Lowrider's tattoo gun, she would needle her name onto him now. A last remembrance, before the cutting began.

Hank was skinnier than a starved hound, just skin wrapped tight around corded muscles and equally narrow bones. Mary-Jo was thankful for that, because it seemed to make her job much easier. His body was like a roadmap, every section clearly marked.

She began at the soft bit underneath his sternum, uncertain how hard to press on the handle. Black-red blood beaded at the tip of the knife, but she realized quickly she was going to have to put more elbow grease into it. She propped her knee up on the edge of the tub and jimmied her opposite foot between the toilet and the too-near cabinet beside it, jockeying for leverage. Once that was settled, she hauled a deep breath into her breast and stabbed Hank like she hated him.

The blade sank clear to the hilt with a crunch, five inches at least, and a whistling gust sang out of Hank's mouth. Mary-Jo yelped, staggered back, and fell over the toilet. The handle of the butterfly knife stuck straight up from Hank's chest. Mary-Jo collected herself, breathed in good air and exhaled the bad, just like the counselor lady at the Goree Unit back at Huntsville advised. Once she felt sufficiently composed, she resumed her position on the edge of the bathtub, gripped the handle again, and started to saw.

Business is business, she told herself, over and over, as Hank gradually split open and the tears spilled down her blood-hot cheeks.

In the end, Mary-Jo cut Hank deep lengthwise, from sternum to groin, and more shallowly across his midsection, to form a seeping red plus sign. The tub—never that white to begin with— was now spattered with blood, as were the walls, and the floor, and Mary-Jo herself. She took a moment to throw the seat up on the john and empty her own guts through a retching series of false starts and, finally, a torrential stream from deeper inside of her than she thought possible. She was slick with sweat from crown to toe. Despite the heat, she juddered like a junky.

"All right, then," she rasped at the ruin of Hank's midriff. "Give me what you got, baby doll. We sure as shit didn't go down Mexico way for nothing."

With that, Mary-Jo Ford dug her fingers beneath the flaps in Hank's gut and pulled them back and apart with a wet snap. To finish the job, she retrieved the knife and cut away at connecting tissues and stubborn organ meat, opening him wider and wider, ever baffled by the glistening red mess inside a body and how in hell any doctor could make sense of it. But she knew a stomach when she saw one, and she saw Hank's now, so she steeled herself to rip it apart when something caught her eye and forced a shuddering shriek out of her throat.

It was, unmistakably, a tiny hand.

The hand moved; balled slowly into a loose fist and released again. It was red and wrinkled and smaller than a newborn baby's. Mary-Jo had popped one out herself, in another life—she knew. In the fraction of second she'd seen the thing, she registered its stubby fingers, even the minuscule nails edged the tips. And it moved. By Christ, it moved.

Stupidly, she whispered, "Hello?"

She wrinkled her nose and shook her head, angry with herself.

Goddamn, she thought, *it's the rock, it's gotta be the rock. I've done gone crazy.*

To verify her conclusion, she rose and leaned back over the eviscerated remains of poor, dead Hank.

The hand remained. The hand still moved.

Mary-Jo slapped a hand, tacky with blood, over her mouth to stifle the next scream.

◎

She wasn't crazy.

She dug into Hank's corpse to rescue whatever struggled inside of him.

◎

At fifteen, in the clinic that frequently served as a maternity ward in the McCulloch County juvie detention center, Mary-Jo Ford gave birth to a baby girl, all red and squalling. The girl-child was gone before Mary-Jo could so much as brush her fingers across the wretched creature's face, but she'd gotten a good enough look to burn it into her brain for the rest of her life. She saw that baby girl almost every time she shut her eyes, even all these years later.

The creature that stirred amidst Hank's ropy, stinking entrails was equally wretched to her judgment, but smaller by half. Its left half was more developed than its right, with an arm and a leg and five digits wiggling at the end of each; the opposite side was shriveled and stick-thin. She could make out its tiny ribcage jutting up beneath translucent flesh, its small round belly poked out above the red mass at its groin. The mass pinned it to Hank's guts.

The face was small and pinched, too small for the proportionally oversized head, upon which not a single hair sprouted. Mary-Jo gazed deep into the thing's tiny black eyes, and she decided they did not see her. It opened its slit of a mouth and mewled, softly.

What are you? she wanted to ask, but she knew there would be no point. Instead, she poked tremulous fingers into the quivering

160

red mass at the thing's middle and peeled it back, revealing what looked like an umbilical cord snaking from its belly into Hank's stomach.

Also revealed to her was the creature's sex: he was a boy.

And, knowing this, no longer a creature.

He was only a boy.

"I'm gunna get you out of there," she said quietly to the child, her eyes and nose starting to drip again. "Hold tight, little fella. I'm gunna get you out."

◎

Pregnancy in men, Mary-Jo reckoned, was a biological impossibility. And Hank, she knew perfectly damn well, was all man.

So, as she cradled the desiccated child in her gore-stained arms on the bed, she concluded that it had always been with Hank. It was always inside of him.

This, if true, made him not Hank's baby, but his baby brother. A little twin, born at last, if thirty some odd years too late.

"I 'spect I ought to call you Hank too, now," she cooed at little Hank.

Little Hank sputtered and shivered, his lame right arm twitching and round, black eyes rolling.

"Hush now. Mary-Jo's gunna take care of you. I'm practically your big sister, don't you know."

Little Hank flopped his lumpy red head against her breast and burbled.

While the baby fussed, as best it could, on a blood-stained motel hand towel atop the bed, Mary-Jo finished what she started with Hank. She split open his stomach sac, sliced down the length of his large intestines. Of the four Easter eggs he'd swallowed, she only recovered three; the last was reduced to a loose flap of latex, its contents absorbed into Hank's body while he slept. The damn thing burst, and he OD'd.

Suddenly panicked the same would happen to her any minute, Mary-Jo gulped down the laxative they'd bought at a corner store. It did its work quickly and efficiently, and after standing naked in the tub under the hot spray for a few minutes—Hank's carved up remains between her feet—she rinsed off the product and lined them up next to the sink. Seven in all, one-eighth less than they promised to deliver.

She bit her lower lip.

Little Hank puled restlessly from the main room.

My Hank, Mary-Jo thought, her face growing warm. *My little Hank.*

The men she and Hank had been muling for were not nice men. They were cartel men, low level chiefs with nothing to lose and no conscience to prickle them. Even Hank had confessed to being afraid of them, but his excitement for bigger, better scores once this trip was done overshadowed his crawling fear. Now Mary-Jo was possessed of enough fear for the both of them. There was nothing now they could do to Hank, Big Hank, but she could conceive of no limits to the things they'd do to her when she explained how one of the pills had gone and popped. No matter that it had killed her man, forced her carve him up like a Christmas turkey.

Business was business. And failing to live up to a promise was bad business.

She washed off the butterfly knife in the bathroom sink, and then she pierced one of the stuffed condoms with the tip of the blade.

"Sit tight, little man," she called out from the bathroom. "Big Sis will be along directly."

She held the package up to her face, almost oblivious to where it recently came from, and snorted deeply from the opening she made with the knife. Hank's twin started to hiccough, alternately chirping and belching. Mary-Jo inhaled until her lungs were full, held it in and relished the numbing cocaine drip at the back of her throat.

And once she recovered, she did it all over again.

○

She was never meant for motherhood, Mary-Jo Ford. It was why they took her baby girl away without ever asking her thoughts on the matter. That was why Little Hank's best shot had to be somebody else, somebody who didn't mule drugs across the border and dissect her own man to get at the product that was useless to her now.

Besides, he wasn't a baby, anyway. He was thirty some odd years old, just like Hank. Not grown, but no infant. An anomaly, a thing that shouldn't be.

Mary-Jo figured she was, too.

Naked, she curled around Little Hank's impossibly small, impossibly fragile body and asked, "Some of us never had a chance, did we?"

She licked her lips, the tongue numb though she could still taste the coppery water from the sink faucet. The broken pill went down the drain easily enough, better with practice. She wasn't sure if it had been one of the ones from her or one she'd cut out of Hank. She'd lost track of them. She reckoned it couldn't have mattered less.

"Try and cry, little fella," she urged the withered twin, squeezing him as hard as she dared. Her breathing slowed even as her heart raced, thumping like a drum against her ribs. "Try and cry, while your big sister has herself a nap. Just a little nap, buddy. Just a little nap."

The woman in the parking lot got to hollering again, screeching about perverts and racists, but all Mary-Jo could hear as she floated away was the gentle, bubbling warble from the lips of the last thing she expected to cut out of the man she might have loved, but didn't.

MISERY

Angel Leigh McCoy on Mehitobel Wilson's "The Remains"

Writing isn't easy. Most of us have to work at our craft for decades before we begin to see any recognition for all that sweat and disappointment. But then, along comes a new star who brings her talent with her from a past life or maybe just from living right in this one.

Mehitobel Wilson's work is emotionally visceral and complex. "The Remains," for example, takes an entirely new look at the demons left behind to haunt the victims of violent crime. She has a clarity of style and language that build the story with efficient grace, and a gentle creative touch that delivers powerful blows. She's a thinking-reader's writer.

I am extremely grateful to Ms. Wilson who agreed to write this brand new story for our anthology. It's been a treat to see her go from first to final draft and hone the piece into something that sings so darkly.

If you haven't read any of her other work, I highly recommend you pick up her collection, *Dangerous Red*. It is full of deep cuts that will leave you bleeding inside. This young writer is someone to watch. As long as she keeps writing, you will see more and more of her work in the world, and eventually, if all goes as I predict, her success as a literary horror writer will rival the likes of Caitlín R. Kiernan and Poppy Z. Brite.

The Remains

Mehitobel Wilson

Danielle sat well back from the breakfast table, not touching it. She held her cup of coffee with both hands and counted down in silence. At zero, she would open her eyes. *Twelve. Eleven. Ten,* and her hands tightened in a spasm around the cup.

One drop jounced forth and landed, scalding, on her wrist. Danielle did not flinch at the heat or wipe her wrist on the robe cinched too tightly around her, but her countdown raced then, hurtled to zero so she could open her eyes, so she could stand up and rush to the front door, and lead the twins outside, away from the slender ghost that was staring at her from his seat across the table.

◉

Eighteen months before, Kyle had not come home. Every day, for six weeks, Danielle had set his place at the table. She had never done that before he was taken. When Kyle had been alive, he and Chase and Annie had gnawed toaster waffles on their way to the bus stop while Danielle had drunk coffee in front of the TV at home, or slept in. After school, they had squashed bags of potato chips between their knees while playing their video games. At night, they had eaten pizza rolls and fish sticks from a communal plate on the coffee table while watching TV, wiping their fingers on paper towels. The puppy ate the paper towels afterward, but at least the kids weren't smearing ketchup on the carpet.

The puppy, Kyle's gift on his tenth birthday, had been an ugly, scrawny, undisciplined thing. Danielle's instinct, whenever the puppy came to mind, was to loathe it, but then a memory would blare through her mind so loudly it rocked her: Kyle, shrieking laughter as he rolled on his back, fending off a wiggle-fueled puppy-lick attack.

The puppy had disappeared first. The front yard had been escape-proof, but anyone could have opened the gate and latched it again when they left. Someone did.

169

When Kyle had not come home, Danielle had embarked upon a devotional course of ritualized motherhood. She had separated the whites from the colors and folded everything the instant the dryer's timer bell rang. She had ironed. She had risen early to cook breakfasts that she couldn't bear to eat herself, but there were always eggs and bacon enough for three children, not for two. She had cooked pot roasts or chicken parmesan for dinner and set four places, not three. She had done the washing up after each meal, hand-drying all four plates, though one had sat bare.

If she had managed to appease some goddess of motherhood, her child would have come home safe.

It hadn't been enough.

Each night, Danielle had climbed the first few stairs leading to the dark second floor of the house. Each night, the whispers from above had stopped her progress. She would stand, one hand on the banister, one across her stomach, and listen to the darkness. Twice, she thought she heard weeping. Both times, she felt an urge to go on up, but then the whispers returned, and the sounds of weeping grew muffled, as if by a pillow or an embrace. So, she turned away. Better not to go up, better to leave well enough alone.

Danielle stopped setting a place for Kyle the first day the ghost sat down with them for breakfast.

◉

Danielle reached zero and opened her eyes. She was alone at the table. From the front of the house, she heard a click and then the creak of hinges, footsteps in the foyer, a hush of rustling nylon. She rose, set her coffee cup on the counter and hurried across the house.

The front door was wide open. Autumn air curled inside, chilling her.

The twins, hand in hand, stood on the porch, their stillness uncanny. They stared in at her, placid, patient.

Danielle looked past them to scan the front yard.

The ghostly man was at the gate, studying the latch. It wasn't the first time, Danielle knew.

He began to raise his head, and Danielle spun away from him, toward the door. She wanted to run back inside, through, out the back, and away; but it wouldn't matter. He'd be anywhere.

Danielle pulled the door shut, glanced up at the little window set into it.

He stood inches from her, on the other side of the glass, in her house, his face framed there, the hateful planes of it all hunger. His hair had grown longer since she saw him in life, and his skin was the same greasy gray as his curls.

Danielle shuddered, focused back on the lock, and made little snake-strike stabs at it with the key.

"Mom." Chase's voice, patient.

Danielle backed across the porch toward the steps, afraid to look at the house, but afraid not to. She held the keys out in space behind her and felt Chase tug them from her stiff fingers as she stared at the black seam between the bottom of the door and the metal kick-strip at the jamb. She wouldn't look at the little window. She wouldn't look at the knob; if she did, and saw it turn, she would lose her mind.

She backed down the steps and into the yard. Unblinking, she watched that black seam so she wouldn't miss it if it widened. She watched it past the corduroy cuffs of Chase's pants as he locked the deadbolt for her, and she watched it past the glitter of his buzz-cut red hair as he reached her side and pressed the key ring into her palm.

The ghost had not returned to the gate, but Danielle trembled as she reached for the latch. She dropped the sleeve of her robe over her hand and let the thick-knitted cuff shield her from touching the polluted metal.

The twins' bus stop was three blocks from the house. Danielle walked behind them, guarding them. The twins themselves were barely visible to her, so intent was she on monitoring the street. She had not been vigilant before, she knew. She had not even known what to guard against, exactly. But now she did—oh, how she knew—and she was hyperaware of every face that passed by, marked the gait and stance of each person on foot, the degree to which drivers turned their heads.

Her gaze flicked back to the children. The twins were silent; their heads down as they walked; Annie's left hand holding Chase's right.

Danielle wished she could remember a time when she had looked upon her children with any measure of peace, but what she remembered instead was irritation, annoyance, exhaustion. She remembered watching to be sure they weren't about to break something, steal something, ruin something she couldn't afford to replace. She remembered being angry at them every time they hurt themselves: Annie's burned wrist, Kyle's fractured collarbone. They'd been stupid to hurt themselves—*didn't I tell you not to*—and she'd had to take them to Urgent Care and beg for extra hours cleaning guest rooms at the motel, which her boss had never granted.

She knew how it felt to find the cut-off notices in the mailbox, and to weigh which they could live without for a bit: electricity or water. She had no choice but to ignore the bills from the clinic and would not notice when the phone got disconnected for nonpayment because she'd long since turned off the ringer to avoid the constant collection calls.

What would she do the next time one of the kids fell off a bicycle they weren't big enough to ride?

The puppy went missing, and Kyle stole a nudie mag. He sold pages from it for a buck apiece so he could print up "Missing: Puppy" flyers and tape them to the perforated necks of stop signs, as high as he could reach. The signs kept falling down; and on his way to school, when he would spy one, curling and sodden beneath a sun-browned boxwood hedge, he would pull it out, smooth it hard against the sidewalk with his fists, and wrap it around the next telephone pole he saw, strapping it to the staple-encrusted wood with a half a mile of shitty dollar-store cellophane tape that would come unstuck before he'd made it the rest of the way to school.

And then Kyle had disappeared.

Danielle's world of fears had shifted. At first, she had watched for any sign of Kyle. Now, she only watched for *him*.

The twins, though, had each other, and they had their doctor, their therapist, psychiatrist, psychologist, one of those. They had the resilience of young minds, the doctor said. Doctor Francis. He wasn't a big believer in drugs, he said, and thank god for that, because those cost, too. The state was financing what they called "limited care" for the twins, and Danielle had a feeling that Doctor Francis might be giving them some free time of his own. She'd watched his nostrils flare as he met the twins and guessed he was calculating his future worth on the talk-show circuit. It hadn't mattered. Any other doctor would have done the same.

Danielle would not tell the doctor, or anyone else, about the ghost. Child Protective Services was already very attentive.

She was completely alone.

◙

Danielle had been fired from her housekeeping job at the motel after the incident with the Bibles. One day she had taken all sixty-eight of them from their rooms, hauled them home with her, and stacked them in the windows, bracketed the doorways. A few lay open, as if to beam the words into the air. She wasn't sure what passages were anathema to evil entities so she had let the books fall open and left it at that.

The Bibles had changed nothing, so she had returned them in grocery bags, left them at the motel's front desk. Maybe they hadn't worked because they'd been *stolen* Bibles, or maybe her own lack of faith had been at fault. Danielle was pretty certain that the man who haunted her would be happy to take a shit all over every one of those books.

She had burned sage in the house. She had poured salt around the perimeter of the yard, piling extra at the gate. She had read about brick dust keeping evil away and had stolen a brick from the neighbor's flower garden. She had knelt on the front walkway and squared the brick against one of the concrete steps. But, when she raised the hammer over her head, she thought about the puppy, dropped the hammer, and kicked the brick into the grass.

None of it mattered, anyway. Danielle understood that she was just closing the barn door, as the saying went.

Losing her job was okay. No guests to recognize her, no questions. Most of all, she hated reading that nasty initial blaze of excitement in their eyes: the thrill of pseudo-celebrity, the frisson of the lowest of gossip fodder, the pulse-quickening of a brush with death, twice removed.

Every tabloid and web forum called the man who had killed her son a monster. She thought that was cheap and easy, a handy way for people to distance themselves from the basic truth that he was a man. Just a human being, and there were billions more. Maybe they weren't like him, but maybe they were.

Salt wouldn't keep *them* out, either.

◙

There were groups on the internet who fancied themselves sleuths, and two weeks after Kyle's disappearance, Danielle had posted a plea in their "Missing: have you seen this child?" section. A few people had posted sympathetic responses and promises of prayer. One had posted a video of a lit candle, the flame guttering in an infinite loop, as some kind of digital vigil. This struck Danielle as crass, and she blocked the post so she wouldn't feel that ungrateful flush of shame and anger when she visited the site.

A month after that, Kyle had his own subforum (complete with a forty-page thread full of goddamn candle posts).

When his killer was taken into custody, the subforum's title was changed: Kyle's name was gone. The killer's name was there instead. He was of far more interest to the forum than Kyle himself.

That may have been the same day the police located Kyle's remains. No one had ever been quite clear with Danielle about that. When she later learned more from the reports on the internet, she understood—the police hadn't been certain that everything they'd found was Kyle.

The killer had given the forum members plenty of fodder. He'd kept a blog with daily posts. He'd had profiles on dating sites, where he'd posted photos of himself wearing makeup and a string bikini. He was everything a murder fan could want.

He had even killed a puppy with a hammer, according to the police. They had found the corpse in his apartment, in the garbage. The news ran a photo of the puppy. Danielle didn't think the twins had seen it, but she didn't ask. She was afraid that, if they had seen the photo, her asking would bring the images back to mind. Better to leave well-enough alone.

The true-crime gossip fanatics pissed their sweatpants with joy, each scrambling to be the first brilliant internet investigator to announce some astonishing tidbit. They dedicated a thread to the puppy and speculated that the man had taken it himself and then approached his prey to say he'd found it. This was most likely true.

They posted the property records of houses in proximity to the killer's and delved into the personal lives and transactions of his neighbors: a fifty-year-old single father, three doors down from the killer, had donated money in 1988 to a college that in 1996 published a magazine of student poetry in which there appeared a haiku about a little boy. The author of the haiku had later become a consultant, and he had a blog hosted by the same free hosting service that hosted the killer's blog. The connections were obvious and damning, the forumites agreed, and they made sure to send their discoveries to the police department investigating the case. They took care to CC the FBI and the host of a cable television true-crime program, just in case the local police tried a cover-up.

Danielle had seen a nature documentary once. There had been a big beast, a yak maybe, dead. In a time-lapse sequence, the yak had been beset by scavengers and maggots and flies and a wild ravaging crawl of bacteria. That was what she saw when she dared to visit the forum.

The moment a thread had been opened with her own name in the subject line—"Kyle's Mother Danielle: CPS visited 2x!"—she had closed her account, deleted her bookmark, and vowed never to visit the site again. She didn't want to see what they said about her and her family.

But by then, she had already read and absorbed far too much. After each silent dinner, Chase and Annie would go play in their room, and Danielle would heave the ancient laptop onto the kitchen table, take a deep breath to quell the dread, and press the power button.

She had read the killer's blog and watched the short videos he'd posted of himself, talking about his day. He prepared spaghetti in one of the videos. He wrote about bad dreams he had been having and about how peeved he was to be forced to waste baseball tickets because the terms of his parole meant the police had to visually verify his whereabouts every two weeks. He wrote that he understood the position of the court, that sure, being a Level 3 sex offender should indeed bring some occasional inconvenience upon him, that he understood he was being punished and all—but that he was irked nonetheless.

He complained that most people who had served their sentences were called *ex-cons*, but people like him were called *sex offenders*. He found this unfair.

He wrote that such punishments, such constant judgment from the courts and the police, even after he had served his time and been released on good terms, might just possibly be responsible for a fellow getting it into his head to go off and rape a little boy, or something.

He wrote that "the System" was so hard on poor convicted child rapists that, on the off chance the parolee was able to slip out from under its heavy thumb from time to time, it was likely that said parolee would simply slaughter any child he raped and then get rid of the evidence.

He wrote that "the System" might consider taking a good hard look at itself and placing blame where blame was due.

Danielle had thought he was misspelling "prosecuted" until she grasped the fact that he truly felt he was being *persecuted*. That he wanted his readers to feel sorry for him, as sorry as he felt for himself. That he was embarrassed about what he saw as his most egregious mistake: that of letting his first victims live.

In the final post on his blog, he had written about his love of cinnamon toast and of socks hot out of the dryer. He'd related what he seemed to think was a hilarious anecdote in which his brand-new twenty-pound bag of birdseed had split as he refilled a feeder, and how seeds were suddenly turning up in the unlikeliest of places, days later. He'd asked if any readers had a favorite brand of ginger ale. He'd said he was looking forward to his upcoming camping trip. He'd said that, all in all, his intent was to harm society as much as he could and then die. He'd said he'd be dying soon. He'd reminded himself to take out the trash.

On the forum, a man claiming to be a police officer on the case posted terse details about the crime scene, and the sleuthy housewives were tantalized beyond their wildest dreams.

National park, remote campsite, hand-written "Reserved: do not disturb" sign attached to a clothesline strung across the trail precisely two hundred and twelve feet from the campsite. Ropes on a tree, tied low, at little-boy height. Circle of stones containing campfire detritus and ashes distinguishable from common wood ash due to their greasy consistency; analyses pending. Hatchet. Lithium-ion battery pack. Skull fragment, approximately three inches square, with attached scalp and reddish hair: DNA analysis pending. Drought conditions resulted in the preservation of deep indentations in the dirt, clustered in formations of three, in a manner suggesting the sustained use of a tripod holding equipment heavier than a still camera. Small human bones, charred, located approximately five feet inside a drainage pipe at another campsite about sixty yards away. Fragments presumed to be bone, analyses pending, strewn in a patch of wild daisies.

There followed a maelstrom of posts: Were the bits of bones in the daisies arranged in a pattern? Did they spell out a message? *No discernible pattern, no indication that they had been arranged. More likely, deposited via shotgun blast.* But the ones in the drainage pipe, surely they had been stacked in a special formation? *It was a functional large-*

bore drainage pipe, people. In other words, water had disturbed any formation there might have been. These are irrelevant questions.

No more posts from that officer appeared.

There was a rumor on the website and, soon after, in local newspapers: a video camera and multiple tapes had been recovered from the suspect's car.

This man had kept Kyle alive for six weeks. He had known before he pulled Kyle into his van that a single tape would not have been enough. He had planned to record hours and hours of footage, and he had done so.

Danielle read all of the rumors. Her compulsion to bear witness to Kyle's trauma, to somehow share the burden of his agonies, as if he might feel a measure of relief, had been too strong to resist.

Finally, there came a point when she had to stop: a journalist claimed to have watched one of the tapes, and had described what he'd seen in detail. It could not have been true, Danielle knew. No monster, no beast, no human being, could do the things the source described—not to her son, not to anyone's child. Not to an enemy, or to a toy. But the simple fact that this reporter had himself imagined such atrocities was the sticking point: if one man could conjure them in his mind—for he certainly had, hadn't he— another could have actually performed them.

This was not a burden she could bear, after all. From then on, Danielle bore her days, spending them mantled in cold shock. One night, her trance had been broken by the slam of the bathroom door overhead. That was the night she wept.

Child Protective Services had indeed come by twice in the year before Kyle had gone. They'd been gathering notes on a case against Danielle's ex for some reason or other, but she hadn't seen him in seven years. Until the caseworker had knocked on her door, Danielle had been pretty sure her ex was long dead. She wasn't any help to them.

The same caseworker had been back five times after Kyle's disappearance: first, because Danielle herself had been a suspect. She had trouble remembering that fact. Those had been very dark days in some other world. Later, they'd just visited to be sure that Danielle hadn't gone insane or mistreated Chase and Annie. They'd been satisfied with their findings and had wished her family well.

Danielle was glad that the check-up phase was long finished by the time the murderer arrived to haunt her house.

The trial had been too much for her to handle. Just too much. On the first day, she could not tear her eyes away from the face of the man who had murdered Kyle.

He was a calm, quiet person, sharp-shouldered in his orange jumpsuit. He looked normal, utterly normal. He sat for the first couple of endless hours with his normal hands clasped before him, his normal forehead tilted against his knuckles, in a normal attitude of peace, perhaps of prayer. His eyes were closed.

Danielle had tunneled her vision at him, desperate to see inside. And he was, after all, the last person to have heard her son's voice.

So she had stared. For hours.

Then, he had jolted in his chair. His head had rocked back hard, as if he had been blasted at close range with a shotgun, and Danielle imagined bone fragments and a hunk of skull with the skin attached flying from him. As she blinked the image away, he twisted his head around and met her gaze.

His face was utterly impassive.

And she felt *him* see inside *her*, instead. He saw that he himself was within her, forever. The wounds he had inflicted would never go away.

She saw that this pleased him. Deeply.

Danielle had scrambled from her seat and run for the door, where the guards caught her, and she had vomited bile and hot water on one's khaki slacks, and they had let her leave.

She had not returned.

But she followed the trial in the news, struggling to remain conscious of the case. Everything in the world, including the case, was a distant remove from her. Kyle, the puppy, daily realities of bills and food and work: none felt present.

The only thing that felt absolutely immediate was the reality of the killer—his placid face, and the infinitesimal uptick of his left eyebrow broadcasting his awareness of what he had done to her.

Everyone had expected an insanity plea. He had represented himself. He had been very low-key and matter-of-fact throughout the trial, expecting the guilty verdicts he indeed received.

But during sentencing, he asked the judge if he could show the jury the videotapes. The prosecution team couldn't believe their luck when the judge agreed and ordered that the tapes be shown in open court.

Anyone who wanted to leave the courtroom before the tapes were shown could do so; they had time to decide while the windows were covered with blackout curtains. Those who opted to leave did so, and the doors had then been locked.

Danielle was at home that day, in her bedroom, ignoring the reporters on the porch. Early on, the police and the prosecution had discussed the tapes with her. She had sat among all these people at a conference table and stayed silent while they argued over her bowed head. She had gotten a cramp in her hand from clutching her knee, and the pain felt stupid and insulting, coming as it did during this pitched discussion about brutal violence done to her son.

The police had screamed at the prosecution team that no one should see the tapes, especially not Danielle. The prosecution had wanted her to be furious and horrified and become the face of the case, making TV appearances with her eyes hollow and her soul in ashes.

She had murmured something in the negative and shaken her head, and one of the cops had driven her home in a squad car.

Danielle didn't think that was the same officer who had committed suicide before the trial, but she wasn't certain. The one who had driven her had seen the tapes and done a lot of the yelling at the conference table. There had been another two cops at the meeting who already looked dead. It had probably been one of them. Danielle understood exactly how they felt. The man was allowed to speak, since he was representing himself.

What he said to the judge after the lights came up was, "This is no longer a jury of my peers. This is a jury of my victims."

What the court said in reply was:

Death.

Danielle sat in front of her television, her legs folded under her. She adjusted the black hood of her sweatshirt, pulling its edges past her cheekbones until the fabric pressed hard against the back of her head. This made a little tunnel through which she could only see the TV. If the ghost was sitting on the sofa, she couldn't see him, and if she couldn't see him, she was all right.

Unless he was standing beside her. That really wouldn't be all right.

She willed herself to focus on the travel show about Hong Kong, but the host's gleeful yammer about prawns and harbor tours grew distant as Danielle became certain that the ghost was looming over her. Reaching for her. If he touched her—

She dropped the remote and gripped the edges of her hood. The tendons in her neck creaked as she, slowly and with intense effort, turned her head to the left.

No ghost. Empty couch, door locked, all lights on, lots of noise about Kowloon's nightlife.

But if she looked back at the TV, what if he was right in front of it?

And what if she continued to hide, and he was there, looking at her, about to touch her? And what if she looked back, and there was nothing? Where would he be, instead?

Because he was there. He was always there.

She heard footsteps overhead. Upstairs, feet running the length of the hallway. A barking laugh. The bathroom door slammed, and then she heard another thud immediately after, as if someone had run into the door, or kicked it.

Danielle groped for her hood-strings and yanked them, cinching the hood tight, collapsing the tunnel. She crossed her arms atop her head and bore down, folding herself into a knot. She kept very still until she slept.

◉

"Mom?"

Annie's small hand pressed on Danielle's shoulder and shook it a little. Danielle blinked, then squeezed her eyes closed and drew back the hood. She opened her eyes and glanced around the room, too bright in the new dawn. Dust motes hung static in a blaze of sunshine from the living room window, and Danielle peered at their arrangement. They seemed random. She saw no figure in the dust.

Annie sighed, shook her head, and went to the kitchen as Danielle went to work unfurling her limbs. Everything ached. She scanned the room for the ghost: all clear.

Massaging her sore shoulder, she thought then of Annie's hand there. When was the last time Annie had touched her? When had she last embraced either of the children? Ages. They had clung to her for a time, but children adapt well, twins especially, she'd read. Their fear had gradually faded, though they did seem much closer to one another than she recalled them being before Kyle's death.

From the kitchen came the sound of whispering. There was a sudden, cacophonous jangle of pots and pans and a loud bang as a cupboard door bashed against its neighbor. A little shriek, and more whispers. A giggle.

Danielle pushed herself from the chair and hurried across the room, plunging through the shaft of sunlight, setting the dust awhirl. She rounded the corner and crossed into the kitchen.

The ghost of the man on death row leaned against the refrigerator. He met her eyes and smiled. His teeth were tan against the sickly gray of his skin. Her body, breath, mind all stopped.

Chase crouched beside the stove, piling cookware back into the cabinet. He was still giggling a little.

Annie had set the cereal on the table and was going for the milk.

Danielle stared, aghast, as her daughter neared the fridge.

Annie reached for the handle. Danielle sucked in air and took a falling step forward, wanted to yell, "No!" wanted to stop her, to get her back, to get her away. Danielle's lungs were turgid and sore with the force of her gasp, and she could not scream at Annie, could not scream at the ghost.

But the ghost kept his eyes fixed on Danielle. She stumbled into him and was glad then that her lungs were full, because she didn't want to breathe him in, to let him inhabit her any more than he already did. She coughed with disgust and spun away, catching hold of the countertop. Her fingers whitened from the force of her grip.

Annie had already opened the fridge and retrieved the milk. Gallon jug in hand, she stood there, looking with mild interest at her mother. Danielle's eyes were wild and wide, her breathing shallow, as she scanned the room. The ghost was nowhere to be seen. She forced herself to settle, closed her eyes, opened them.

Annie set the half-empty jug on the kitchen table and crossed to her mother. She slipped her cold hand into Danielle's. The milk had chilled her skin. She looked up, and Danielle met her eyes. They were curious, patient eyes. Danielle read no concern in them; the twins were used to her being like this, she supposed. They both were beyond concern, now.

181

Danielle watched Chase slam the cabinet door closed, stand up, and make a grand show of dusting off his hands. He saw her looking, grinned broadly, and gave a *what-are-ya-gunna-do?* shrug that almost made her smile too.

The light was in his hair.

Danielle looked from one twin to the other, and saw that, no matter where the ghost may be—for he was always, always there, even if she couldn't see him—he was only haunting her. They knew nothing of him. And if anyone was frightening the twins, it was Danielle herself.

She flung her arms around Annie and squeezed her tight. She buried her face in Annie's unruly fluff of hair and kissed the top of her head. Then she went to Chase and hugged him as hard as she could. He hugged her back, and it felt lovely.

Danielle grabbed the back of the fourth chair at the breakfast table and dragged it across the kitchen. She opened the back door, thrust the chair through it, and gave it a kick. It tumbled down the back steps and landed on its side. She closed the door and locked it.

The twins looked at each other. Chase whispered something to Annie, and she laughed and nodded.

The ghost loomed beside the refrigerator again.

Chase slammed himself into his chair with such force that it slid a few inches to the right; without missing a beat, he grabbed the edge of the table and slung himself right back in front of his cereal bowl. He snatched up the box and dumped cereal into his bowl with one hand, catching the sugared bits that fell to the table and jamming them into his mouth with the other.

Annie settled into her chair, pushed her nylon book bag and windbreaker a few inches across the floor in a hissing scuff until they were clear of the chair, then reached for the milk jug. Danielle watched her pour milk into the bowl, taking care to cover the little pattern of ivy within it, then gently shake the cereal over the surface, little frosted wheat lily pads floating in a pond. Annie spooned up each individual flake, then, when there were none left, repeated the whole performance.

Danielle noticed the puff of Annie's frizzy curls shadowing her clear brow, the shine of milk on Chase's skinny wrist from where he'd wiped his mouth. She listened to the scrape of shoes on the chair rungs, to the spatting drip of milk as it fell from each lifted spoonful, to the sop-chaw of the twins, always chewing with their mouths open.

Danielle took a clean bowl from the dishwasher, sat down at the table with Chase and Annie, reached for the cereal, and said to the two of them, "Good morning."

Rachel Karyo on Caitlín R. Kiernan's "Rats Live on No Evil Star"

Several of my favorite horror stories are found in Caitlín R. Kiernan's *Tales of Pain and Wonder*. But "Tears Seven Times Salt," "Postcards from the King of Tides," and "Estate" have already received much critical acclaim, so for my *Deep Cuts* recommendation I nominate "Rats Live on No Evil Star." "Rats…" tells the story of Olan, a "lean and crazy man," living in a rough neighborhood, terrified of the "long-legged thing" he sees down by the train tracks and the "searching noise" he hears in the night. There's so much to admire about this story: arresting language ("…the camera flash of rage…"), poetic imagery ("Morning like clotted milk…"), interesting characters, and moments of shivery horror. There's something sublime about the sentences, the atmosphere. Kiernan is so brilliant and original. Her work blows me away, and her courage inspires me to take more risks in my own writing.

Beavers

Rachel Karyo

The first beaver arrived on a snowy Monday morning. The baby was on her play mat, batting at her psychedelic hanging toys. Sara was folding freshly dried towels. Sara's husband had forgotten to lock the front door when he left for work, so the Beaver let himself in.

"She should be on her stomach," the Beaver said.

Sara wondered when the whole world would stop offering unsolicited advice on parenting.

185

"Tummy time is so important for babies," the Beaver continued. "You can put a little pillow under her chest if she gets tired or frustrated."

Sara picked up her daughter and said, "Carrot gets plenty of tummy time." And then, she wondered how much was enough.

Carrot opened her mouth wide and started banging it against Sara's collar bone.

The Beaver's whiskers quivered, and he said, "The little one is hungry!"

"I'm going to feed her and put her down for a nap," Sara said, looking pointedly towards the front door.

"Excellent. Then we can speak without interruption." The Beaver followed Sara into the kitchen. When he saw the Enfamil, he scowled.

Sara said, "We tried everything. I saw three lactation consultants and the only breastfeeding doctor in Westchester." Her voice pitched high, defensive.

The Beaver nodded. "Ah, that must have been very difficult."

They all went upstairs to the nursery, and soon, Carrot was drinking, making happy gulping sounds like a fish tank.

"You seem sad," said the Beaver.

"I'm just tired." Lately, even the air had felt heavy. Sara wanted to lie down and sleep for days, for weeks, for months. Her husband, Ben, kept encouraging her to hire a babysitter so she could get some rest. But how could she sleep with a stranger in the house?

When the bottle was half empty, Sara wrestled the plastic nipple out of Carrot's mouth, sat her up, and tapped her back.

The Beaver looked on approvingly. "You're doing an outstanding job. So *attentive*, so *in tune* with your baby's needs."

Carrot burped and a thin stream of milk trickled from her mouth onto Sara's already stained lounge pants. Sara dabbed at the baby's lips with a cloth then allowed her to return to the bottle. Carrot drank greedily, grumbling between swallows.

Eyeing Sara's pants, the Beaver asked, "Don't you ever get time to yourself? Where is your mother?"

Sara explained that during her third trimester of pregnancy, her parents had moved to the Caribbean. "I'm happy for them, really. They've worked hard all their lives; they should enjoy their retirement," said Sara, which was what she always said, and how she sort of felt.

"You would think that enjoying their retirement would mean spending quality time with their granddaughter," said the Beaver, which was something Sara never said, but did sometimes feel.

"My parents disappoint me, too," said the Beaver. Sara asked him how, and he described his father's temper and his mother's coldness. The Beaver complained about his wife, her hyper-sensitivity, and their constant bickering.

"Ben and I don't spend enough time with each other to fight," said Sara. It was a good talk, the kind of open-hearted truth-telling conversation that transforms strangers into friends.

They spent the rest of the day together, and when the Beaver left, Sara was sorry to see him go.

◎

On Tuesday morning, the world outside was frozen solid. The tree branches and pine needles glistened in the sunlight as if they were sealed in glass. Every so often, icicles crashed upon the roof.

In the living room, two small Beavers were playing tag.

"Mrs. Beaver has the flu, so I had to get these rascals out of the house," said the Beaver. Before Sara could respond, he hugged her calf and said, "You're a lifesaver."

Sara took Carrot into the kitchen, fixed breakfast and a bottle, and turned on *Free to Be...You and Me*, an album Sara had loved as a child. It was nice, the crystalized world outside the window, the toasted bread smell of the kitchen, the dishwasher humming, and countertop sparkling.

"Parents are People" started playing, a song about how mommies can be anything they want to be: *ranchers or poetry makers or doctors or teachers or cleaners or bakers.*

Sara's mommy had been a scientist, the only working mother on their block. She had been surprised and disappointed when Sara had quit her job after Carrot was born. Sara had explained over the phone that she *wanted* to stay at home with her baby, felt fortunate that she could.

"I'm just not sure it's healthy for you, being cooped up alone in the house with a baby all day," warned her mother.

Her father agreed, "In most societies, childcare is shared work. But whatever makes you happy."

They had invited Sara, Ben, and Carrot to visit them on their

187

Virgin Islands estate, a handsome terra-cotta villa built into the side of a remote tropical mountain. Their home overlooked Coral Bay, a Neverland lagoon, where rich retired Baby Boomers played with pirate ships.

But, Ben couldn't get time off work, and anyway, Sara's parents drove him crazy. He'd said Sara and Carrot could go without him, but Sara didn't feel right abandoning him alone at home.

Sara heard a loud crash from upstairs, so she picked up Carrot, went to investigate, and stiffened when she saw the overturned bookcase, the picture books strewn across the nursery floor. One of the Beaver's sons was tearing apart *Where the Wild Things Are*; the other was hunched over the bookcase, gnawing at a shelf.

Sara felt her face flush and her scalp tingle. She wanted to grab the little beasts and chuck them across the room.

The Beaver rushed in. "I'm so sorry. I was just resting my eyes." He frowned at his boys. "Little buddies, what were you thinking?"

Sara took a deep breath. She told the Beaver not to worry. She put Carrot in her crib and began straightening up the room. The baby jerked her limbs and said, "Ack ack ack."

"Just a minute, baby girl," promised Sara, trying to keep the irritation out of her voice.

"Are you OK?" asked the Beaver.

"Sometimes, I think Carrot might be better off in daycare or with a nanny," said Sara.

"Why? You're a *wonderful* mother," said the Beaver.

"I love Carrot," said Sara. *I just hate myself*, she thought.

She didn't really hate herself. Or, at least, not always. She was just tired. Most nights, Ben slept through Carrot's crying, while Sara was startled wide awake.

The house glowed eerily in the dark. The nursery, so cheery and innocent by day, became haunted after hours. Sara tried to ignore the pin-eyed teddy bears and nodding dolls, the rocking horse with its muzzled grimace. Carrot's room smelled of stale diapers and medicinal creams, and Sara imagined how it might feel to be a baby in a crib, helpless as a turtle on its back. While Carrot mouthed the rubber nipple, Sara studied her own hands—those pale slabs of meat. Deep in the night, she could hardly even feel them as they held the bottle or tapped the baby's back. Sometimes, it was like the hands belonged to somebody else.

◉

Wednesday morning, Ben overslept and was late leaving for work. Sara and Carrot walked him to the front door, and when he opened it, the Beaver was waiting on the porch.

Sara held her breath, wondered what her husband would say. But Ben simply kissed his wife and daughter goodbye and walked out the door, as if the Beaver wasn't even there.

After breakfast, Sara discovered a half dozen beavers in the living room. She wanted to ask the Beaver about them, but he was nowhere to be found. So, Sara grabbed supplies, and she and Carrot camped out in the nursery with the door locked.

Sara sang Carrot songs, read her books, gave her tummy time. She tried to ignore the skittering of claws outside the door. She tried not to notice the sounds of tearing and scratching.

All day, Sara waited for the Beaver to knock, to check on them. But he never came.

In the early evening, the beavers finally left. The house was a wreck. Ben was due home at any moment.

Sara put Carrot in her crib and turned on the mobile, a gift from Sara's parents. It lit up and began rotating. Electronic organ music played. The googly-eyed monkey leered at the demented circus clown. The lion chased the pony.

Carrot stared, completely rapt, and Sara wondered if the baby was fascinated or terrified.

Sara vacuumed up the coarse dark beaver hair from the living room carpet. She reunited the cushions with the sofa. Next to the piano, the beavers had constructed a mound of shredded newsprint, broken sticks, wood chips, and toilet paper. When Sara came close to it, she gagged at the smell: like rotting worms and fish tank slime.

She stuffed everything into heavy-duty trash bags, then washed her hands for a long time under steaming water. When she'd finished, her hands looked pink and swollen—a pair of floating, boneless, hag fish.

◉

On Thursday morning, three beavers in the kitchen were molesting the Tupperware, two were wrestling beneath the dining room table, one was pleasuring itself in the bath tub, and six or seven were running around aimlessly while screaming like wild animals.

Sara found the Beaver snoring in the pantry. She wanted to stomp on his furry little head. She wanted to shake him until his bones rattled in his pelt. But then, she remembered how the Beaver had asked, "Are you OK?" with such concern.

Sara had to get out of the house. She grabbed Carrot and fled, leaving so quickly she forgot to pack diapers and formula.

Eight hours later, when they finally returned, the beavers were gone. Sara settled Carrot in front of the TV and hurried about trying to straighten up before her husband came home. How could she ever explain such a mess?

◎

That night, when Ben slid his hands under Sara's nightgown, she imagined the Beaver's face floating up before her, as if from the bottom of a well. She squeezed her eyes shut and tried to concentrate on the two human bodies in bed. But, she couldn't clear her head of tails, claws and fur, quivering whiskers and twitching ears, impossibly rapid animal heartbeats.

◎

Friday morning, Sara and Carrot attended their first "Mommy and Me" music class. The teacher played guitar and sang songs like "Wiggly Piggly" and "Rock Around the Alphabet" while the mommies, daddies, and (mostly) nannies waltzed, skipped, and marched their babies around the room.

Sara felt silly.

Carrot appeared astonished.

One of the other mothers recognized Sara from prenatal yoga. She asked for Sara's number and promised to call.

"That would be great," said Sara, and it would be. A mom-friend. Her first.

Driving home, Sara planned the play date: mid-morning, a fresh pot of coffee, mini muffins. They could take pictures of the babies lying side by side on the play mat. Hopefully her friend, like Ben, wouldn't notice the beavers. But how would Sara explain the wiry hairs, the fishy stench, the weird piles of sticks?

Back at the house, there were beavers everywhere. Paw and tail prints covered the floors, furniture, and lower portions of the walls. The windows were fogged from hot mammal breath.

Sara found the Beaver in the kitchen, squatting on the countertop, his head in the sink. He was lapping water directly from the faucet.

"There are too many beavers in this house," she told him. He raised his head to look at her. Water dribbled from his whiskers. Before he could answer, one of his sons scurried across the countertop and accidentally overturned the knife block. Knives flew through the air, and when they landed, one sliced off the tip of his brother's tail.

"See?" Sara shouted at the Beaver.

The Beaver ignored her, grabbed a dishtowel, rushed to his screeching son, and tied a tail tourniquet.

Sara took Carrot and her computer into the master bedroom, locked the door, and Googled "How to get rid of beavers."

At *Professional Wildlife Removal*, Sara read: "There is no magic spray or device that you can use to make them go away." On a threaded discussion board at *Homesteading Today*, she found much innuendo about female anatomy and several recommendations for dynamite and lead poisoning; "Alligators work well too."

As she researched, Sara's long hair kept falling across her face; it was driving her crazy. She left Carrot on the bed and went to the dresser to find an elastic.

As she pulled her hair into a sloppy ponytail, she heard the sickening thud of a baby hitting the floor.

After a breathless moment of silence, Carrot began to wail.

Sara hugged her daughter to her chest and walked her around the bedroom. "I'm sorry I'm sorry I'm sorry I'm sorry," she whispered to Carrot, too afraid to examine her child's head for lumps or bruises.

What made her think she could care for an infant, she who had never even held a baby before Carrot was born? Sara walked Carrot down the hallway, shushing and apologizing. The pediatrician had warned her not to leave the baby on a high surface, unattended. *What had she been thinking?*

Beavers rushed by, brushing against her legs, nearly tripping her.

Why didn't she hire a babysitter like a normal person? Why didn't she return to work where she couldn't hurt anybody? Why didn't she cut her hair short like a good mother? *And why were there so many Goddamn beavers in the house?*

Sara went downstairs to the kitchen and picked up the phone. She intended to call her husband, but then she remembered he was in meetings all day. Sara put down the phone.

She started picking up the knives from the kitchen floor. The shiny steel blades distracted Carrot, and she finally stopped crying.

In the silence, all Sara could hear was the gnawing and thumping of the beavers in the other room.

One of the knives was crusted with blood from the tail slicing. Sara held onto that knife and, carrying Carrot, walked slowly into the living room.

The animals stopped what they were doing and formed a loose circle around Sara and Carrot. Squeezing the steel handle so tightly her knuckles turned white, Sara said, "You need to get out of my house."

The Beaver stepped forward and asked, "Is Carrot all right? I thought I heard her crying."

Sara glared at him and said, "She's fine. Now, get the hell out."

"Sara, please. Watch your language," said the Beaver, covering his injured son's ears.

Sara took a step closer to the Beaver, brandishing the knife.

The Beaver's son took a step closer to Sara, brandishing ten sharp claws. Then, he leapt upward and slashed Carrot's leg.

Sara remembered how, before Carrot was even born, the ultrasound technician had admired those beautiful baby legs.

Sara growled, low and mean.

The Beaver's son turned to run, but before he could get away Sara sliced off the rest of his tail.

Oh shit, she thought. She had only meant to nick it, to show she meant business, to scare them all away.

The severed tail was leaking blood onto the beige carpet. It looked like a raw slab of meat, like a war offering, and Sara wondered if she should put it on ice, so that it might be sewn back on later. She tried to remember where she had last seen the Nature's Miracle stain remover.

But, all other thoughts disappeared when Sara saw the Beavers: their eyes were hard, and their teeth were bared, and they were coming at her.

The hair on the back of Sara's neck stood up, and the knife handle felt slippery in her slick palm.

Sara asked, "Can we talk?"

192

But the Beavers didn't answer. They scratched and bit at her bare feet.

Instinctively, Sara kicked at the animals, slashed at them with steel. She sliced another tail, and the rodent squealed.

Ugh, what sort of an example she was setting for Carrot? Sara was a strict ovo-lacto vegetarian, a Sierra Club member, a Prius Driver, a Moby fan. She wanted to teach her daughter to plant beans, to like Daddy Long Legs, to recycle paper, to love Charlotte and Wilbur.

But who had time to worry about that? Certainly not Sara—the sudden target of all those tree-cutting teeth and Freddy Krueger claws.

One thing they never tell you before you become a parent is that it's hard to fight while holding a crying baby. Sara wished she could call a brief "Time Out," just so she could grab the Baby Bjorn carrier.

Then a sudden, sharp pain in the small of her back made Sara whirl around. It was the Beaver.

"You!" said Sara. "I've had it with you. You're a terrible friend and an *irresponsible father.*"

"You're one to talk. You *do not* give Carrot enough tummy time. You let her watch too much TV. You're moody and inconsistent and—"

Sara was about to interrupt his rant with a deep cut to the throat, when she heard the front door open and Ben call, "Honey, I'm home."

The beavers turned and fled—a quick moving stream of matted fur, crusted blood, and briny sweat.

Sara glanced down at her lounge pants, now reduced to shredded rags.

Ben walked into the living room and stared at his wife and baby.

"I know how this must look," said Sara, unsure about what to do with the knife.

Ben dropped his briefcase to the floor.

Kelly A. Harmon on Shirley Jackson's "The Lottery"

Written in 1948, Shirley Jackson's "The Lottery" begins almost benignly. A small town gathers together excited (and nervous) to prepare for the *lottery*, a decades-old tradition intended to ensure a good harvest. The excitement's almost party-like, and it feels as though this story is going to be about something wholesome and uplifting in rural America. Then, the lottery box comes out. One man from each family takes a slip of paper from the box to determine if his family is chosen. Then, each member of the chosen family draws from the box. The one holding the marked lot is immediately stoned to death by the community. It seems so mundane on the surface, which makes it even more terrifying. What's more horrific than knowing your friends—your family—are willing to kill you to promote their own well-being, based on the strength of an old proverb: *Lottery in June, corn be heavy soon*?

Lucky Clover

Kelly A. Harmon

"Any idea where we are?" Mick asked. He took another drag off his Camel, turned up the Ramones on his buzzing speakers, and pushed the accelerator to the floor. The car leapt forward in a burst of speed, then settled into a noisy rumble down the highway.

Sean shook the accordion pleats out of the road map and tried to decipher how lost they were. Unfolding the map between the passenger window and the gear stick proved nearly impossible with his seat pushed so far forward. Mick's boxes and bags filled the small hatchback to the sagging headliner. The top-left corner of the map flapped in the gale-force wind blowing through Mick's wide-open window and didn't help matters.

"Maryland," Sean answered, head buried in the map. He traced a blue line south to north across the center fold. The road pitched north on the map, but Interstate 70 ran east to west. They were headed in the wrong direction.

Thanks to Mick, they'd lost at least two hours.

"Smartass," Mick said. "We've been in Maryland for almost an hour. Even I figured that out." He sucked hard on the cigarette, smoking it down to the filter, and then flicked it out the window. "This is the last time I'm taking you on a road trip," he added, shaking his head. "Can't take you anywhere without you getting us lost."

Sean knew better than to argue. He already regretted having agreed to the trip. He was tired of taking the blame for all that had gone wrong. And tired of shelling out dough for everything, especially gasoline, since Mick felt he'd done his part by driving. At least, Mick bought his own cigarettes; Mick's two to three packs a day would have bankrupted him. No wonder Mick didn't have the cash to pay for anything else.

"We're not lost," Sean said, then thought, *But if you had read the fuckin' map correctly earlier, we'd be a lot further down the road.* "You need to take exit 53 South when you come to it." He looked up to see the ramp for exit 53 pass by.

"Dammit!" Mick said, pulling hard to the right and onto the shoulder. Horns blared all around like the trumpets of Jericho. Tires squealed as a car eked by their fender. The driver flipped Mick the finger as he roared past them.

Mick stomped hard on the brakes, shaking his fist at the other driver, and almost scraping the guardrail.

Sean pitched forward, his hands smashing into the dashboard, crumpling the map. He choked as the seatbelt caught him on the side of his neck.

"Jesus, Mick! Calm down, will you? You nearly strangled me."

"I'd have bloodied your nose if you weren't wearing the belt," Mick said, laughing. "Aren't you glad I made you wear it?"

"And you'd be laughing then, too, you moron." Sean shook his wrists, willed the tingling to stop. "You're going to get us killed. Quit driving like a maniac."

Mick shoved the gear stick into reverse and turned around in his seat, left hand on the wheel. With his right, he pushed Sean's duffel out of his field of vision and started backing up.

"What are you doing?"

"Going back to take the turn we missed, thanks to you, fuck-up." Mick jammed his foot down on the accelerator and reversed up the soft shoulder.

"Don't be an ass, Mick. Just play the clover."

"Take the wrong ramp twice over just to get back on this road? No way. Reversing it is faster." He punched the accelerator again and the car leapt backward. Rocks kicked out from under the front tires and a plume of dust rose up.

"And illegal," Sean said. "Not to mention dangerous." He folded the map and shoved it into the door-panel pocket. "Play the clover, Mick."

"No way," Mick said, shaking his head. "No cop, no stop." The car rumbled backward up the shoulder, dipping to the right once as it swagged off the tar-and-chip pavement and onto rutted dirt before Mick corrected.

Sean crossed his arms on his chest. "I'm not paying the fine this time if you get another ticket. Besides, it's lucky to drive around a clover."

Mick slammed on the brakes again, saying something under his breath. Sean thought he heard "pussy" but wasn't sure. Joey Ramone screamed that he wanted to be sedated. Sean thought he wouldn't mind a little of that himself. The road trip wasn't going at all like they'd planned, and he didn't know how much more of Mick's attitude he could take.

"You and your damned Irish superstition," Mick said.

"You're Irish, too."

Mick stared straight ahead, his face as hard as fossilized limestone from County Clare. He said, "Faith, hope, or love?"

"It's a *four*-leaf clover. Don't forget luck. Make a wish on your way around."

Mick shook another Camel out of the soft pack and pulled it out with his lips. He pushed the cigarette lighter in, and without even looking, merged back into westbound traffic—accompanied by the sound of horns.

Sean grabbed the dashboard and screamed, "Are you trying to get us killed? Or just trying to piss me off?"

The lighter clicked. Mick leaned forward and grabbed it,

moving the cylinder to his face. He angled the cigarette down with his teeth and pressed the tip of it against the glowing brand. The sweet scent of fresh-lit tobacco filled the car. Mick filled his lungs and pushed the lighter back into place. When he exhaled, slowly, he blew the smoke in Sean's face.

"You're a dick," Mick said. "You know that?" He leaned forward and cranked the volume knob all the way to the right.

"Me?" Sean had to shout to be heard over the music. "I'm a dick because I don't want to get killed? Or am I a dick because I don't want to break the law?" He waved a pointed finger toward the back of the car. "Maybe I'm a dick because I don't want to piss off the guy behind us, just in case he has a gun!"

"Right," Mick said, "you're a triple dick. A real prize for the ladies." He blew more smoke in Sean's direction. "It would have been so much easier to back up and take the ramp. We'd have been on our way by now. Instead, we've got to play the clover leaf, round and round, to get back where we started. What a waste of time."

Mick laid on the horn as a driver merging onto the highway cut him off. "Asshole!" Mick yelled, merging onto the exit ramp. He sped up, turning into the curve.

Sean grabbed the door's armrest and pressed his left hand against the dash, bracing himself into the seat, wrist white with the pressure.

"Get your hand off the dash," Mick said, smashing his fist down on Sean's splayed fingers.

"Dammit," Sean said, pulling his hand back.

"I am not going to get us killed," Mick said, pulling the car back onto the highway. He sucked on his Camel, then, with an expert hand, guided the cigarette into the stream of air rushing by outside the rolled-down window, close enough to whip the ash off, but far enough not to rip out the cherry. He returned it to his mouth, letting saliva stick it to his bottom lip. "This is the last trip we're taking together," he said. "After this, I'm through with you. Pussy."

Sean laughed. "You think that's some kind of punishment? Depriving me of your sainted company? What a joke. You're damned right this is the last trip we're taking together. Just get me home in one piece so we can go our separate ways. The last thing we need is a freakin' accident that smears us together for eternity.

You know?" Sean shook his head. "Sometimes…"

Mick accelerated sharply, slamming Sean back against the seat. He laughed, then did it again. "Sometimes, what?"

"Sometimes…" Sean grabbed the dashboard again. "Slow down, man. You are so going to get us killed."

Mick laughed and floored the accelerator around the final ramp of the clover.

The Ford's tires squealed.

Joey Ramone yelled right along with them.

"Sometimes, what?" Mick screamed.

Sean said, "You're a real prick! You can't see how stupid the shit you do is. I wish…" He shook his head, knowing that what he said wouldn't make a difference to Mick no matter what. "You are so blind…"

The turn faced them into the setting sun, and blinding light blazed in through the windshield.

Mick shielded his eyes with his left hand and stomped on the brakes.

The car careened around the bend of the clover loop, tires hiccupping across pavement, grasping for purchase, as forward momentum pushed the car in a straight line. They hit the short curb and jumped off the road, shearing through the guardrail.

The Ford Escort turned over and over into oncoming traffic.

◉

"You still feel guilt over your friend's death," the doctor said, pulling the avocado-green visitor chair closer to Sean's hospital bed. He propped a wire-bound notebook on his knee and pulled out a mechanical pencil.

"I could have done more," Sean said, picking at the hospital-white blanket. "I could have tried harder to stop him."

"You said he was driving recklessly. What could you have done? Grabbed the wheel? Put your foot over his on the brake?"

Sean sat silent for several moments. The doctor ceased writing in his tablet and waited.

"I wished him dead."

"Your best friend?" The doctor raised his eyebrows.

"Yeah," he nodded. "We've been best buds since fifth grade when Mr. Baker gave us detention together."

"There's nothing like shared misery to bond friendships," the doctor said. "But there was more than that, no?"

Sean nodded. "Sure. Class projects, sleep-overs." He laughed. "Sock fights." He lifted a hand to mimic a throw, then winced at the pain in his ribs.

"But you grew out of that."

"Mm-hmm," Sean said with a smirk. "Got our first jobs together at Jack-in-the-Box. And got fired from there together, too. Girl chasing on Friday nights. Summer vacations." Sean sobered. "He saved my life once, at the pool. I dove in and pushed off the bottom…but my foot went through the filter grate and got stuck. He jumped in and dragged me to the surface."

The doctor looked at him with an expectant expression, waiting for Sean to continue.

Sean just closed his eyes and leaned back against the pillows.

"Well," the doctor said, laying down his pencil. "It seems we've come to the heart of it. It's not the guilt of Mick's death that's causing you grief; it's betrayal: he saved your life once, and you feel as though you've taken his."

Sean whispered, "What should I do?"

Was he dreaming, or did he hear the doctor say, "Wish him back," before sleep claimed him?

○

Sunlight glared off row after row of monuments in the Catholic graveyard. Sean squinted his eyes, feeling the skin pull taut on the right side of his face where black stitches pulled the ruined skin together. He laid a bruised hand atop the carved lamb on Mick's tombstone.

"You shit," he said. "This wasn't supposed to happen. We were supposed to part ways, like a divorce. Irreconcilable differences." He swallowed hard. "Death is bullshit."

Sean had missed the funeral, so doped for pain from his shattered left leg that he couldn't leave the hospital. Five days of his life gone that he'd never get back.

Getting past Mick's death was going to be mighty hard. A fancy new stone and fresh-turned earth didn't feel real enough.

Michael Casey Dunn
b. July 17, 1991 - d. September 23, 2009
Death is not a foe, but an inevitable adventure.

The chiseled words—created deep shadows on the face of the stone in the harsh glare of the afternoon sun. No comfort in that epitaph; Mick's father had probably chosen it. He'd remarked on more than one occasion that their road trips would get them into trouble. This kind of trouble, he probably hadn't considered.

Sean wiped his eyes, careful not to touch his broken nose.

"I didn't even get a chance to say goodbye," he said. "They told me you died on impact—no pain. I hope so, buddy, 'cause I can tell you, pain sucks.

"I hope your cloud is comfortable. It's just one more thing to pin on me if it's not. That's all I've been thinking about: you condemning me for this. Ever since they told me you were dead, it's played through my mind like a movie on repeat. That and the fact that I'll never see your ugly mug again.

"I've been giving this a lot of thought. I think you may be partly right. The accident is sort of my fault. I mean, you were driving way too fast. But, I did make the wish. Though, I didn't realize what it was at the time."

Sean brushed aside a speck of dirt. "It all comes down to the clover, Mick. Four-leaf clovers make wishes come true. I'll do what I can to make it right, man. I'll do what I can."

Sean limped to his car and got in.

All night and half the next morning, he drove, a newly-purchased *Best of the Ramones* recording in the CD player. When he got to exit 53 on I-70, he took the westbound loop of the clover.

The skid marks were still there, as was the new guardrail the state had made Mick's parents pay for.

Sean said aloud, "I wish Mick were alive." He drove all the way around, back to eastbound exit 53.

Then, he drove the clover again, "I wish Mick were alive."

By the time he made the third loop, Sean was crying. "Son-of-a-bitch!" he yelled before, more quietly, "I wish Mick were alive..."

...so they could kill Mick's old man, and then Sean's. Teach them a lesson. No kid should grow up with a drunk for a father, especially a drunken cop with handcuffs and a nightstick, like Mick's dad. Or like his own, a longshoreman with fists like hammers.

"Goddammit!" Sean yelled. That was never going to happen. Wouldn't have happened, even if Mick had lived. But they could dream. And keep their secrets. Together. Just the two of them, against the world.

Because, when you had a friend like Mick, you couldn't have any other friends.

Now what was he going to do?

After the fourth loop, Sean made fists and pounded them on the steering wheel. He cried, "Why? Why did you fucking have to die?"

He drove the loop again, hands tight on the wheel, Ramones turned up loud like Mick used to like it. Joey screamed for sedation as the car approached the westbound ramp, and Sean accelerated into the turn.

The sun burned his eyes as he shouted, "I wish you were here, you stupid son-of-a-bitch! I wish you were here!"

The temperature in the car dropped ten degrees. A shiver ran up Sean's spine, and the hair on his neck stood on end. His hands started shaking on the wheel.

Yet, there was no sign of Mick.

Sean took a deep breath through his mouth, exhaled with an audible sigh as he weighed his options. He was tired. He was hungry. And he was disappointed.

He turned off the Ramones. Inside the car, there was silence, with only the monotonous sound of the tires on the pavement to mar the simplicity of it. Sean stared straight ahead. A moment later, he smiled. He followed that with a half-muttered, "Heh," then a chuckle, and finished with a stream of laughter. Once he'd started laughing, he almost couldn't stop.

Had he been expecting Mick to appear in the seat next to him? What if he *had* just popped out of thin air? Jesus! That would have scared him to death. He might have had an accident. Might have killed Mick all over again. Might have killed himself.

Clovers. Wishes. Mick had just lost control. Sean's wish hadn't caused anything, and another wish couldn't undo it. Stupid, lunatic idea.

Mick would have laughed his ass off at such a lame idea, and then, he'd have lit a Camel and called Sean an idiot.

Sean exited the clover and headed for home.

◎

At the used record shop, rap music blasted from the speakers placed at the end of each aisle, and the teen-star wannabes gyrated to the pounding bass beat stolen from some '80s top-10 song Sean couldn't remember the name of.

No originality, Sean thought. He tuned it out, wishing the store would play something more to his taste. He plucked a Smithereens CD off a shelf and studied it.

A figure in the corner of the cover art caught his attention.

Mick? Impossible.

He dropped the CD back onto the shelf as if it had burned him. Then, looking up, he saw Mick hurry down the aisle on the other side of the CD bins.

"Mick!" he called, but Mick continued down the aisle as if he hadn't heard.

Sean hurried after him, but his bum leg prevented him from catching up.

Had it been Mick? Or a guy who looked a lot like Mick?

Sean paused at the end of the row and looked left, then right.

Where had he gone? Sean could have sworn he saw Mick go that way. He searched down a few more aisles.

"Mick?"

Sean checked the Country and Western aisle, but Mick wasn't there.

Of course, he isn't, Sean thought. *Mick wouldn't have been caught dead in the Country-Western aisle when he was alive.* A hysterical giggle bubbled up from Sean's chest, and he felt a surge of panic.

"Mick!" he yelled.

Several people gave him strange looks.

Sean left the store and headed for his car, pulling his cell phone from his pocket and hitting the speed dial for Mick. After a moment, he heard the three-tone intro and the monotone announcement that the number had been disconnected.

◎

Sean pulled into the driveway and pushed the gearshift into park. The car ran by automatic transmission; no more shifting his own gears, thanks to Mick. He struggled with the parking brake, his left leg shaking with the effort of pressing the pedal, then he laid his head back and closed his eyes.

The Smithereens blasted out of the speakers—new speakers, no buzz here, not like in Mick's rattletrap.

Sean pounded his good thigh with a clenched fist. When would his mind stop making the comparisons? All roads led to Mick, it seemed.

He clicked off the radio, threw open the door, and pushed himself up from the seat. *No more low-riding cars either,* he thought, struggling to stand on his weak leg. Eighteen years old and half broken, like an old man.

At least, he was alive. Unlike Mick.

Sean looked up at the front porch and his heart began a wild beat, thumping like a fist against his breastbone.

Mick sat on the front steps of the house, smoking a cigarette.

Sean felt himself trembling. The short walk across the lawn took longer than usual.

Dried blood streaked Mick's blond hair brown and splattered over his left shoulder, nearly obliterating the Ramones logo on his t-shirt.

Sean tried to keep the quaver from his voice. "Mick? What are you doing here?" The purple bruise straddling Mick's forehead appeared vivid, almost fresh.

Sean felt himself tremble, even as he explored the possibilities. Mick was dead. He was never coming back, which meant this visitor was a ghost, or Sean was going crazy.

"I'm here to collect." Mick sucked on the end of the cigarette, the tip burning bright scarlet in the shade of the porch awning. He smiled that I'm-right-and-you're-wrong smile Sean had always hated.

"Collect what?" Sean limped closer, pocketed his keys. "You're dead."

Mick's smile deepened. "Do I look dead? I'm just a little banged up." He pointed at Sean with the cigarette. "That was some stunt you pulled, driving us into the sun like that."

"You're not blaming the accident on me."

"But I am, Sean," Mick said, putting the Camel to his lips.

"You were driving too fast."

"You forced me to take the clover, and then you wished me blind. Of course the accident was your fault."

Sean felt a twinge of pain behind his forehead. He lifted his right hand and rubbed, sliding three fingers up the center and down the bridge of his nose. He shook his head. Released the breath he'd been holding. "Get lost, Mick. You're a fucking hallucination. I'm not up for this right now."

"I'll be back." Mick stood, took a last drag from the cigarette and tossed the butt at Sean's feet.

Sean stomped it out, but when he moved his foot away, there was no cigarette butt there. He struggled up the steps to the porch, giving Mick a wide berth, opened the door, and hurried inside.

When Sean looked out through the screen door, Mick had vanished. Sean crept back out onto the porch to look up and down the street, but Mick was nowhere to be seen.

In the aftermath of Mick's departure, silence pervaded the neighborhood. No birdsong, no shushing of leaves in the breeze, no road noise off Holabird Avenue.

A slow dread chilled Sean, filling the ache around his heart with fear. He fled into the house and locked the door.

◉

A squeak from the open window in his bedroom woke Sean.

He scanned the room for anything out of the ordinary and saw the red hot glow of a cigarette hovering over the chair near his desk. His heart clanged once against his ribcage, paused, then galloped in a relentless rhythm.

In the moments it took for his eyes to adjust, Sean watched Mick materialize out of the darkness, lips clasping the lit cigarette. A thin curl of smoke rose toward the ceiling.

"What are you doing here?" Sean said.

Mick's cigarette bobbed as he answered. "Making sure I collect. I told you I intend to. You owe me."

"Even if you're right," Sean said, "I don't know what you expect from me." He ran a hand threw his hair. "Besides, it's your own fault the accident happened."

Mick stood and walked toward the open window. Faint moonlight illuminated a semi-circle of carpet just beyond the drapes. He took one last drag on the cigarette and flicked it outside, then knelt to examine a box sitting in the puddle of a moonbeam.

"What are you doing with my CDs?"

"Your mom gave them to me," Sean said. "They were here when I got out of the hospital."

Mick picked up a Black Flag CD. "I could never live without my music."

"Take them. They're yours. Your folks moved away before I had the chance to give them back."

Mick shook his head, pulled another cigarette from the soft pack in his T-shirt's breast pocket and lit up. "You're just racking up the debt, Sean."

"I still don't know what you expect me to do."

"You'll figure it out," Mick said. "You always were the smarter of us two."

He rose, and the Black Flag CD toppled back into the box on the floor. He put one foot up on the sill and grasped the window frame in his hands, then turned to face Sean still lying in his bed.

In the moonlight, Sean could see the livid bruise, the bloodstained T-shirt Mick wore.

"Until next time," Mick said, crawling out the window to the waiting oak.

Sean heard a step on the branch, the rustle of leaves as Mick departed, then he sprang out of bed and bent his head through the open window. He saw nothing, heard nothing.

Mick had vanished, like the smoke from one of his cigarettes.

Sean shivered, closed the window, and crawled back into bed, yanking the covers up over his shoulders.

He was nearly asleep when he had a thought, *I hope Mom doesn't smell the smoke from Mick's cigarettes.* It was a thought he'd had many times over the years.

Then, like a jolt of caffeine, Sean was wide awake. He hadn't smelled the cigarette himself, didn't detect any odor of it right then. The room smelled as fresh as if his mom had just changed the sheets.

Sean lay there, shaking, wide awake until the sun came up and sleep finally claimed him. His last thought was that Mick said he would pay...and he was. He was paying. The question was, how long would Mick make him pay?

◉

Sean awoke to Joey Ramone singing about Sheena the punk rocker. It came from outside, but the music blared so loudly, it rattled the window of his bedroom.

Why wasn't his mother yelling?

He got out of bed, went to the window, and opened it. The music roiled out of the speakers of his car. He hadn't known they could play so loud.

Dammit. Any more of that and his brand new subwoofers

would buzz like Mick's. All four car windows gaped open, and Sean could just barely discern a stream of smoke spilling out the passenger side.

Who was in his car? As if he didn't know.

He dressed as fast as he could and limped down the stairs. His mother was reading the newspaper at the kitchen table, a cup of coffee at her elbow.

"Isn't the music bothering you?" he asked.

"What music?" she said, not looking up from the editorial page of *The Baltimore Sun*. "Better close your windows," she added, reaching for her coffee. "It looks like rain."

Just as Sean opened the screen door and stepped out on the porch, it began to pour.

Great, he thought, *buzzing speakers and wet upholstery: a winning combination*. Add in the Ghost of Mick Past, and he'd hit the trifecta.

He hurried to the car and clambered into the driver's seat as fast as he could.

"Go. Away." Sean shoved the key in the ignition and started the car. He lowered the volume and closed the windows.

The bruises and bloody wound on Mick's face glowed in contrast to the pallid whiteness of his dead flesh. He curled a graying lip in a facsimile of a smile.

"Not until you pay," he said. "You owe me." He took a last drag on his cigarette and flicked it out the closed window. It disappeared as if it had made it through the glass.

"I've paid," Sean said. "I've paid with my leg; I've paid with my face; I've paid with my peace of mind."

He put the car in reverse and backed out of the driveway. Raindrops pattered on the windshield to the Ramones' throbbing beat.

"Where are we going?" Mick asked.

"I'm going out for a drive," Sean said. "You, I hope, are going to Hell."

"No such luck," Mick said, lighting up another cigarette. "I'm here to stay—at least until you pay up."

Sean could smell his own stench, the fear of sitting in an enclosed space with a dead friend—and the faint, pungent odor of long-extinguished butts in the ashtray, but the fresh, sweet aroma of new-lit tobacco eluded him. Was Mick in the car with him, or wasn't he? Had he been in the house last week, or not?

Sean hadn't known where he was driving to, but the split second he realized he honestly didn't know what reality was, he made a decision. He signaled and pulled into the turn lane for the interstate.

Exit 53, he thought, *here we come.*

○

Pouring rain sluiced over the windshield wipers, making everything harder to see.

Sean was driving fast—faster than he usually drove. Fast like Mick. He lit a Camel and sucked hard on it, filling the car with smoke. His eyes burned. The exit 53 ramp was approaching fast.

The Ramones blasted through the speakers.

Mick's hands were on the dashboard, his face white in the dim glow of the dash lights. "What are you doing, man?"

"Fixing something," Sean said, raising a shaking hand to brush the hair from his eyes. "I'm gonna wish you back to Hell."

"Be careful what you wish for," Mick said. "You wish me to Hell, and you'll find yourself there with me."

Sean accelerated. "I just want some peace of mind, Mick."

"That wish won't buy it," Mick said, relaxing back against the seat. "You send me to Hell, and you'll regret it every day for the rest of your life, and then some."

"Tell me what you want!"

After a moment, Mick said, "Admit it's your fault I'm dead."

Sean shook his head. "You always were a jerk, Mick."

Mick just smiled.

Sean kept his eyes on the road. "Saying the accident was my fault and believing it are two different things."

"Sure," Mick said. "But admitting it puts you on the road to redemption, so to speak."

"Right," Sean said, his words dripping sarcasm. "If I admit I killed you, it will make me feel better."

"No. If you admit you killed me, you'll recognize that you owe me. You fucked up; you pay up. Them's the rules."

"And where does that get us?" Sean put the Camel to his lips and drew deep, exhaling while Mick spoke.

"Once you realize it's your fault, you have no choice but to use your last wish for *me*…not for yourself."

"Fuck!" Sean said. "You want me to own up to killing you,

then throw away my chance for some peace of mind—for an apparition? You always were a selfish bastard."

Mick laughed. "Yeah. But you used to like this selfish bastard. I had my finer points." He winked.

Sean couldn't help it; he laughed, then shook his head.

Exit 53 approached. Sean signaled and jerked the speeding car onto the ramp.

He pressed the button to lower the driver's window, then took one last, long draw on his cigarette and tossed it out the window. He shut off the radio with a jab of his finger, and turned his head to face Mick, his countenance solemn.

Mick looked scared. "Do the right thing, dude," he said.

"I will." Sean looked Mick right in the eyes. "Wishing you dead will bring me the peace I need."

He accelerated into the turn and punched the brakes hard.

Tires squealed on the wet pavement.

"No!" yelled Mick.

At almost the last second, Sean smiled. "I wish you peace, Mick."

The car smashed through the guardrail and tumbled, end over end, down the embankment into oncoming traffic.

Sean heard the click of a lighter and the crumpling of a cellophane wrapper. The aroma of fresh-lit tobacco assailed him.

"This is the last time I'm taking you on a road trip," Mick said. "Can't take you anywhere without you getting us lost."

Scathe meic Beorh on Joyce Carol Oates's "Thanksgiving"

In her collection titled *Haunted: Tales of the Grotesque*, Joyce Carol Oates includes her story "Thanksgiving." When I first discovered this story, I had been reading horror for thirty-five years. Poe, Lovecraft, Machen, Gilman, Hawthorne, Le Fanu—you name the writer, I have likely read at least one story. I read "Thanksgiving" by Oates five years ago, and not only did the thing terrify me as few other tales have, I haven't been able to stop thinking about it. I thought I had gotten over being 'impressionable.' Apparently not. Since my reading, I have discovered the point of the story (I think), but that knowledge does nothing to assuage my fear of the nightmarish grocery store encountered by the protagonist. I dare anyone to read this well-wrought piece and not be reminded of at least one time when a busy holiday supermarket seemed like some other place altogether.

Pinprick

Scathe meic Beorh

A wee girl with two pinpricks for a nose smiled at me through her narrow mansion window, her big black eyes glistening like carrion beetles in the morning sunshine. Her fingers and the stone sill where she stood were smeared with fresh blood. She had killed something, but her features showed a lunacy that would send her to relatives—if what she had slain was human—and give her a slap on the wrist if 'twas only her dog.

It turned out to be human, and 'twas my lot in life to be hired by the butler, a Mr. Renault, as the child's personal coachman. My first assignment was, the following morning, to drive Hanna from her home in Rathmines, Dublin, through the Wicklow Mountains to her uncle's manor in Corsillagh. An outrider had gone ahead with the revolting news.

It would be a long day's journey forcing us to pass through *Gleann na Gruagh*, a gloomy glen haunted by highwaymen and other denizens of low social esteem. Under no circumstance whatever was I to allow her to exit the four-in-hand (her privy needs while traveling to be met with a chamber pot).

I dozed an hour at most that night, my mind unable to extricate itself from wondering who the babe had axed to death that sunny morn.

○

As one may imagine, when we reached the darkest portion of the glen, we were indeed waylaid and told to stand and deliver, for 'twas our money or our lives. Hanna swung open the door of the coach and smiled, and the masked highwaymen smiled with their eyes, taken aback by her sweetness. She then drew two flintlocks and slew them who had hailed us so boldly—a ball entering an eye socket of one, the breast of the other.

"Pinprick!" I said. "Get back in! *Quickly!* They were not the only two cutthroats living here!"

"I like that you call me Pinprick, Mister Coachman," she said as she swung herself back into her seat and slammed the door shut. "I have a crossbow and full quiver, Mister Coachman. What do you have up there?"

"Nothing to your concern," I replied as I snapped the reins so hard all four horses whinnied in anger. I figured then why I had been sent on the precarious journey alone. No need for extra servants when not required!

"I don't like mean people, Mister Coachman. You should be nice to me. My fingers do bad things to people who speak harshly. To me."

"So I hear," I whispered, hoping she hadn't heard me.

"I heard you," she said.

○

Inexplicably, we escaped the glen without further incident. We were moving along at a fair clip when, to the curdling of my blood,

I registered a piercing scream which nearly unseated me. It was followed by a "Stop!"

Did I stop? Of course I stopped. My father went to his grave providing me with an education, which included knowing when I was out of my depth with *terrible enfants*.

"*There once was a man from Kilkennyyy*," Hanna sang as she relieved herself behind a spiny blackthorn, "*who thought he would never get anyyy...*"

I plugged my ears with my forefingers and closed my eyes. This was not happening to me. *This was not happening to me.*

"Listen to my rhyme, Mister Coachman."

"Must I, Pinprick?" I heard myself ask.

"If you choose not," the wee murderess replied, brushing my sleeve with fingers still bloodstained from the morning before. *Why hadn't someone washed her hands? God in Heaven!* I begged my guardian angels to guide me safely to her awaiting Uncle Pilchard.

I suddenly felt an indomitable angelic presence, which indeed was comforting, and my belief remained constant that God would not put upon His children any more than we can bear. But why had I been chosen, of those with far better credentials (fellow murderers, for example), to escort a diminutive Elizabeth Bathory! Surely this was another instance, as with Job, where the Devil had wagered with God concerning my ability to endure the unthinkable—and God had accepted the challenge!

"Mister Coachman?"

"Yes, Miss Pilchard?"

"Please call me Pinprick."

"Yes, Miss Pinprick."

"Pinprick by itself will do."

"Right. *Pinprick.* What can I do for you?" I opened the coach door and released the stairs for her.

"Well..." she replied as she rolled her eyes, "I'm hungry, and the basket of food prepared for me is not to my liking. I don't care for soda bread and apples much."

My blood went icy. This meant that we would have to stop at Kilmacullough, which was only down the way, and purchase whatever would be to her heart's delight.

"I wish to use my crossbow and kill something to eat. Like Robin Hood," she said.

I went light-headed and fell against the lacquered coach, the sweat on my ungloved hand causing me to slip quickly along the surface so that my next contact was an eyebrow on the brass lamp.

"Mister Coachman?" She snapped her head to gaze into a nearby stand of gorse. "Did you see something that frightened you?"

"Yes, as a matter of fact, I *did* see something frightening."

"What was it?" She bounced on her toes, an unsettling glee in her voice. "*Ooooo!* You're bleeding!"

I staunched the seepage of blood with my kerchief.

"What did you see that terrified you?"

Not answering her, which made her pinch her lips together and glare at me, I found strength enough to help her back to her seat and to find mine.

It would've only been a few more leagues, and we'd have arrived, safe if not sound. But we needed to stop again so that she could kill something. What would she kill? And how would we cook it? We'd be all night reaching our destination at that rate, and my post would most likely be lost. I may even be put into custody for kidnapping.

We drove on.

"Stop at the wee wood near Kilmacull, Mister Coachman," cried Hanna, head thrust out of the window. "We're near there now. I can tell by the sweeter air. And, we just passed Bloodland."

I couldn't help myself. "Bloodland?" I cried, trying to direct my voice backward at full gallop.

"It's nothing, Mister Coachman," she cried back, and we rode on in silence.

I reflected upon driving straight past 'the wee wood near Kilmacull,' but then considered that a crossbow arrow could easily pierce the roof of the coach.

"Good thinking," she said.

I froze where I sat.

"Here, Mister Coachman. Pull over here. By the wee wood."

Seeing a copse of oak growing in front of farmland, I said not a word, halted the team, dismounted, and prepared to water them. I was glad 'twas near Summer Solstice, for we had many hours of light left, though my pocket watch showed half past five.

"Do you like my crossbow, Mister Coachman?"

I turned and saw that the medieval weapon, which had singly altered the face of warfare in that distant era, was pointed—loaded with an arrow—at my privy parts. I hopped like a man on fire and hid myself behind the nearest tree.

"I wasn't going to shoot you, Mister Coachman."

"What were you going…going to do then? *Frighten me to death?*"

"Maybe. And, careful with your tone," she replied. "I have funny fingers. They like to dance." Then, she tromped off into the wood.

◉

The team 'ostled properly, I climbed back into my seat and, shaking like sheep fuzz in a breeze, packed my Oom Paul pipe with a rich cherry tobacco, lit it, and tried to relax.

"Mister Coachman!"

I do not remember taking myself down from the four-in-hand. Nor do I remember running into the wood. After the memory of Hanna's scream coloring the surrounds like a nightmare, my next recollection is seeing a handsome lad crawling toward me, his eyes bulging as he gasped for air, an arrow piercing his left jugular and spine.

"I got one!" Hanna cried. "One of the shepherd lads! Oh, will he be tender enough to eat? I hope I haven't made a mistake, Mister Coachman." She fired another arrow from the evil contraption, this one squarely entering his heart. He fell with a thump to the dewy grass.

"*Mmmm*, smells wonderful, doesn't it? I so love the scent of freshly spilled blood. They wouldn't let me eat—"

I had the crossbow in one hand and Hanna in the other, dragging her by the collar back to the coach. How I accomplished it I do not, to this day, know, but soon I had the child tied securely and placed in her seat.

She screamed throughout the next leg of our journey, and at first, I wished I had gagged her. But, when her screams turned to tears, I could not be quite so hard-hearted. I would rather have not stopped—yet again—risking a mishap to my person, but she was, after all, just a wee girl.

◉

When we finally arrived, two tall footmen, several servants, and Hanna's uncle all appeared as if they greeted the 'Ooser' itself. I was ushered into the Great House, for fear that I was dying, and a

215

quick glimpse into an outsized wall mirror showed me the reason for their pallid complexions. Though I knew the reflected figure to be me, the green skin and disheveled hair of a lunatic were completely incongruent with my usual demeanor.

"Sir!" Lord Perrault took me by the arm and led me to a sitting room decorated with a bevy of Pinprick's dour-faced and dark-eyed cousins. "What is the meaning of your arrival here with my niece?"

"Arrival?" I was still very much dazed and on display for this audience of crows.

"Aye! Were you not properly briefed?"

"What…should I have been briefed about, sir?" I managed to ask.

A chorus of whispers circled the room; black-haired heads tipped toward one another as Pinprick's noble family members consulted. Lord Perrault looked rather helplessly around at his brood, perhaps seeking someone else to do the talking. When no such savior rose to the occasion, he cleared his throat loudly, and said, "Based upon your, ah, *curriculum vitae*, shall we say, you were hired to perform a certain *service* for the family."

"I'm afraid I do not follow you, sir," I replied. "I've done as requested. The child is quite safe."

The gentleman closed his eyes. Beads of sweat had erupted over his features. "Are…you not John Copper, newly released from Dublin Castle gaol to, shall we say, *serve* the Pilchard-Perrault clan with a most necessary but particularly…unsavory duty?"

"Copper? *Copper*, did you say? No, my surname is *Coppe*. I am John *Coppe*."

"Oh, God in Heaven," he replied. He put his hand to his forehead and began to pace, back and forth, obviously deep in thought. "There has been a terrible mistake. The rush and bustle of yesterday, surely. All the confusion. May…may I ask, Mr. Coppe, how came you to be hired?"

"A reputable reference made an appointment for me a fortnight ago," I said.

"That damned butler Renault!" came Perrault's reply, and his jowls jounced with each word. "His infernal senility has caused us far too much pain this time round!"

"Sir," I said, "if I may be permitted. I am quite sure that I do not understand what has happened. Mr. Renault was very cordial, if a bit flustered. Might I inquire into the particulars, even a wee bit, in order to clear my own mind?"

Lord Perrault again consulted his family with a look. They, in turn, all looked at me, taking in my bedraggled state with unblinking, coal-black eyes. I shrank under their scrutiny, finding not even a hint of sympathy in any one of them.

I assume Perrault received familial approval that was invisible to me, because he placed his large hand on my shoulder. "You, sir—or I should say the murderer John Copper—were hired to dispatch that devil Hanna somewhere on the highway from Dublin."

"Dispatch?" I whispered.

"Say you something, Mr. Coppe?"

◙

Having, with a purloined bag of currency, made amends to the clans of the two murdered thieves—one of which, ironically, had been John Copper. He had apparently decided not to make himself present for his Pilchard Manor assignment, despite the fact that it was Perrault who had secured his release from gaol so he could perform that particular duty.

Hanna and I today abide in a comfortable stone cottage hidden in the olden oaks and ash of *Gleann na Gruagh*. Though my education and my father's memory may be sullied by my present profession, I could not see the disturbed child assassinated over a condition of mind completely out of her control.

We do well for ourselves when the affluent travel through this perpetually shadowed woodland. Furthermore, Hanna has taught me to fashion and fletch crossbow arrows.

—*John Coppe, Highwayman*

Patricia Lillie on Melanie Tem's "Secrets"

Melanie Tem's stories start out innocently enough. Her people aren't perfect. Their lives and problems could very well be those of your next-door neighbors—or your own. Then, Tem slowly and meticulously peels away the layers and reveals dark secrets. Whether her vehicle is the supernatural or human emotion, Tem's horrors leave you hoping these are not your neighbors—or yourself. In "Secrets," Grace is surrounded by secrets. After the death of her husband, she discovers his secrets. Christy, Grace's once loving daughter, is silent and locked alone in her room with her secrets. Hidden in the Beatle's *White Album*, Grace finds the answer she needs. When you love someone, you can't allow them to keep secrets. Currently available in *The Ice Downstream and Other Stories*, eBook edition, published by Crossroads Press, *Secrets* first appeared in the Spring 1991 issue of *Cemetery Dance Magazine*.

Abby

Patricia Lillie

Life with a teenager with an Autism Spectrum Disorder is, on the best of days, quirky. Don't get me wrong. Abby is high functioning, and I know things could be much worse. Other than periodic meltdowns, we have it relatively easy and have learned to deal with, if not understand, the way she works.

There are the non-sequiturs. In Tim Burton's version of *Charlie and the Chocolate Factory*, Grandpa Joe is talking about working for Willie Wonka, when out of the blue, Grandma Georgina says, "I love grapes."

I adore that scene. Abby and Grandma Georgina have similar conversational skills. At noisy family gatherings, Abby might bring all discussion to a halt by loudly announcing, "In third grade, I sat behind David Besom. He had red hair."

Her father or I look at her and quietly say, "I love grapes." It's a signal, and most times she laughs and turns her attention back to what is going on around her. Abby does know that, by other people's standards, she's not quite right. She's okay with that.

There's what we call "Abby's Pause Mode". She walks through the house and stops, usually in the middle of a doorway. She stands there, stock still, and grins her lopsided grin, until one of us says, "Hey! You stuck?"

"Noooo," she laughs and continues on her way. If we're busy and don't notice she's on pause, she retreats into Abby-land. We find her stopped, still grinning, but no longer still. She sways, front to back, elbows bent, hands in front of her body. Her fingers dance; her eyelids flutter; and, if it's been too long, her eyes roll back in her head. At these times, it's harder to call her back.

"Abby!" Wait a beat. "ABBY!"

"Huh."

"You stuck?"

"We haven't had any snow days this year." Her replies are mundane and often of the "grapes" variety, and we assume they have something to do with happenings in Abby-land.

We go with it the best we can. "Nope. And as far as I'm concerned we don't need any."

"I want at least one." She grins and moves off to wherever she was going before her little holiday.

And obsessive? You may think you obsess. You may have friends who obsess to the point you've suggested they require medication. But, they're all slackers compared to a teenager with ASD.

A postcard reminds us it's time to have our eyes checked, and she starts up.

"Did you make our eye appointments?"

"When are you going to make our eye appointments?"

"You really should make our eye appointments."

"We need our eyes checked."

On and on, until I say, "Yes! I made the appointments!" Obsession over eye check-ups leads to obsession over the dentist, the ear doctor, and the anything-else-she-can-think-of doctor. Regularly scheduled maintenance is very important to Abby.

There's more. Some of it, like the rocking, are typical ASD behaviors; some of it is Abby-specific. She doesn't sleep through the night. Most nights, she wakes up, gets out of bed, and spends an hour or so at her computer. Often, she sits in her bed and sings. Or rocks. Mentally and emotionally, in many ways she's twelve; in others, she's completely seventeen. It keeps things interesting. Worse is when she's excited about something. It becomes the only subject of conversation for weeks, even months.

"Abby, did you empty the dishwasher?"

"Twyla's birthday party is in three weeks."

"Abby, dinner's ready!"

"I'm going to wrap Twyla's present in red."

"Abby, do you know you're a banana?"

"Twyla's mom is going to take us to the party."

"It's okay, Abby. I love bananas. A lot."

"Twyla's favorite color is red."

You get the picture.

Our life has a rhythm; it's an odd rhythm, but it works. It's my excuse for not noticing sooner that something was wrong. Most people with normal kids would have caught on at the first sign of weird. We're so used to weird, we took it all in stride.

If I'm at the computer paying bills, lightning could strike the house and, as long as the electricity stays on, I won't notice. Even so, when I looked up and saw Abby in my office doorway, I knew she hadn't been there long, maybe a minute. Not long enough for her to go from simple pause to deep Abby-land. Yet, there she was, already into the eye-rolling stage.

"Abby? Abby! ABBY!" Three *Abby's* deep is bad.

"You stuck?"

"He's watching."

That was a new one. I wasn't sure I'd heard her correctly. "What?"

"He's hungry."

"Who's hungry?"

"Idunno," she said and shrugged.

In Abby-speak, that word—and it is one word—combined with a shrug does not mean she doesn't know the answer. It means she doesn't want to talk about it, and it's always her final answer.

She walked away.

"Hey!" I called. "What did you want?"

She stopped and looked back, puzzled.

"Did you need me for something?" I asked.

"I forget." She gave me her crazy grin and left.

Have I mentioned that Abby never forgets? Anything. Ever.

A few days later, I got a call from Abby's teacher. Daytime calls from Ms. Colley were always bad and usually meant Abby had had a meltdown.

"What's up?" I asked. I closed my eyes and hoped for a *minor* meltdown. Things were crazy at work, and I didn't have time to go get her.

"Um," Ms. Colley said. "I have a sort of odd question."

"I'm Abby's mother. Define odd."

She laughed. "Good point. So, has Abby been watching movies that she's not ready to cope with or process?"

I panicked. My first thought was *sex*. Attempts to discuss the subject with Abby, explaining appropriate and inappropriate behavior, had proven frustrating. I could never tell how much she understood or how much she already knew. But she was seventeen, *and* she was obsessed with the idea of having a boyfriend, even though she didn't fully grasp the reality.

The previous year, thanks to a pregnant cousin, she'd figured out that one doesn't have to be married to have a baby. After that, she'd told everyone she knew—and a few people she didn't know—she wanted one. Dealing with that was loads of fun.

"What kind of movies?"

"Oh, the scary, gory, bloody, spattery kind."

I was relieved. Bad movies, I could deal with. I was fairly sure Abby would never take an ax to a cabin full of teenagers.

"Not that I know of," I said. "What happened?"

"Abby disrupted the math lesson with…lurid talk," Ms. Colley said. "The two things she kept repeating were, 'He rips their throats out,' and 'When he eats them, their insides get splattered all over.' No matter how many times I told her to change the channel, or just to stop, she kept going."

Change the channel was Ms. Colley's version of *I love grapes*.

"She didn't stop until Twyla cried. Then Abby cried, and they both had meltdowns."

I was speechless. And appalled. We both knew Abby didn't—

couldn't—just make things up. She could only lie in reply to yes or no questions, and she was bad at that. She could repeat verbatim things she heard or describe in great detail things she saw or did. Even when she went off on a tangent and imagination came into play, the what-ifs were always easily attributed to something we knew she'd heard, seen, or done.

"Are you still there?" Ms. Colley asked.

"Yeah. I'm clueless. We don't watch many blood-and-gore movies and never when Abby's around. Besides, she's pretty self-censoring. If we watch anything that gets scary or makes her uncomfortable, she goes to her room and puts in an *Anne of Green Gables* DVD. Maybe she watched something on Netflix when she was home alone. I'll check into it. Do you need me to come get her?"

"No. They're both sitting in the Quiet Corner now. I think Abby feels bad for upsetting Twyla. They seem to be comforting each other. I just wanted you to know what happened."

We hung up, and I thought about it. I dwelled on it—Abby-level dwelling. We didn't have cable, so television was limited to Netflix, only hooked up in the living room, and DVDs. I wasn't getting any work done, so I opened my Netflix account and checked the list of recently viewed items. Nothing there I didn't recognize, nothing that explained Abby's storytelling.

When I got home, she was at the kitchen table doing a word search.

"Abby, what happened at school today?"

"Nothing."

"Don't tell me 'nothing.' Ms. Colley called me."

"Twyla doesn't like moving pictures. They freak her out."

I understood that. Twyla couldn't cope with television or movies. Her parents kept the television in a locked cabinet and only watched it when she was asleep or gone. "What does that have to do with what happened at school?"

"I shouldn't have told her about the moving pictures. It was mean."

"What are you talking about? What moving pictures?"

"Idunno." Shrug.

Great. "Abby, we really need to talk about this."

"Mom. I really need to finish this." She went back to her puzzle. And that was that.

I checked her room; maybe somebody at school had lent her a movie. I looked in her player and at her DVD collection. *Anne of Green Gables, Emily of New Moon, A Little Princess*—all I found were the sweet, slightly sappy movies Abby liked. I checked her known hiding places but only found a half-eaten bag of chocolate chips. (One minor mystery solved; I knew I'd bought those.)

Later, when Abby was in bed, I told my husband what had happened. Jim couldn't come up with an explanation either. We decided to take the wait-and-see route and not worry until we were sure there was something to worry about. It's worked for us before.

The night the lights went out, Jim and I were out to dinner with friends. Abby was home alone—we had only planned on being gone a couple of hours, not long enough to need a sitter. We waited about fifteen minutes in the dark, but when the lights didn't come back on, we made our apologies and left. Not only did we want to check on Abby, but Jim was a policeman. A prolonged power outage meant alarm drops and people getting the stupids. There was a good chance he would be called in to work.

With Friday night traffic and no street lights, our ten-minute drive home took over a half hour. I asked what good it was to be married to a cop if you couldn't have lights and sirens when you needed them. Jim just snorted. I made the same joke often.

The house was, of course, pitch dark, and Abby didn't answer when we called. Jim grabbed his flashlight, and we headed upstairs.

She sat cross-legged on her bed, rocking. Her fingers danced. Her eyelids fluttered, and her eyes showed only white. To someone who didn't know Abby, it would have looked like a seizure, but we knew she was deep in Abby-land.

The thing was, we had always assumed Abby-land was a happy place. When in Abby-land, she always smiled; in fact, she looked downright blissful. We were often sorry to call her home.

That night, however, her lips were pinched, in a straight line. On the side of her face, a jaw muscle throbbed. Her forehead was furrowed, her eyebrows so close together they became a uni-brow. Anything but blissful, her expression was one of intense—and worried—concentration.

"Abby! ABBY!"

She gave no sign she heard us and continued to rock.

I reached out to shake her, something we usually tried to avoid, but before I could, the lights flashed on, and she stilled. Her face was slack, her expression blank.

"He's finished," she said, voice flat.

"What? Who's finished?" Jim asked.

"The ceiling's red. Twyla would like it."

"Abby. Look at me." I tried to keep my voice calm, steady. "What ceiling?"

She did look at us then, and her face lit up with that big, loopy Abby grin. "How was your dinner? Was it good?"

"Abby." I must have failed at the soothing mom-voice, because Jim interrupted me.

"We didn't get to eat. The lights went off before we even ordered our food."

"Me too," Abby said. "Sandwiches?"

Tuna on toast wasn't in our plans for the evening, but it was one of Abby's specialties, and she enjoyed making it for us.

Jim took his first bite and pronounced it, "Delicious!"

Abby glowed.

It was a normal family night, a happy family night. I relaxed and decided to go with the flow. Whatever was going on with my daughter, I couldn't solve it then anyway.

○

"Nancy and Kyle will be sad," Abby said at breakfast.

"I love grapes." Still on my first cup of coffee, I wasn't paying attention.

"He was really hungry."

She had Jim's attention. "Who? Abby, who was hungry?"

"Twyla would like the ceiling, but I don't think Nancy will."

"Abby. Look at me. What are you talking about?" Jim used the serious dad-voice.

"Idunno."

He couldn't get another word out of her.

When the school bus arrived, she didn't even say good-bye.

I'd known Nancy and Kyle all my life. Small towns are like that.

"Four kids. What were we thinking?" Nancy had told me. "We need a kid-free life—at least for a week." Nancy and Kyle had left for a second honeymoon. Nancy's mother stayed with the children.

When none of the kids showed up at school, and nobody answered the phone, the school called the police. The dispatcher sent a patrol car over to check on them.

Small towns are like that, too.

◉

Cops see horrible things. Jim seldom shared them with me, but when he needed to talk, I listened. Even on those occasions, I knew he spared me the worst of the details. This time was different.

He sat still—rigid—his head down and his voice emotionless. "They were...ripped apart. All five of them. The children...Nancy and Kyle's babies...and the blood. So much blood. On the floor. On the walls. It was like...like...something...ate them."

He was quiet for a moment, then raised his head and looked at me. "There was blood all over the fucking ceiling."

My senses—the sound of Jim's voice, the glare of the room's lights, the lingering smell of dinner—became physical, solid, and pressed against me, heavy, smothering me.

Is this how Abby feels when she has a meltdown?

When I could breathe again, Jim was still beside me, holding my hand. We sat like that, in silence, for I don't know how long. It felt like forever.

◉

I've taken sick leave from work, and I sleep while Abby's at school. She's safe there. Ms. Colley doesn't allow rocking in class. The bus ride to and from school is short, and Abby's well-buckled in.

But, when she's at home, I watch.

"He's hungry," she keeps saying.

Every time I catch her rocking or swaying or retreating to Abby-land, I stop her.

"He's hungry."

"Who?" I ask every time, but I never get more than *Idunno*.

My nights, I spend in the big chair in the corner of her room. When she wakes up, I make her lie down, and we talk about silly things. Or I read to her. Jim and I don't discuss it.

◉

Yesterday, Abby got her snow day.

I was tired and cranky, and to make matters worse, it was the day of our eye exams.

"Maybe they're there."

"Abby, everything is closed."

"Maybe just the school is closed. You should call. Maybe they're there."

"They called us. They are closed. I have to reschedule our appointments."

"Mom, can you call now and reschedule?"

"ABBY! They're closed! I will call tomorrow. JUST DROP IT!"

She hates to be yelled at. She stiffened and went into Pause Mode.

"ABBY!"

"He's very angry," she said, softly.

"WHO? WHO IS ANGRY?"

"Idunno." She shrugged and ran to her room.

I wanted to curl up into a ball and sleep—or cry—but I knew I should apologize to my daughter. I followed her.

Abby was sitting on her bed, rocking.

"ABBY!"

"Huh."

I took a deep breath and tried to sound cheerful. "I'm sorry I yelled. We have a snow day; let's make the most of it. We'll bake cookies. Brownies. Watch movies. Make mac-and-cheese."

Mac-and-cheese always got her attention.

We spent the day doing all that and anything else I could think of to keep us busy. The whole time, I kept up a stream of happy chatter. No pauses, no rocking, no time to think.

Perky did not come naturally to me. I was exhausted.

◙

Last night, Jim and I took shifts with Abby, two hours to sleep, two hours on watch. I struggled to stay awake during my watches, but I was almost sure I managed it—almost sure there was no rocking.

This morning, there was no real talk in our house, just grunts and monosyllables, the conversation of the sleep deprived—until Abby left for school.

As the bus pulled up, just before she went out the door, she turned to me, grinned that big lopsided grin, and said, "Twyla's birthday party is today. She loves red. Her mom is picking us up. And five is just enough."

The door slammed, and she was gone before I could ask, "Enough for what?"

Satyros Phil Brucato on Lucy Taylor's "Wall of Words"

Lucy Taylor appears to be one of the lost voices in modern horror...which is a damn shame, as she writes with chilling clarity and a gift for messy surprises. I almost nominated the title tale from this collection, but "Wall of Words" won out over that story, thanks to its haunting strangeness. Where "The Flesh Artist" is a grotesque but conventional tale of misogyny and revenge, "Wall of Words" remains indescribable. Though smaller in scope, it reminds me of Clive Barker's "In the Hills, The Cities"...not because of its subject matter but because of its nightmarish take on ordinary life. *The Flesh Artist* holds a place of honor in my collection. If you can find a copy of this book, by all means, grab it...and please tell Lucy I said hello! — *"Wall of Words" Lucy Taylor, from The Flesh Artist, Silver Salamander Press, 1994.*

◎◎◎

Clown Balloons

Satyros Phil Brucato

The floor at my feet is littered with clown-balloon corpses. Bright rubber screams into nightmare shapes. My ears ring. My wrists throb. This is my damnation, to twist and strangle rubber 'til my brain runs dry.

It isn't working, though. I'm running out of balloons.

◎

I may have been eight when the clown first appeared, a looming bright Satan against a sea of children. Flies buzzed lazy in the summer heat, but if the clown felt dizzy in his painted prison, it

229

didn't show. He laughed instead and did magic tricks, his face swollen and flat behind red-slashed masking.

Marcie Meyers, the Birthday Girl, flounced about, all pink and pretty, but it seemed like the clown was intent on me.

My world tilted. I recall that much. Sickness bloomed in my belly, greasy-sweet from too much cake. The birthday-hat elastic bit into my chin and throat. I wanted the bathroom. I wanted to go home. I nearly wet my pants when the clown leapt suddenly from the bushes, scattering children in a screeching herd.

Laughing harder, he beckoned us back…and trusting, we returned to him. The Birthday Parents beamed and reassured us as the clown went back to work. The other children giggled and clustered beside him. I held back, though, sniffling. His laughter held tiny screams just for me.

I stood apart. Is that why he had watched me?

I didn't need to see his eyes to know that he watched me. The feeling was clear enough. His eyes burned my skin like sunburn, prickled like peroxide on a scrape. When I dared a glance, our eyes met and locked. He seemed to giggle, then, but that may have been my imagination.

Then he fetched his balloons, and it all grew worse.

I didn't want to be there. To be watching. To be caught. I didn't want to see him pull things from nowhere, to see the sun glare on bright baggy clothes. To feel flaming eyes set on black-rimmed white—eyes that scurried over me like roaches. I tried to brush that gaze away.

"*Timmy!*" cried Birthday Mom. "Don't touch yourself there! It isn't nice!"

"Can I go inside?" I begged, or something like it. "I gotta…"

"I see," she said, and she led me by the hand. But she *didn't* see. Not really. The clown did, though. I caught him smiling at me as we went inside.

When we came back from the bathroom, I heard balloons scream. I wanted to stay inside, but she wouldn't let me. She said it was time to have fun, time to laugh, time to play. Marcie wanted all her friends to be there, and I didn't want to miss the *clown*, did I?

How little we recall kid fears.

He caught my eye as I came out through the door. He'd been waiting for my return. At the middle of the yard, he tortured two balloons in his white-gloved hands, much to the other children's delight.

I winced as tiny screams broke me into goosebumps. My friends didn't notice, but I did. Dancing Marcie held a balloon-beast in her eager hands. Bruce and Katrina did, too. The clown gave his weeping balloons a final, vicious twist, then handed the result toward me.

It was hideous.

The clown was a master of his art. His creations were bent and broken things, agonizingly alive. The balloon-beasts quivered and mewled. Wet eyes pleaded for release. The one in Marcie's hands looked worst of all.

I wanted to puke.

So I did.

It took forever 'til Mom showed up to take me home. I burned as the other kids laughed. Even the clown seemed amused. I wished he'd stop looking at me! On the ground at his feet, balloon-things writhed. The clown smirked as he squashed one beneath his oversized shoe. It squealed before it burst. Bright blood spattered the white of his pants. Why didn't anyone see it but me? And still, he brought freakish things to life, handing them out like treats. Like sacrifices. He seemed to sneer beneath his paint as he wrenched pathetic beasts from garish rubber. That grin promised similar treatment to me.

Later.

I still felt him watching me as Mom came to take me home. Marcie never forgave me for puking blue birthday cake at her party.

The clown came to see me that night in my dreams. Red, wet, sticky dreams smelling of greasepaint.

◎

Bruce Taylor called me "Party Puker." Katrina Watkins called me "Timmy Toilet-Face." Marcie called me things I never expected from a girl, and Gary Bright did a lunchtime impression of me that got him sent to Mr. Jordan's office. I was out-cast all that month, and it would be a long time before anyone invited me to a birthday party again.

I still can't eat cake, even now.

It wasn't over, though. There was more.

I was in my backyard, pitching dirt clods at my G.I. Joes a week later or so, when I heard the squeak of rubber behind me.

"I *know* you want a balloon, Timmy."

Nobody saw the clown with me, then. Nobody saw his hands on me. His eyes. His blazing white suit. I didn't scream or cry or run away. I could see the sweat sheen on greasepaint as he held me close. The whisker-tips beneath it. His hot clown suit smelled unwashed against the pine-needle scene of my back yard.

I recall a finch feeding worms to her children that day.

◉

In high school, I could never come through. I graduated virginal, not quite a man. I'd go out on dates, sure, but when things got close the smell of greasepaint turned me small and useless for the night. Word spread between the girls by my junior year. I didn't date again 'til college. My girlfriends, though, couldn't hear the squeak of rubber in my room back home. I didn't share that part of me at all.

The clown, I'd soon learned, had passed his gift of creation on to me that back-yard afternoon. Now *I* could make animals, too. I hid balloons underneath my bed, and when I returned from dates with Jane or Alexa or Sherri or Mo, I'd dig out the bag and blow up and twist balloons until the skin pulled back beneath my nails and my head swam dizzily. Then I'd put the suffering things out of their misery with a pin, muffling their bursting bodies with my pillow before I slept.

I didn't want to do clown things.

◉

Once, in college, feeling brave, I dropped some acid. Big mistake. The room soon filled with balloons and the laughter of clowns. Colored light crawled across the walls like blood. My feet brushed the bones of long-dead children as the clown stood, laughing, at the center of the room and blew bubbles shaped like heads.

Balloon-creatures writhed, broken, at his feet.

All around me, stoned girls watched my eyes and giggled when I met their gaze. My friends weren't *really* my friends, it seemed. I stared at the floor to avoid their eyes.

I just wanted my balloons.

"I know you *really* want to be a clown, Timmy," said the bubble-blowing trickster. I don't think he was right, but back then, I wasn't sure.

"Hey, Tim," said a soft voice. Gypsy Alison, from my chem class. She took my hand in her own warm one. "Let's get you some air," she offered. "It's kinda close in here." I didn't disagree.

Outside, we walked hand-in-hand as dying stars fell to the wet cement. Branches shook with nighttime wind. Our clothes clung, tight in drizzling rain. We brushed damp hair from one another's faces as we kissed beneath a streetlight.

The next time I recall seeing Gypsy Alison, she covered her face and ran away from me. When I saw the clown again shortly afterward, he looked pleased. Although I never learned what else happened that night, I also never touched acid again.

I made many balloon-things on my wedding night. My new wife Helen never saw them. I went outside and popped them in an alley while she slept. If the clown was there then, I didn't see him.

I see him a lot now, though. At the edges of my sight, he waves at me. I buy plenty of balloons and then fashion horrors to make him go away. Sometimes, I miss pieces of them when I'm cleaning up. Helen finds them and wonders where the rubber scraps come from. I haven't dreamed up a good enough lie.

"I know you really want to be a *clown*, Timmy," he insists. No matter how far away he stands, I smell rancid greasepaint, sweat, and birthday cake. My fingers ache, stained and stinking of cheap balloon rubber.

Helen keeps to her side of the bed now, watching me with chilly eyes. Maybe I should have told her about greasepaint and pine needles. If I had, she might not look at me that way.

I *should* tell her, but I can't anymore. It's too late. Things have changed. The clown leers from every shadowed corner, now.

Maybe I should tell Helen that I'm running out of balloons.

But I can't.

So I sit in my den, surrounded by gasping shapes wrung from rubber, nightmares that look at me with glistening eyes. It's late out, too late to buy balloons. The clown's shadow falls across my shoulder. He brings the taste of sweet sugar cake and the tang of pine needles, and he's chuckling.

Only two balloons left. Two balloons between me and my young son's bedroom door.

Please help me, God.

I really don't want to do clown things.

Rob M. Miller on Monica J. O'Rourke's "Jasmine & Garlic"

Buckets-of-blood stories are often derivative, not particularly scary, and even silly. But when quality meets gore, the results can be incredible. During 2001, at the World Horror Convention in Seattle, Washington, I met Monica J. O'Rourke, an incredible woman, who was gracious enough to spend time with a young developing writer. Soon after, Monica shared with me a preview of her short "Jasmine & Garlic," a riveting piece of extreme horror that can be accessed on Smashwords. Monica's story, since my first read, has ever since served as a template when it comes to putting together an in-your-face piece of disturbed and disturbing fiction. With more than a hundred published shorts and a number of books, Monica's been a long-standing staple in the horror community, but still almost an undiscovered gem. Her work's primed to explode with a whole new crop of readers.

I Am Victim

Rob M. Miller

THE ALLEY WAS TYPICAL. It sat long, dark, and bleak, collapsed underneath a cloud-filled, soot-covered night's sky, from the air looking like an elongated, straight-lined incision—an infected cut.

Trash bins, syringes, and probably a billion cigarette carcasses—not to mention the dog-*and-whatever-else*-shit—filled its entire length.

Past the first fifteen feet, no clear line of sight could be made into its depths, and no vehicle had any hope of penetrating its maze.

Piss and mud puddles, along with scattered patches of broken glass sat as anti-personnel mines warning off all pedestrians. The city must've forgotten about the place, as it had so many others, as if the lofty urban-managers in power had simply said, "Screw it."

Or, perhaps the owners of the buildings sharing the alley's borders hadn't paid the waste bill in the past thirty-or-so years…say since 2003, preferring to have their own pseudo land-fill in closer proximity.

Noise came from the alley-adjacent sidewalk and street: blaring horns, curses, flirtations, whore-hounding pimps, sirens from futile efforts of succor, as well as the street talk of excited teenagers, full of hope and spunk, feeling foolishly-secure in their burgeoning freedom, as if they were adults…as if they were *really* prepared to take on the night.

No sounds, though, came from the long alley. But if one were to linger, one might start to hear little things: the rustling of Styrofoam blown about by a careless wind; or the mewling, perhaps, of cats in heat; the scampering of vomit-eating rats; and maybe a subtle, subliminal warning of: *Abandon all hope, all ye muthas that would enter.*

◉

He lay limp over the top of an old crate, a rusty nail from the semi-rotted box imbedded painfully in his stomach. Some of his shattered teeth were visible to him on the ground, eerily easy to see in the faint light, looking like the hand-thrown toss of some shaman's bones, enthusiastically prognosticating even more pain to come.

He didn't expect any rescue, knew in fact there would be none.

There never was. Not for him.

Never for him.

What did amaze was how aware he could be. One would think, that with his unique nervous system, with his one-of-a-kind neuro-set of synapses, that he wouldn't feel what was being done. Unfortunately, one would be wrong. He felt it *all*.

True, he kept a certain sense of distance, but just enough for him to function, a kind of omni-awareness that couldn't be described. Sufficient to say, *nothing* escaped his notice: not the crying children of Borneo and not the piece of scum masturbating as he watched the show.

His show.

"Don't quit," a young curly-haired man called from where he leaned against a brick wall. "Make him squeal...make him fuckin' beg and squeal."

"I don't think this piece-of-shit can talk," an Italian-looking greasy-haired youth called back. "Hell, I'm gettin' tired of workin' the bastard." He glanced at the broken, wickedly-pointed broom-handle in his hand, threw it down, then started massaging his aching forearm, all the while watching the body-slimed piece of wood as it rolled into a goopy pile of oily-looking water.

Then, with a disgusted look on his face, and with an award-winning amount of boisterous hawking, he spat out a sizeable blob of phlegm onto the broken man's back.

Curly nodded in approval at his friend's display of contempt. Then an idea hit, one fostered by anger and the throbbing bulge in his pants.

"Fucking piece of garbage. Hold his goddamned head up. He looks thirsty."

"Got it, meego," Greasy answered. Reaching down, he seized the toy's hair and snatched his head up.

Still, he wasn't satisfied. He hadn't made the man beg; he'd only broken his body. The meat's glassy-looking eyes said so. "Get ready for a splashing, you fucking freak."

Curly was ready. He'd wasted no time moving to the front of the freak's held-up head.

"Yeah, baby, I'm buildin'...I'm geeet...t...t...tin' reeaddy...yeah, that's it. Ohhh, yeah." Though the *smack-smack-smack* of his beating, pounding hand echoed weakly throughout the alley, it was more than audible enough for the both of them to enjoy, the freak, too, if he wasn't totally lost in shock.

Greasy couldn't help himself.

He fell into his friend's cock-beating rhythm, jerking the toy's head in tandem. "Yeah, that's it, STAIN! Get ready. It's commin' to the top. Cummin' for YOU." Greasy—in time to the humiliation—banged the man's head on the crate.

"Ohhh...baby...yeah!" Curly felt himself building. *Soon. Any second.* "Fu...fuck...fuckin' CHRIST." Curly, eyes glazed with hate, let fly a massive glob of hot-load jism all over the man's face.

"You son-of-a-bitchin' dog," Greasy yelled, half-dropping half-slamming the toy's head. "You got some on my hand. You, ASSHOLE."

"Don't get mad. Friend's got to share, right?" Curly laughed as he packed his tool away.

Greasy wiped his hand on what was left of the toy's tattered T-shirt.

"What the flying-fuck is wrong with this guy, anyway?"

Greasy stood with a stupid *I-dunno* look on his face.

They didn't get it.

Usually when they went to have a good time, they knew they were going to be in for some *real* choice-cut begging.

But not from this guy.

Not from the moment they'd first jumped him.

They'd been eye-balling his ass for a couple of days, seeing him around the hood, periodically talking with people, or they with him. Asking for chits and shit, they'd guessed.

Just being a bum wouldn't have necessarily caught their attention. There were plenty of those. They'd *had* plenty of those, along with others, more up-scale, that they'd used...rolled, murdered.

This guy had been just right.

Made for them somehow.

Deserving.

A freak.

From the moment they'd seen the man's albino skin, their wheels had started turning. Then, when they had gotten closer and seen the rest, the guy's fate had been sealed.

The man's eyes were colorless, and he had scars all over his face and hands, jagged, torturous lines that criss-crossed themselves, almost like a spider-web, as if he were some kind of savage from New Zealand or something. Weird. The world didn't need freaks like that.

Snatching his ass had simply been a matter of timing.

"Maybe he's mental," Greasy offered, lazily walking around, pacing in a half-moon circuit, looking at the silent, dying piece of freak-shit before him.

"Don't know. Maybe. He's sure as hell something..." Curly paused a moment letting his last word trail off. Then louder: "Probably right. Just off somewhere, gone in his mind. Sailing on a lake or something."

"Maybe so. But not for long. I got something for him. Gonna be sailing down to Hell in a minute." Greasy unzipped his pants.

"You gotta be shittin' me. Whatcha think you're doing, anyway?"

"What's it look like? You had yours, now I'm gonna have mine."

Curly stared, hands crossed, with a thin, wicked grin. "Go for it, bud."

Greasy glared at the man's bared buttocks. He couldn't really see the man's anus. Not enough light. Just a bit from the lone glow-globe they had brought and stuck on the side of a battered, low-hanging fire-escape.

What he could see wasn't pretty. Just fun. He had worked the albino over pretty good with the broom-handle, jagged, splintered edge leading the way, shoving it in-and-out with a fervor that had surprised even him. The damage had been a kick. He'd seen it, done it, many times before: chunks of meat coming out, blood-soaked, shit-smelling—fun.

But with this guy, he'd felt something else.

Anger.

He didn't know why. Strange. But his lust was afire, could hardly wait to stick it to this guy...in him. Teach the motherfucker his place.

Greasy shoved down his baggy pants. He never wore underwear. Then, as an afterthought, he said, "Check the guy's pockets. Maybe he's got a rubber."

"Done." Curly fumbled through the pockets of the large Army field-jacket he wore, that he'd taken from the toy when they'd jumped him only a half-hour earlier. "Nada, bud. But hold a minute, will ya?"

"What for?"

"This, meego," Curly said, pulling out a small baggie from his khakis. "This shit here," Curly pointed with his chin at his buddy's stiff wood, then at the toy's ass, "is too fuckin' wild to watch straight."

"Gimme some of that," Greasy said before breaking out in a short-stepping shuffle toward his friend, his body moving carefully to not trip over the pants around his ankles. Getting to his bud, he held up a fist, thumb-side up.

Curly poured the contents onto Greasy's index finger.

"Nothing like a little BLUE to get you pumpin'."

"No shit." Greasy bobbed his head to a silent cadence as he moved the powder around in some semblance of a line. He was glad he couldn't smell anymore. Made alleys like that bearable. But thank God, he could still suck-it-up. "Yeahhh. Now that's the shit." He snorted the blue-colored crystal-powder up his ruined nose. "Whoooo!" he yelled, immediately feeling the stuff hit his system with all the damn strength that made it the rave-of-the-age.

"Mother-fucking-awesome!" Curly yelled, finishing his own snort. "Now go and get it on, baby. Let the Greeking commence."

Greasy shuffled back to the toy, stared at the mess he'd made, and spat. "Fuck. I'm going to end up ballin' a cheek. What a mess." Bending down, he pulled a clip-it blade from his pant's pocket and flicked it open. *Snap.* Standing, he grabbed a hunk of the toy's T-shirt and stuck his blade in. A few cuts later, he held a swatch of dirty cotton and quickly worked to daub some of the goop, just enough to make the way clear.

"Careful now. Don't want to catch nothing."

"So fuckin' what," Greasy answered, slicking his cock with some spittle. "Somethin' starts burnin', I'll just go down to the clinic and get a nice dose of one-shot-cures-all."

Watching his partner getting into his work, and with the BLUE really kicking in, Curly's heart started to pound, and he felt his own 'Charlie' coming back on the rise. There was something strange about watching the toy getting *it.* They had really torn the man up, and they weren't done. But it was like…like nothing they could do would be enough. Something about this dude just sparked him off, made something inside him want to hurt the bastard more and more.

Curly's mouth salivated as he enjoyed the show. *What a jump,* he thought. He felt his heart beating like a hammer in his BLUE-charged penis. *I think I'm gonna have to get a piece of that.*

◉

He could feel what was being done to his body. Could feel it in all its dark-praising glory—all its pain. That was his job, his charge, and yet, he was still distant. He wondered for a moment what was happening. Internal bleeding, obviously. His insides were all ripped, torn, and gouged. Infection, too, from that dirty mini-spear shoved up him, plus his own mixed-in fecal matter, were already spreading their poison . He felt his life-juice leaking on the inside, as well as all the places where it was coming out of him...coating his legs, helping to lubricate the asshole's thing in a ménage-à-trois of blood, flesh, and shit.

He took note, automatically recording every grunt from the panting pig behind him...in him. Every grunt.

Then he started to spasm, his body choking out, gagging on something. *What now? Oh, my shattered teeth.* How could he have forgotten those? *Must've let my mind wander.* But to where...Calcutta? Bonn? Tokyo? Someplace more local perhaps? Oregon, maybe. To the woman getting raped, almost as violently as he, a mere five hundred yards away, in some nasty little apartment-cube? To her baby, screaming in the background, soiled, laying on a blanket, wondering what was happening? His only diversion: a bottle of sour milk waiting to make his little day.

He felt it all.

ALL.

That was his job. And it was a full day's work. To feel it all, to remember all the pains of the past, as well as the pains being administered in the present. And he did...every stripe, every wail, every burning, pleading scream that had ever escaped a human throat...every fallen tear, every word-cut heart. It was all in him. It was him.

He *was* PERSONIFICATION.

His cicatrix made sure of it, a series of lines that was his personal harrow-of-record, marking him with their all too-visible web. They made him look like a savage, like some freaked-out worshipper of Barker's Pinhead. Scars, channeling all the sorrow to the pinpoint needling of nerves, mercifully unreadable to the humans who looked at them and thought *him* to be some vile thing.

The *rat-a-tat-tat* of flesh-butchering ammunition rippled through his guts, every moment of every day. And gagging, that suffocating feeling, the terror...of...of smoke, black and thick, acrid, mercilessly substituting itself as air, incinerating his lungs as he felt...what so many...what *so* many had felt during the sacking of Troy, the nightmare of Masada.

Buchenwald.

He felt it all.

Spears, swords, and knives...piercing his body from the battles of Arbela, Syracuse, Thermoplæ. Maces and clubs smashing his skull. The sharpened-edge that had pierced and opened so many pregnant, begging mothers…in Egypt, in Bethlehem.

When he willed it, he could focus, feel it happen, as if it were *now*, the looking up in terror at the dark savage sun as his heart was ripped from its housing, then offered high as a visceral sacrifice.

Laser blasts sliced him, self-cauterizing dismemberment, leaving him drawn-and quartered, with not a molecule of air left in his body during Moon War I.

Dresden lived within. Bataan. The known and unknown victims of the Cold War.

Gettysburg.

And every word. Every cutting remark, bold-faced lie, and heart-wrecking plea.

He could hear them in his mind, every damned second of every cursed day-and-night. Words. Torturous words. As painful in their own right as the race-cleansing gas of Dachau. They all reverberated in his thoughts, from tormentor and victim, demanding remembrance. Awaiting the Great Day.

I was only joking, I didn't really want to dance with you, you're ugly…You fucking bitch-whore-cunt…Please, daddy, please. My head hurts; don't hit me again…I don't care what you say, it's not my baby…Don't worry; you're only being re-located…Depends on your definition of is…trust me…I'm sorry, I'm sorry. I won't cheat again…Pleeease don—don—don't kill me…THERE IS NO GOD.

Every lying treatise dwelled within…every filthy Dear-John-Dear-Jane letter, every evil bull written, every duplicitous I'll-be-working-late-don't-wait-up phone message…every evil radio transmission, every computer- typewriter- morse-generated lie…they were all etched into his very being.

He was faithful. He kept the record within. He was, in truth, the Great Ledger, the Maker's personal walking, talking, *feeling* book of accounts.

After all the ages, one haunting question still nagged.

Why?

It was a foolish question. One for which there was no answer, save to the Searcher-of-Hearts.

Why do people do this to one another? Wasn't it enough that man had to face natural death? Enough they could get sick? That they toiled—just to eat?

A foolish question.

He remembered having it when he'd seen the rivers, the endless rivers of tears cascading down the face of Adam as he wailed out his sorrow to the Everlasting.

He remembered having it before even then. About his own kind. When he'd fought against his brothers after they'd dared to follow the beautiful one.

What waste.

Why?

Certainly, part of the reason behind man's folly, was the other side. Locusts, flies, lying-birds, scorpions—*devils*. They helped to cause so much, like what they have done...*are* doing, working *within* Curly and Greasy, the gloating fiends.

Still—there was no excuse.

Man could resist.

One day, there would be an accounting and a reckoning. Man had been warned: "Forget not to show love unto strangers: for thereby some have entertained angels unawares."

Some did far worse than entertain.

◉

"Ready for a smoke?" Greasy asked.

"Yeah, well...maybe another hit of BLUE." Looking down, Curly grimaced. He was a mess. Gore soaked. "I'm kinda grossed out. You didn't say our 'girl' here was split."

"A little pay-back s'all...fer shootin' your squirt on my hand." Pulling out a pack of Black Jack 5s, Greasy packed 'em down hard. "Better leave the BLUE alone for now. Too much of that nitro, and we'll be about as assed-out as this motherfucker."

"Fine." Curly glanced at the messy heap strewn-out on the ground.

"Hey, ya hear something?" Greasy asked just after tearing open his new pack of cigs.

"Think I did. Fucker's still alive! Think he's saying something." Curly moved to the crumpled pile on the ground.

Curly was immediately joined by his friend, the both of them bending down, leaning close to hear what was coming from the ruined man's devastated mouth.

They were right.

The toy was speaking, repeating something. A message that sounded like—

"'Why?' Is that what this pigshit's saying? 'Why?'"

"Sounds like it, meego," Greasy chuckled in answer.

"Why? MOTHERFUCKER. I'll tell you why. Because we can. That's why." Curly spat out the words. *Why?* The question freaked him out somehow. Gave him the creeps. Made him feel…as if he'd…done something wrong.   Who'd this piece of shit think he was, anyway? *Why?*

"Can't believe this fucker's still alive. After all we've done…well fuckin' goddamn-it-to-Shirley, this sonuvabitch is tough. I'll tell you wha—" Greasy stopped. His buddy wasn't paying attention, just stood, staring at the lump with some kind of strange look on his face. Greasy called out, good and loud: "HEY!"

"Yeah, man," Curly answered. "I hear ya. Fuck this white-ass-piece-of-whipped-shit." Curly would never in this life know that the man lying before him could see the telltale sparkle in his eyes, his friend's eyes, the sign of devils within.

"What do you want to do? Kill him?" As if by magic, Greasy's clip-it was again in-hand, its serrated edge looking raw and hungry.

"Already done that," Curly answered. "Just a matter of time." Then, looking down and feeling again that strange compulsive urge to inflict, he said, "Go ahead and take out his eyes."

Greasy nodded, smiling.

◎

The nameless OPEN-24-HOURS restaurant was small and cozy. A little dirty at first glance, but that was a lie. The place was just old, and like many old things, its parts were stained and marred, a bit ragged about the edges. But it was relatively clean. He hoped to find out what the food tasted like—and soon.

It had been a rough night, one not without its sense of irony. He never really got any rest, never experienced a moment's peace. After a ravishing, however, for what seemed like the barest flicker of time, he often did feel better.

It had something to do with the re-knitting of himself.

He briefly ran his tongue over his teeth. They felt firm, strong and secure, and new. So unlike how they had just hours before, when they'd been broken after catching that two-by-four.

He remembered dying, if it could be called that. Then awakening, feeling his fluids flowing back into his body, his flesh re-establishing itself, eyes reforming, the *crackle-pop-crackle* of his bones as they re-meshed and went back into the right sockets, everything moving as if under the guiding hands of an all-mighty sculptor, which really, was the truth.

The re-vitalized feeling was a token of the Promise, a refutation of the evil he had to endure, for now.

His clothes were different, had just been on him when he had come-to. Old-looking frayed jeans now covered skinny legs. Dirt-encrusted boots that had seen better days were now on his feet, and an old, plain-blue T-shirt, covered over with a heavily-stained red-flannel long-sleeve, dressed his torso.

The clothes were the usual. Like he'd always worn, garments meant for the day-and-times, region and climate he found himself in. The only thing that ever set his attire apart as being noticeable was their poverty-stricken look.

And then the only oddities that marked *him* as being different from the rest of the world's poor, were his eyes and albino-skin, and naturally, his scars. His hair, always thin, always silver in color, often changed its style after a ravishment: going from long to short, curly to straight. Today it was long and drawn back, tied into a ponytail by a dirty rubber-band he'd found in the alley.

What he had discovered, ages ago, was that people didn't remember him much after he'd left their presence. Something for the best. Most of his work was impersonal, absorbing the terrible blows the world-over, and never forgetting one jot or one tittle of any dark deed done. But, like last night, he also suffered personal attacks, personal assaults of cruelty. His bad brothers, devils all, got a kick out of it.

"Can I help you?" The waitress stood beside his table, face full of contempt. She had taken her time coming, more'n-likely hoping he'd just give up and leave. Time was on the outer edges of morning; there were hardly any people present, a family or two, a few truckers. He'd been kept waiting for an hour. He would remember.

"Biscuits-and-gravy, please." Looking at the girl's face, he could see himself in her eyes: ugly, scar-marked, bizarre in his albino flesh and no-color eyes. Beneath her.

He could also *see* her: Christian, by profession, twenty-something, married, and screwing everything in sight, all the while telling her hubby that his fears were just in his head. He could feel her husband's wounded heart. It tore him.

"Comin' right up."

He knew it would be. She'd want him out of here—quick.

Glancing out the window from his booth, he watched the trees, the birds in the air, tried to focus on his environment, tried not to let his mind wander. He didn't want to internalize just yet. Since his re-knitting, he'd felt a bit good. Horribly good, his body freshly touched by the Great Lord. But within, it was all still there, an open raw wound, with salt aplenty, constantly poured on. He could feel it all—locally, globally…historically, everything but the future.

That was always fresh.

A poor good-hearted cop, just shot dead, so some kid could join a neighborhood crew. A corpse-loving mortuary-worker having his way with a poor widower's wife, hours before the funeral, thinking nobody would ever know.

But he knew.

It was torture.

He could do nothing about any of it. Not yet. All he could do was watch, know, record—and *feel*.

The pain racked him. But he would bear it. It was his charge, after all. But he didn't want to. Not now. He wanted to enjoy what few moments of slight reprieve were left to him.

Breathing in, he enjoyed the wafting smells of the restaurant: the bacon, the grits, the eggs, T-bone steaks, and…all the rest. Even the subtlest of the restaurant's smells were there for him to enjoy: the spicy, biting scent of Tabasco, the morning-smell of coffee, and the fruity-tangy aroma of ketchup.

He focused best he could and tried to ignore the whore-killing truck driver at the end of the counter, all covered in demon-stink.

He failed.

It was bound to happen, did in fact, most every day. The other side liked to taunt him, rub in his lot.

He stared at the large-bellied, dark-hearted, dark-filled man.

And saw it.

A sparkle in the man's eyes, a sparkle recently seen. *Checking up on me,* he thought.

He could see the waitress heading his way, coming out the kitchen, behind where the truck driver sat, biscuits-and-gravy at-hand.

He'd been right; they'd worked up his order good and fast.

The truck driver, or rather what he was packing inside, gave him a knowing-grin, then toasted him with his coffee.

"The Lord rebuke thee," he whispered. *For now.*

For a moment, the driver looked blank-faced, then turned back to his grits, completely unaware of his actions a moment before.

"Here's your chow," the waitress said, voice flat, hands putting his food down hard on the table.

"Thank you."

The waitress didn't give the expected you're-welcome. Instead, she just walked away.

He ate with a gusto rarely experienced. It wasn't that he was starved, though he always felt that way. It was more from simply wanting to enjoy a breakfast.

Too soon, he was finished and standing at the register. He wasn't concerned about paying for the meal. Somehow he always had the right amount needed, the exact amount to keep his body going.

Reaching into a pocket, he pulled out a few dirty bills and some coins and set them on the counter. He knew the pile would precisely meet the bill.

"Anything else we can do?" the waitress asked from behind the register.

"How about one of those mints?" he asked, pointing at a small box of Peppermint Patties. He knew he wasn't going to get one, but he clung to the thin-hope anyway. Sometimes, he felt he needed more than just what it took to keep his body moving. Sometimes, he felt a treat would be nice, would be like ambrosia to his lips and tongue.

"You can read the sign, mister. A quarter a piece."

"Too bad. I'm tapped."

"We all have it tough."

"Hey, sir."

Turning around, he saw a young girl, ten or so, sitting at a booth with her mother. *Ahhh! How sweet,* he thought. He could sense the child's goodness. It flowed out of her like spring water.

"Yes, little lady?" he said, going to bended knee.

The girl got up and came over. He could see her mother watching with a wise and wary eye. He sniffed a breath of her goodness, as well, and knowing what he looked like, wasn't offended by her suspicion.

247

"Hi, my name's Tara. What's yours?"

"I am Victim."

"That's a funny name."

"So is Tara. Do you know what Tara means?"

"No."

The girl looked sweet as could be standing in her summer-print dress. "It means 'Tower.'"

"Really? My mother says the Lord is my high-tower."

"Does she now?"

"Anyway, I couldn't help but overhear that you're short a quarter. That you wanted a mint."

"That's right, little one."

"Well, today is your day. I happen to have a quarter."

The girl stood tall and proud, holding her hand out, quarter between two grace-filled fingers.

Glancing at the mother, he saw her smile and give an OK-nod, and he took it. It was the best thing he'd received in a long, long time.

"Thank you very much, dear lady."

"You're welcome." The girl smiled and stole a quick glance back at her mother, saw the still-young woman mouth to her, "Go-ahead; it's okay." The girl turned back. "I want you to know…" she hesitated, some shyness taking hold.

"Yes?" he asked, heart melting.

"I just wanted you to know that Jesus loves you. For you to not ever, ever forget." Happy with herself: for her message, her kindness, her bravery…for doing something good and for making her mother smile, she scampered back to her table.

He stood up, heart breaking with joy. He faced the waitress, grabbed a mint, and held up his new quarter between thumb and finger. "Here."

"Big-man had to take the little girl's money, huh?"

"Yes," he said, hardly able to restrain a hearty laugh.

The born-again adulteress, with folded arms, stared. If she'd been able to look any further down her nose, she'd be looking at her own tits.

Ignoring her, he turned around and walked to the mother and daughter sitting at the table.

"Hello, I won't be a moment," he said to the mother.

"Take your time," she returned.

He looked at the girl. "Tara, you know what you told me?"

"Yes."

"I wanted to say that I know. I *do* know. And I will never, never forget. I promise."

"I won't either," she answered, smile beaming.

"You two have a wonderful day."

◉

The parting pleasantries had been nice, but short. He moved to leave the table, and the restaurant. He rarely engaged in conversation with people, and when he did, he kept it brief. He had work to endure. He did notice, however, that the truck driver was nowhere in sight.

Good.

As he left the restaurant, he glanced into the heavens, far beyond the morning blue-sky, and said under his breath, "Thank you."

He knew his lot was hard. That was why he'd been chosen. The Great One had known he'd be faithful.

It was a hard lot, to stand by—to just watch and feel and remember.

There were Guardians, and they did what they could, sometimes able to strike back into the heart-of-darkness. But his task was different. He had to stand...and take it, to take it all, and never strike back.

It was hard.

But there was the Promise.

And that, he held dear to. Will it be today? Tomorrow? Another hundred, thousand, ten thousand years? He didn't know. Only that it would come to pass.

He used to have a different name, a long time ago. A beautiful name. Unpronounceable by the human tongue. He missed it.

He walked across the near-empty parking lot, direction picked by instinct. It didn't really matter where he went. But, he was thankful. He'd been touched by his Lord, allowed to experience, even if so fleetingly...*goodness*.

Looking about at nothing in particular—he spoke. He spoke to remind himself, he spoke in gratitude, spoke to spite evil. "For those who have, and who will be redeemed, there will one day, be rest. For all others, though, there *will* be me.

"Now…today…I am Victim. But one day, *when* the Word returns, my name *will* change again. And let those who have delighted in their evil tremble.

"For then, I *will* be…Vengeance."

More *Deep Cuts* Recommendations

Our slush pile contained a number of gems in the form of recommendations we loved. We'd be cheating our readers if we didn't include them, especially since the writers put so much thought into them. We hope you find it in yourself to unearth and read all these horror stories by women writers.

—Editors

◉

Fifteen years ago, I read **Lisa Tuttle's "The Extra Hour"** in Peter Crowther's *Destination Unknown*, and it's stuck with me ever since, informing both my fiction and my daily life. Whenever I think I just need a little more time in the day, or a bubble on the side of reality where I can do my own thing without guilt or disruption, or a place where I can take a hell of a long nap without losing an ounce of time in real life, I think of that story—which means I think of it *every single day*. I re-read "The Extra Hour" just now, and discovered that in the years since I'd last read it, the ending had changed. (And maybe it had: I'd left it to its own devices, tucked away in that anthology. A lot of time has passed out here.) Everything that I had loved about it was still there, though. The concept is pure in its simplicity: a woman, craving more hours in the day, finds a magical room in which she can have all the hours she needs. There is a crafted, subtle timelessness to the prose and setting that perfectly suits the subject matter. The voice of the narrator is beacon-clear and absorbs attention at the outset. The story is a fantasy gone foul, but even when life in the magic room starts to get horrific, it's still so beguiling to me. It's just such an easy, but profound, "what if" scenario, and such a pleasure to read.

—Mehitobel Wilson

I discovered **Ann Radcliffe** by accident when I picked up an anthology titled *The Witches Brew*, containing **"The Haunted Chamber."** After reading her work, I wanted to write like she did. Upon further research, I discovered Ann Radcliffe's style had influenced other writers such as Mary Shelley, Baudelaire, and H.P. Lovecraft. Her way with description and the supernatural showed me those elements missing in my own work. It's no wonder she's hailed as the Mother of Gothic Fiction. Ann Radcliffe's ability to infuse an aura of romanticism into scenes of terror leaves me in awe. Her works contain little physical horror as she relies on the supernatural. This style is similar to my own in that I prefer to describe the shadow, which can be far more frightening than the monster itself.

—Hollie Snider

I came across the story **"Green Thumb"** by **Nancy Kress** in a collection entitled *Terrors*. What struck me most about it was how Kress managed to keep a reader simultaneously curious and on edge at every point. She accomplished this by keeping the events strange and disturbing but also mysterious. The reader was given just enough of a glimpse into the twisted central character to know he was engaged in a seemingly ordinary hobby for rather unordinary purposes, but the exact nature of both his hobby and his motives weren't revealed until a scene towards the end. Yet, the most horrifying surprise took place after the primary mystery of the story was revealed. There's an unforeseeable twist that completely changes the reader's perspective on all the events preceding it. "Green Thumb" is a frightening and very original horror story that is well worth seeking out.

—Kelly Chase

Almost a decade ago, I read **"The Quest for Blank Claveringi"** by **Patricia Highsmith** for the first time. I ran across this incredible story in the anthology *Masterpieces of Terror and the Supernatural*, edited by Marvin Kaye. Highsmith, perhaps best known for her gripping five-novel crime series about the murderer Tom Ripley, penned "Claveringi" mid-career, in 1967.

The story remains one of my all-time favorites. For writers, it is an unforgettable lesson that an antagonist's danger has more to do with how relentlessly she (or it) pursues her goal than with her natural attributes or the advantages of her species. For readers, it's just a damn scary story.

—Chandler Kaiden

Lyn Venable scared us, not with monsters or magic, serial killers or super-science. She scared us with *ourselves*. With only a handful of published stories to her credit between 1952 and 1957, she nevertheless has a proven record of unsettling, introspective horror perhaps best exemplified in her 1953 masterpiece, **"Time Enough at Last."** In a world where one of the simplest pleasures is finding time to be alone, Venable reminded us that we should enjoy the things we have, rather than dwelling on the things we don't. Originally published in the January 1953 edition of the science fiction magazine *If: Worlds of Science Fiction*, "Time Enough at Last," went on to become one of the earliest (and most highly-regarded) episodes of *The Twilight Zone*.

—Christian Larsen

I recommend the story called **"The Bearded Ones"** by **Felicity Dowker**. It was originally published in a small press anthology from Tasmaniac Publications called *Festive Fear*, and is reprinted in Dowker's debut collection *Bread & Circuses*, from Ticonderoga Publications.

The story showcases Dowker's formidable horror talent, her skill at evoking magic and dread, and her delicious penchant for revenge. "The Bearded Ones" takes seemingly innocuous and commonplace themes, like the joy of Christmas, and peels back its skin to reveal the disturbing flesh beneath that most of us never stop to consider. From the innocence of children to the injustice of being wronged, this story runs the gamut of the human condition. And it will forever change how you feel about Santa Claus.

—Alan Baxter

The horror story by a woman that most influenced my own writing is a wonderful, almost-haunted-house story I discovered in college, **Elizabeth Bowen's "The Cat Jumps."** A modern, cheerfully rational married couple throws a party in their new home, the site of a notorious murder. There are no walking dead in this story, no blood, and no graphic accounts of violence— just deeply disturbing hints, fragments of conversation, and a growing sense of menace. Today, as a middle-aged woman, I am more critical of the story. Bowen seems just a bit too sympathetic to the brutal misogyny it depicts. But "The Cat Jumps" remains the best example I know of an author allowing the readers' own imagination to invoke horror.

—Pamela Troy

I adore the work of **Barbie Wilde**, mostly known for her film and television roles. Her short story **"Sister Cilice"** appeared in the *Hellraiser* themed anthology *Hellbound Hearts*. Wilde rises above the mostly male-penned stories in the collection to provide a touching but altogether very twisted piece. To write a story on the character (a female cenobite) that gave Wilde cult status not only gives that character extra depth, but also shows Wilde's understanding of emotion and desire, two factors that make a good horror tale. For someone whose literary career is now stepping from the shadows of the great Clive Barker, Wilde shows she has a lot to offer readers.

—Daniel I. Russell

The mark of powerful writing is the ability to elicit a physical response from the reader. There are wonderful works that make us laugh or cry or think, but what about those things that just makes you cringe. When a writer can make our stomachs tense, make our bowels clench, send intense shivers slicing through our nervous system—those are the words we remember.

The writing of **Fran Friel** exemplifies this concept, and her flash piece **"Close Shave,"** originally published in *Insidious Reflections* (2006), accomplishes—in less than 300 words—a gut response few writers could match.

—Jonathan H. Roberts

One of my favorite short stories is **"Stillborn"** by **Nina Kiriki Hoffman**, which appeared in *Borderlands*, edited by Thomas E. Monteleone. In it, a boy forms a bond with his mummified little brother against the horribleness of the outside world. Nina's concise, effective prose style ratchets up that disturbing premise to a mind-bending denouement. Using only a thousand words, she reaches off the page, grabs the reader by the throat, and doesn't let go.

—Lee Forsythe

The horror story I'd like to recommend is **"Gestella"** by **Susan Palwick**. It is a haunting story of a rapidly-aging female werewolf and the marriage that deteriorates as quickly as she ages. Tragic and moving, I read this story more than five years ago, but it's one of the few short stories that has lingered in my memory for that long. Fiction usually doesn't make me cry, but this one made me bawl. This is the level of effect I would love to have on my readers. It was originally published in *Starlight 3* by Tor, edited by Patrick Nielsen Hayden.

—David Steffen

Sarah Orne Jewett is a must-read for anyone who appreciates a woman's touch with tales of the supernatural. Her **"The Foreigner,"** first published in *The Atlantic Monthly* (vol. 86, issue 514, August 1900), is a masterpiece of moodiness, both subtly strange and achingly sad, and it lingers in the memory like a ghost. I discovered her in an American literature class, and through studying Jewett I learned how to write supernatural tales of my own. Jewett influenced H.P. Lovecraft, and through him, every horror author since her lifetime.

—Molly Moss

The most riveting horror short story I have ever encountered was **"The Unremembered"** by **Chesya Burke**. I first read the story in Burke's anthology *Let's Play White*, published by Apex Publications. As the African-American mother of a special needs child, the story of Nosipha and her special angel Jeli, brought tears to my eyes. I understand what it is to be in Nosipha's shoes, as the world views your child to be just a brown body, not capable of many feelings, accomplishments, or worth. The thought of watching your baby die, no matter how much relief you know it will bring to her tormented flesh, is truly horrifying. Burke turned a heart wrenching situation into a blessed one, by giving Jeli and her uncooperative body a larger purpose in life, her race and the entire universe.

—Rhonda Jackson Joseph

Tanith Lee was the queen of horror-fairytale mash-ups long before they were trendy. With her short stories and novels alike, all of her fantasy has an air of darkness, and all her horror at least a hint of the mythic. Her work is rife with sensuous demons, terrible monsters, sinister villains and elements of the macabre. I fell in love with her murky writings as a teenager, adoring collections of her twisted fables as *The Gorgon and Other Beastly Tales*. I read each story several times over—**"Anna Medea"** being one of my favourites. She had a definite influence on my own writing, an influence that shows itself every time my stories delve into darkness.

—Chantal Boudreau

I am a fan of stories where the horror is off page and the isolated town becomes more than a setting. Although towns like Dunwich, Dunnett Landing, or Oxrun Station are better known, I return to Tiverton and Sudleigh, rural villages created by regionalist **Alice Brown** (1856-1948). Even in her own lifetime, Brown was underappreciated. Her short story **"Old Lemuel's Journey"** is a ghost story, with time travel and philosophical implications, that first appeared in *Atlantic Monthly*, June 1920. Miserly Lemuel Wood is dying, but he's so cheap that he refuses to pay for any further house calls by the doctor, since it would be a waste of money. He slips into a brief coma, and when he reawakens, the worst has passed and he is healthy with a changed outlook. He claims he saw his future, begging the question: Can a man be haunted by his own future self?

—David Goudsward

One of the most frightening stories I have ever read is **"Where Are You Going, Where Have You Been"** by **Joyce Carol Oates**. While many academics may resist the urge to call Oates a horror writer, the terror and tension she creates on the page and the horrors she hints at that are surely coming just after the story is over are certainly frightening. Heavily anthologized, this gem was collected in *The Vintage Book of Contemporary American Short Stories*, edited by Tobias Wolff. When you're done reading this literary darkness, you will certainly pull your children closer, and make sure the front door is securely locked.

—Richard Thomas

Mary Lavin's brilliant use of dialectic niceties in **"The Green Grave and the Black Grave,"** published in the *Atlantic Monthly*, 1940, had me entranced from the first paragraph. The cadence, syntax, and calculated repetition of the peculiar maritime narrative sets her work apart and affords it a timeless quality missing from many contemporary pieces.

Lavin's story is featured in *Great Irish Stories of the Supernatural* (Pan Books, 1993)—a book I purchased second-hand for a few dollars when the title stopped me dead in my tracks. I simply had to have it. As a lover of speculative fiction, for me, Lavin's particular brand of horror finds its success not in what is shown, but rather in what remains unseen. The poetic banter of Lavin's father-son fishers—and the grisly, yet unsentimental, subject matter—strikes a chord with my macabre desire to guess at what truths the black grave *really* holds.

—Carmen Tudor

"Brazo de Dios" by **Elizabeth Massie**, published in *Borderlands 3* and edited by Thomas F. Monteleone, has stuck with me since I first stumbled upon it in junior high. Weaned on a steady diet of supernatural-based horror in my formative years, Massie's tale rooted in real life terror wasn't the sort of horror I was accustomed to—but I loved it just as much as stories about demonic clowns and French Quarter vampires. In "Brazo de Dios," a young, Christian missionary is abducted by a South American military regime. As the young woman awaits her fate in a dank cell, listening to others being tortured, she contemplates her life and the mysterious man who presides over her capture. Massie's writing and amplification of the human element and all its grey areas pulled me in. In just 15 pages, Massie defined her main character with a richer history and more harrowing "dark night of the soul" than some authors convey in 300 pages.

—Lana Cooper

While I've written in spurts since I was about thirteen, I only decided to try to write and publish horror early last year. January, 2011, I was surfing *Chiaroscuro* e-zine and discovered the story **"Pugelbone"** by **Nadia Bulkin**. The story set a high standard of storytelling craft that I wish to achieve as a writer.

It was macabre and elegant, with a scary visual sensibility like the best of Munsch or Goya—and it reminded me why I love horror. Bulkin's prose created a believable yet darkly fantastic world, while maintaining a deep sympathy for the characters she'd created. It's a wonderful talent, and "Pugelbone" is the kind of story that makes me think "I wish I could write one damn thing that's that GOOD."

—Selene MacLeod

The authors of the anthology, *The Monster's Corner*, were asked to write stories from the monster's point of view. In her story, **"The Screaming Room," Sarah Pinborough** chose Medusa. I loved this story because I found Pinborough's rendering to be completely unexpected. Instead of depicting Medusa as a vicious, man-hating monster, she portrays her as a lonely woman, longing for the arrival of her next lover.

Medusa's reality may be flawed—to her the men are suitors, not enemies, and the sounds they make are songs, not scream. It is a reality full of passion and desire—two things not often associated with Medusa. Pinborough's style is beautifully understated and as sensual as her protagonist's. She engages and tantalizes, making the reader want more. And, to me, this is the mark of a truly exceptional story.

—Meghan Arcuri-Moran

My recommendation is **"Aftermath"** by **Joy Kennedy-O'Neill**, published in *Strange Horizons* February 2012. This is a zombie story with an original slant: the infected are cured and brought back to life. They—and everyone else—have to try and find a way to live with what they did when they were mindless, cannibalistic monsters.

This is an immersive story full of deft, realistic details of a world attempting to recover: radio stations won't play songs like "Love Bites," the ex-zombies smile with closed lips because their teeth are broken from gnawing on bones. The protagonist is desperately trying to get back to normal and to be thankful that she got her husband back, while still mourning her young daughter. The narrative is interspersed with terrifying, claustrophobic flashbacks, and the ending packs a powerful emotional blow, leaving the reader with a truly horrifying image.

—Michelle Ann King

I'll never forget reading **"Calcutta, Lord of Nerves"** by **Poppy Z. Brite** in *Still Dead* in 1992. The mood stuck with me for days. I could taste the air and feel the streets' energy. The story wrapped round all my senses. Yup. Even my sixth sense—the feeling of doom crept inside. Such is the power of perfectly rendered prose. I had to read more of Brite, and grabbed everything in my small town bookstore. I'd found a voice that broke open barriers. It was okay for the characters not to be middle class white guys. These people were imperfect. Lost. Searching. Broken. Soulful. This encouraged me to find my voice and explore new worlds. At the time, "Calcutta, Lord of Nerves" was well esteemed. But that was twenty years ago, and anyone with just the right mindset will fall in love with this timeless story just as I did.

—John Palisano

Sometimes great things come in small packages, as with the story **"Taking Care of Michael"** by **J. L. Comeau**, a sneaky little slice of horror originally published in the anthology *Borderlands 2*, edited by Thomas F. Monteleone. With each word precisely placed to give this flash fiction piece great depth, Comeau weaves a tragic tale of a child left to care for her disabled brother after her mother sits on the couch to watch television and never gets up. This has to be one of the most disturbing stories I have ever read. At no more than two pages long, the visceral images haunted me for days. Depressing, horrific, and dreadful, this story shows us that one does not need gratuitous blood and guts to genuinely shock the reader. This clever, dark tale is what I look for in any collection of fiction. A true gem not to be overlooked.

—Robert Essig

My deep cut is **"Apocalypse Scenario #683: The Box"** by **Mira Grant** (pseudonym of Seanan McGuire). Grant's outstanding *Newsflesh* trilogy (*Feed, Deadline,* and the recently released *Blackout*) is easily my favorite new horror series. I love the fresh take on the zombie theme, where zombie popularlty in pop culture works to prepare everyone when the undead rise for real. I stumbled upon

"Apocalypse Scenario #683: The Box" while anxiously anticipating the release of the last book in the *Newsflesh* trilogy. It tells the story of a group of friends that gather weekly to plot the hypothetical end of the world. The only problem is that one of the group hasn't shown up for a few weeks, and soon everyone is wondering if their innocent get-together might be turning into more than a game. It is a quick gem of a story that is sure to spark some interesting conversations.

—Steven Voelker

Shirley Jackson wrote many famous stories. My favorite is a lesser-known, brief, enigmatic story, **"The Witch,"** from *The Lottery: Adventures of the Daemon Lover*. On a commuter train a mom, distracted by her infant daughter, allows a man to sit next to her four-year-old son. At first charming, the stranger's chat with the boy turns gruesome, and the mom asks the man to leave. I often return to this tiny masterpiece to study its depiction of menace. It exemplifies a quiet, inexorable horror I love. I'm in awe of the economy with which Jackson evokes a deep undercurrent of dread. Expert juxtaposition of the man's violent story, a sense of maternal affection, and the boy's delight make it work on many levels at once. The joy and innocence contrast with horror to make the story resonate with conflicting emotions. It is the light which makes the darkness so compelling.

—S.P. Miskowski

Kaaron Warren is an Australian author, so many in the U.S. may be unfamiliar, which is shame. She's fantastic, and her story I'm recommending is the novella **"The Grinding House."** To me, it's one of the best short horror stories since Stephen King's *The Mist*. A friend recommended this book to me, and I pounced on it, since he was the one who first introduced me to King. Warren has a real talent for taking ordinary people and putting them in messy situations, both supernatural and organic. "The Grinding House" is a post-apocalyptic tale of sorts, in which no one is safe from the creepy disease plaguing Australia. It's gross, scary, and even makes you think a little.

—Tyler L. Duniho

The story I wish to honour is **"Cafe Endless: Spring Rain"** by **Nancy Holder**, a haunting story about a sadomasochistic Japanese vampire. I came across this story in the wonderful vampire erotica anthology *Love in Vein*, which was edited by the equally amazing author Poppy Z. Brite. The anthology as a whole captured my attention and imagination as a hard-core vampire enthusiast, but this is one of the stories that stayed with me long after I'd put the book away. Holder is a powerful and well-respected writer in the fantasy and horror genres, being a four-time winner of the Bram Stoker Award for superior achievement in horror writing. She won Best Short Story in 1991 for "Lady Madonna," in 1993 for "I Hear the Mermaids Singing," and in 1994 for "Cafe Endless: Spring Rain."

—Liz Strange

I divide fear (rational fear, anyway) into two spheres: fear of the unknown and fear of the inevitable. **Judith Merril's "That Only a Mother"** (*Astounding Science Fiction*, June 1948) marries these disparate concepts perfectly, while capitalizing on the public's nascent fear of nuclear fallout, years ahead of popular culture. The story concerns the day-to-day life of a new mother as she corresponds with her husband, a deployed serviceman. Off-handed allusions to "accidents," mutations, and a rise in infanticides suggest that all is not well with the world's children; between this, and the woman's (unconsciously) evasive and rationalizing language (and, indeed, the title itself), we know something's wrong with her baby, but what is it? We must wait until the end, and, helpless, we do. Merril's tale is a narrow, dim passageway; the path is straight, the exit obvious, but the way forward is dark, and something unseen waits there.

—Desmond Warzel

I still remember the feelings of awe and excitement the first time I discovered **"Greedy Choke Puppy"** in the collection *Skin Folk* by **Nalo Hopkinson** (who, incidentally, deserves much greater recognition outside the genre fiction community). I then progressed to her novels, including *Brown Girl in the Ring*. The thing that struck me the most was the unique voice that narrated the story, as well as the way Nalo infused West Indian elements and

261

mythology with the main creature, the *soucouyant*, which has vampire-like elements but is a far more sinister entity.

Although I devoured fiction from Anne Rice, Poppy Z. Brite, and Tanith Lee growing up, Nalo's works have a special place in my heart because her perspective, that of the ultimate outsider and Other, resonated with me (and still does) as I have been an outsider my whole life—and her works taught me to embrace that.

—Anita Siraki

I first read **Ursula K. Le Guin's "The Ones Who Walk Away from Omelas"** in an American Literature Anthology when I was an over-read English major. The story has this slow build that I try to integrate into my writing. When the story's big reveal happens, my jaw was left hanging. A story that has the potential to leave a horror enthusiast like myself gaping is a story that needs to be studied.

I have since read the story a few times, and every time, I am baffled by how Le Guin is able to describe something as horrible without resorting to the typical *Saw*-level gore porn we have accepted as horror today. For any aspiring writer, I recommend this story to show how to subtly reveal a horror plot and how to let the story drive itself.

—Eric Ponvelle

"Eyes of Emerald: The Bride" is one of nine interlocking short stories in the *Book of the Beast*, which in turn is part of *The Secret Books of Paradys, Books I and II* by **Tanith Lee**. This book turned up in an obscure thrift store on an otherwise dull day—and has provided fresh inspiration during countless readings since. In this story Tanith Lee subtly, yet unmistakably, challenges traditional female societal roles, wending her way to the ugly heart of the matter by way of horror dressed up in an elevated and beautiful writing style. This story's terror is carefully baited with fascinating imagery that embraces and encloses the reader like a Venus flytrap. The expected bloodbath will come, yes, perhaps …eventually. But first, something almost worse: a slow, excruciating buildup of dread, set against the gloom the of gray stone, wrapped in cloth-of silver, and haunted by eyes of malevolent green.

—Kelly Dunn

I've long been a fan of **Sarah Joan Berniker**'s work, from the early days when I workshopped with her in Francis Ford Coppola's Zoetrope Studios. She's had some success with short works over the years, including winning a lofty prize in a *Playboy Magazine* short story contest. It is difficult to choose from her array of stories, but I'll have to settle on the odd and surreal **"Pearlstock,"** a front yard carny, freak-show extravaganza published in *Dark Recesses Press*, Issue #7, sometime in 2007. Some people can write, and some people can tell stories. Sarah spins an intricate web of intrigue in wide open places, catches you in it, off-guard, even though you know it's there, secures you in tight, and then feeds on you when she's good and ready.

—Boyd Harris

While **Angela Carter**'s "The Company of Wolves" is widely anthologized, another Carter short story changed the way I thought about horror and about fiction writing. **"The Fall River Axe Murders"** blends history, speculation, and poetic language as it retells the final hours before "Lizzie Borden took an axe . . ." Carter brings those agonizing hours to life: the oppressive heat, the spoiled mutton, and the choking closeness of four family members in a house about to become a tomb.

Her recreation of claustrophobic horror is so vivid that the ultimate outbreak of violence seems inevitable. But the violence never happens, at least not on camera. Carter never shows the bodies, the bloodied couch, the infamous "whacking" at all. Anyone can look up pictures of the Borden family post-mortem, but Carter shows the hidden horror of a home where "the angel of death" has come to roost.

—April Asbury

Few short stories have captured me as thoroughly as **Suzy McKee Charnas**'s **"Unicorn Tapestry."** This 1980 Nebula winner haunted me for days after I read it in *Vampires: Two Centuries of Great Vampire Stories*, edited by Alan Ryan. This compelling story draws the reader into its embrace with the cunning of a vampire. Charnas introduces the enigmatic Weyland through his psychotherapist, Floria, during her treatment for his self-diagnosed condition of vampirism. But, as her mysterious patient reveals the details of his life and nimbly lays waste to her attempts to unravel his delusions, Floria's fascination escalates into horror, as did mine.

Their dance with words eventually leads to a dance with death in a heart-pounding and unexpected conclusion that left me mourning for these characters and what they shared. Even now, after all this time, I think of Weyland. "Unicorn Tapestry" is currently available in Charnas's *The Vampire Tapestries*.

—Roh Morgan

When I first got into hardcore horror, I happened upon a copy of *Splatterpunks 2: Over the Edge*. The first story, **Wildy Petoud's** **"Accident d'Amour,"** blew my mind. My eyes were opened to a type of fiction that was all at once filled with hate, rage, and violence, but also stunningly beautiful. I knew immediately what was missing with my work.

Petoud's language bounced in my brain for days, and I couldn't help but pick apart the story in the hopes that my work could become half as striking. I owe thanks to a number of authors for inspiration, but Petoud's angry little story is quite possibly the first that actively pushed me to write better. Every horror author, hell, every fan of quality fiction, owes it to her or himself to track down this collection and feast their eyes on this story.

—Shawn Rutledge

I discovered **Lucy Taylor** at a World Horror Conference in the 1980s, and I was immediately riveted by her fiction. In my favorite story of hers, **"The Safety of Unknown Cities"** in *Unnatural Acts*, Val, a woman with her own inner demons, is searching for The City, a real life Sodom and Gomorrah, that exists in an area that is not only physically remote, but also in another dimension. She finally finds someone who can lead her there, Majeen, a beautiful hermaphrodite with cat-like eyes.

Their journey to The City, along with their escape from a villain, made a huge impression on me and has remained in my memory for a good twenty years. Though this tale would be called bizarre by most standards, Taylor captures human nature in a way few writers do. It affected my writing by making me go beyond the surface of appearances.

—Sally Bosco

One of my favorite authors is **Elizabeth Massie**. Her collection *The Fear Report* was released by Necon E-books and contains her Bram Stoker® short story winner, **"Stephen."** After reading this collection, I fell in love with her work. Her story "Stephen" elicits different feelings in the reader. Everything from pity, hope, and despair to finally acceptance of Anne's actions in the story.

The character Anne is someone I could relate to, especially her feelings of despair and need for someone to care for her. Furthermore, Massie's ability to write not just horror, but other genres, makes her a powerhouse writer and someone that new authors can look up to. Massie is an extremely talented and creative person, a wonderful writer and artist. Her artwork is as powerful as her writing.

—Laura J. Hickman

This exquisite story—**"The White Maniac: A Doctor's Tale"** by **Waif Wander** (Mary Fortune) and touted as Australia's first 'vampire' story—was first published in 1867 by *The Australian Journal*. I discovered it in *Macabre: A Journey Through Australia's Darkest Fears* (2010) and fell in love.

The elegance with which Fortune crafts this cut-off world of absolute white, how she brings this visual prison alive with texture, form, movement and sensation, giving this achromatic world a *soul*... then destroys it with a gesture of love, both beautiful and obscene, lingers still. In a time when Australian women writers were dismissed and maligned, Mary Fortune readily surrendered her name and her gender for her love of storytelling. So fiercely did she protect her pseudonym, her identity wasn't discovered until the 1950s. To me, that altruism inspires, revealing the soul of a *true* writer: where the story is all that matters.

—Amanda J. Spedding

Even now **"Singing My Sister Down"** by **Margo Lanagan** makes me cry. I had this itch. Short things that needed to be written. But I knew nothing about short stories. I only knew novels. So I pulled down all my collections and read, reread, studied and wrote. I needed more. My bookshelf held Stephens, Clives, Peters, Roberts and Rays. No one with boobs and a uterus? The shame.

265

I purchased *Black Juice,* and over coffee read the first story. I wept. I shuddered, marveled, and when it was over, I ached. In horror our darkness creeps out, our fears, and those twisted things that torment. "Singing My Sister Down" depicts the horror of suffocation, of punishment, of death. But the loss, grief and regret, frustration and pain, these horrors won't go away when you lift the bed skirts. They sing to you that familiar melody that crushes your chest, strips your breath.

—E. L. Kemper

As an accomplished writer, **Lisa Tuttle** is not unrecognized, but I think her story **"The Replacements"** is a forgotten hit. "Replacements" exposes the terrible tendencies of human violence and the underside of irrational cravings of the human heart by introducing a strange creature to a realistic story. Tuttle fathoms a world where need, want, desire, and intimacy are wrought in loneliness; where people fill existential voids with any captive to stop the craving. In the process, she exposes the ugliness of the human heart.

At every reading, I'm struck by how "Replacements" challenges readers to move beyond repulsion/attraction to the creatures appearing inexplicably around the city. This quiet horror story inverts the paradigm: instead of examining the creature, readers are disgusted by human behavior, not other-worldly existences. Stories that explore the insidious evils hiding beneath the surface of human existence inspire me to keep reading and writing.

—E. F. Schraeder

The short horror story **"A Reversal of Fortune"** by **Holly Black** (in the collection *The Poison Eater,* published by Big Mouth House, 2010) impressed me by presenting a protagonist who was at first quite repulsive. Nikki is a white-trash teen girl who lives in a trailer court and works in a candy store in the mall, where she can eat all the candy she can stomach—and she does.

When Nikki's dog, Boo, is hit by a neighbor's car, she doesn't have the money, so she strikes a bargain with the devil, who appears as an eccentric old man. The devil promises to heal Boo if Nikki wins a wager, and Nikki picks an eating contest. Nikki displays grim determination and bests the devil, matching his trickery with her own. Rare is the writer who can make me like and respect a deeply flawed character.

—Sonny Zae

My influential horror story snuck up on me as I binged on apocalyptic fiction while writing my dystopian horror novel. **"The Screwfly Solution"** is told intimately through the eyes of a married couple. The story slowly reveals the depth of horror in store for women as men's impulses are twisted against them.

The writer never flinches from taking the story to its darkest extreme and no exception is made for the couple through whom we experience this terrible world. **James Tiptree Jr.** (pseudonym of Alice Bradley Sheldon) wrote stories full of emotion and depth. She is best known for her science-fiction, but all her stories held elements of darkness. "The Screwfly Solution" was included in the *Masters of Horror* anthology. Though an accomplished writer, she felt it necessary to hide behind a man's name. I love that with this anthology we acknowledge the women who have helped us stand on equal footing with male writers.

—H.E. Roulo

Deep Cuts Supporters

In the early 1900s, professional short story writers were those who earned three cents a word. That pay goal didn't change until 2004 when the Science Fiction & Fantasy Writers of America (SFWA) raised it to five cents. As you can see, writing short fiction is more about passion than payout.

Throughout history, artists have depended on patrons to support them as they pursued their visions, but for the most part, writers have been relegated—sometimes figuratively but often literally— to the garret and poverty. Poe and Lovecraft are two greats that come to mind. Fortunately, for today's writers, the patronage system has come to the masses through websites such as Kickstarter. This site allows artists, writers, musicians, and inventors to promote their projects, collect donations, and solicit pre-orders. Supporters can contribute as little as a $1, and in return, they earn a reward related to the project.

That's what we did with *Deep Cuts*. We took our project to the Internet, made our case for the validity of our project, and achieved our monetary goal. This allowed us to pay the writers—not just five cents a word but six. *Deep Cuts* would not be what it is without our Kickstarter supporters, and we owe them a debt of gratitude.

Linda Addison
Alana
Angelina
Aurora Septon
Cathie A. Aymar
Bailey
Lauren Bennetts
Greg Berry
Folly Blaine
Bill Bodden
The Boo-Monster
Steve Breault
Jason & Sunni Brock
Satyros Phil Brucato

Brian "Chainsaw" Campbell
Jason Carl
Nicole Carnegie
James Chambers
Colleen Welch-Brown
Shawn Colton
Wendie Conjura
Paris Crenshaw
David L. Day
Elena DeGarmo
Guy Anthony De Marco
DENISE
Dhaunae
Lisa DiSabatino

Kelly Dunn
Benjamin Kane Etheridge
Aaron M. Fisk
H.B. Flyte
Lisa Foland
Fran Friel
Lady Gallo
—In memory of Yvonne K
GhostGirls
In memory of
   Charlotte Perkins Gilman
Tina Marlene Goodman
Damien Walters Grintalis
Eric J. Guignard
Peter Halasz
John E. Hambly
Guido Henkel
Laura J. Hickman
Laurel Anne Hill
Aaron Matthew Holmes
Ingrid
Linda Gibson Judd
Kaae
Robyn "Rat" King
Ty King
Kim Kirsch
Jason M. Light
LJH
Lucas
Jeffrey J. Mariotte
Kevin McAlonan
Chanté McCoy
Michael McIntosh
Alison J. McKenzie
S.P. Miskowski
—In memory of Det. Tim
Bayliss

Daniel Mitchel-Slentz
Christine Morgan
Roh Morgan
Terry Morris
Lisa Morton
Craig Moya
William "Billy" Michael
Murphy
Yvonne Navarro
Gene O'Neill
John W. Oliver
John Palisano
Ripley Patton
Amanda Power
Rebecca Rahne
Loren Rhoads
Shauna Roberts
Gord Rollo
Nathan Rosen
Martel Sardina
Scary White Girl
Diana Septon
In memory of Sonia Shah
S.L. Schmitz
Chris Snyder
Randy Standke
Peggy Stankovich
Sasha Elan Stimmel
Robert E. Stutts
Sean Sweeney
Eric Takehara
Juan Valdez
Allana Vee
Mike Welham
Rocky Wood
Jeremy Zimmerman

Deep Cuts Bios

COLLEEN ANDERSON lives in Vancouver, BC and has over 100 published stories and poems appearing in magazines and anthologies, including *Heroic Fantasy Quarterly*, *Chizine*, and *ON Spec*. She has a BFA in creative writing and edits for Chizine Publications. She is a 2011 and 2012 Aurora finalist in poetry. Like many writers, Colleen caters to the ubiquitous cat. New work will be coming out in *BullSpec*, *Chilling Tales 2*, *Artifacts and Relics: Extreme Sorcery* and through Zharmae Publishing. Current projects include a new series of poems on witches (in progress) as well as her just-published reprint collection *Embers Amongst the Fallen*. She is also co-editor, along with Steven Vernon, of the yearly Canadian anthology *Tesseracts 17* put out by Edge Publishing and to be published in 2013. (www.colleenanderson.wordpress.com)

R.S. (Rod) BELCHER has been an award-winning newspaper and magazine editor; reporter and freelance writer. He was the grand prize winner of the Star Trek: Strange New Worlds contest. His story "Orphans" appears in Strange New Worlds 9, by Simon and Schuster in 2006. His first novel, *The Six-Gun Tarot*, was published by Tor Book in January of 2013. He lives in Roanoke Virginia with his children, Jonathan, Emily and Stephanie.

SCATHE MEIC BEORH is an author, professional storyteller, and founder of *Bradburyesque Quarterly*. His influences include William Blake, Arthur Machen, T. S. Eliot, W. B. Yeats, and George Mackay Brown, as well as a wide sweep of film directors. First a writer of poetry, he has most recently worked in other literary forms. His work may be found in anthologies, magazines, and both public and private libraries the world over.

SATYROS PHIL BRUCATO, aka Phil Brucato or just plain Satyr, sold his first professional story to Marion Zimmer Bradley's *Sword & Sorceress IX* anthology in 1990. During White Wolf's "classic WOD" period, he co-created the *Mage, Sorcerers Crusade, Werewolf, Changeling* and *Vampire: Dark Ages* lines, contributing to over 80 books for the Wolf. The next decade saw him author *Deliria: Faerie Tales for a New Millennium, Everyday Heroes, Goblin Markets: The Glitter Trade,* and popular columns for *Realms of Fantasy, Witches & Pagans,* and *NewWitch* magazine. His fiction has appeared in *Weird Tales, Steampunk Tales,* a slew of collections, and the *Bad-Ass Fairies* series. Recently, he co-edited the benefit collection *Ravens in the Library,* founded Silver Satyr Games, and produced the webcomic series *Arpeggio* (arpeggiothecomic.com). Satyr lives in Seattle with his partner Sandra Buskirk and their cats.

JAMES CHAMBERS's tales of horror, crime, fantasy, and science fiction have been published in numerous anthologies and magazines. In 2011 Dark Regions Press published his collection of four Lovecraft-inspired novellas, *The Engines of Sacrifice. Publisher's Weekly* described it as "chillingly evocative." Most recently, Dark Quest Books has published his zombie novellas, *The Dead Bear Witness* and *Tears of Blood,* the first two volumes in the Corpse Fauna novella series. Chambers is also the author of the short story collections *Resurrection House,* published in 2009 by Dark Regions Press, and *The Midnight Hour: Saint Lawn Hill and Other Tales* with illustrator Jason Whitley. His stories have appeared in the award-winning anthology series *Bad-Ass Faeries* and *Defending the Future,* and he has also written numerous comic books including *Leonard Nimoy's Primortals,* the critically acclaimed "The Revenant" in *Shadow House,* and *The Midnight Hour. His work has also appeared in Bad Cop No Donut, Dark Furies, The Dead Walk, The Dead Walk Again, The Domino Lady: Sex as a Weapon, Dragon's Lure, The Green Hornet Chronicles, Hardboiled Cthulhu, In An Iron Cage, New Blood, Warfear, Weird Trails,* and the magazines *Bare Bone, Cthulhu Sex,* and *Allen K's Inhuman.* He is a member of the Horror Writers Association and the chairman of its membership committee. His website is jameschambersonline.com.

SAMAEL GYRE is a mysterious literary terrorist and shaman of the dark arts of Ficta Mystica. He knows your secrets and intends to spill them wide. He is known solely through his work, which is too extreme for some. He gets around and lives closer than you'd think. There are no known photographs of him; his biography is rumored to be classified. His work has appeared in various anthologies, and there is said to be a novel in the works.

Samael Gyre can be reached via Gene Stewart at genestewart.com/wordpress and will reach you in various dark places.

KELLY A. HARMON used to write truthful, honest stories about authors and thespians, senators and statesmen, movie stars and murderers. Now she writes lies, which is infinitely more satisfying, but lacks the convenience of doorstep delivery, especially on rainy days. She has published short fiction in several anthologies including the EPIC Award Winning *Bad Ass Fairies 3: In All Their Glory; Hellebore and Rue, Black Dragon, White Dragon,* and *Triangulation: Dark Glass.* Her story "Lies" short-listed for the Aeon Award. Her award-winning novella, "Blood Soup," and other short fiction are available widely in many formats. Ms. Harmon is a former magazine and newspaper reporter and editor. She has published articles at *SciFi Weekly, eArticles,* and magazines and newspapers up and down the East Coast and abroad. Read more about Ms. Harmon at her Web site: kellyaharmon.com.

MICHAEL HAYNES lives in Central Ohio where he helps keep IT systems running for a large corporation during the day and puts his characters through the wringer by night. An ardent short story reader and writer, Michael has had over twenty stories accepted for publication during 2012 by venues such as *Orson Scott Card's Intergalactic Medicine Show, Daily Science Fiction, Nature,* and many others. His website is michaelhaynes.info.

NANCY HOLDER, New York Times Bestselling author, has had work appear on the New York Times, USA Today, LA Times, amazon.com, LOCUS, and other bestseller lists. A five-time winner of the Bram Stoker Award from the Horror Writers Association, she has also received accolades from the American Library Association, the American Reading Association, the New York Public Library, and Romantic Times. She and Debbie Viguié co-authored the New York Times bestselling series *Wicked* for Simon and Schuster.

They have continued their collaboration with the *Crusade* series, also for Simon and Schuster, and the *Wolf Springs Chronicles* for Delacorte (2011.) She is also the author of the young adult horror series *Possessions* for Razorbill.

She has sold many novels and book projects set in the *Buffy the Vampire Slayer, Angel, Saving Grace, Hellboy,* and *Smallville* universes. She has sold approximately two hundred short stories and essays on writing and popular culture.

Her anthology, *Outsiders,* co-edited with Nancy Kilpatrick, was nominated for the Bram Stoker Award in 2005. *Pretty Little Devils* and *The Watcher's Guide Volume 1* appeared in the New York Public Library's Books for the Teen Age, and The Watcher's Guide Volume 1 also appeared on the Los Angeles Times Bestseller List in 1999. *Saving Grace: Tough Love* won the 2011 Scribe Award for General Fiction/Best Original Novel. Nancy teaches in the Stonecoast MFA Creative Writing Program, offered through the University of Southern Maine.

She has previously taught at UCSD and has served on the Clarion Board of Directors. She lives in San Diego, California, with her daughter Belle, their two Corgis, Panda and Tater; and their cats, David and Kittnen Snow. She and Belle are active in Girl Scouts and dog obedience training.

RACHEL KARYO. When Rachel Karyo was a young child, her older cousins thought it good fun to lock her in a closet with a plastic punching bag clown. Rachel was terrified of that clown--it bobbed back and forth, it seemed to be laughing and crying at the same time. Perhaps not surprisingly, Rachel developed a chronic case of coulrophobia and grew up to be a writer. Rachel has worked as a journalist, copywriter, editorial assistant and English teacher. She recently attended the Sarah Lawrence College Summer Writers Seminar and is an Amherst Writers and Artists affiliate. Rachel lives with her family in Westchester County, New York.

ED KURTZ is the author of *Bleed* (Abattoir Press), *Control* (Thunderstorm Books), and numerous short stories. His work has appeared in *Dark Moon Digest, Needle: A Magazine of Noir, BEAT to a PULP, Shotgun Honey, Horror Factory, Mutation Nation,* and *Psychos: Serial Killers, Depraved Madmen, and the Criminally Insane.* Ed resides in Texas, where he is at work on his next novel and running his genre imprint, Redrum Horror. Visit Ed Kurtz online at edkurtzbleeds.wordpress.com.

PATRICIA LILLIE used to write picture books. Now, she

makes bad things happen to nice people—but only on paper. She lives in Northeastern Ohio and is working towards an MFA in Writing Popular Fiction at Seton Hill University. "Abby" is her first published story for readers over the age of six. You can visit her online at patricialillie.com.

E.S. MAGILL (co-editor) likes to wear the two hats of writer and editor. She is the editor of *The Haunted Mansion Project: Year One*, an anthology of essays and short stories based on the experiences of a dozen horror writers who attended a writers retreat at a haunted mansion. She is also the former reviews editor and columnist for *Dark Wisdom* magazine. Her most current short fiction can be found in the Horror Writers Association's anthology *Blood Lite III*. She has an M.A. in English, specializing in the postmodern gothic. By day, she teaches middle school English; night is a whole other story. Southern California is home to her and her husband Greg and their menagerie of cats and Corvettes. Find her at facebook.com/esmagill.

CHRIS MARRS (co-editor) lives on the West Coast of British Columbia, has two kids, two jobs, and two cats. Before the kids took over, Chris used to write a lot and had two stories published. Now that the kids are older, Chris is back to writing a lot, usually very late into the night and accompanied by copious amounts of coffee. In the past year, Chris had two pieces of flash fiction published in *Necon E-books Flash Fiction Anthology Best of 2011* and another piece of flash fiction published in *100 Horrors, Tales of Horror in The Blink of An Eye*. Also, a short story of hers recently appeared in *Behind Locked Doors*, an anthology by Wicked East Press. Chris is a supporting member of the HWA. You can find her at facebook.com/chris.marrs.14.

ANGEL LEIGH MCCOY (co-editor) is the producer and lead editor at www.WilyWriters.com, a professional speculative fiction e-zine. She also writes, and her fiction has appeared in numerous places. During the day, she is a narrative designer at ArenaNet, part of a vast team effort to make the coolest MMORPG ever: *Guild Wars 2*. Angel lives with Boo, Simon, and Lapis Lazuli in Seattle, where the long, dark winters feed her penchant for all things spooky and cozy. Visit her at www.angelmccoy.com.

ANJA MILLEN (cover artist) was born somewhere at the end of the world, so-called Germany, and spent her entire youth there, followed by some years as a cook in France. In 1984, Anja started to visualize her own world in paintings and sketches. Strange, monstrous, nifty, and sometimes beautiful. After visiting the European Academy of Art, the school of design and art, she discovered the wonderful, unlimited world of digital art in 1998. For a few years, she has banned the demons in her head also with photography—still learning, still going crazy from all those surreal fantasies in her mind. Anja is currently living in a cave, on top of the highest mountain, scratching little stick men in the wall, and thinking of publishing a volume of photographs or an illustrated book. Her art is shown and featured in different virtual galleries. She is currently working with musicians creating their CD cover art. Anja made MMORPG concept arts and character studies for the RPG genre and is looking forward to creating book covers for fantasy novels.

ROB M. MILLER was born and raised in the hood of Portland, Oregon. Over the years, he has been victimized by violent bad guys, has victimized violent bad guys, been a U.S. Army Infantryman, taught martial arts, worked security, video store clerked, washed windows, retreaded tires, and stocked products in a grocery store. After two years of freelance stringer work for a military newspaper, he tired of nonfiction and decided to use his love of the dark, his personal terrors, and his talent with words, to do something more beneficial for his fellow man: *scare the hell out of him.* Rob's continuing his quest to write tales of dark woe in the Pacific Northwest, from where he moderates an online writing group (www.writers-in-action.spruz.com). His work can be found in various American and U.K. anthologies. Come give him a visit at www.jaggeddarkness.com.

LISA MORTON began her career as a professional writer in 1988 with the horror-fantasy feature film *Meet the Hollowheads* (aka *Life on the Edge*), on which she also served as Associate Producer. For the Disney Channel's 1992 *Adventures in Dinosaur City*, she served as screenwriter, Associate Producer, Songwriter, and Miniatures Coordinator. Lisa has also written numerous episodes of the animated television series *Sky Dancers, Dragon Flyz,* and *Van-Pires.* For stage she has written and co-produced the acclaimed horror one-acts *Spirits of the Season, Sane Reaction* and *The Territorial Imperative,* and has adapted and directed Philip K. Dick's *Radio Free Albemuth* and Theodore Sturgeon's *The Graveyard Reader;* her full-length science fiction comedy *Trashers* was an L.A. Weekly "Recommended" pick. Her short fiction has appeared in dozens of books and magazines, including Dark Delicacies: *Original Tales of Terror and the Macabre, Mondo Zombie, Dark Passions: Hot Blood XIII, The Mammoth Book of Zombie Apocalypse!,* and the forthcoming *Blood Lite 3.* Her first book, *The Cinema of Tsui Hark,* about the legendary Hong Kong director/producer of such classics as *Peking Opera Blues* and *A Chinese Ghost Story,* was published by McFarland, who also published *The Halloween Encyclopedia* in 2003 and *A Hallowe'en Anthology: Literary and Historical Writings Over the Centuries* in 2008.

Her television movie *Tornado Warning* was chosen by the Pax cable station to launch their 2002 fall season, and 2005 saw the release of three horror films, the vampire thriller *Blood Angels,* the mutant shark story *Blue Demon,* and *The Glass Trap,* about genetically altered fire ants.

Lisa was awarded the 2006 Bram Stoker Award for Short Fiction for her story "Tested" (which first appeared in *Cemetery Dance* magazine), and the 2008 Bram Stoker Award for Non-fiction for *A Hallowe'en Anthology.* For the first anthology she edited, 2009's *Midnight Walk,* Lisa received a Black Quill Award for Best Dark Genre Anthology, and she won the 2009 Bram Stoker Award for Long Fiction for her novella *The Lucid Dreaming.* In 2010, she received her fourth Stoker Award, this time in the First Novel category for *The Castle of Los Angeles.*

Her first collection, *Monsters of L.A.,* was published by Bad Moon Books in 2011, and garnered Lisa her seventh Bram Stoker Award nomination. Her most recent book is *Witch Hunts: A Graphic History of the Burning Times* (co-written with Rocky Wood and illustrated by Greg Chapman), and forthcoming from Reaktion Books is *Trick or Treat?: A History of Halloween.*

Lisa is currently Vice President of the Horror Writers Association, and she lives in North Hollywood, California.

YVONNE NAVARRO lives in southern Arizona, where by

day she works on historic Fort Huachuca. She is the author of twenty-two published novels and well over a hundred short stories, and has written about everything from vampires to psychologically disturbed husbands to the end of the world. Her work has won the HWA's Bram Stoker Award plus a number of other writing awards.

Visit yvonnenavarro.com to keep up with slices of a crazy life that includes her husband, author Weston Ochse, three Great Danes (Goblin, Ghost and Ghoulie), a people-loving parakeet named BirdZilla, painting, and lots of ice cream, Smarties, and white zinfandel.

Also at facebook.com/yvonne.navarro.001

Her most recent work is *Concrete Savior*, the second book in the Dark Redemption Series. She has both lived in real haunted houses and weekended with friends in a seriously haunted mansion, just like those dumb blondes in B-movies.

SANDRA M. ODELL is a 45-year old, happily married mother of two teenage boys, an avid reader, compulsive writer, and rabid chocoholic. Her work has appeared in *Jim Baen's UNIVERSE, Ideomancer,* and *Andromeda Spaceways Inflight Magazine,* been produced by *The Drabblecast* and *Pseudopod,* and her short story collection, *The Twelve Ways of Christmas,* was released by Hydra House Books in 2012. Find out more about her work and her love of audio fiction, at her blog: sandramodell.com.

C.W. SMITH is a writer from Southwest Virginia. From 2008-2010, he contributed creative non-fiction to *The New River Voice.* He does not have children.

SARA TAYLOR is a socially anxious product of rural Virginia. She traded her good health for a BFA in Creative Writing from Randolph College, and is now furiously attempting to earn an MA in the same from The University of East Anglia before the faculty realizes she isn't the reincarnation of Ernest Hemingway, as stated on her application. Her short stories have been published in anthologies from Seedpod Publishing, Storm Moon Press, and Cruentus Libri, as well as in print and online magazines. She currently lives in the UK.

MEHITOBEL WILSON has been publishing horror fiction

since 1998. You may find her work in *Psychos: Serial Killers, Depraved Madmen, and the Criminally Insane* (Black Dog & Levinthal, 2012), *Necro Files: Two Decades of Extreme Horror, Zombies: Encounters with the Hungry Dead, Sins of the Sirens, Damned: An Anthology of the Lost,* and *Dead But Dreaming.* Selected stories have been collected in *Dangerous Red,* which is now available in a range of e-book formats from various retailers. She contains most of the planet's caffeine and salt. If you can't pronounce her name, call her "Bel."

STEPHEN WOODWORTH, a graduate of the Clarion West Writers Workshop, is the author of the *New York Times* best-selling Violet Series of paranormal thrillers, including *Through Violet Eyes, With Red Hands, In Golden Blood,* and *From Black Rooms.* His short fiction has appeared in such publications as *Weird Tales, Realms of Fantasy, Fantasy & Science Fiction, Year's Best Fantasy 9, The Dead That Walk,* and *Mutation Nation.*

We editors thank you all for your cheerful support.

Made in the USA
Charleston, SC
28 January 2013